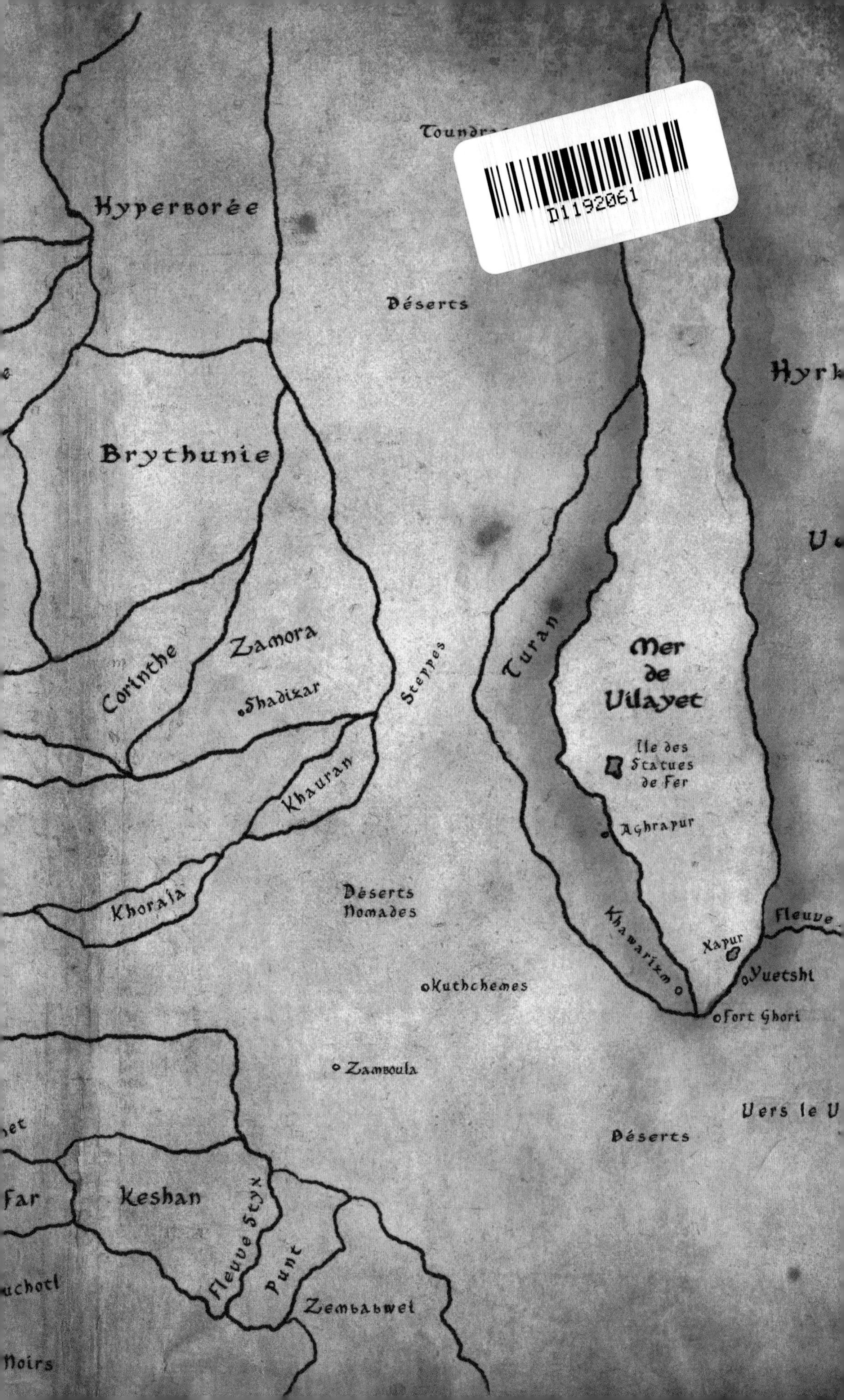

Hyperborée
Déserts
Brythunie
Zamora
Corinthe
Shadizar
Steppes
Turan
Mer de Vilayet
Île des Statues de Fer
Khauran
Aghrapur
Déserts Nomades
Khoraja
Khawarizm
Xapur
Fleuve
Yuetshi
Kuthchemes
Fort Ghori
Zamboula
Déserts
Keshan
Fleuve Styx
Punt
Zembabwei

THE CIMMERIAN

VOLUME 2

PEOPLE OF THE BLACK CIRCLE

THE FROST-GIANT'S DAUGHTER

Publisher's Cataloging-in-Publication Data

Names: Runberg, Sylvain, author. | Recht, Robin, author. | Howard, Robert E.
(Robert Ervin), 1906-1936, author. | Park, Jae Kwang, illustrator.
Title: The Cimmerian , Vol. 2 / written by Jean-David Morvan, Robert E. Howard,
and Régis Hautière; illustrated by Pierre Alary, Olivier Vatine, and Didier Cassegrain.
Description: Contains "The People of the Black Circle" and "The Frost Giant's Daughter" | Portland, OR: Ablaze Publishing, 2021.
Identifiers: ISBN: 978-1-950912-34-6
Subjects: LCSH: Conan (Fictitious character)--Comic books, strips, etc. | Cimmerians. | Fantasy fiction.
Graphic novels. | Comic books, strips, etc. | BISAC COMICS & GRAPHIC NOVELS / Fantasy
Classification: LCC PN6728.C65 R86 2021 | DDC 741.5--dc23

THE CIMMERIAN

PEOPLE OF THE BLACK CIRCLE

WRITER
SYLVAIN RUNBERG

ARTIST
JAE KWANG PARK

COLORIST
HIROYUKI OOSHIMA

LETTERER
DEZI SIENTY

THE FROST GIANT'S DAUGHTER

WRITER AND ARTIST
ROBIN RECHT

LETTERER
DEZI SIENTY

ADAPTED FROM THE WORK OF
ROBERT E. HOWARD

EDITOR
RICH YOUNG & PATRICE LOUINET

SPECIAL THANKS
**ETIENNE BONNIN,
IVANKA HAHNENBERGER,
PATRICE LOUINET,
JULIA SKORCZ**

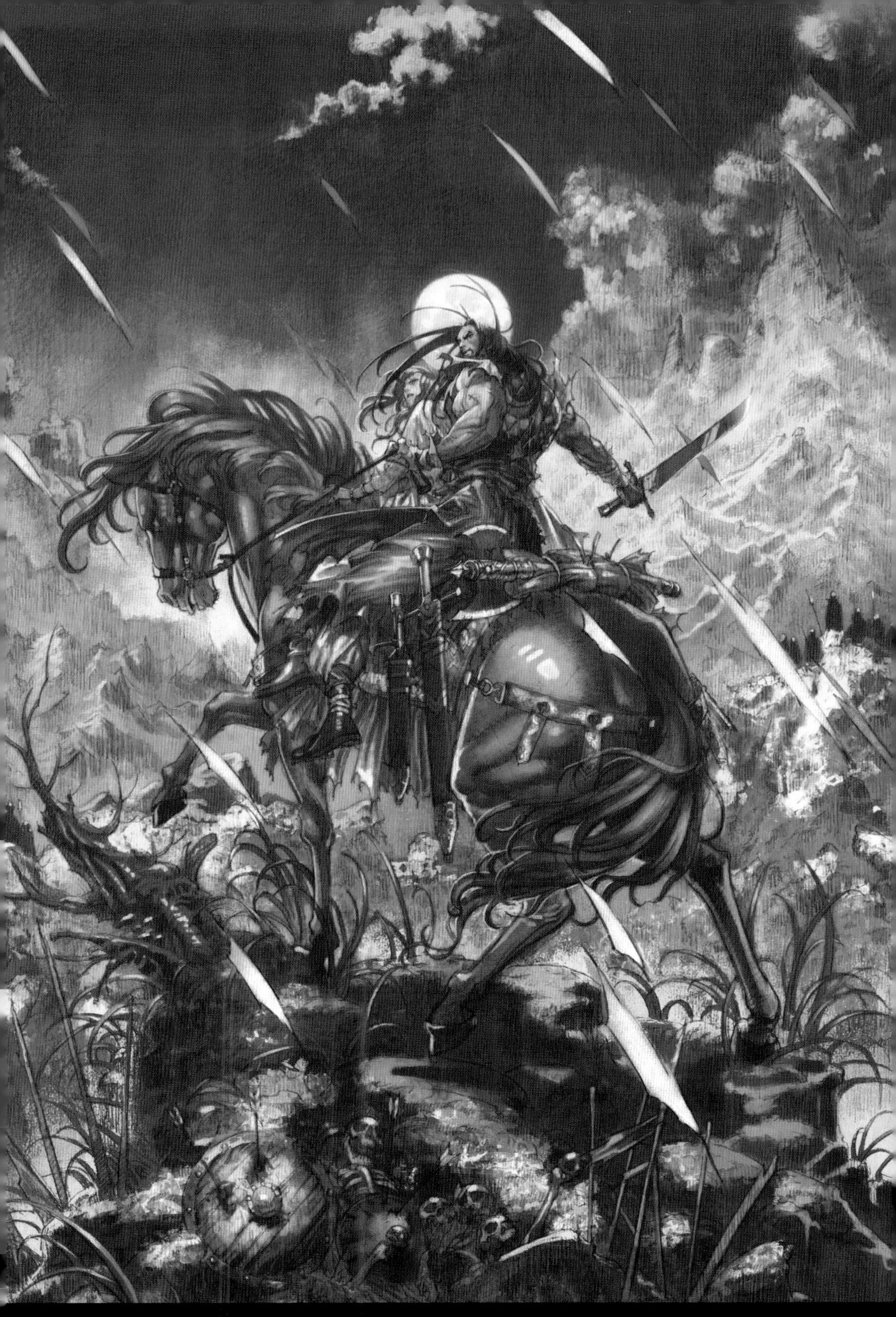

PEOPLE OF THE BLACK CIRCLE

In the kingdom of Vendhya, the king has just died, struck down by the spells of the black prophets of Yimsha. The king's sister, Yasmina, decides to avenge him...and contacts Conan, then chief of the Afghuli tribe. But several of Conan's warriors have just been killed by the men of the kingdom of Vendhya, further complicating the matter. The princess thought she could use the Cimmerian, but rather it is she who will serve his interests

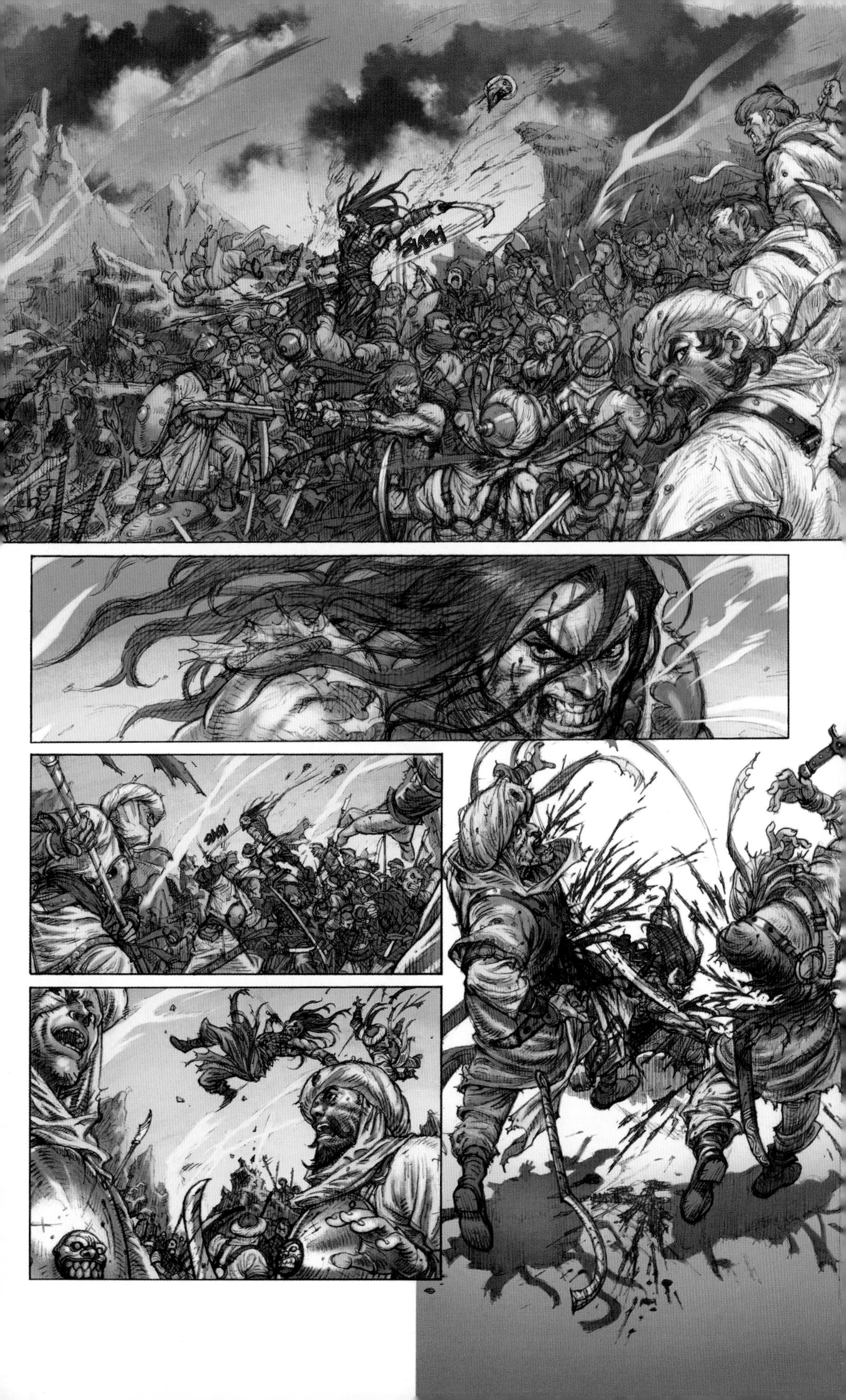
SLASH

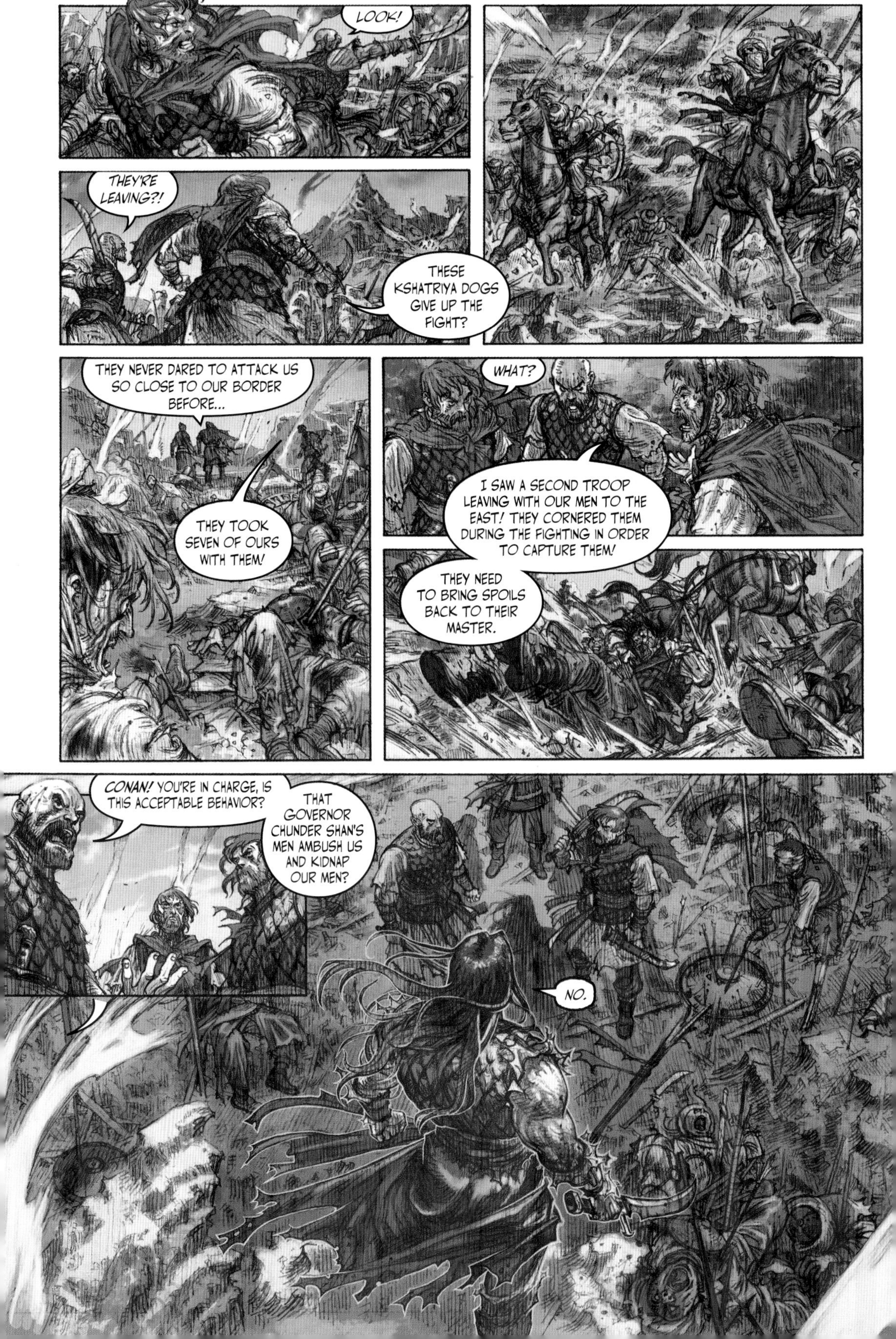
LOOK!
THEY'RE LEAVING?!
THESE KSHATRIYA DOGS GIVE UP THE FIGHT?
THEY NEVER DARED TO ATTACK US SO CLOSE TO OUR BORDER BEFORE...
THEY TOOK SEVEN OF OURS WITH THEM!
WHAT?
I SAW A SECOND TROOP LEAVING WITH OUR MEN TO THE EAST! THEY CORNERED THEM DURING THE FIGHTING IN ORDER TO CAPTURE THEM!
THEY NEED TO BRING SPOILS BACK TO THEIR MASTER.
CONAN! YOU'RE IN CHARGE, IS THIS ACCEPTABLE BEHAVIOR?
THAT GOVERNOR CHUNDER SHAN'S MEN AMBUSH US AND KIDNAP OUR MEN?
NO.

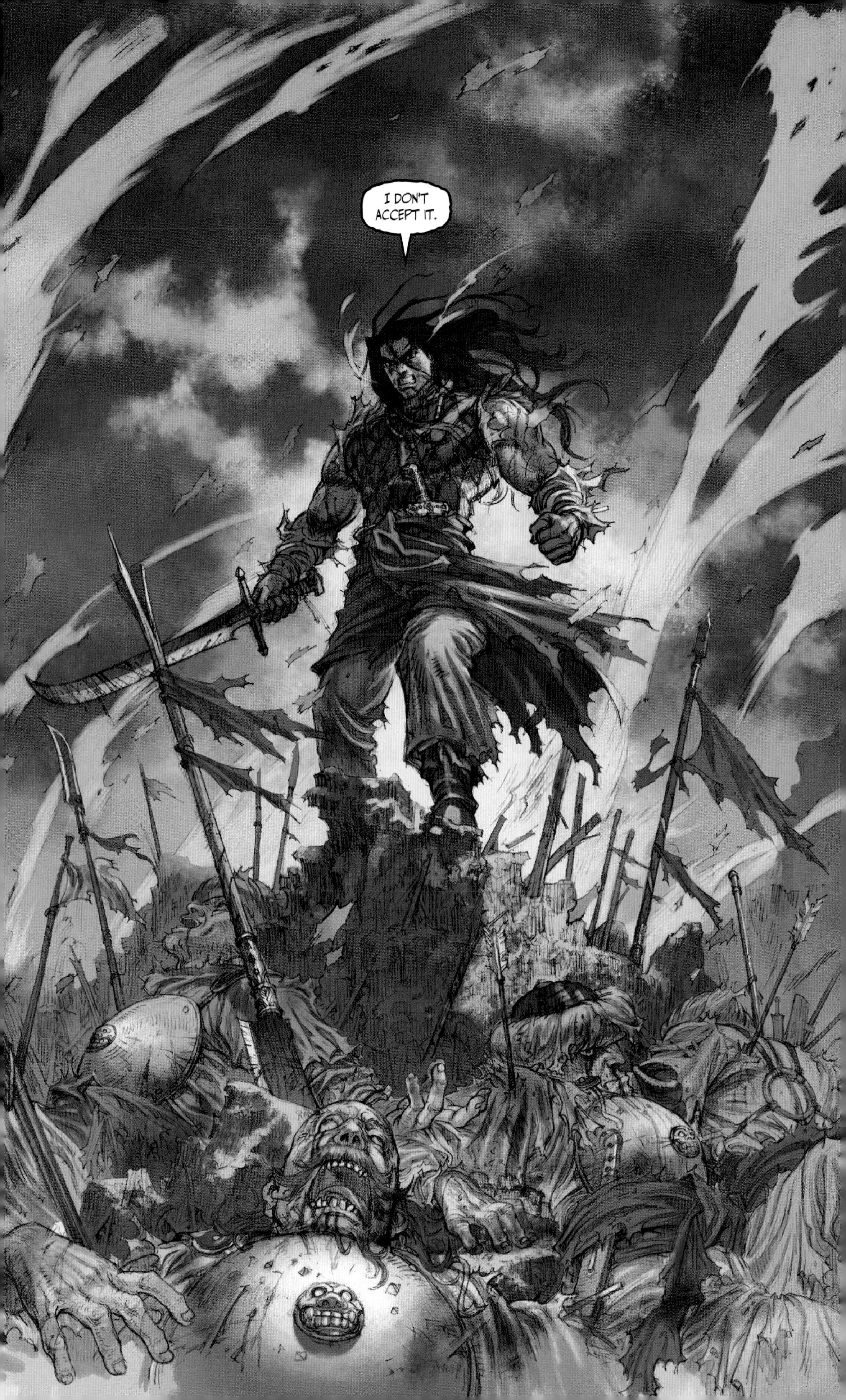
I DON'T ACCEPT IT.

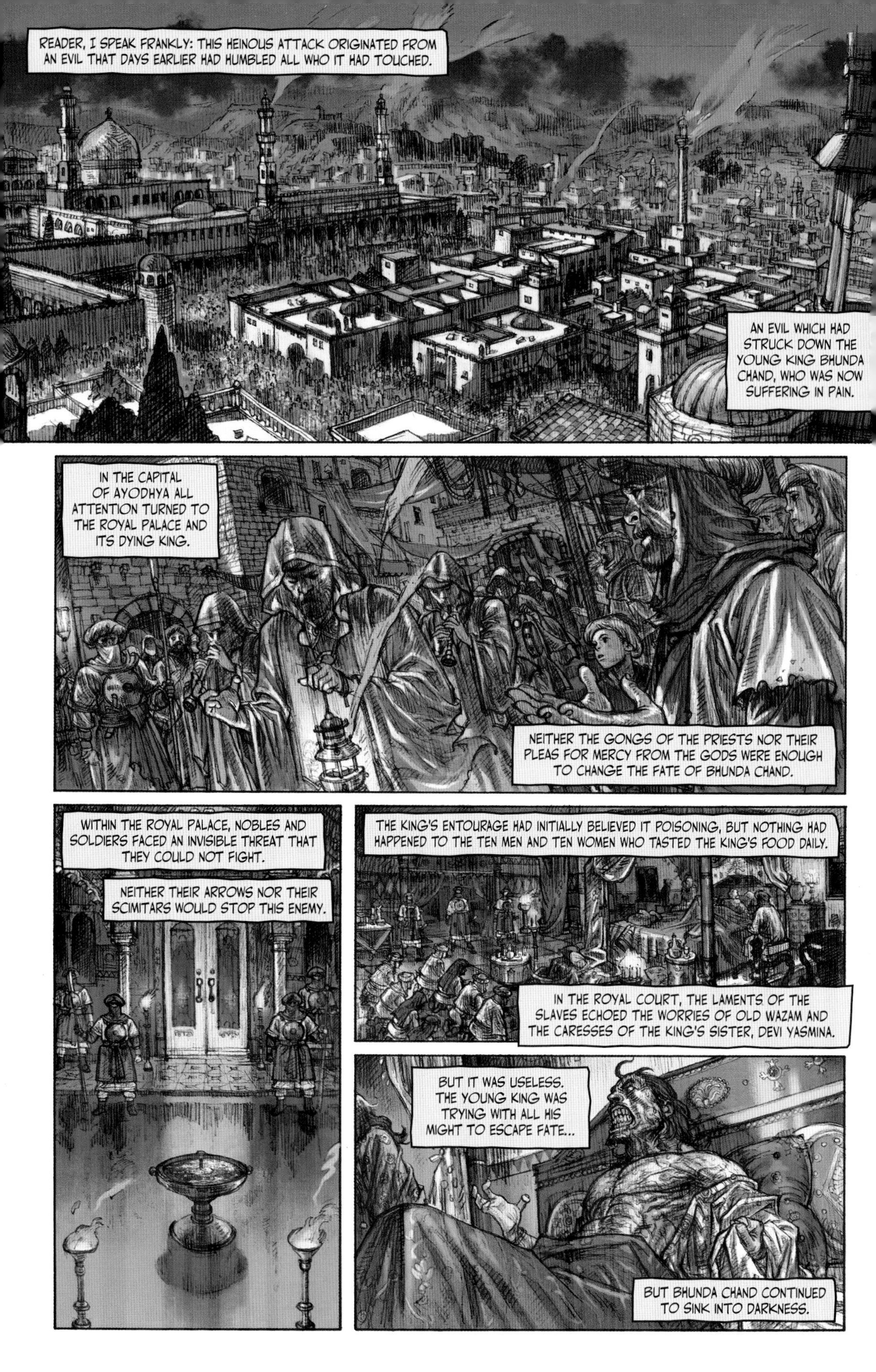
READER, I SPEAK FRANKLY: THIS HEINOUS ATTACK ORIGINATED FROM AN EVIL THAT DAYS EARLIER HAD HUMBLED ALL WHO IT HAD TOUCHED.
AN EVIL WHICH HAD STRUCK DOWN THE YOUNG KING BHUNDA CHAND, WHO WAS NOW SUFFERING IN PAIN.
IN THE CAPITAL OF AYODHYA ALL ATTENTION TURNED TO THE ROYAL PALACE AND ITS DYING KING.
NEITHER THE GONGS OF THE PRIESTS NOR THEIR PLEAS FOR MERCY FROM THE GODS WERE ENOUGH TO CHANGE THE FATE OF BHUNDA CHAND.
WITHIN THE ROYAL PALACE, NOBLES AND SOLDIERS FACED AN INVISIBLE THREAT THAT THEY COULD NOT FIGHT.
NEITHER THEIR ARROWS NOR THEIR SCIMITARS WOULD STOP THIS ENEMY.
THE KING'S ENTOURAGE HAD INITIALLY BELIEVED IT POISONING, BUT NOTHING HAD HAPPENED TO THE TEN MEN AND TEN WOMEN WHO TASTED THE KING'S FOOD DAILY.
IN THE ROYAL COURT, THE LAMENTS OF THE SLAVES ECHOED THE WORRIES OF OLD WAZAM AND THE CARESSES OF THE KING'S SISTER, DEVI YASMINA.
BUT IT WAS USELESS. THE YOUNG KING WAS TRYING WITH ALL HIS MIGHT TO ESCAPE FATE...
BUT BHUNDA CHAND CONTINUED TO SINK INTO DARKNESS.

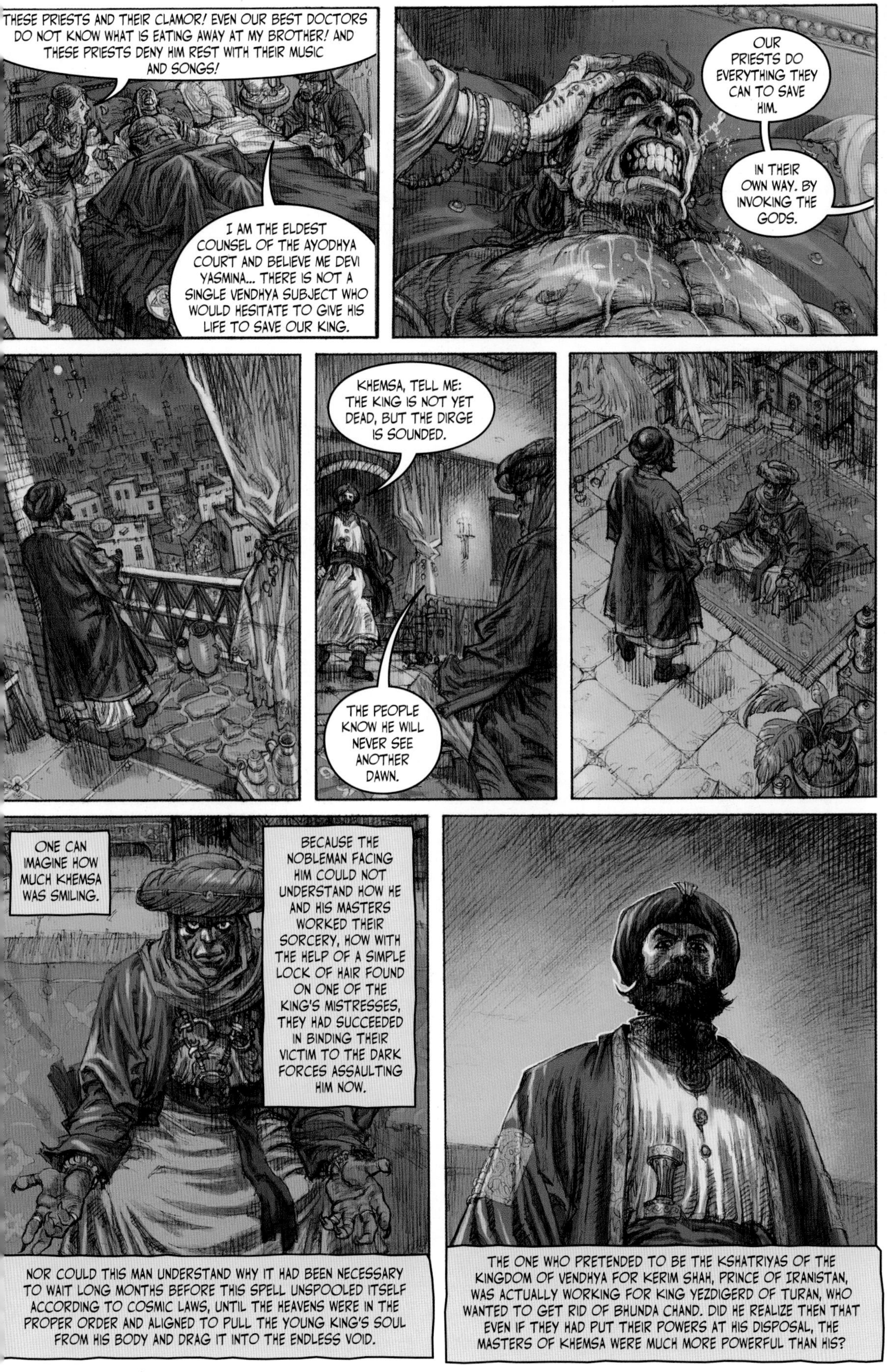
THESE PRIESTS AND THEIR CLAMOR! EVEN OUR BEST DOCTORS DO NOT KNOW WHAT IS EATING AWAY AT MY BROTHER! AND THESE PRIESTS DENY HIM REST WITH THEIR MUSIC AND SONGS!
I AM THE ELDEST COUNSEL OF THE AYODHYA COURT AND BELIEVE ME DEVI YASMINA... THERE IS NOT A SINGLE VENDHYA SUBJECT WHO WOULD HESITATE TO GIVE HIS LIFE TO SAVE OUR KING.
OUR PRIESTS DO EVERYTHING THEY CAN TO SAVE HIM.
IN THEIR OWN WAY. BY INVOKING THE GODS.
KHEMSA, TELL ME: THE KING IS NOT YET DEAD, BUT THE DIRGE IS SOUNDED.
THE PEOPLE KNOW HE WILL NEVER SEE ANOTHER DAWN.
ONE CAN IMAGINE HOW MUCH KHEMSA WAS SMILING.
BECAUSE THE NOBLEMAN FACING HIM COULD NOT UNDERSTAND HOW HE AND HIS MASTERS WORKED THEIR SORCERY, HOW WITH THE HELP OF A SIMPLE LOCK OF HAIR FOUND ON ONE OF THE KING'S MISTRESSES, THEY HAD SUCCEEDED IN BINDING THEIR VICTIM TO THE DARK FORCES ASSAULTING HIM NOW.
NOR COULD THIS MAN UNDERSTAND WHY IT HAD BEEN NECESSARY TO WAIT LONG MONTHS BEFORE THIS SPELL UNSPOOLED ITSELF ACCORDING TO COSMIC LAWS, UNTIL THE HEAVENS WERE IN THE PROPER ORDER AND ALIGNED TO PULL THE YOUNG KING'S SOUL FROM HIS BODY AND DRAG IT INTO THE ENDLESS VOID.
THE ONE WHO PRETENDED TO BE THE KSHATRIYAS OF THE KINGDOM OF VENDHYA FOR KERIM SHAH, PRINCE OF IRANISTAN, WAS ACTUALLY WORKING FOR KING YEZDIGERD OF TURAN, WHO WANTED TO GET RID OF BHUNDA CHAND. DID HE REALIZE THEN THAT EVEN IF THEY HAD PUT THEIR POWERS AT HIS DISPOSAL, THE MASTERS OF KHEMSA WERE MUCH MORE POWERFUL THAN HIS?

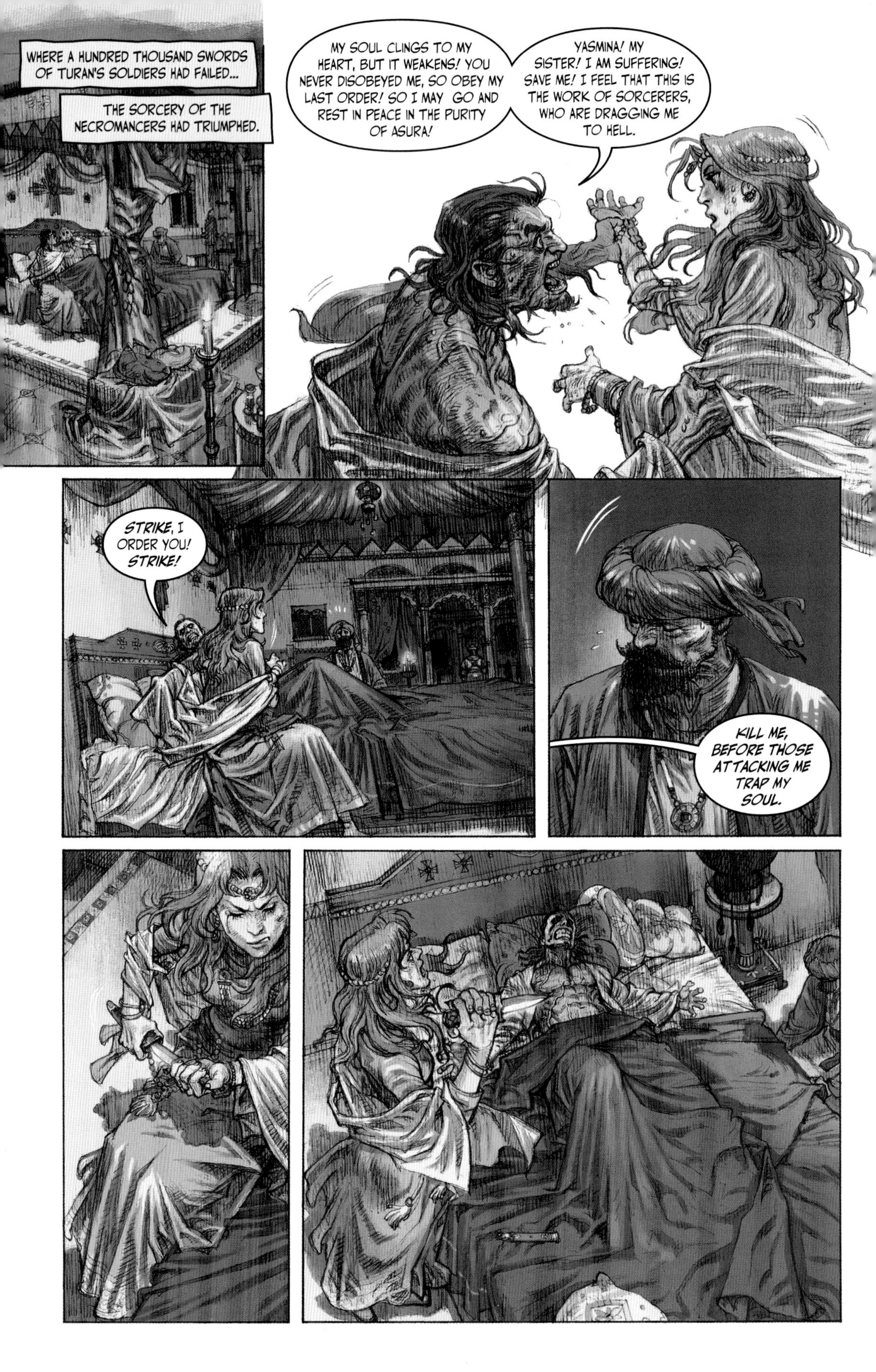
WHERE A HUNDRED THOUSAND SWORDS OF TURAN'S SOLDIERS HAD FAILED...
THE SORCERY OF THE NECROMANCERS HAD TRIUMPHED.
MY SOUL CLINGS TO MY HEART, BUT IT WEAKENS! YOU NEVER DISOBEYED ME, SO OBEY MY LAST ORDER! SO I MAY GO AND REST IN PEACE IN THE PURITY OF ASURA!
YASMINA! MY SISTER! I AM SUFFERING! SAVE ME! I FEEL THAT THIS IS THE WORK OF SORCERERS, WHO ARE DRAGGING ME TO HELL.
STRIKE, I ORDER YOU! STRIKE!
KILL ME, BEFORE THOSE ATTACKING ME TRAP MY SOUL.

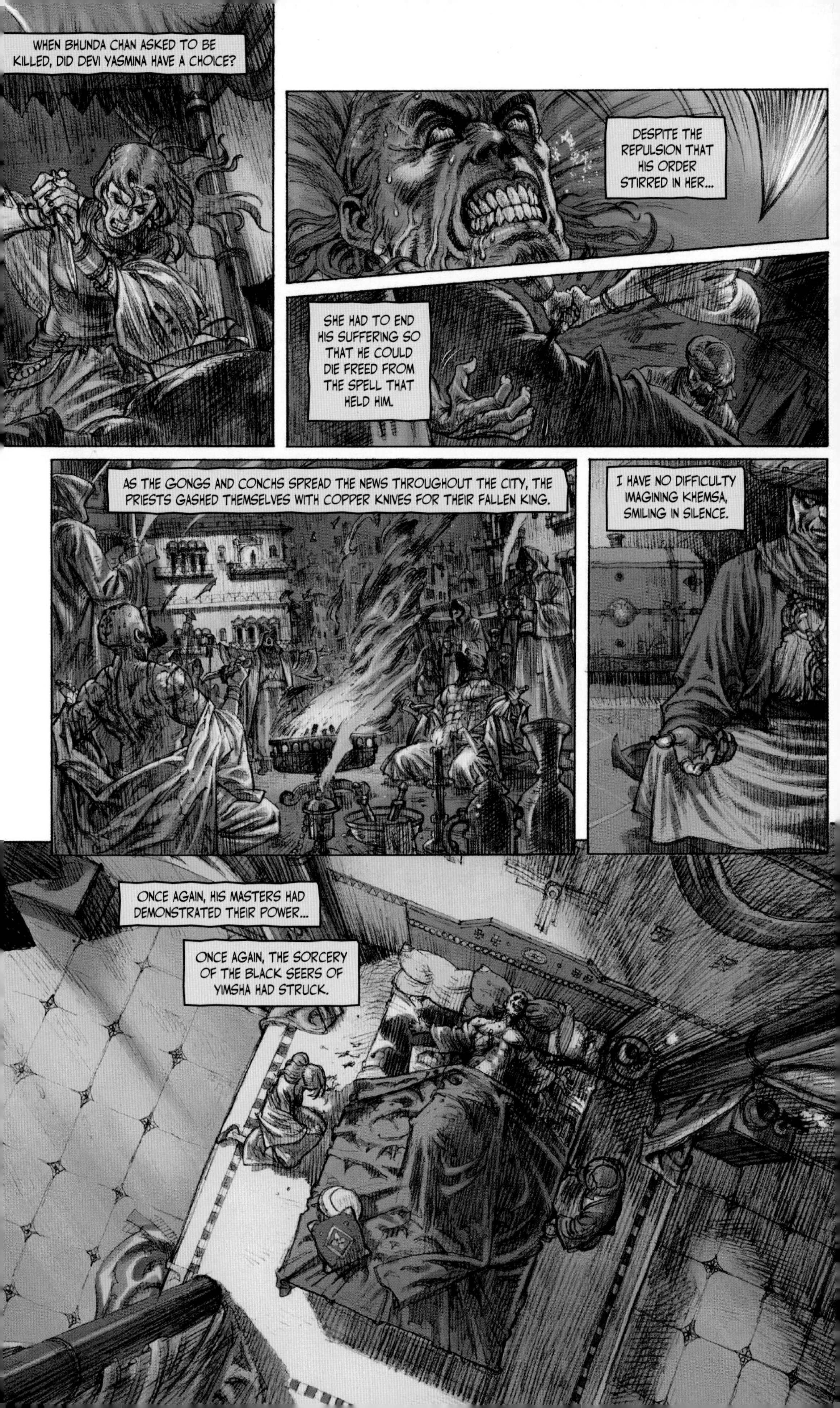
WHEN BHUNDA CHAN ASKED TO BE KILLED, DID DEVI YASMINA HAVE A CHOICE?
DESPITE THE REPULSION THAT HIS ORDER STIRRED IN HER...
SHE HAD TO END HIS SUFFERING SO THAT HE COULD DIE FREED FROM THE SPELL THAT HELD HIM.
AS THE GONGS AND CONCHS SPREAD THE NEWS THROUGHOUT THE CITY, THE PRIESTS GASHED THEMSELVES WITH COPPER KNIVES FOR THEIR FALLEN KING.
I HAVE NO DIFFICULTY IMAGINING KHEMSA, SMILING IN SILENCE.
ONCE AGAIN, HIS MASTERS HAD DEMONSTRATED THEIR POWER...
ONCE AGAIN, THE SORCERY OF THE BLACK SEERS OF YIMSHA HAD STRUCK.

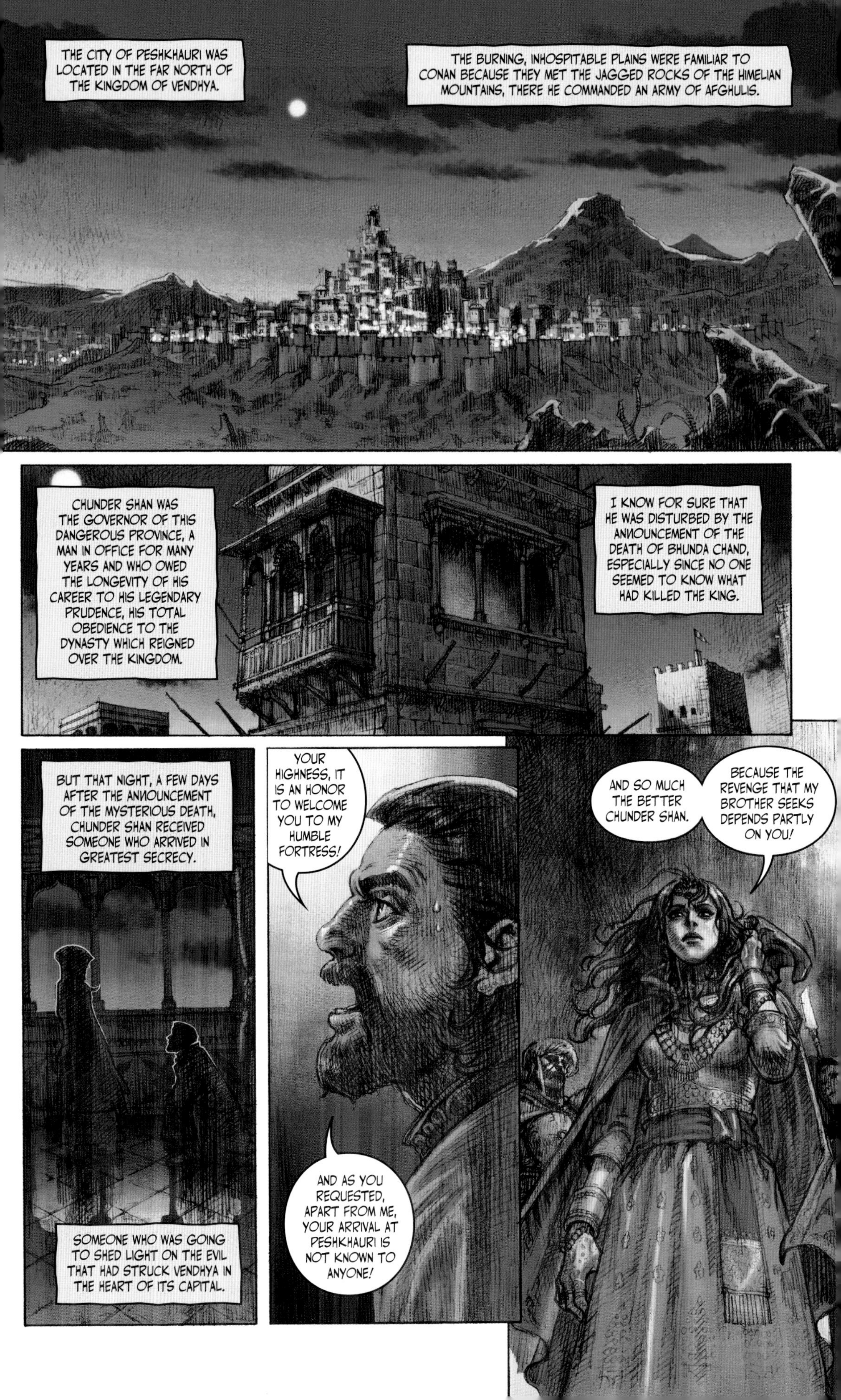

THE CITY OF PESHKHAURI WAS LOCATED IN THE FAR NORTH OF THE KINGDOM OF VENDHYA.
THE BURNING, INHOSPITABLE PLAINS WERE FAMILIAR TO CONAN BECAUSE THEY MET THE JAGGED ROCKS OF THE HIMELIAN MOUNTAINS, THERE HE COMMANDED AN ARMY OF AFGHULIS.
CHUNDER SHAN WAS THE GOVERNOR OF THIS DANGEROUS PROVINCE, A MAN IN OFFICE FOR MANY YEARS AND WHO OWED THE LONGEVITY OF HIS CAREER TO HIS LEGENDARY PRUDENCE, HIS TOTAL OBEDIENCE TO THE DYNASTY WHICH REIGNED OVER THE KINGDOM.
I KNOW FOR SURE THAT HE WAS DISTURBED BY THE ANNOUNCEMENT OF THE DEATH OF BHUNDA CHAND, ESPECIALLY SINCE NO ONE SEEMED TO KNOW WHAT HAD KILLED THE KING.
BUT THAT NIGHT, A FEW DAYS AFTER THE ANNOUNCEMENT OF THE MYSTERIOUS DEATH, CHUNDER SHAN RECEIVED SOMEONE WHO ARRIVED IN GREATEST SECRECY.
SOMEONE WHO WAS GOING TO SHED LIGHT ON THE EVIL THAT HAD STRUCK VENDHYA IN THE HEART OF ITS CAPITAL.
YOUR HIGHNESS, IT IS AN HONOR TO WELCOME YOU TO MY HUMBLE FORTRESS!
AND AS YOU REQUESTED, APART FROM ME, YOUR ARRIVAL AT PESHKHAURI IS NOT KNOWN TO ANYONE!
AND SO MUCH THE BETTER CHUNDER SHAN.
BECAUSE THE REVENGE THAT MY BROTHER SEEKS DEPENDS PARTLY ON YOU!

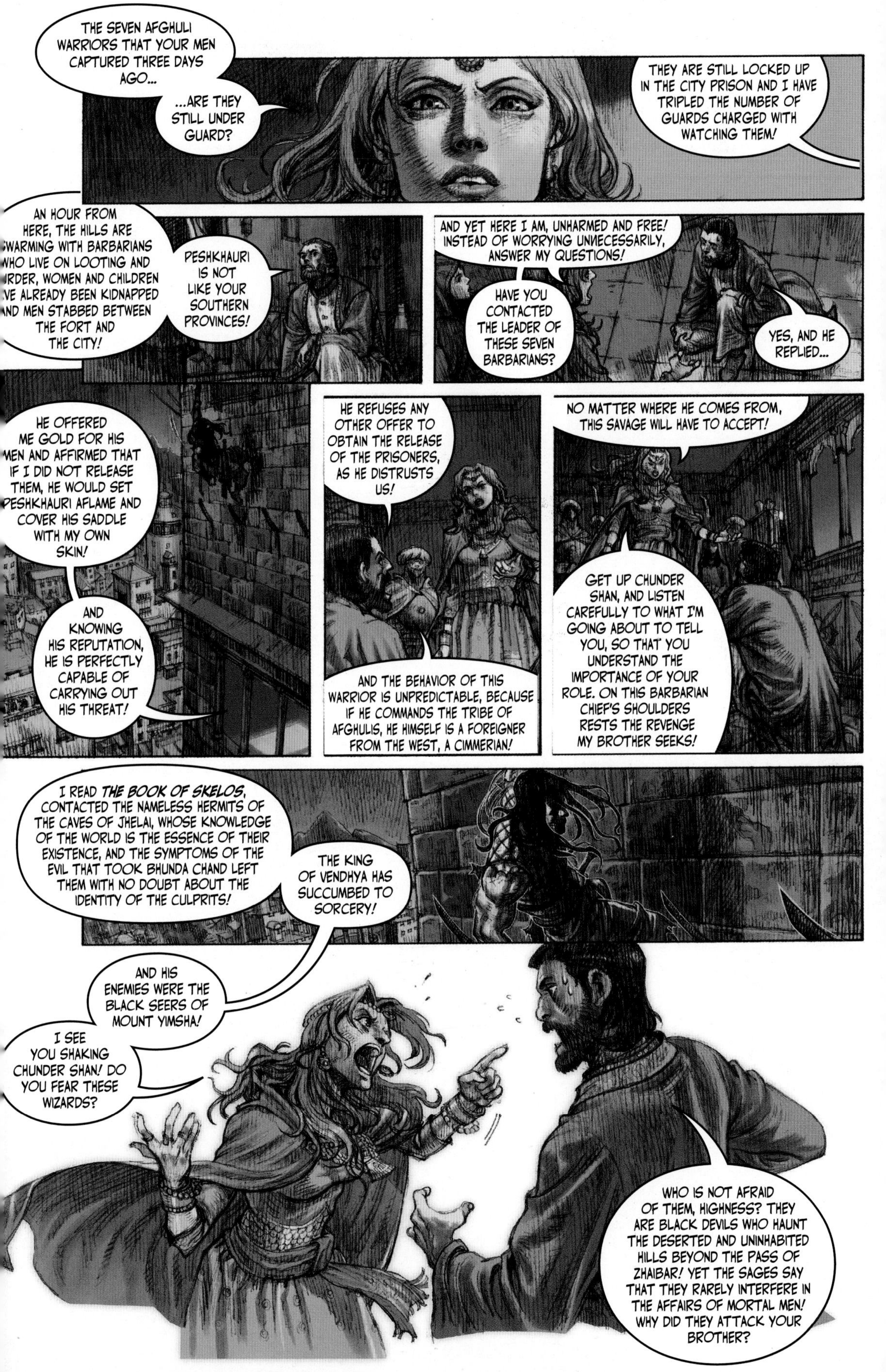
THE SEVEN AFGHULI WARRIORS THAT YOUR MEN CAPTURED THREE DAYS AGO...
...ARE THEY STILL UNDER GUARD?
THEY ARE STILL LOCKED UP IN THE CITY PRISON AND I HAVE TRIPLED THE NUMBER OF GUARDS CHARGED WITH WATCHING THEM!
AN HOUR FROM HERE, THE HILLS ARE SWARMING WITH BARBARIANS WHO LIVE ON LOOTING AND MURDER, WOMEN AND CHILDREN HAVE ALREADY BEEN KIDNAPPED AND MEN STABBED BETWEEN THE FORT AND THE CITY!
PESHKHAURI IS NOT LIKE YOUR SOUTHERN PROVINCES!
AND YET HERE I AM, UNHARMED AND FREE! INSTEAD OF WORRYING UNNECESSARILY, ANSWER MY QUESTIONS!
HAVE YOU CONTACTED THE LEADER OF THESE SEVEN BARBARIANS?
YES, AND HE REPLIED...
HE OFFERED ME GOLD FOR HIS MEN AND AFFIRMED THAT IF I DID NOT RELEASE THEM, HE WOULD SET PESHKHAURI AFLAME AND COVER HIS SADDLE WITH MY OWN SKIN!
AND KNOWING HIS REPUTATION, HE IS PERFECTLY CAPABLE OF CARRYING OUT HIS THREAT!
HE REFUSES ANY OTHER OFFER TO OBTAIN THE RELEASE OF THE PRISONERS, AS HE DISTRUSTS US!
AND THE BEHAVIOR OF THIS WARRIOR IS UNPREDICTABLE, BECAUSE IF HE COMMANDS THE TRIBE OF AFGHULIS, HE HIMSELF IS A FOREIGNER FROM THE WEST, A CIMMERIAN!
NO MATTER WHERE HE COMES FROM, THIS SAVAGE WILL HAVE TO ACCEPT!
GET UP CHUNDER SHAN, AND LISTEN CAREFULLY TO WHAT I'M GOING ABOUT TO TELL YOU, SO THAT YOU UNDERSTAND THE IMPORTANCE OF YOUR ROLE. ON THIS BARBARIAN CHIEF'S SHOULDERS RESTS THE REVENGE MY BROTHER SEEKS!
I READ *THE BOOK OF SKELOS*, CONTACTED THE NAMELESS HERMITS OF THE CAVES OF JHELAI, WHOSE KNOWLEDGE OF THE WORLD IS THE ESSENCE OF THEIR EXISTENCE, AND THE SYMPTOMS OF THE EVIL THAT TOOK BHUNDA CHAND LEFT THEM WITH NO DOUBT ABOUT THE IDENTITY OF THE CULPRITS!
THE KING OF VENDHYA HAS SUCCUMBED TO SORCERY!
AND HIS ENEMIES WERE THE BLACK SEERS OF MOUNT YIMSHA!
I SEE YOU SHAKING CHUNDER SHAN! DO YOU FEAR THESE WIZARDS?
WHO IS NOT AFRAID OF THEM, HIGHNESS? THEY ARE BLACK DEVILS WHO HAUNT THE DESERTED AND UNINHABITED HILLS BEYOND THE PASS OF ZHAIBAR! YET THE SAGES SAY THAT THEY RARELY INTERFERE IN THE AFFAIRS OF MORTAL MEN! WHY DID THEY ATTACK YOUR BROTHER?

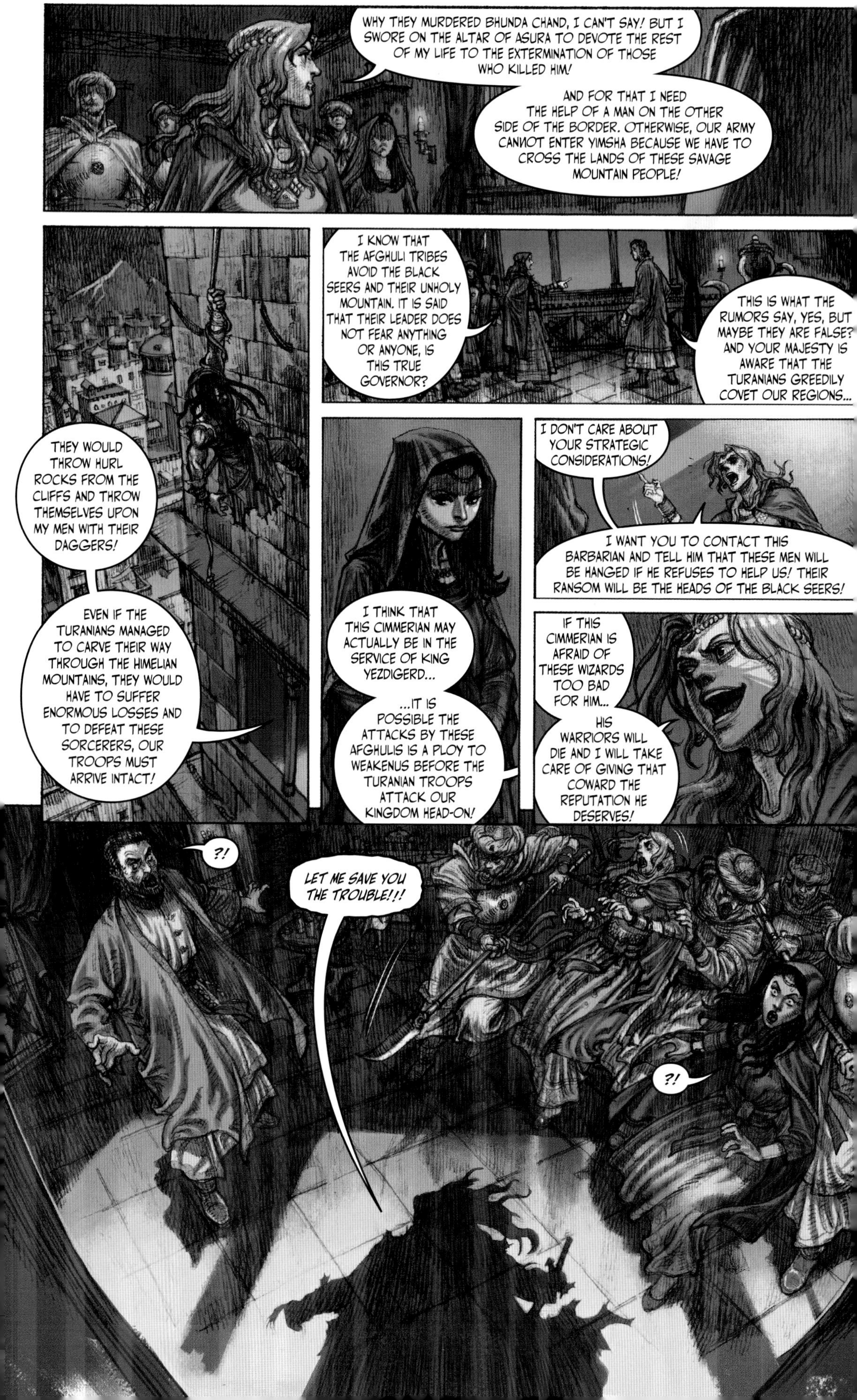

WHY THEY MURDERED BHUNDA CHAND, I CAN'T SAY! BUT I SWORE ON THE ALTAR OF ASURA TO DEVOTE THE REST OF MY LIFE TO THE EXTERMINATION OF THOSE WHO KILLED HIM!
AND FOR THAT I NEED THE HELP OF A MAN ON THE OTHER SIDE OF THE BORDER. OTHERWISE, OUR ARMY CANNOT ENTER YIMSHA BECAUSE WE HAVE TO CROSS THE LANDS OF THESE SAVAGE MOUNTAIN PEOPLE!
I KNOW THAT THE AFGHULI TRIBES AVOID THE BLACK SEERS AND THEIR UNHOLY MOUNTAIN. IT IS SAID THAT THEIR LEADER DOES NOT FEAR ANYTHING OR ANYONE, IS THIS TRUE GOVERNOR?
THIS IS WHAT THE RUMORS SAY, YES, BUT MAYBE THEY ARE FALSE? AND YOUR MAJESTY IS AWARE THAT THE TURANIANS GREEDILY COVET OUR REGIONS...
THEY WOULD THROW HURL ROCKS FROM THE CLIFFS AND THROW THEMSELVES UPON MY MEN WITH THEIR DAGGERS!
EVEN IF THE TURANIANS MANAGED TO CARVE THEIR WAY THROUGH THE HIMELIAN MOUNTAINS, THEY WOULD HAVE TO SUFFER ENORMOUS LOSSES AND TO DEFEAT THESE SORCERERS, OUR TROOPS MUST ARRIVE INTACT!
I THINK THAT THIS CIMMERIAN MAY ACTUALLY BE IN THE SERVICE OF KING YEZDIGERD...
...IT IS POSSIBLE THE ATTACKS BY THESE AFGHULIS IS A PLOY TO WEAKENUS BEFORE THE TURANIAN TROOPS ATTACK OUR KINGDOM HEAD-ON!
I DON'T CARE ABOUT YOUR STRATEGIC CONSIDERATIONS!
I WANT YOU TO CONTACT THIS BARBARIAN AND TELL HIM THAT THESE MEN WILL BE HANGED IF HE REFUSES TO HELP US! THEIR RANSOM WILL BE THE HEADS OF THE BLACK SEERS!
IF THIS CIMMERIAN IS AFRAID OF THESE WIZARDS TOO BAD FOR HIM...
HIS WARRIORS WILL DIE AND I WILL TAKE CARE OF GIVING THAT COWARD THE REPUTATION HE DESERVES!
?!
LET ME SAVE YOU THE TROUBLE!!!
?!

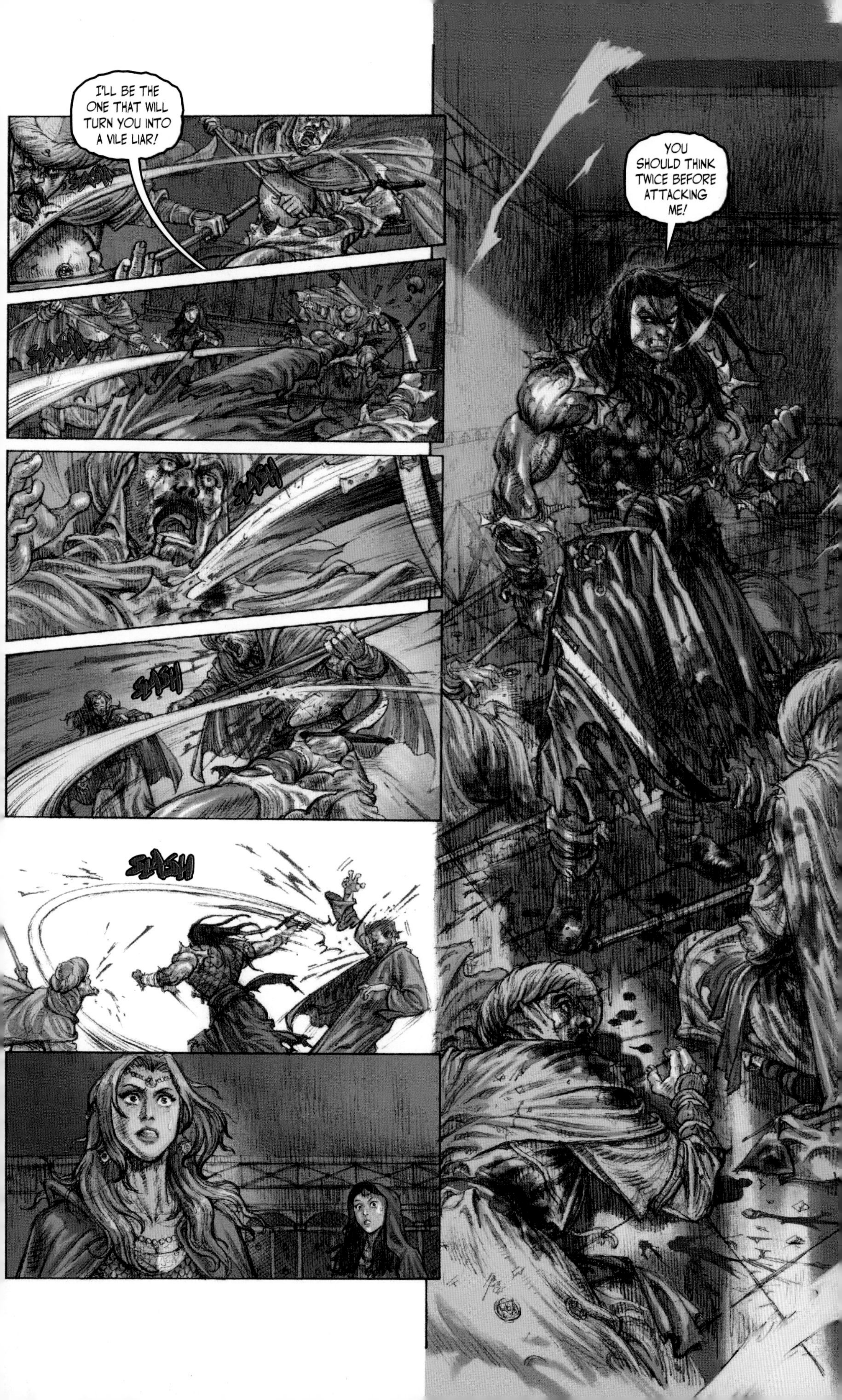
I'LL BE THE ONE THAT WILL TURN YOU INTO A VILE LIAR!
SLASH
SLASH
SLASH
SLASH
SLASH
YOU SHOULD THINK TWICE BEFORE ATTACKING ME!

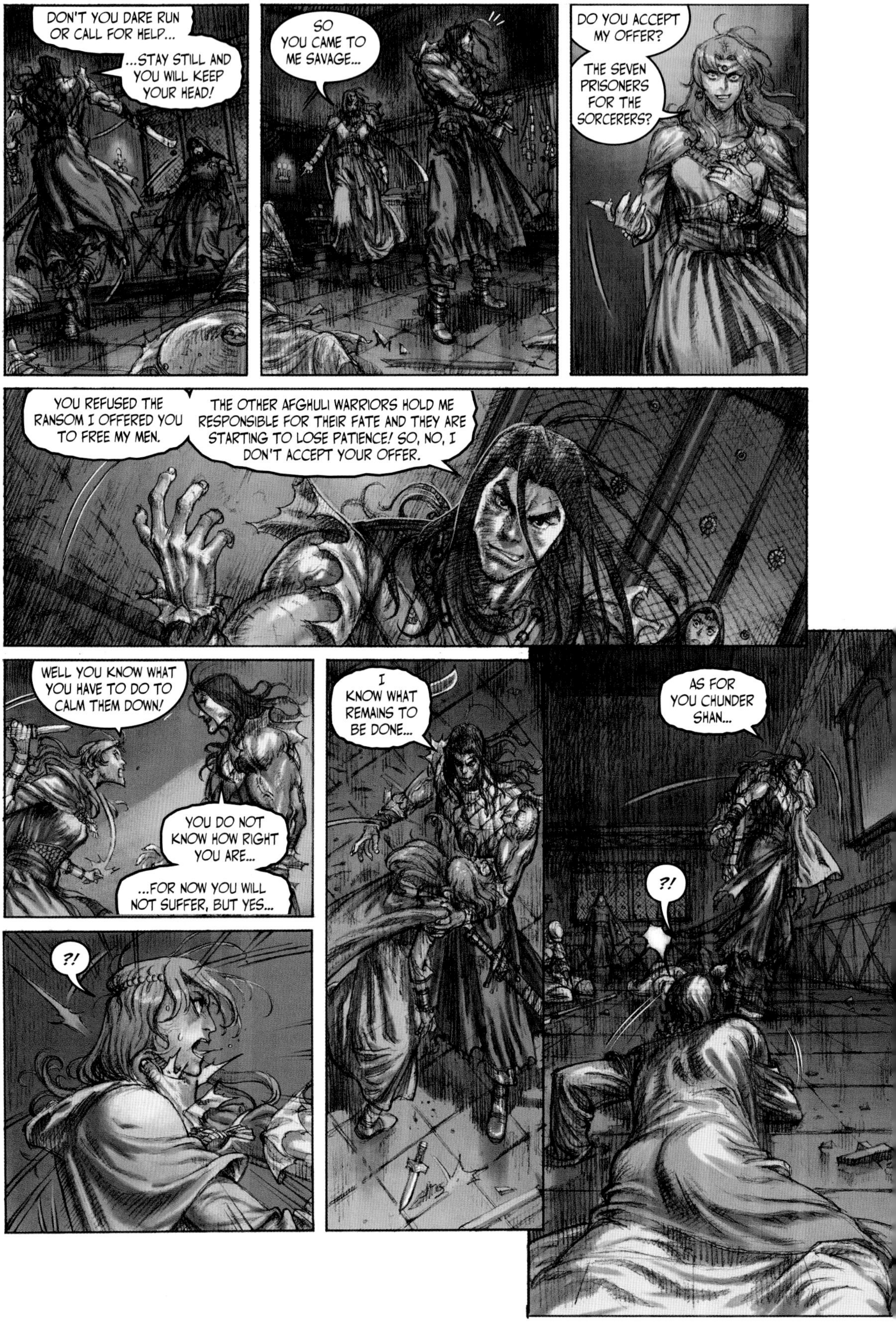
DON'T YOU DARE RUN OR CALL FOR HELP...
...STAY STILL AND YOU WILL KEEP YOUR HEAD!
SO YOU CAME TO ME SAVAGE...
DO YOU ACCEPT MY OFFER?
THE SEVEN PRISONERS FOR THE SORCERERS?
YOU REFUSED THE RANSOM I OFFERED YOU TO FREE MY MEN.
THE OTHER AFGHULI WARRIORS HOLD ME RESPONSIBLE FOR THEIR FATE AND THEY ARE STARTING TO LOSE PATIENCE! SO, NO, I DON'T ACCEPT YOUR OFFER.
WELL YOU KNOW WHAT YOU HAVE TO DO TO CALM THEM DOWN!
YOU DO NOT KNOW HOW RIGHT YOU ARE...
...FOR NOW YOU WILL NOT SUFFER, BUT YES...
?!
I KNOW WHAT REMAINS TO BE DONE...
AS FOR YOU CHUNDER SHAN...
?!

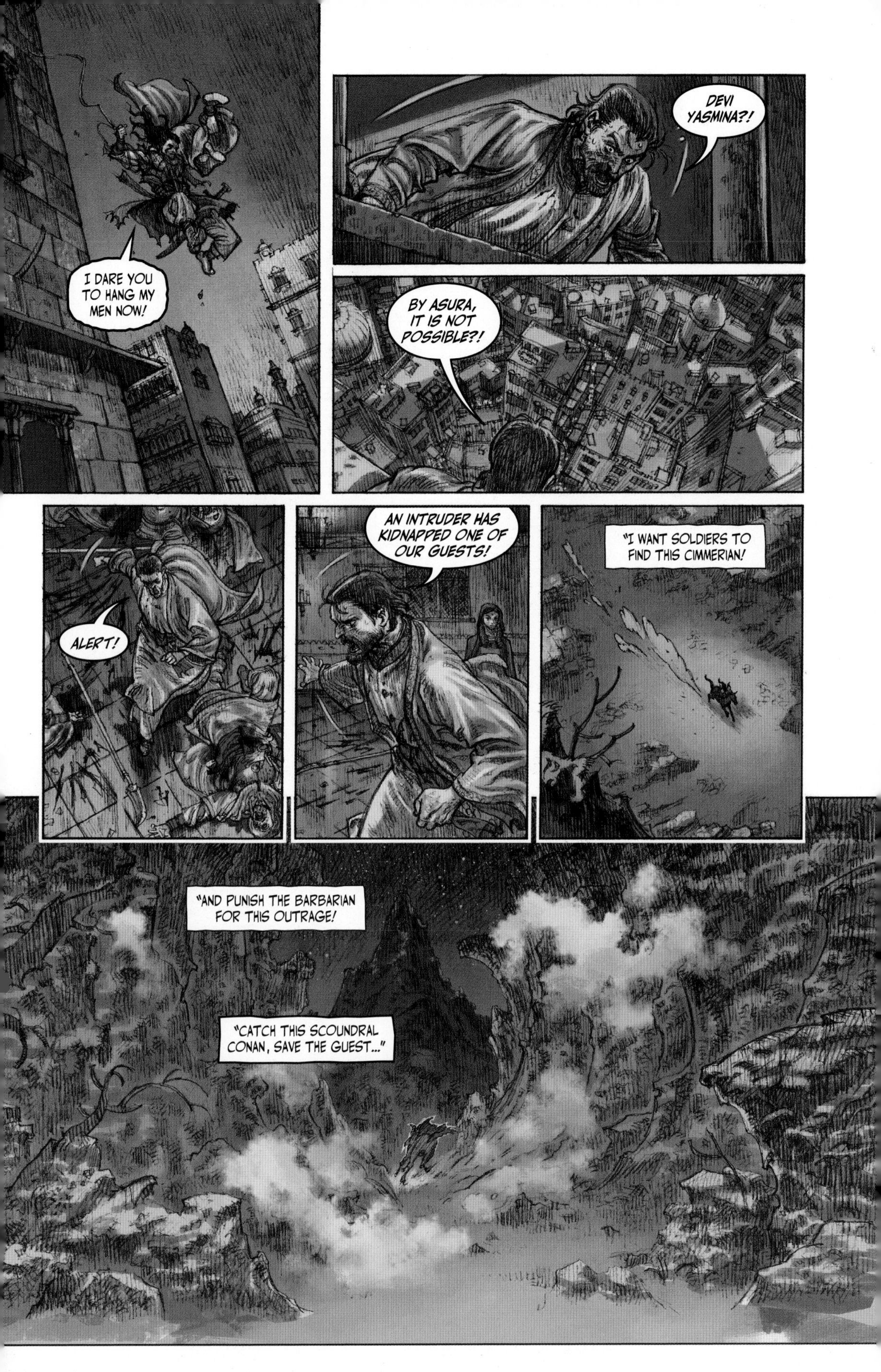
I DARE YOU TO HANG MY MEN NOW!
DEVI YASMINA?!
BY ASURA, IT IS NOT POSSIBLE?!
ALERT!
AN INTRUDER HAS KIDNAPPED ONE OF OUR GUESTS!
"I WANT SOLDIERS TO FIND THIS CIMMERIAN!
"AND PUNISH THE BARBARIAN FOR THIS OUTRAGE!
"CATCH THIS SCOUNDRAL CONAN, SAVE THE GUEST..."

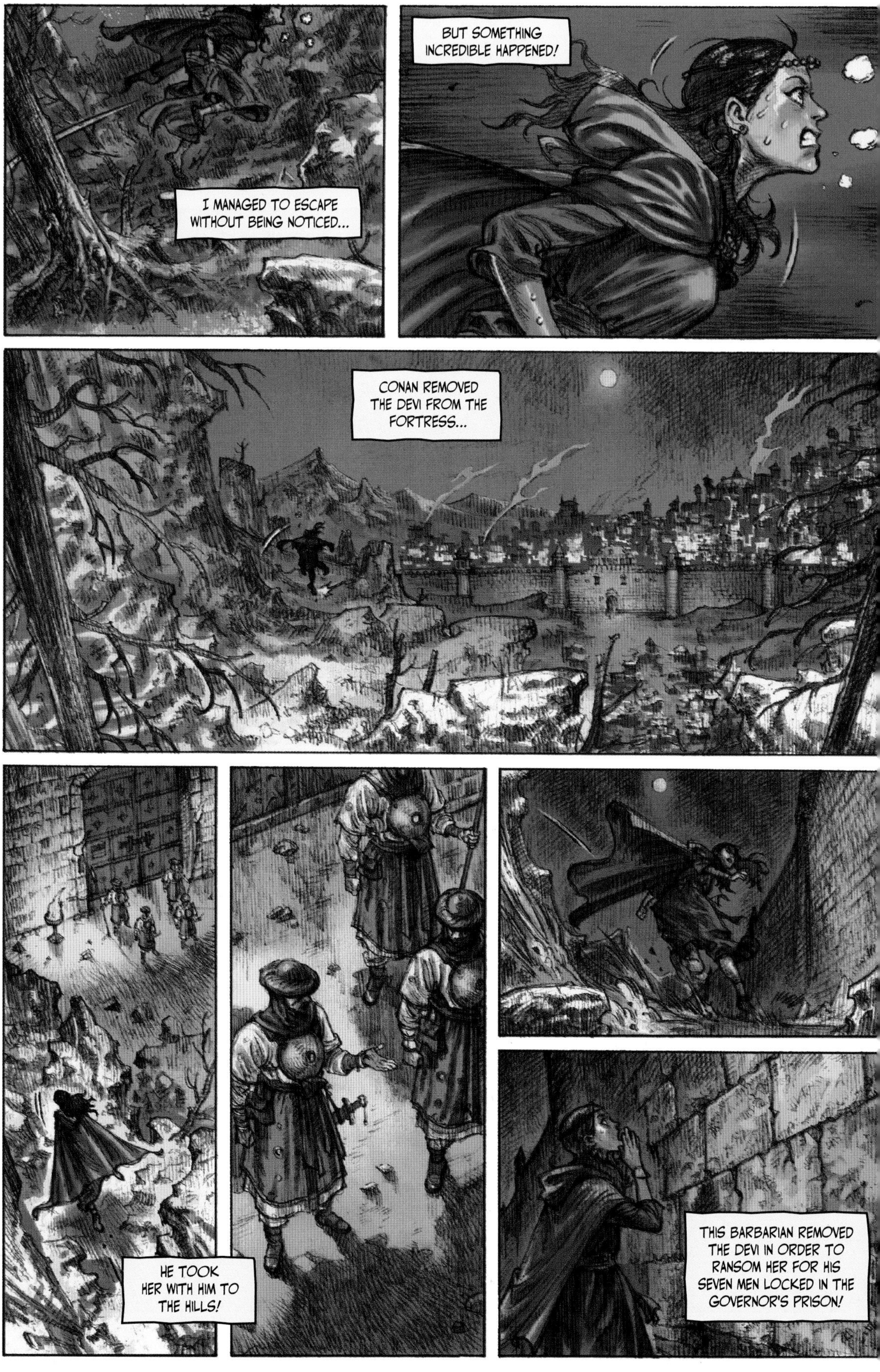
I MANAGED TO ESCAPE WITHOUT BEING NOTICED...
BUT SOMETHING INCREDIBLE HAPPENED!
CONAN REMOVED THE DEVI FROM THE FORTRESS...
HE TOOK HER WITH HIM TO THE HILLS!
THIS BARBARIAN REMOVED THE DEVI IN ORDER TO RANSOM HER FOR HIS SEVEN MEN LOCKED IN THE GOVERNOR'S PRISON!

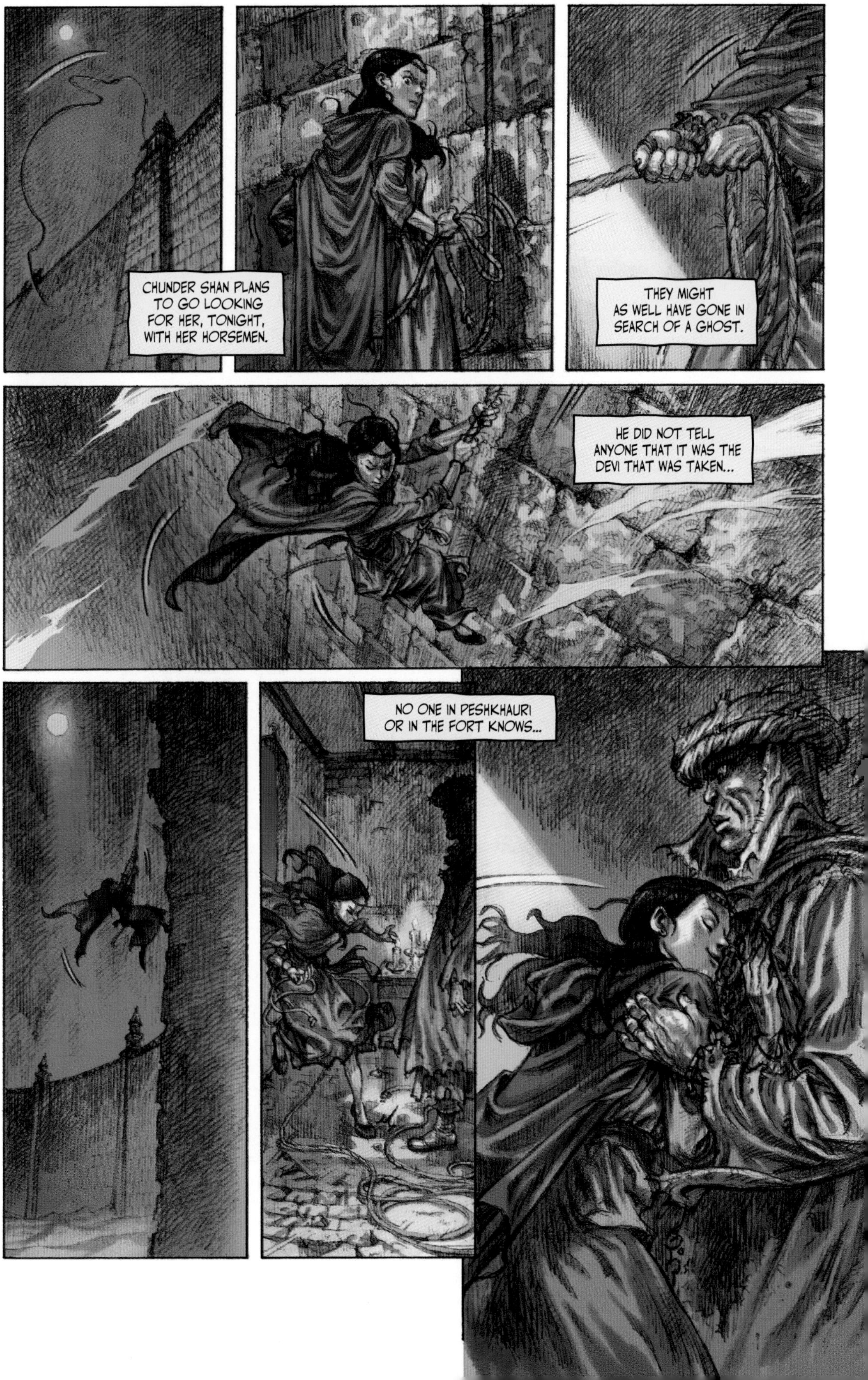
CHUNDER SHAN PLANS TO GO LOOKING FOR HER, TONIGHT, WITH HER HORSEMEN.
THEY MIGHT AS WELL HAVE GONE IN SEARCH OF A GHOST.
HE DID NOT TELL ANYONE THAT IT WAS THE DEVI THAT WAS TAKEN...
NO ONE IN PESHKHAURI OR IN THE FORT KNOWS...

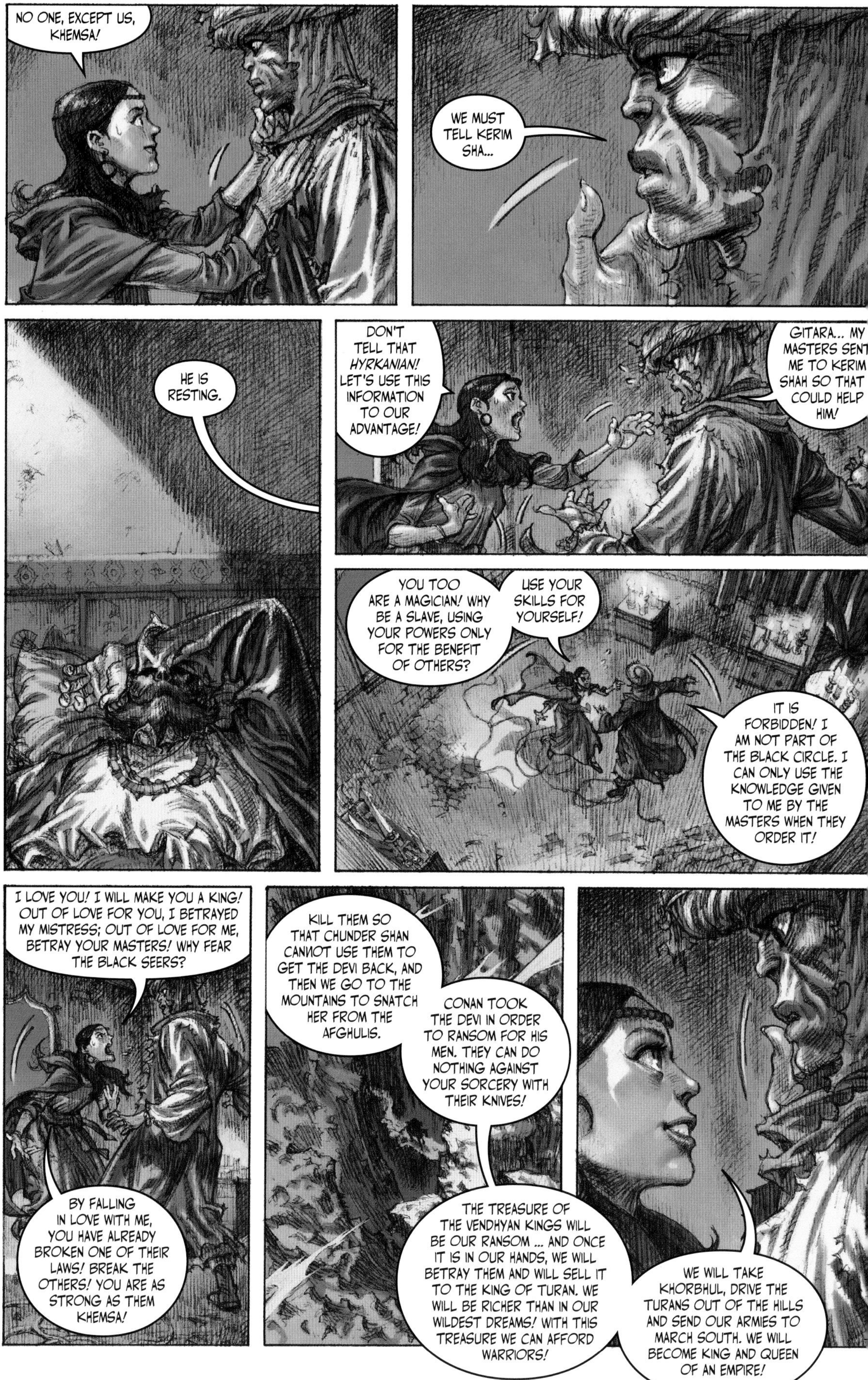
NO ONE, EXCEPT US, KHEMSA!
WE MUST TELL KERIM SHA...
HE IS RESTING.
DON'T TELL THAT *HYRKANIAN!* LET'S USE THIS INFORMATION TO OUR ADVANTAGE!
GITARA... MY MASTERS SENT ME TO KERIM SHAH SO THAT I COULD HELP HIM!
YOU TOO ARE A MAGICIAN! WHY BE A SLAVE, USING YOUR POWERS ONLY FOR THE BENEFIT OF OTHERS?
USE YOUR SKILLS FOR YOURSELF!
IT IS FORBIDDEN! I AM NOT PART OF THE BLACK CIRCLE. I CAN ONLY USE THE KNOWLEDGE GIVEN TO ME BY THE MASTERS WHEN THEY ORDER IT!
I LOVE YOU! I WILL MAKE YOU A KING! OUT OF LOVE FOR YOU, I BETRAYED MY MISTRESS; OUT OF LOVE FOR ME, BETRAY YOUR MASTERS! WHY FEAR THE BLACK SEERS?
BY FALLING IN LOVE WITH ME, YOU HAVE ALREADY BROKEN ONE OF THEIR LAWS! BREAK THE OTHERS! YOU ARE AS STRONG AS THEM KHEMSA!
KILL THEM SO THAT CHUNDER SHAN CANNOT USE THEM TO GET THE DEVI BACK, AND THEN WE GO TO THE MOUNTAINS TO SNATCH HER FROM THE AFGHULIS.
CONAN TOOK THE DEVI IN ORDER TO RANSOM FOR HIS MEN. THEY CAN DO NOTHING AGAINST YOUR SORCERY WITH THEIR KNIVES!
THE TREASURE OF THE VENDHYAN KINGS WILL BE OUR RANSOM ... AND ONCE IT IS IN OUR HANDS, WE WILL BETRAY THEM AND WILL SELL IT TO THE KING OF TURAN. WE WILL BE RICHER THAN IN OUR WILDEST DREAMS! WITH THIS TREASURE WE CAN AFFORD WARRIORS!
WE WILL TAKE KHORBHUL, DRIVE THE TURANS OUT OF THE HILLS AND SEND OUR ARMIES TO MARCH SOUTH. WE WILL BECOME KING AND QUEEN OF AN EMPIRE!

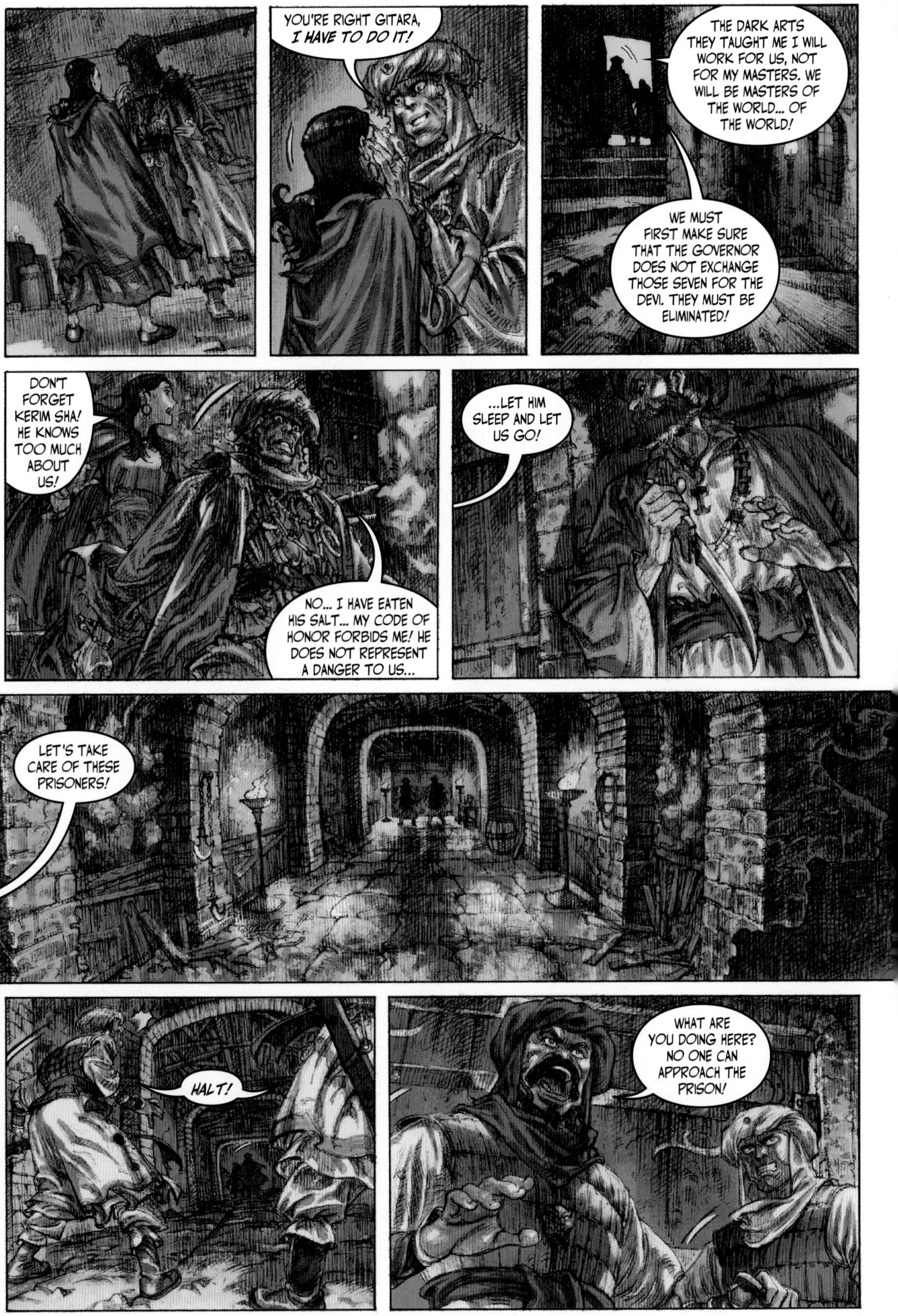
YOU'RE RIGHT GITARA, I HAVE TO DO IT!
THE DARK ARTS THEY TAUGHT ME I WILL WORK FOR US, NOT FOR MY MASTERS. WE WILL BE MASTERS OF THE WORLD... OF THE WORLD!
WE MUST FIRST MAKE SURE THAT THE GOVERNOR DOES NOT EXCHANGE THOSE SEVEN FOR THE DEVI. THEY MUST BE ELIMINATED!
DON'T FORGET KERIM SHA! HE KNOWS TOO MUCH ABOUT US!
NO... I HAVE EATEN HIS SALT... MY CODE OF HONOR FORBIDS ME! HE DOES NOT REPRESENT A DANGER TO US...
...LET HIM SLEEP AND LET US GO!
LET'S TAKE CARE OF THESE PRISONERS!
HALT!
WHAT ARE YOU DOING HERE? NO ONE CAN APPROACH THE PRISON!

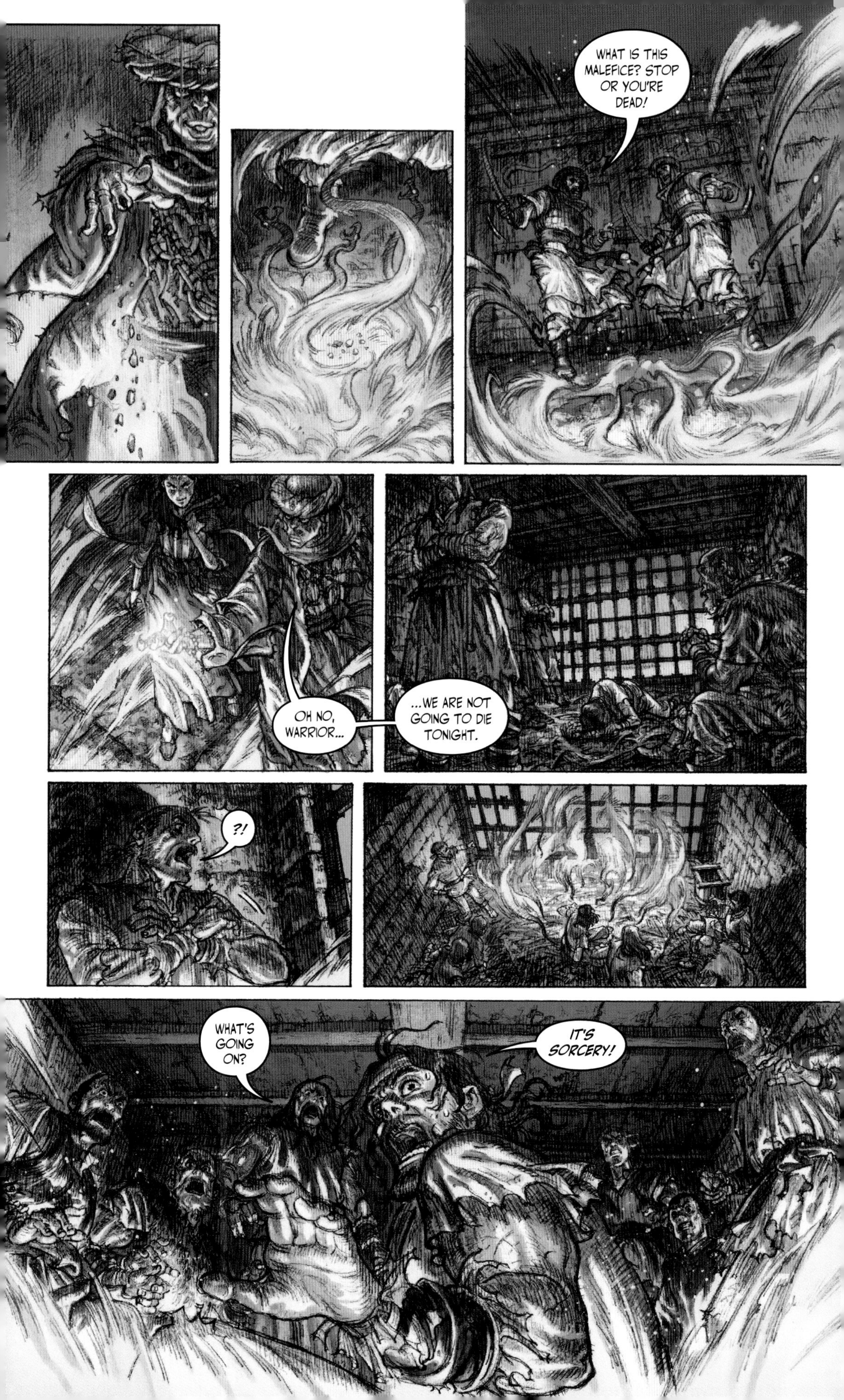
WHAT IS THIS MALEFICE? STOP OR YOU'RE DEAD!
OH NO, WARRIOR...
...WE ARE NOT GOING TO DIE TONIGHT.
?!
WHAT'S GOING ON?
IT'S SORCERY!

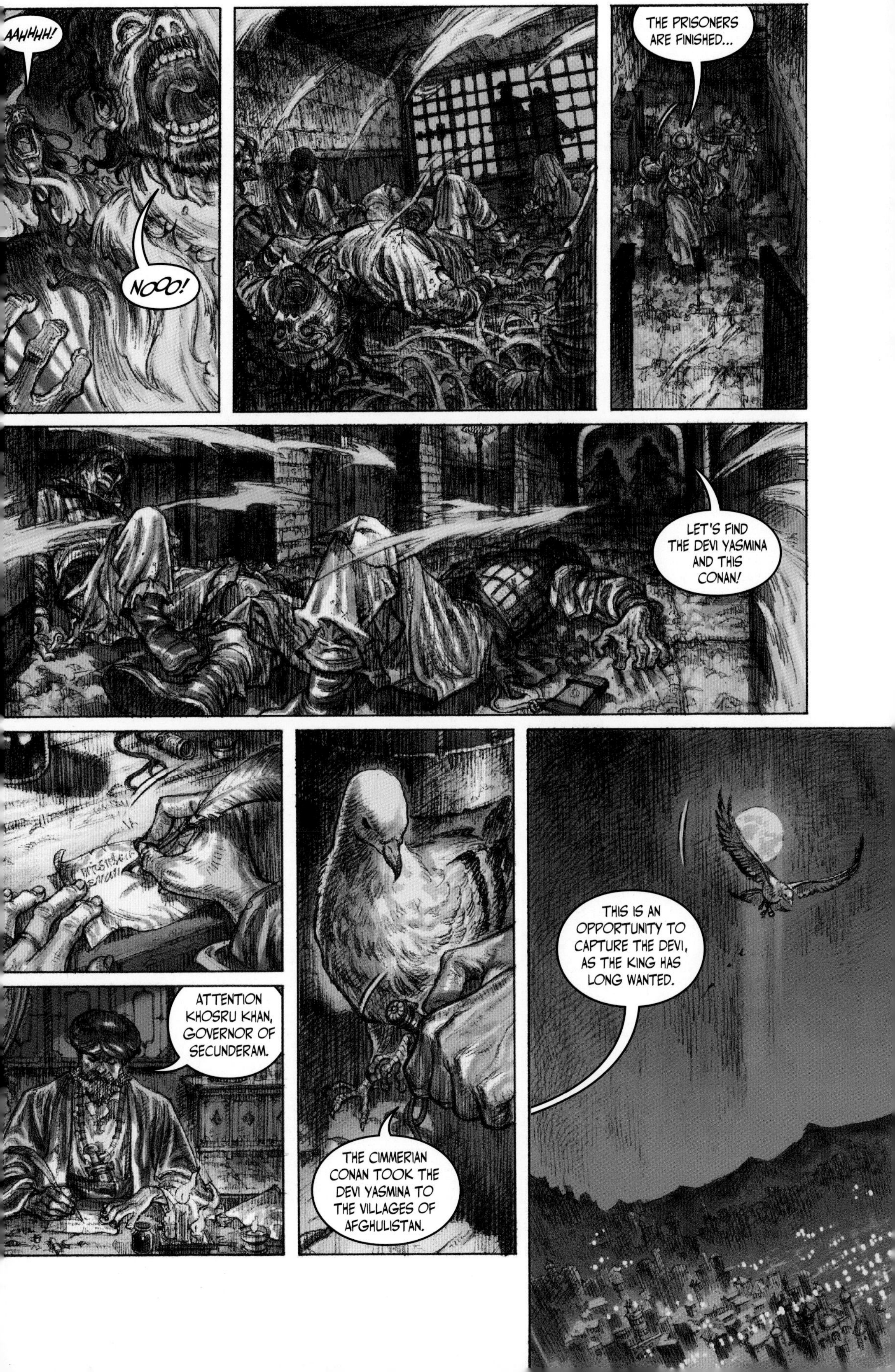
AAHHHH!
NOOO!
THE PRISONERS ARE FINISHED...
LET'S FIND THE DEVI YASMINA AND THIS CONAN!
ATTENTION KHOSRU KHAN, GOVERNOR OF SECUNDERAM.
THE CIMMERIAN CONAN TOOK THE DEVI YASMINA TO THE VILLAGES OF AFGHULISTAN.
THIS IS AN OPPORTUNITY TO CAPTURE THE DEVI, AS THE KING HAS LONG WANTED.

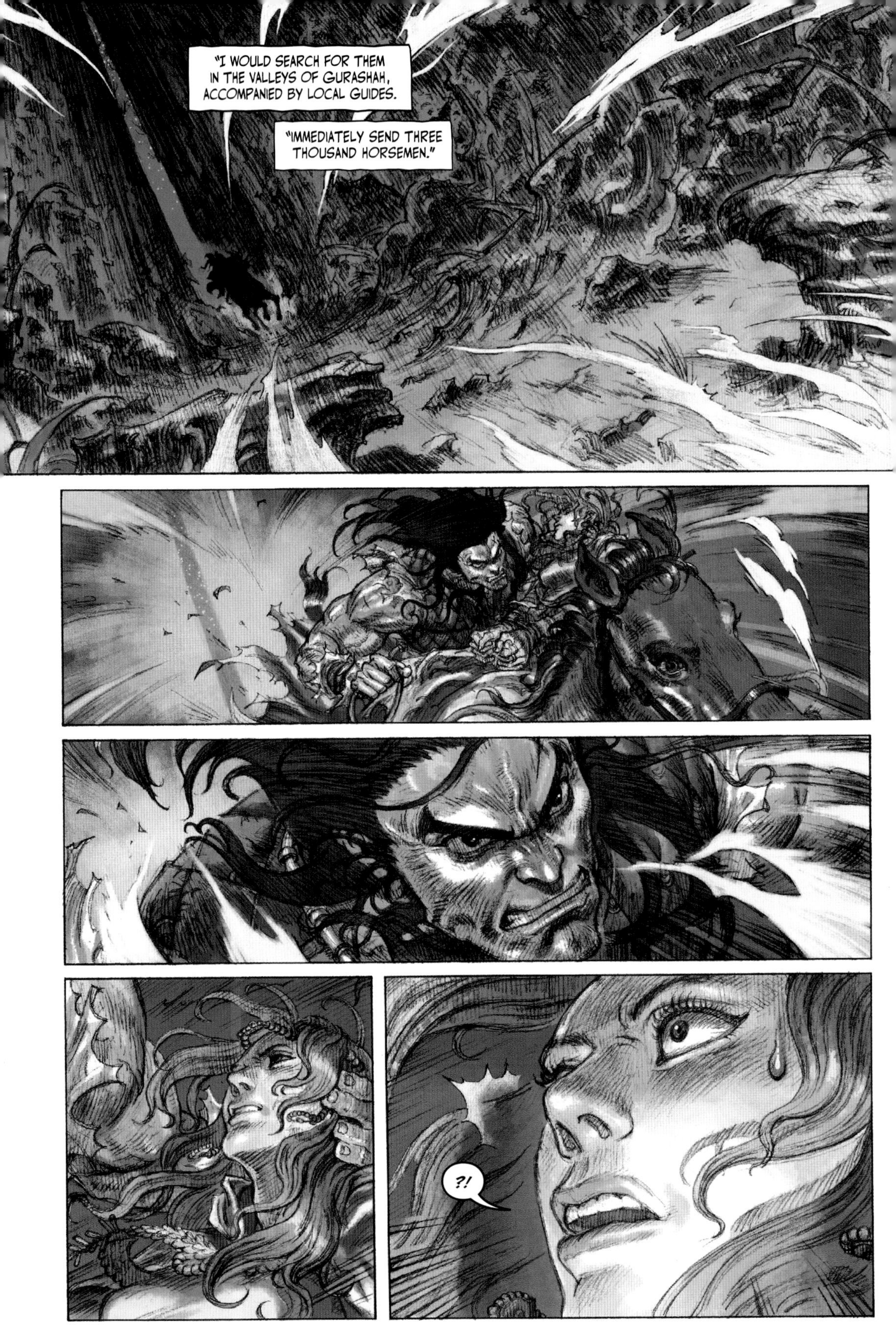

"I WOULD SEARCH FOR THEM IN THE VALLEYS OF GURASHAH, ACCOMPANIED BY LOCAL GUIDES.
"IMMEDIATELY SEND THREE THOUSAND HORSEMEN."
?!

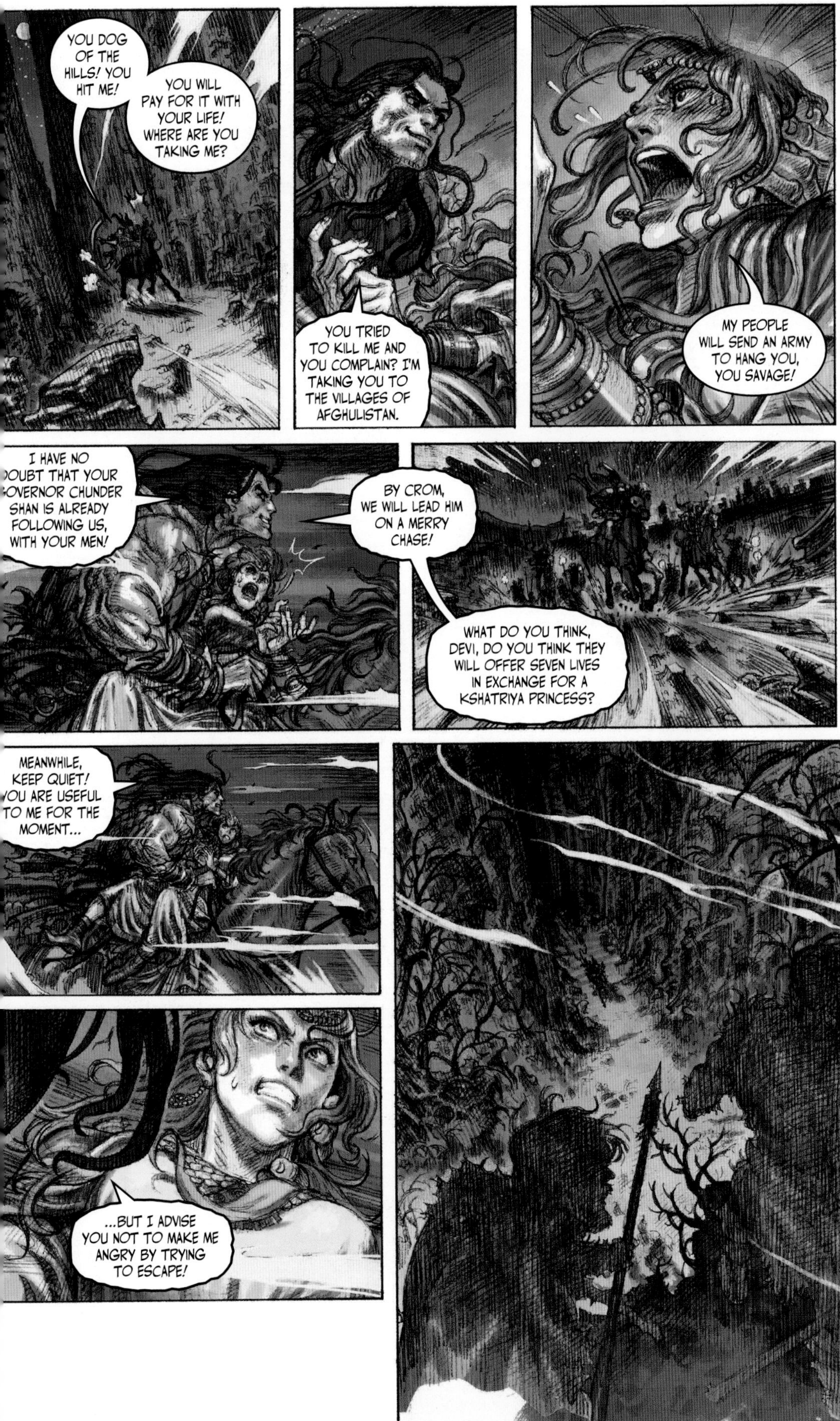
YOU DOG OF THE HILLS! YOU HIT ME!
YOU WILL PAY FOR IT WITH YOUR LIFE! WHERE ARE YOU TAKING ME?
YOU TRIED TO KILL ME AND YOU COMPLAIN? I'M TAKING YOU TO THE VILLAGES OF AFGHULISTAN.
MY PEOPLE WILL SEND AN ARMY TO HANG YOU, YOU SAVAGE!
I HAVE NO DOUBT THAT YOUR GOVERNOR CHUNDER SHAN IS ALREADY FOLLOWING US, WITH YOUR MEN!
BY CROM, WE WILL LEAD HIM ON A MERRY CHASE!
WHAT DO YOU THINK, DEVI, DO YOU THINK THEY WILL OFFER SEVEN LIVES IN EXCHANGE FOR A KSHATRIYA PRINCESS?
MEANWHILE, KEEP QUIET! YOU ARE USEFUL TO ME FOR THE MOMENT...
...BUT I ADVISE YOU NOT TO MAKE ME ANGRY BY TRYING TO ESCAPE!

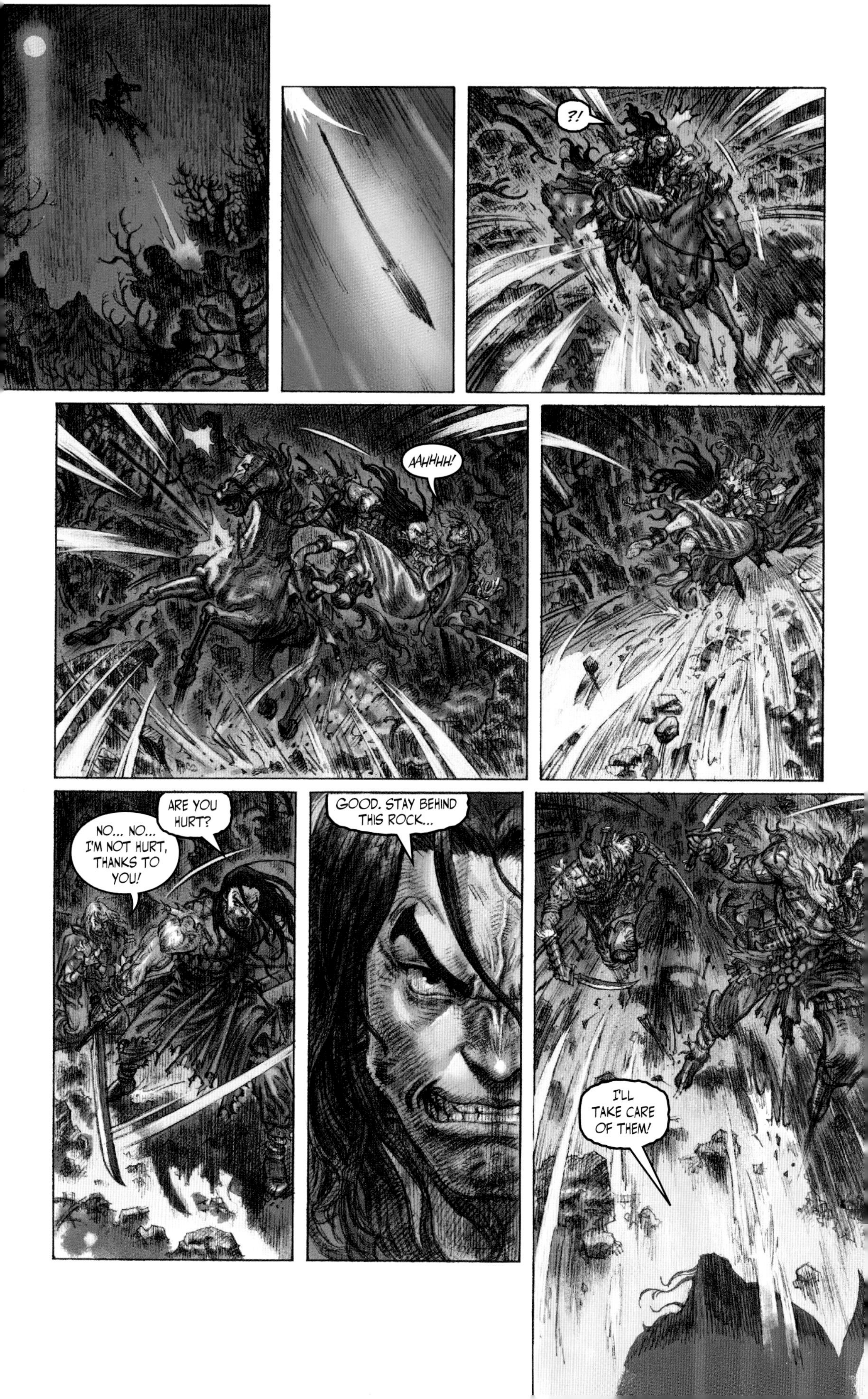
?!
AAHHHH!
ARE YOU HURT?
NO... NO... I'M NOT HURT, THANKS TO YOU!
GOOD. STAY BEHIND THIS ROCK...
I'LL TAKE CARE OF THEM!

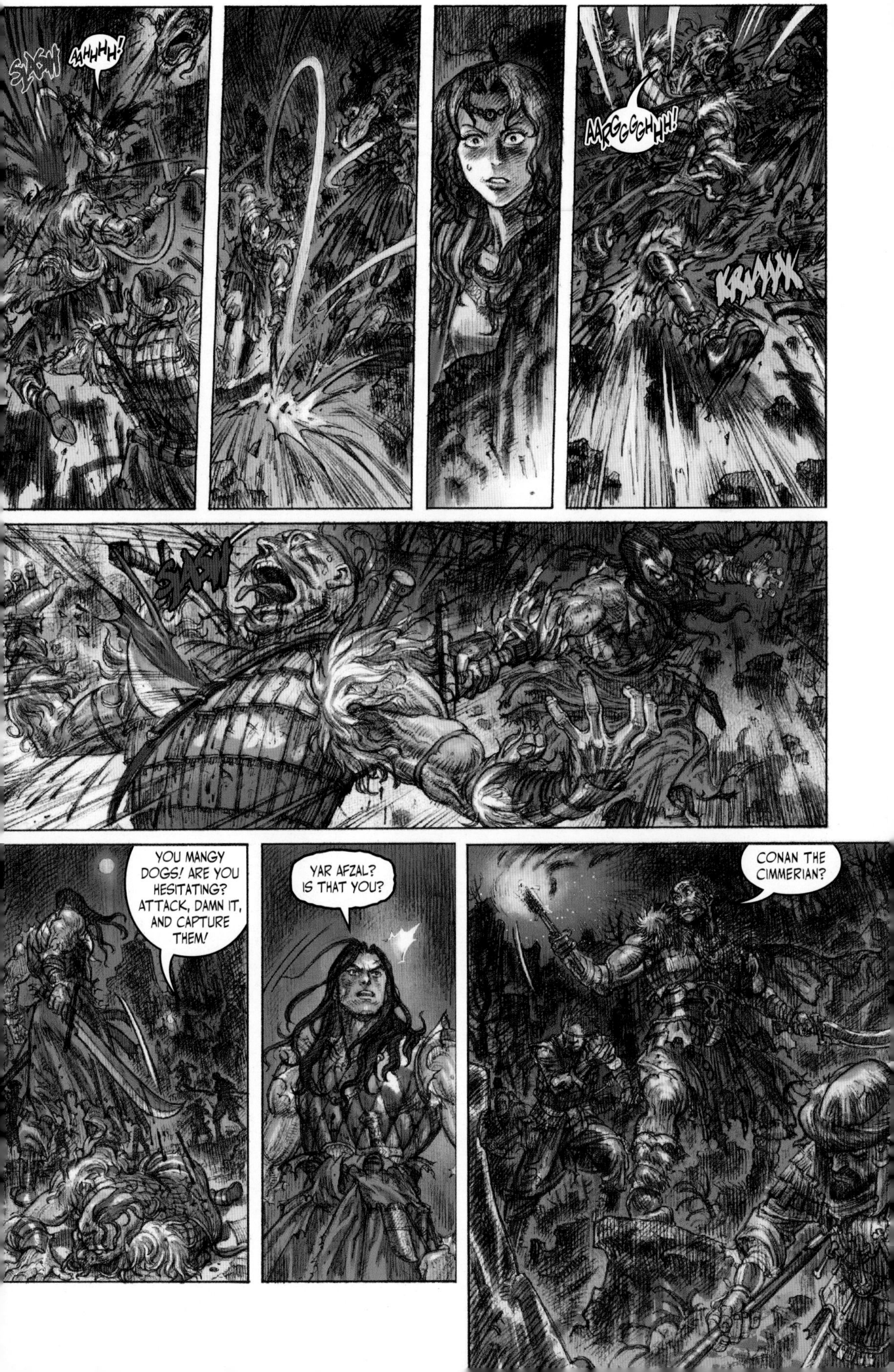
AAHHHH!
AARGGGHHH!
YOU MANGY DOGS! ARE YOU HESITATING? ATTACK, DAMN IT, AND CAPTURE THEM!
YAR AFZAL? IS THAT YOU?
CONAN THE CIMMERIAN?

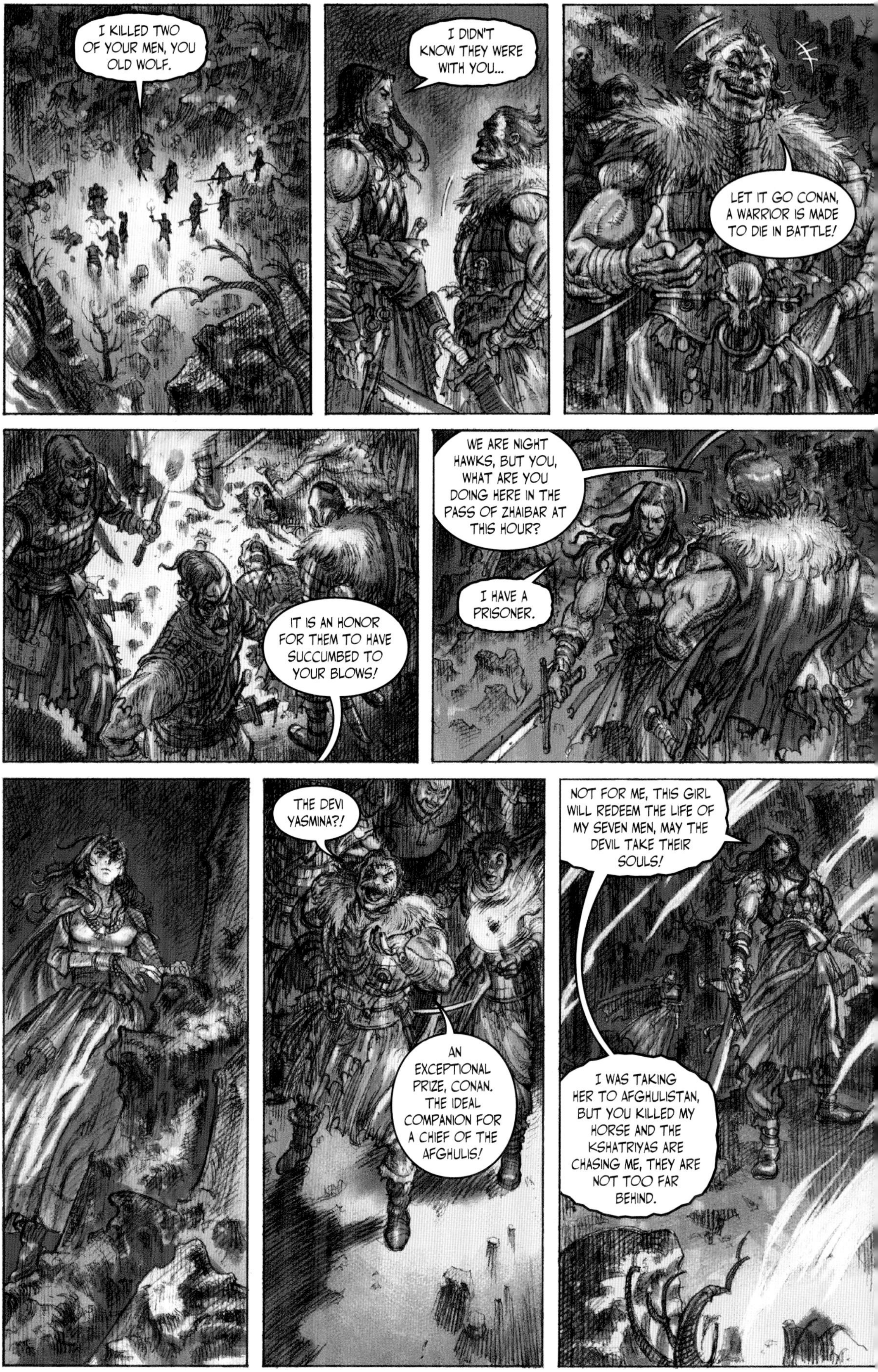
I KILLED TWO OF YOUR MEN, YOU OLD WOLF.
I DIDN'T KNOW THEY WERE WITH YOU...
LET IT GO CONAN, A WARRIOR IS MADE TO DIE IN BATTLE!
IT IS AN HONOR FOR THEM TO HAVE SUCCUMBED TO YOUR BLOWS!
WE ARE NIGHT HAWKS, BUT YOU, WHAT ARE YOU DOING HERE IN THE PASS OF ZHAIBAR AT THIS HOUR?
I HAVE A PRISONER.
THE DEVI YASMINA?!
AN EXCEPTIONAL PRIZE, CONAN. THE IDEAL COMPANION FOR A CHIEF OF THE AFGHULIS!
NOT FOR ME, THIS GIRL WILL REDEEM THE LIFE OF MY SEVEN MEN, MAY THE DEVIL TAKE THEIR SOULS!
I WAS TAKING HER TO AFGHULISTAN, BUT YOU KILLED MY HORSE AND THE KSHATRIYAS ARE CHASING ME, THEY ARE NOT TOO FAR BEHIND.

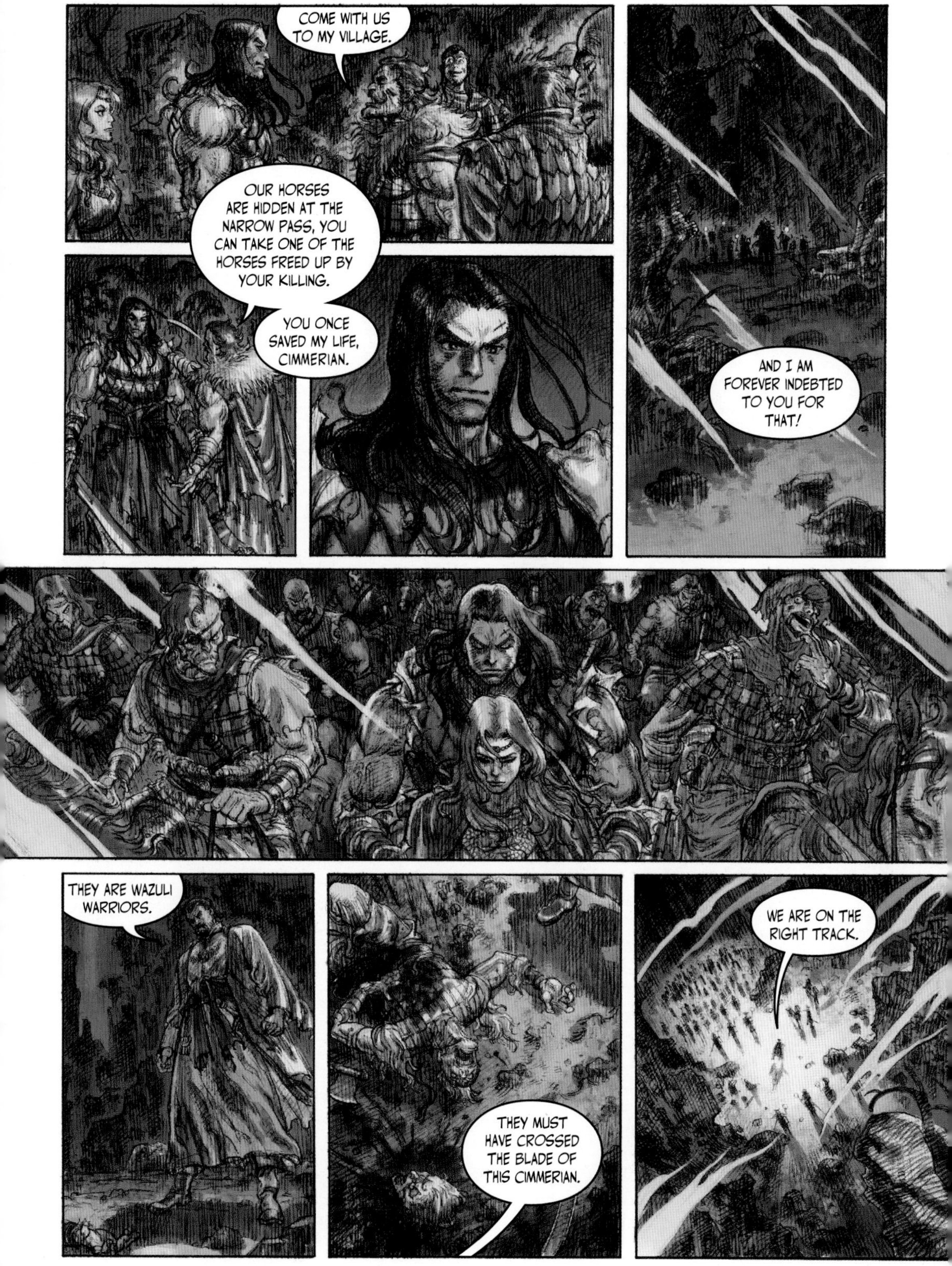
COME WITH US TO MY VILLAGE.
OUR HORSES ARE HIDDEN AT THE NARROW PASS, YOU CAN TAKE ONE OF THE HORSES FREED UP BY YOUR KILLING.
YOU ONCE SAVED MY LIFE, CIMMERIAN.
AND I AM FOREVER INDEBTED TO YOU FOR THAT!
THEY ARE WAZULI WARRIORS.
THEY MUST HAVE CROSSED THE BLADE OF THIS CIMMERIAN.
WE ARE ON THE RIGHT TRACK.

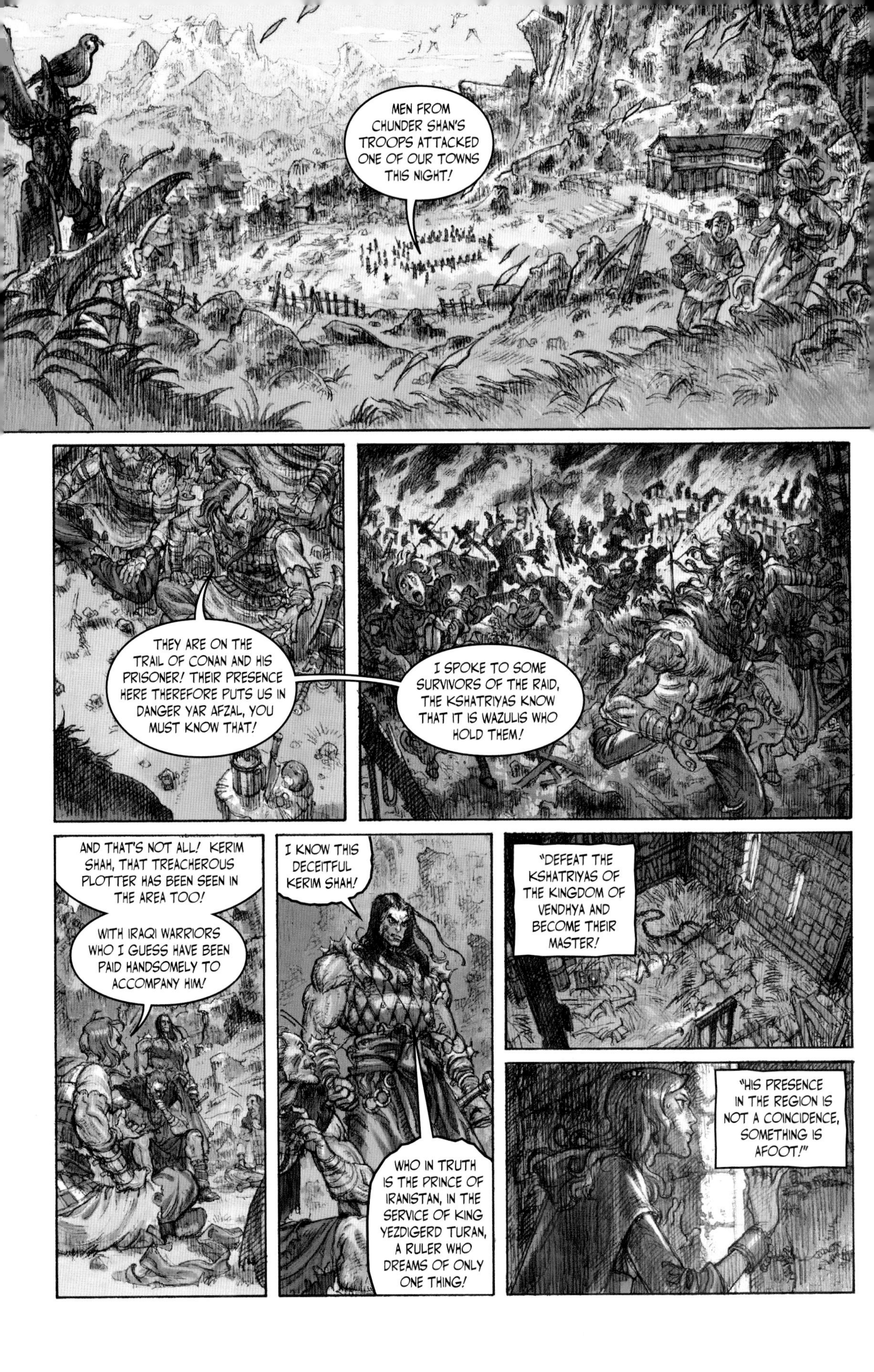

MEN FROM CHUNDER SHAN'S TROOPS ATTACKED ONE OF OUR TOWNS THIS NIGHT!
THEY ARE ON THE TRAIL OF CONAN AND HIS PRISONER! THEIR PRESENCE HERE THEREFORE PUTS US IN DANGER YAR AFZAL, YOU MUST KNOW THAT!
I SPOKE TO SOME SURVIVORS OF THE RAID, THE KSHATRIYAS KNOW THAT IT IS WAZULIS WHO HOLD THEM!
AND THAT'S NOT ALL! KERIM SHAH, THAT TREACHEROUS PLOTTER HAS BEEN SEEN IN THE AREA TOO!
WITH IRAQI WARRIORS WHO I GUESS HAVE BEEN PAID HANDSOMELY TO ACCOMPANY HIM!
I KNOW THIS DECEITFUL KERIM SHAH!
WHO IN TRUTH IS THE PRINCE OF IRANISTAN, IN THE SERVICE OF KING YEZDIGERD TURAN, A RULER WHO DREAMS OF ONLY ONE THING!
"DEFEAT THE KSHATRIYAS OF THE KINGDOM OF VENDHYA AND BECOME THEIR MASTER!
"HIS PRESENCE IN THE REGION IS NOT A COINCIDENCE, SOMETHING IS AFOOT!"

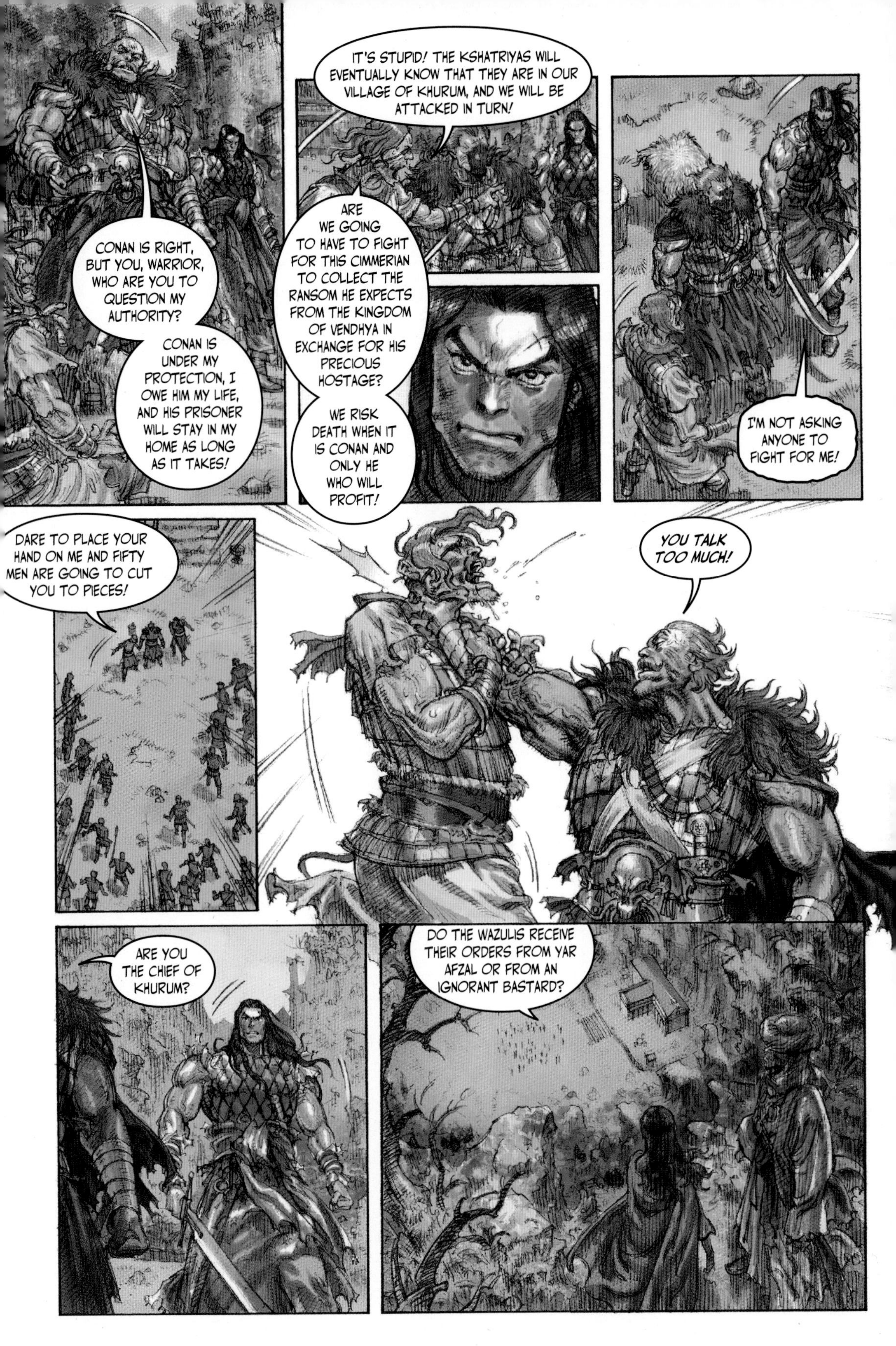
CONAN IS RIGHT, BUT YOU, WARRIOR, WHO ARE YOU TO QUESTION MY AUTHORITY?
CONAN IS UNDER MY PROTECTION, I OWE HIM MY LIFE, AND HIS PRISONER WILL STAY IN MY HOME AS LONG AS IT TAKES!
IT'S STUPID! THE KSHATRIYAS WILL EVENTUALLY KNOW THAT THEY ARE IN OUR VILLAGE OF KHURUM, AND WE WILL BE ATTACKED IN TURN!
ARE WE GOING TO HAVE TO FIGHT FOR THIS CIMMERIAN TO COLLECT THE RANSOM HE EXPECTS FROM THE KINGDOM OF VENDHYA IN EXCHANGE FOR HIS PRECIOUS HOSTAGE?
WE RISK DEATH WHEN IT IS CONAN AND ONLY HE WHO WILL PROFIT!
I'M NOT ASKING ANYONE TO FIGHT FOR ME!
DARE TO PLACE YOUR HAND ON ME AND FIFTY MEN ARE GOING TO CUT YOU TO PIECES!
YOU TALK TOO MUCH!
ARE YOU THE CHIEF OF KHURUM?
DO THE WAZULIS RECEIVE THEIR ORDERS FROM YAR AFZAL OR FROM AN IGNORANT BASTARD?

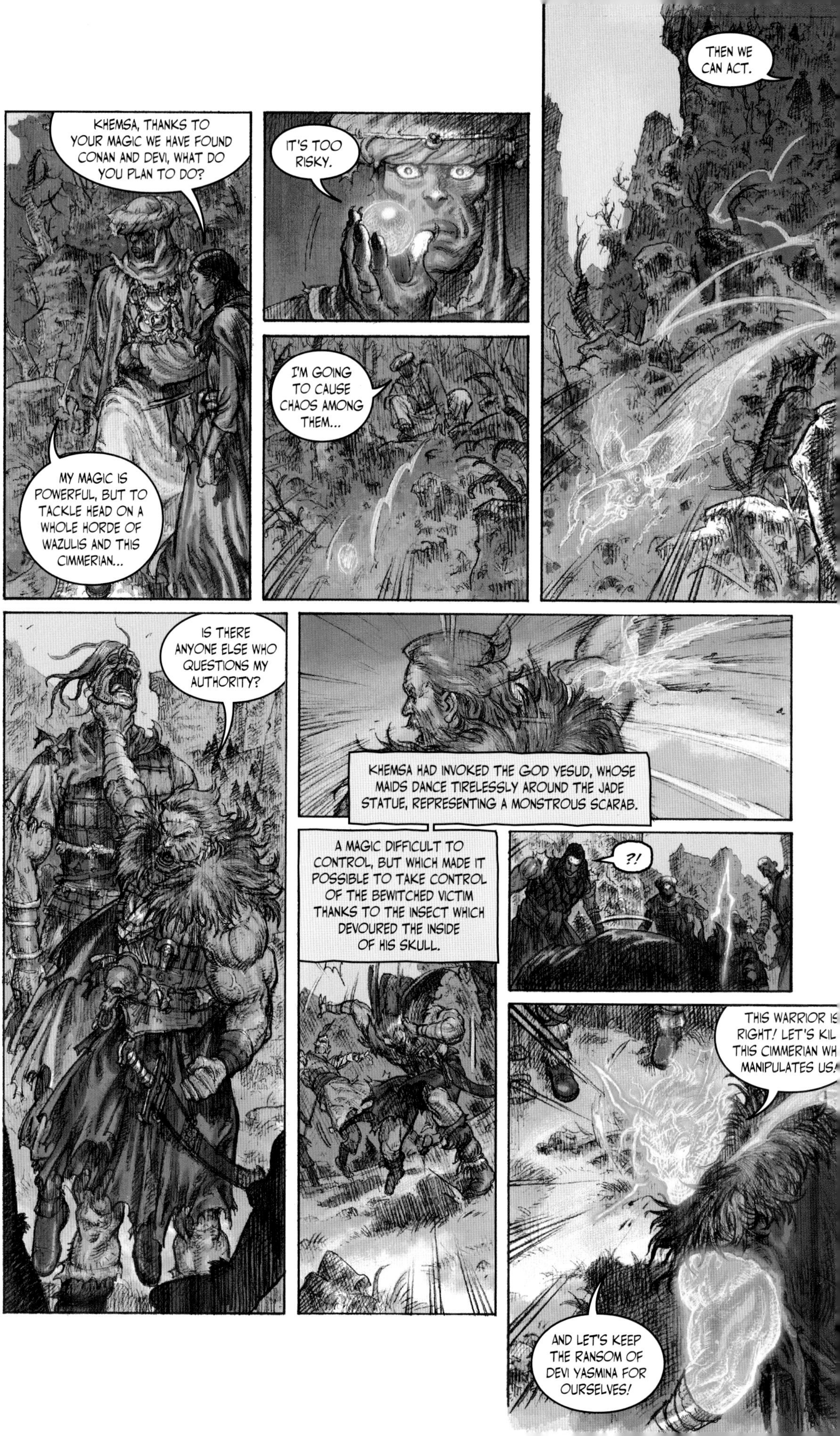

KHEMSA, THANKS TO YOUR MAGIC WE HAVE FOUND CONAN AND DEVI, WHAT DO YOU PLAN TO DO?
MY MAGIC IS POWERFUL, BUT TO TACKLE HEAD ON A WHOLE HORDE OF WAZULIS AND THIS CIMMERIAN...
IT'S TOO RISKY.
I'M GOING TO CAUSE CHAOS AMONG THEM...
THEN WE CAN ACT.
IS THERE ANYONE ELSE WHO QUESTIONS MY AUTHORITY?
KHEMSA HAD INVOKED THE GOD YESUD, WHOSE MAIDS DANCE TIRELESSLY AROUND THE JADE STATUE, REPRESENTING A MONSTROUS SCARAB.
A MAGIC DIFFICULT TO CONTROL, BUT WHICH MADE IT POSSIBLE TO TAKE CONTROL OF THE BEWITCHED VICTIM THANKS TO THE INSECT WHICH DEVOURED THE INSIDE OF HIS SKULL.
?!
THIS WARRIOR IS RIGHT! LET'S KIL THIS CIMMERIAN WH MANIPULATES US.
AND LET'S KEEP THE RANSOM OF DEVI YASMINA FOR OURSELVES!

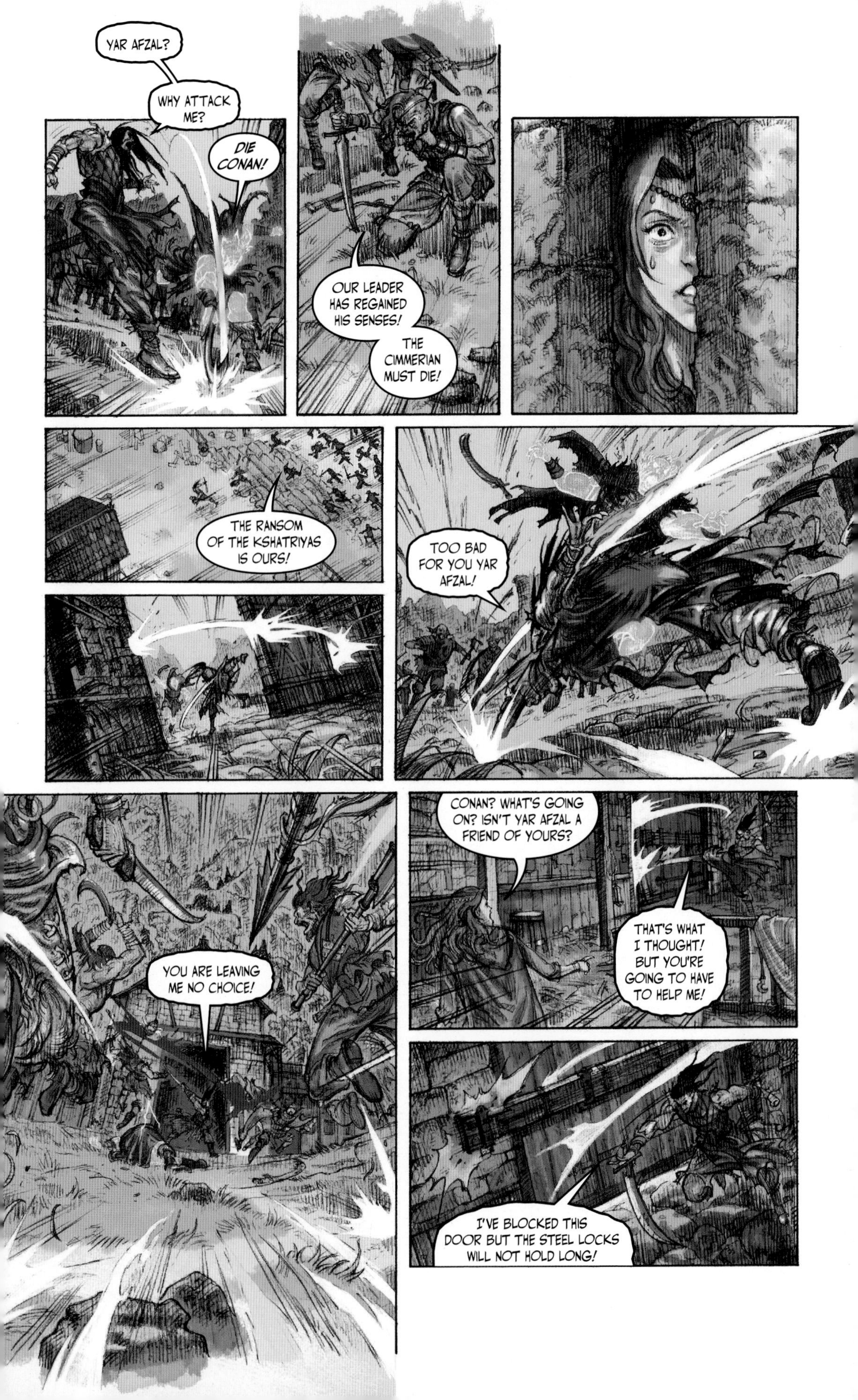
YAR AFZAL?
WHY ATTACK ME?
DIE CONAN!
OUR LEADER HAS REGAINED HIS SENSES!
THE CIMMERIAN MUST DIE!
THE RANSOM OF THE KSHATRIYAS IS OURS!
TOO BAD FOR YOU YAR AFZAL!
YOU ARE LEAVING ME NO CHOICE!
CONAN? WHAT'S GOING ON? ISN'T YAR AFZAL A FRIEND OF YOURS?
THAT'S WHAT I THOUGHT! BUT YOU'RE GOING TO HAVE TO HELP ME!
I'VE BLOCKED THIS DOOR BUT THE STEEL LOCKS WILL NOT HOLD LONG!

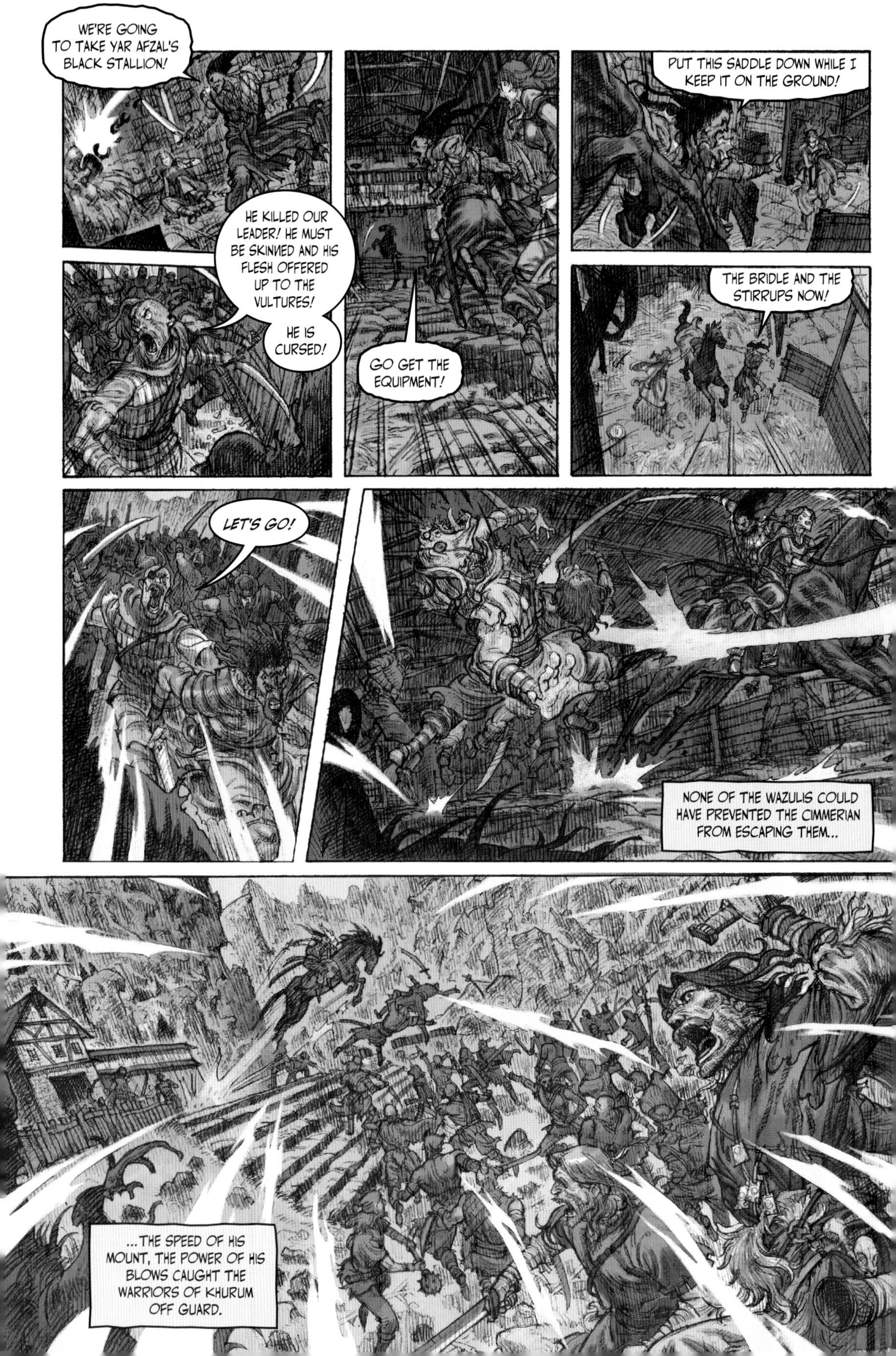
WE'RE GOING TO TAKE YAR AFZAL'S BLACK STALLION!
PUT THIS SADDLE DOWN WHILE I KEEP IT ON THE GROUND!
HE KILLED OUR LEADER! HE MUST BE SKINNED AND HIS FLESH OFFERED UP TO THE VULTURES!
HE IS CURSED!
GO GET THE EQUIPMENT!
THE BRIDLE AND THE STIRRUPS NOW!
LET'S GO!
NONE OF THE WAZULIS COULD HAVE PREVENTED THE CIMMERIAN FROM ESCAPING THEM...
...THE SPEED OF HIS MOUNT, THE POWER OF HIS BLOWS CAUGHT THE WARRIORS OF KHURUM OFF GUARD.

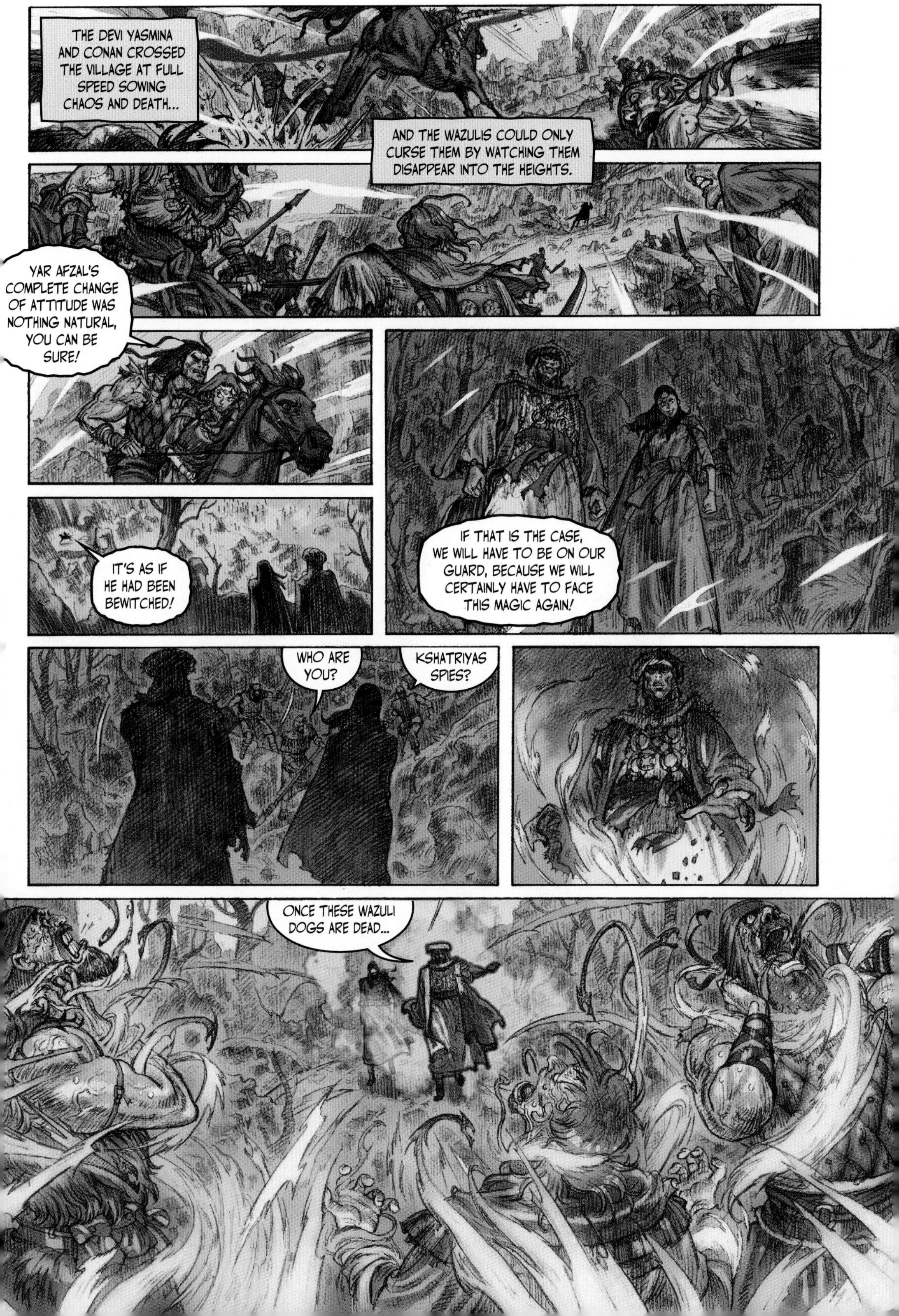
THE DEVI YASMINA AND CONAN CROSSED THE VILLAGE AT FULL SPEED SOWING CHAOS AND DEATH...
AND THE WAZULIS COULD ONLY CURSE THEM BY WATCHING THEM DISAPPEAR INTO THE HEIGHTS.
YAR AFZAL'S COMPLETE CHANGE OF ATTITUDE WAS NOTHING NATURAL, YOU CAN BE SURE!
IT'S AS IF HE HAD BEEN BEWITCHED!
IF THAT IS THE CASE, WE WILL HAVE TO BE ON OUR GUARD, BECAUSE WE WILL CERTAINLY HAVE TO FACE THIS MAGIC AGAIN!
WHO ARE YOU?
KSHATRIYAS SPIES?
ONCE THESE WAZULI DOGS ARE DEAD...

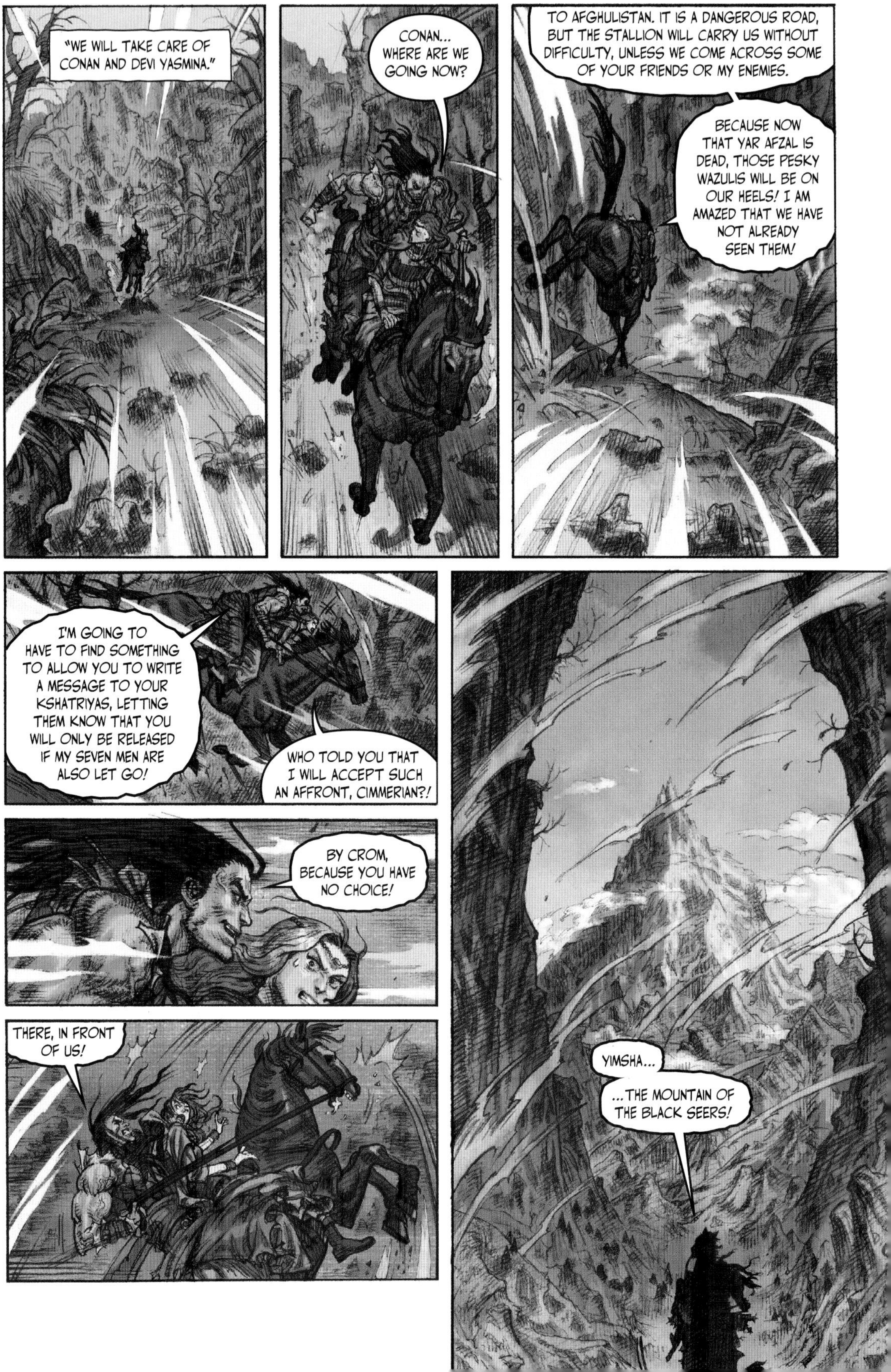
"WE WILL TAKE CARE OF CONAN AND DEVI YASMINA."
CONAN... WHERE ARE WE GOING NOW?
TO AFGHULISTAN. IT IS A DANGEROUS ROAD, BUT THE STALLION WILL CARRY US WITHOUT DIFFICULTY, UNLESS WE COME ACROSS SOME OF YOUR FRIENDS OR MY ENEMIES.
BECAUSE NOW THAT YAR AFZAL IS DEAD, THOSE PESKY WAZULIS WILL BE ON OUR HEELS! I AM AMAZED THAT WE HAVE NOT ALREADY SEEN THEM!
I'M GOING TO HAVE TO FIND SOMETHING TO ALLOW YOU TO WRITE A MESSAGE TO YOUR KSHATRIYAS, LETTING THEM KNOW THAT YOU WILL ONLY BE RELEASED IF MY SEVEN MEN ARE ALSO LET GO!
WHO TOLD YOU THAT I WILL ACCEPT SUCH AN AFFRONT, CIMMERIAN?!
BY CROM, BECAUSE YOU HAVE NO CHOICE!
THERE, IN FRONT OF US!
YIMSHA...
...THE MOUNTAIN OF THE BLACK SEERS!

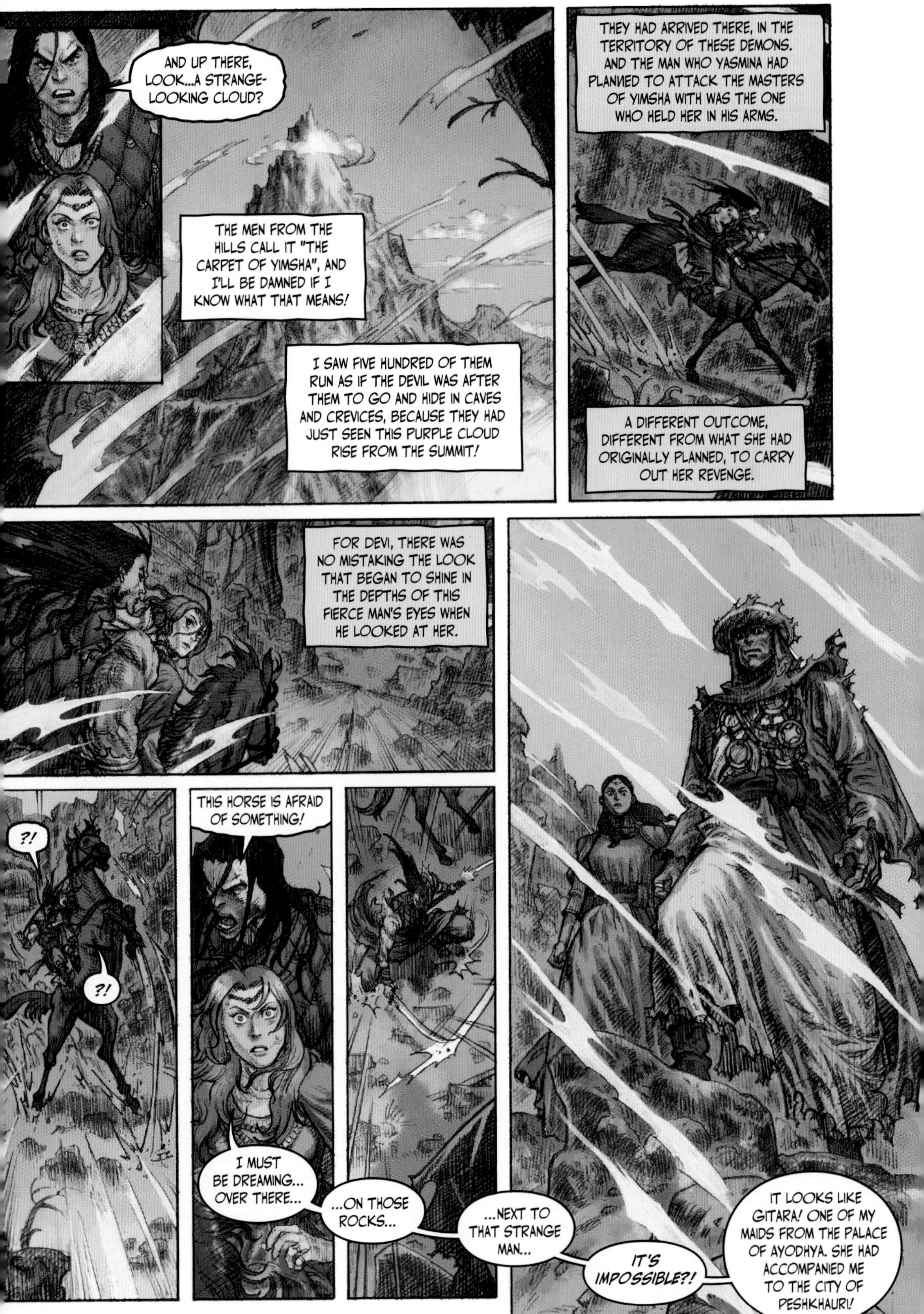
AND UP THERE, LOOK...A STRANGE-LOOKING CLOUD?
THE MEN FROM THE HILLS CALL IT "THE CARPET OF YIMSHA", AND I'LL BE DAMNED IF I KNOW WHAT THAT MEANS!
I SAW FIVE HUNDRED OF THEM RUN AS IF THE DEVIL WAS AFTER THEM TO GO AND HIDE IN CAVES AND CREVICES, BECAUSE THEY HAD JUST SEEN THIS PURPLE CLOUD RISE FROM THE SUMMIT!
THEY HAD ARRIVED THERE, IN THE TERRITORY OF THESE DEMONS. AND THE MAN WHO YASMINA HAD PLANNED TO ATTACK THE MASTERS OF YIMSHA WITH WAS THE ONE WHO HELD HER IN HIS ARMS.
A DIFFERENT OUTCOME, DIFFERENT FROM WHAT SHE HAD ORIGINALLY PLANNED, TO CARRY OUT HER REVENGE.
FOR DEVI, THERE WAS NO MISTAKING THE LOOK THAT BEGAN TO SHINE IN THE DEPTHS OF THIS FIERCE MAN'S EYES WHEN HE LOOKED AT HER.
?!
?!
THIS HORSE IS AFRAID OF SOMETHING!
I MUST BE DREAMING... OVER THERE...
...ON THOSE ROCKS...
...NEXT TO THAT STRANGE MAN...
IT'S IMPOSSIBLE?!
IT LOOKS LIKE GITARA! ONE OF MY MAIDS FROM THE PALACE OF AYODHYA. SHE HAD ACCOMPANIED ME TO THE CITY OF PESHKHAURI!

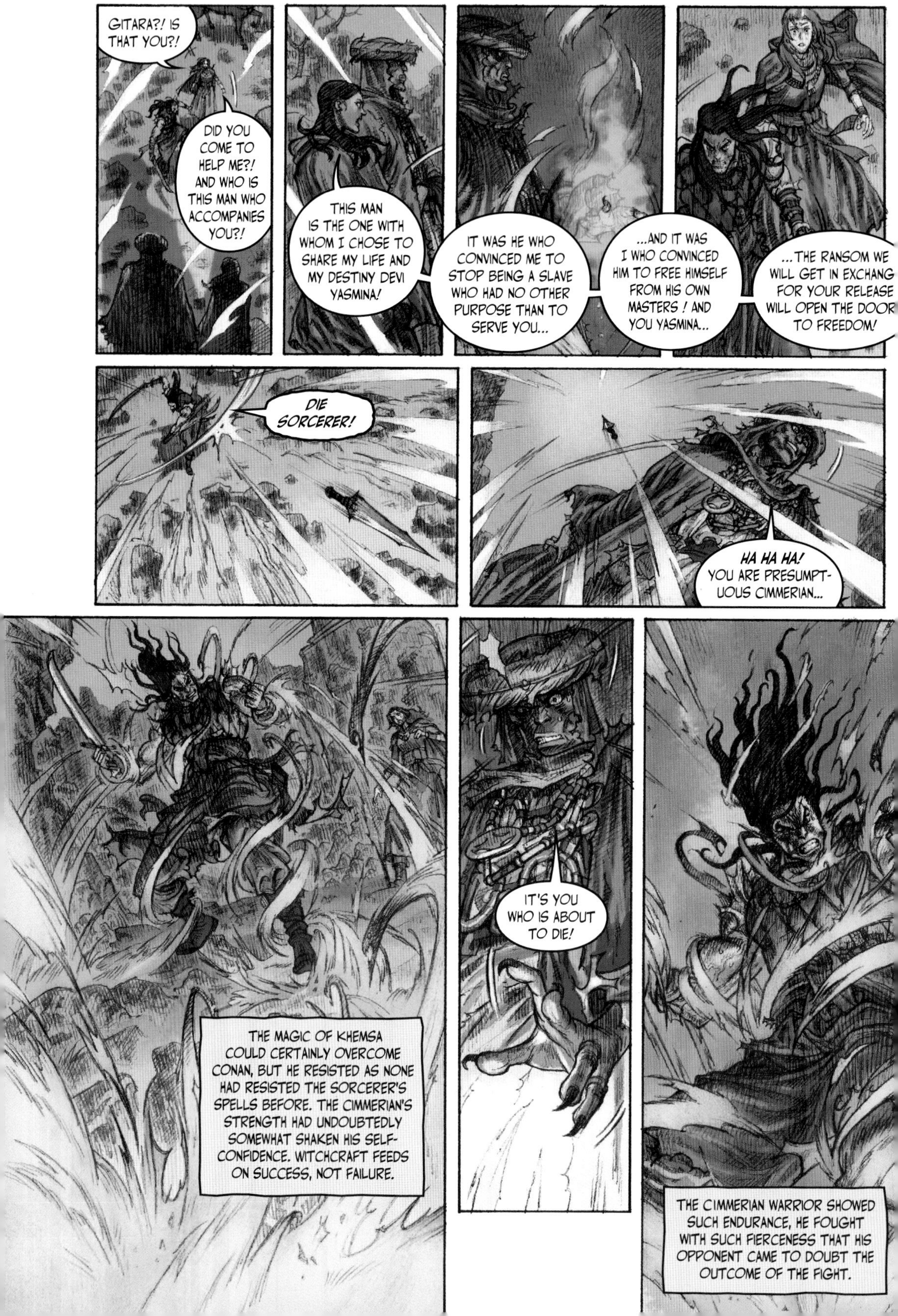
GITARA?! IS THAT YOU?!
DID YOU COME TO HELP ME?! AND WHO IS THIS MAN WHO ACCOMPANIES YOU?!
THIS MAN IS THE ONE WITH WHOM I CHOSE TO SHARE MY LIFE AND MY DESTINY DEVI YASMINA!
IT WAS HE WHO CONVINCED ME TO STOP BEING A SLAVE WHO HAD NO OTHER PURPOSE THAN TO SERVE YOU...
...AND IT WAS I WHO CONVINCED HIM TO FREE HIMSELF FROM HIS OWN MASTERS ! AND YOU YASMINA...
...THE RANSOM WE WILL GET IN EXCHANG FOR YOUR RELEASE WILL OPEN THE DOOR TO FREEDOM!
DIE SORCERER!
HA HA HA! YOU ARE PRESUMPT-UOUS CIMMERIAN...
THE MAGIC OF KHEMSA COULD CERTAINLY OVERCOME CONAN, BUT HE RESISTED AS NONE HAD RESISTED THE SORCERER'S SPELLS BEFORE. THE CIMMERIAN'S STRENGTH HAD UNDOUBTEDLY SOMEWHAT SHAKEN HIS SELF-CONFIDENCE. WITCHCRAFT FEEDS ON SUCCESS, NOT FAILURE.
IT'S YOU WHO IS ABOUT TO DIE!
THE CIMMERIAN WARRIOR SHOWED SUCH ENDURANCE, HE FOUGHT WITH SUCH FIERCENESS THAT HIS OPPONENT CAME TO DOUBT THE OUTCOME OF THE FIGHT.

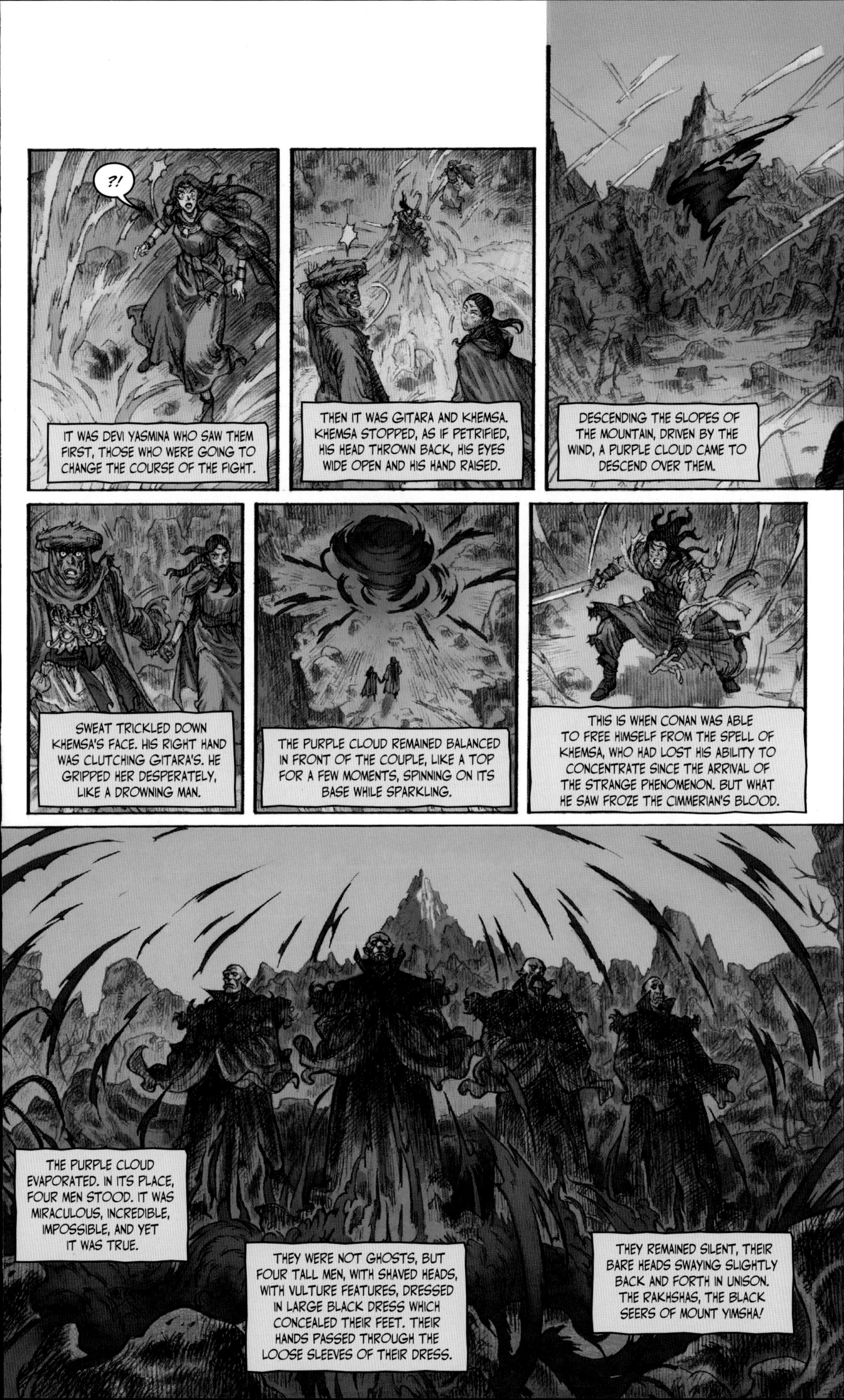
?!
IT WAS DEVI YASMINA WHO SAW THEM FIRST, THOSE WHO WERE GOING TO CHANGE THE COURSE OF THE FIGHT.
THEN IT WAS GITARA AND KHEMSA. KHEMSA STOPPED, AS IF PETRIFIED, HIS HEAD THROWN BACK, HIS EYES WIDE OPEN AND HIS HAND RAISED.
DESCENDING THE SLOPES OF THE MOUNTAIN, DRIVEN BY THE WIND, A PURPLE CLOUD CAME TO DESCEND OVER THEM.
SWEAT TRICKLED DOWN KHEMSA'S FACE. HIS RIGHT HAND WAS CLUTCHING GITARA'S. HE GRIPPED HER DESPERATELY, LIKE A DROWNING MAN.
THE PURPLE CLOUD REMAINED BALANCED IN FRONT OF THE COUPLE, LIKE A TOP FOR A FEW MOMENTS, SPINNING ON ITS BASE WHILE SPARKLING.
THIS IS WHEN CONAN WAS ABLE TO FREE HIMSELF FROM THE SPELL OF KHEMSA, WHO HAD LOST HIS ABILITY TO CONCENTRATE SINCE THE ARRIVAL OF THE STRANGE PHENOMENON. BUT WHAT HE SAW FROZE THE CIMMERIAN'S BLOOD.
THE PURPLE CLOUD EVAPORATED. IN ITS PLACE, FOUR MEN STOOD. IT WAS MIRACULOUS, INCREDIBLE, IMPOSSIBLE, AND YET IT WAS TRUE.
THEY WERE NOT GHOSTS, BUT FOUR TALL MEN, WITH SHAVED HEADS, WITH VULTURE FEATURES, DRESSED IN LARGE BLACK DRESS WHICH CONCEALED THEIR FEET. THEIR HANDS PASSED THROUGH THE LOOSE SLEEVES OF THEIR DRESS.
THEY REMAINED SILENT, THEIR BARE HEADS SWAYING SLIGHTLY BACK AND FORTH IN UNISON. THE RAKHSHAS, THE BLACK SEERS OF MOUNT YIMSHA!

THESE ARE YOUR MASTERS, AREN'T THEY MY LOVE? WELL IT'S TIME! YOU HAVE TO DESTROY THEM!

THEN NOTHING CAN STOP US!

WE WILL BE INVINCIBLE!

FOR THE FIRST TIME, YASMINA APPROACHED CONAN, INSTINCTIVELY SEEKING PROTECTION FROM HIM, WHO RESPONDED TO HER REQUEST, WITHOUT A WORD, HIS EYES FIXED ON THE DEATH FIGHT BEFORE THEM.

PUSHED TO HIS LIMITS BY HIS FORMER MASTERS, KHEMSA FOUGHT FOR HIS LIFE, CALLING ON ALL HIS MAGIC...

...ALL THE TERRIFYING KNOWLEDGE THEY HAD INSTILLED IN HIM DURING ALL THE LONG AND PAINFUL YEARS WHEN HE WAS ONLY A NEOPHYTE AND THEIR SERVANT.

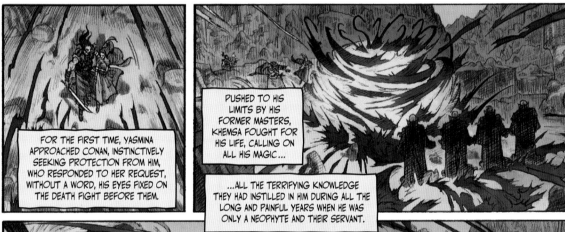

BUT THE BLACK SEERS HAD ALREADY DETECTED THE WEAKNESS OF THEIR OPPONENT AND THEY DID NOT HESITATE TO USE IT.

KRAAAAAAAAKK

GITARA, THE WOMAN WHO HAD MANAGED TO CONQUER THE HEART OF KHEMSA, WOULD BE THE ONE THROUGH WHOM DEFEAT WOULD COME.

ANOTHER SORCERER TOOK A STEP FORWARD AND STAMPED THE GROUND WITH HIS FOOT. AT THE SAME TIME A RUMBLE WAS HEARD, WHICH QUICKLY TURNED INTO A FORMIDABLE CRACK.

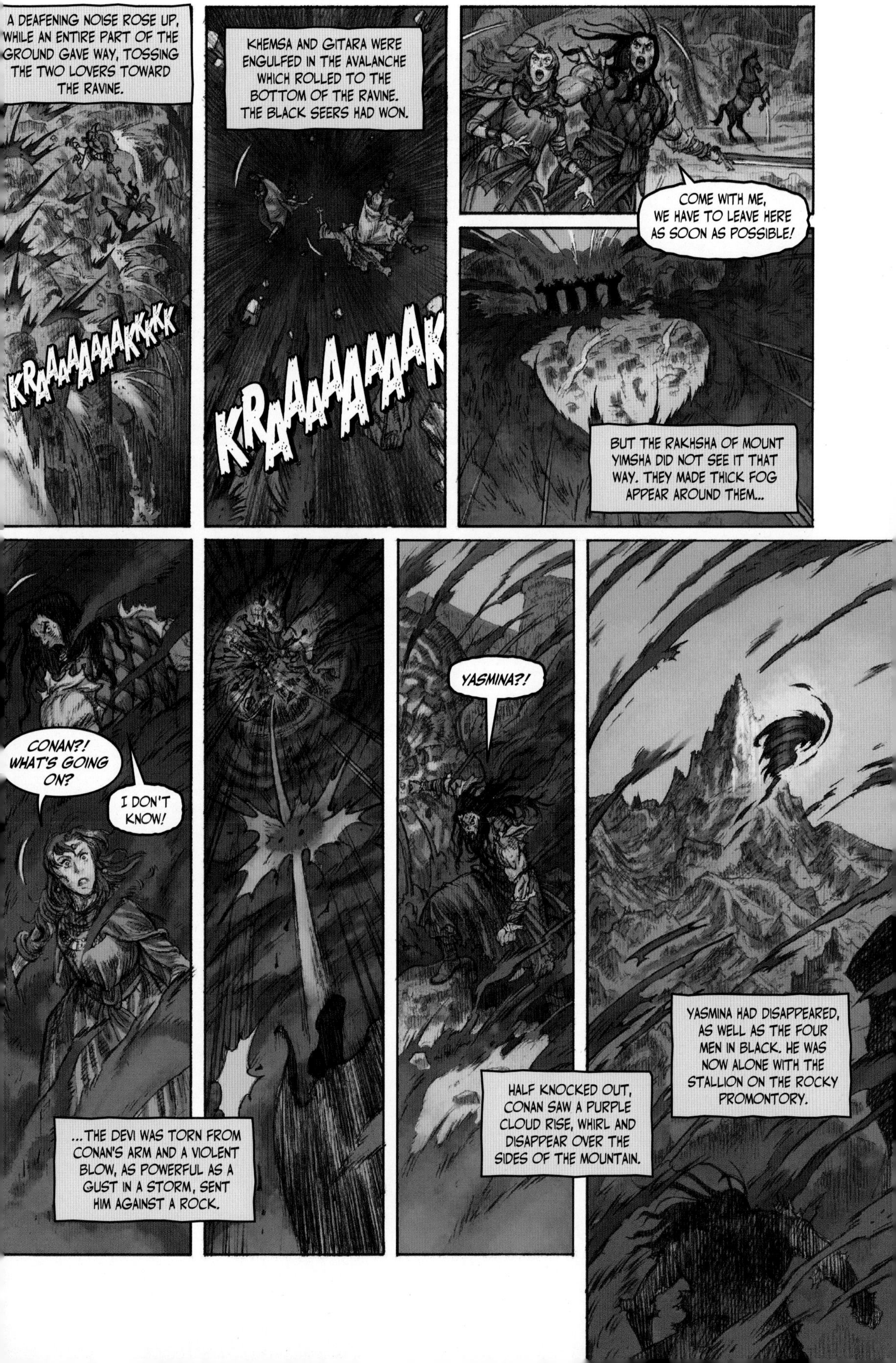
A DEAFENING NOISE ROSE UP, WHILE AN ENTIRE PART OF THE GROUND GAVE WAY, TOSSING THE TWO LOVERS TOWARD THE RAVINE.
KRAAAAAAAKKKKK
KHEMSA AND GITARA WERE ENGULFED IN THE AVALANCHE WHICH ROLLED TO THE BOTTOM OF THE RAVINE. THE BLACK SEERS HAD WON.
KRAAAAAAAAK
COME WITH ME, WE HAVE TO LEAVE HERE AS SOON AS POSSIBLE!
BUT THE RAKHSHA OF MOUNT YIMSHA DID NOT SEE IT THAT WAY. THEY MADE THICK FOG APPEAR AROUND THEM...
CONAN?! WHAT'S GOING ON?
I DON'T KNOW!
...THE DEVI WAS TORN FROM CONAN'S ARM AND A VIOLENT BLOW, AS POWERFUL AS A GUST IN A STORM, SENT HIM AGAINST A ROCK.
YASMINA?!
HALF KNOCKED OUT, CONAN SAW A PURPLE CLOUD RISE, WHIRL AND DISAPPEAR OVER THE SIDES OF THE MOUNTAIN.
YASMINA HAD DISAPPEARED, AS WELL AS THE FOUR MEN IN BLACK. HE WAS NOW ALONE WITH THE STALLION ON THE ROCKY PROMONTORY.

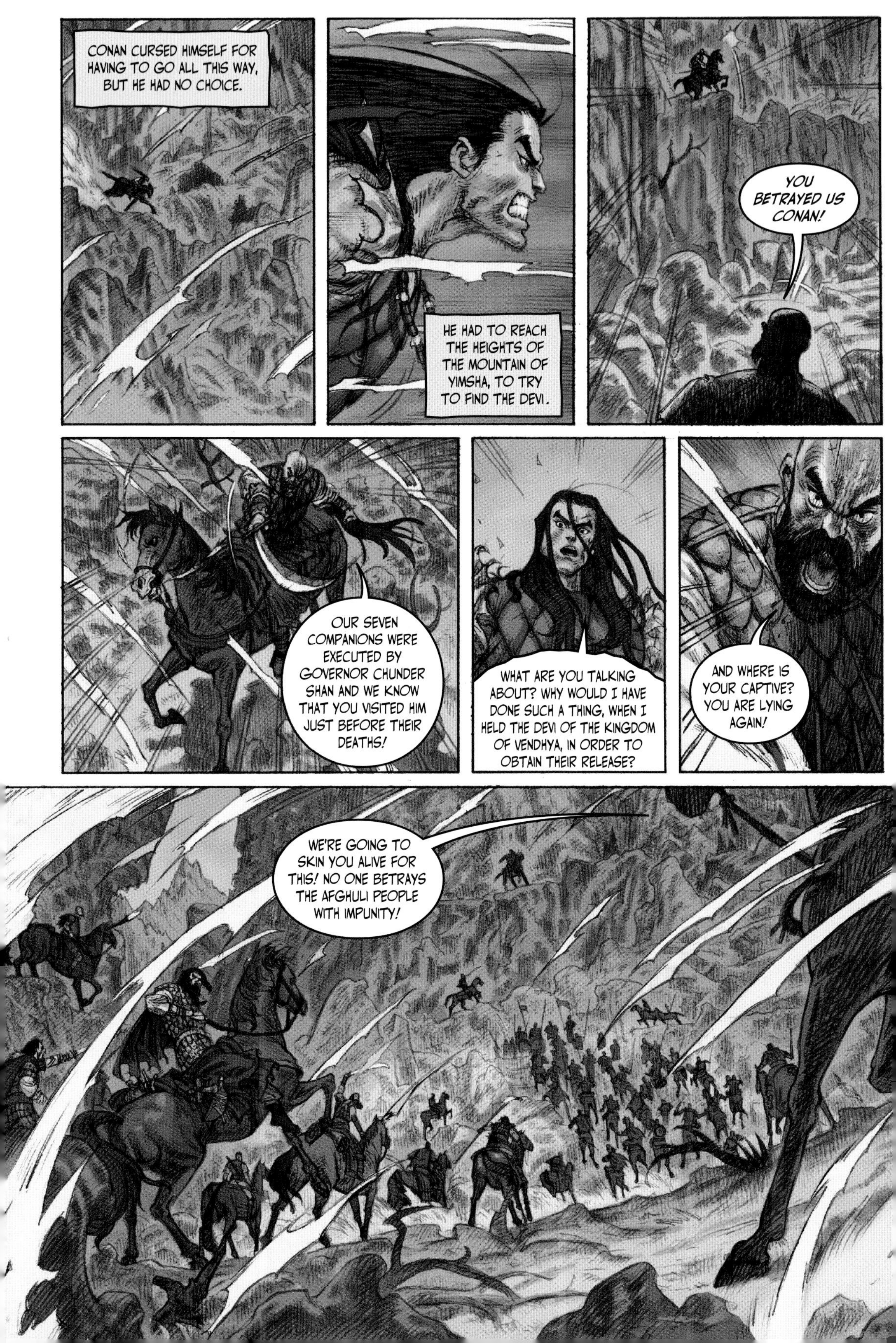
CONAN CURSED HIMSELF FOR HAVING TO GO ALL THIS WAY, BUT HE HAD NO CHOICE.
HE HAD TO REACH THE HEIGHTS OF THE MOUNTAIN OF YIMSHA, TO TRY TO FIND THE DEVI.
YOU BETRAYED US CONAN!
OUR SEVEN COMPANIONS WERE EXECUTED BY GOVERNOR CHUNDER SHAN AND WE KNOW THAT YOU VISITED HIM JUST BEFORE THEIR DEATHS!
WHAT ARE YOU TALKING ABOUT? WHY WOULD I HAVE DONE SUCH A THING, WHEN I HELD THE DEVI OF THE KINGDOM OF VENDHYA, IN ORDER TO OBTAIN THEIR RELEASE?
AND WHERE IS YOUR CAPTIVE? YOU ARE LYING AGAIN!
WE'RE GOING TO SKIN YOU ALIVE FOR THIS! NO ONE BETRAYS THE AFGHULI PEOPLE WITH IMPUNITY!

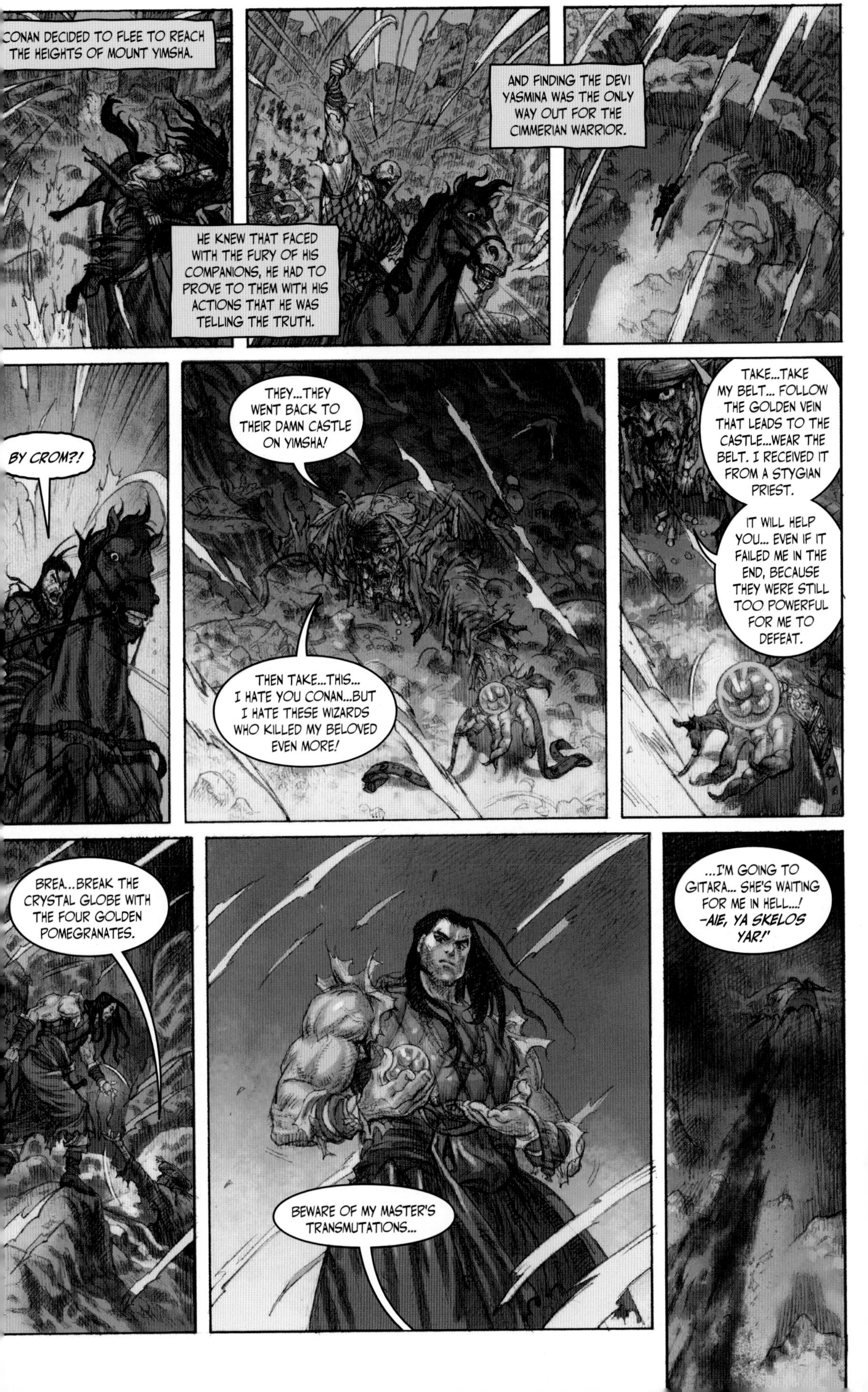
CONAN DECIDED TO FLEE TO REACH THE HEIGHTS OF MOUNT YIMSHA.
HE KNEW THAT FACED WITH THE FURY OF HIS COMPANIONS, HE HAD TO PROVE TO THEM WITH HIS ACTIONS THAT HE WAS TELLING THE TRUTH.
AND FINDING THE DEVI YASMINA WAS THE ONLY WAY OUT FOR THE CIMMERIAN WARRIOR.
BY CROM?!
THEY...THEY WENT BACK TO THEIR DAMN CASTLE ON YIMSHA!
THEN TAKE...THIS... I HATE YOU CONAN...BUT I HATE THESE WIZARDS WHO KILLED MY BELOVED EVEN MORE!
TAKE...TAKE MY BELT... FOLLOW THE GOLDEN VEIN THAT LEADS TO THE CASTLE...WEAR THE BELT. I RECEIVED IT FROM A STYGIAN PRIEST.
IT WILL HELP YOU... EVEN IF IT FAILED ME IN THE END, BECAUSE THEY WERE STILL TOO POWERFUL FOR ME TO DEFEAT.
BREA...BREAK THE CRYSTAL GLOBE WITH THE FOUR GOLDEN POMEGRANATES.
BEWARE OF MY MASTER'S TRANSMUTATIONS...
...I'M GOING TO GITARA... SHE'S WAITING FOR ME IN HELL...!
-AIE, YA SKELOS YAR!'

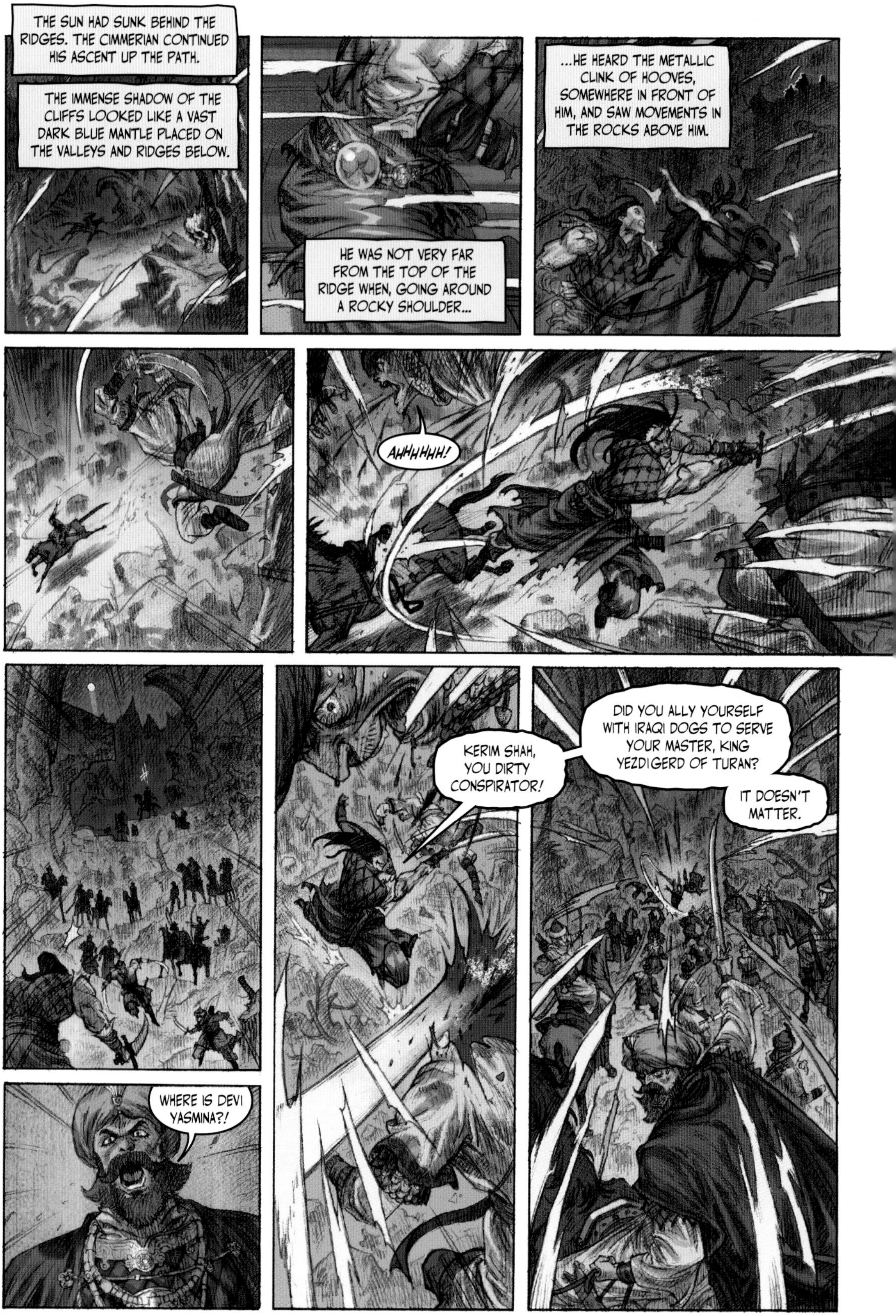

THE SUN HAD SUNK BEHIND THE RIDGES. THE CIMMERIAN CONTINUED HIS ASCENT UP THE PATH.
THE IMMENSE SHADOW OF THE CLIFFS LOOKED LIKE A VAST DARK BLUE MANTLE PLACED ON THE VALLEYS AND RIDGES BELOW.
HE WAS NOT VERY FAR FROM THE TOP OF THE RIDGE WHEN, GOING AROUND A ROCKY SHOULDER...
...HE HEARD THE METALLIC CLINK OF HOOVES, SOMEWHERE IN FRONT OF HIM, AND SAW MOVEMENTS IN THE ROCKS ABOVE HIM.
AHHHHHH!
KERIM SHAH, YOU DIRTY CONSPIRATOR!
DID YOU ALLY YOURSELF WITH IRAQI DOGS TO SERVE YOUR MASTER, KING YEZDIGERD OF TURAN?
IT DOESN'T MATTER.
WHERE IS DEVI YASMINA?!

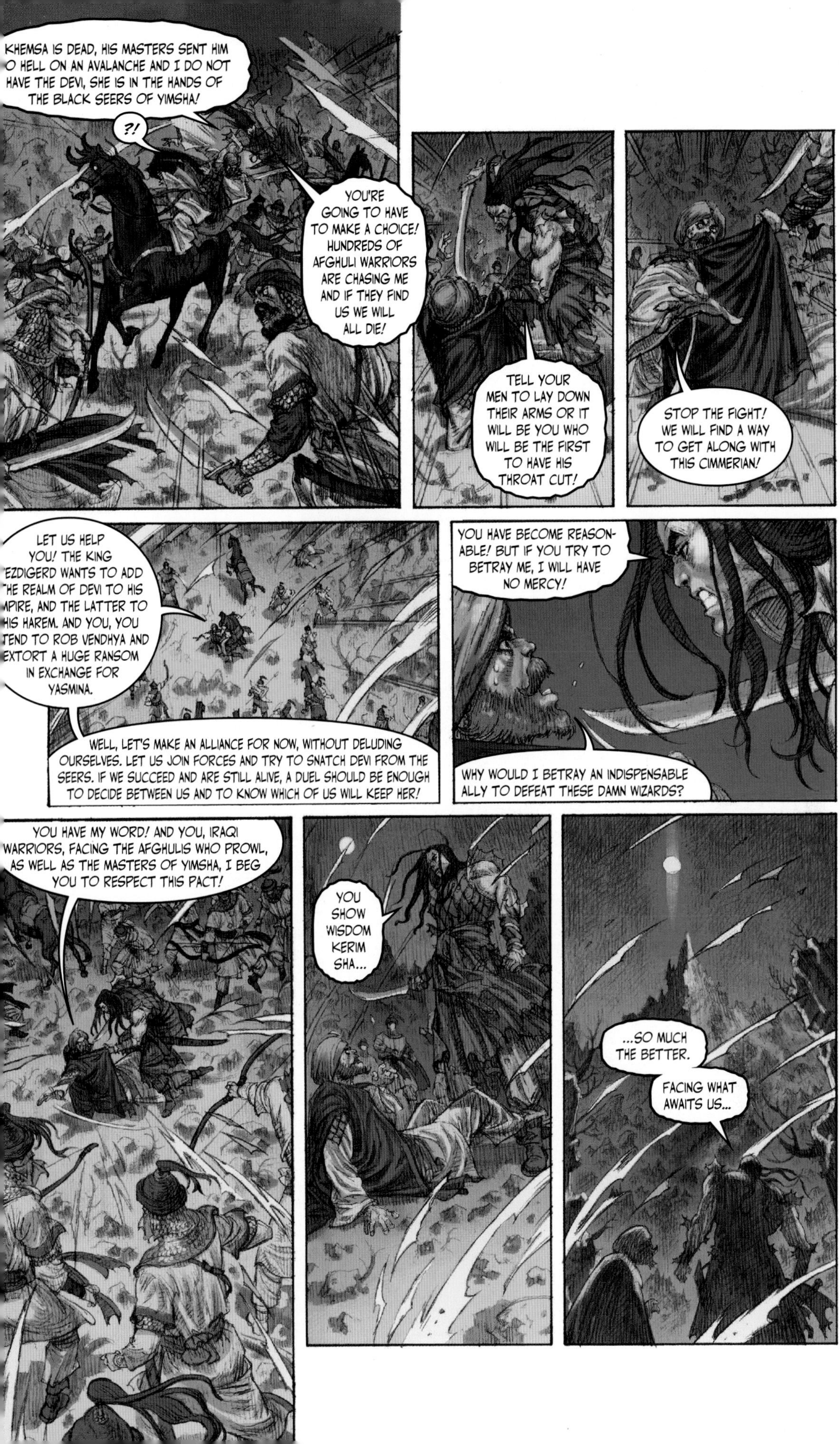
KHEMSA IS DEAD, HIS MASTERS SENT HIM O HELL ON AN AVALANCHE AND I DO NOT HAVE THE DEVI, SHE IS IN THE HANDS OF THE BLACK SEERS OF YIMSHA!
?!
YOU'RE GOING TO HAVE TO MAKE A CHOICE! HUNDREDS OF AFGHULI WARRIORS ARE CHASING ME AND IF THEY FIND US WE WILL ALL DIE!
TELL YOUR MEN TO LAY DOWN THEIR ARMS OR IT WILL BE YOU WHO WILL BE THE FIRST TO HAVE HIS THROAT CUT!
STOP THE FIGHT! WE WILL FIND A WAY TO GET ALONG WITH THIS CIMMERIAN!
LET US HELP YOU! THE KING 'EZDIGERD WANTS TO ADD THE REALM OF DEVI TO HIS MPIRE, AND THE LATTER TO HIS HAREM. AND YOU, YOU TEND TO ROB VENDHYA AND EXTORT A HUGE RANSOM IN EXCHANGE FOR YASMINA.
WELL, LET'S MAKE AN ALLIANCE FOR NOW, WITHOUT DELUDING OURSELVES. LET US JOIN FORCES AND TRY TO SNATCH DEVI FROM THE SEERS. IF WE SUCCEED AND ARE STILL ALIVE, A DUEL SHOULD BE ENOUGH TO DECIDE BETWEEN US AND TO KNOW WHICH OF US WILL KEEP HER!
YOU HAVE BECOME REASONABLE! BUT IF YOU TRY TO BETRAY ME, I WILL HAVE NO MERCY!
WHY WOULD I BETRAY AN INDISPENSABLE ALLY TO DEFEAT THESE DAMN WIZARDS?
YOU HAVE MY WORD! AND YOU, IRAQI WARRIORS, FACING THE AFGHULIS WHO PROWL, AS WELL AS THE MASTERS OF YIMSHA, I BEG YOU TO RESPECT THIS PACT!
YOU SHOW WISDOM KERIM SHA...
...SO MUCH THE BETTER.
FACING WHAT AWAITS US...

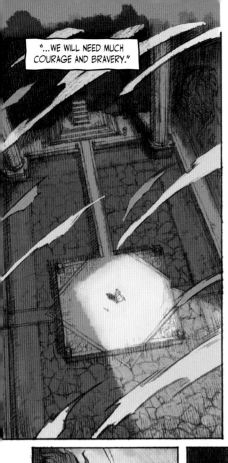

"...WE WILL NEED MUCH COURAGE AND BRAVERY."

?!

WHO ARE YOU?

WHY DID YOU BRING ME HERE?

I AM THE MASTER OF YIMSHA.

WERE YOU NOT LOOKING FOR ME?

IF YOU ARE ONE OF THE BLACK SEERS... YES! YOU KILLED MY BROTHER! WHY DID YOU PERSECUTE HIM? HE NEVER HURT YOU!

THE PRIESTS SAY THAT THE SEERS ARE ABOVE HUMAN AFFAIRS. WHY THEN DID YOU KILL THE KING OF VENDHYA?

SO IS YEZDIGERD YOUR VASSAL?

IS THE DOG WHO COMES TO EAT THE REMAINS OF THE OFFERINGS IN THE TEMPLE COURTYARD THE VASSAL OF THE GOD?

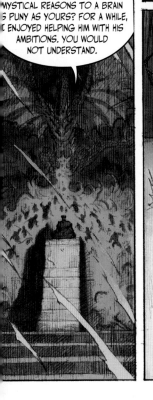

HOW COULD A SIMPLE HUMAN UNDERSTAND THE MOTIVATIONS OF A SEER? MY ACOLYTES IN THE TEMPLES OF TURAN, WHO ACTUALLY HIDE BEHIND THE PRIESTS OF TARIM, URGED ME TO ACT IN FAVOR OF YEZDIGERD.

FOR REASONS THAT ONLY CONCERN ME, I GRANTED THEIR REQUEST. HOW CAN I EXPLAIN MY MYSTICAL REASONS TO A BRAIN AS PUNY AS YOURS? FOR A WHILE, I ENJOYED HELPING HIM WITH HIS AMBITIONS. YOU WOULD NOT UNDERSTAND.

WELL DIE, DEMON!!

I'M TIRED OF YEZDIGERD...

...I'VE TURNED TO OTHER FORMS OF AMUSEMENT.

?!

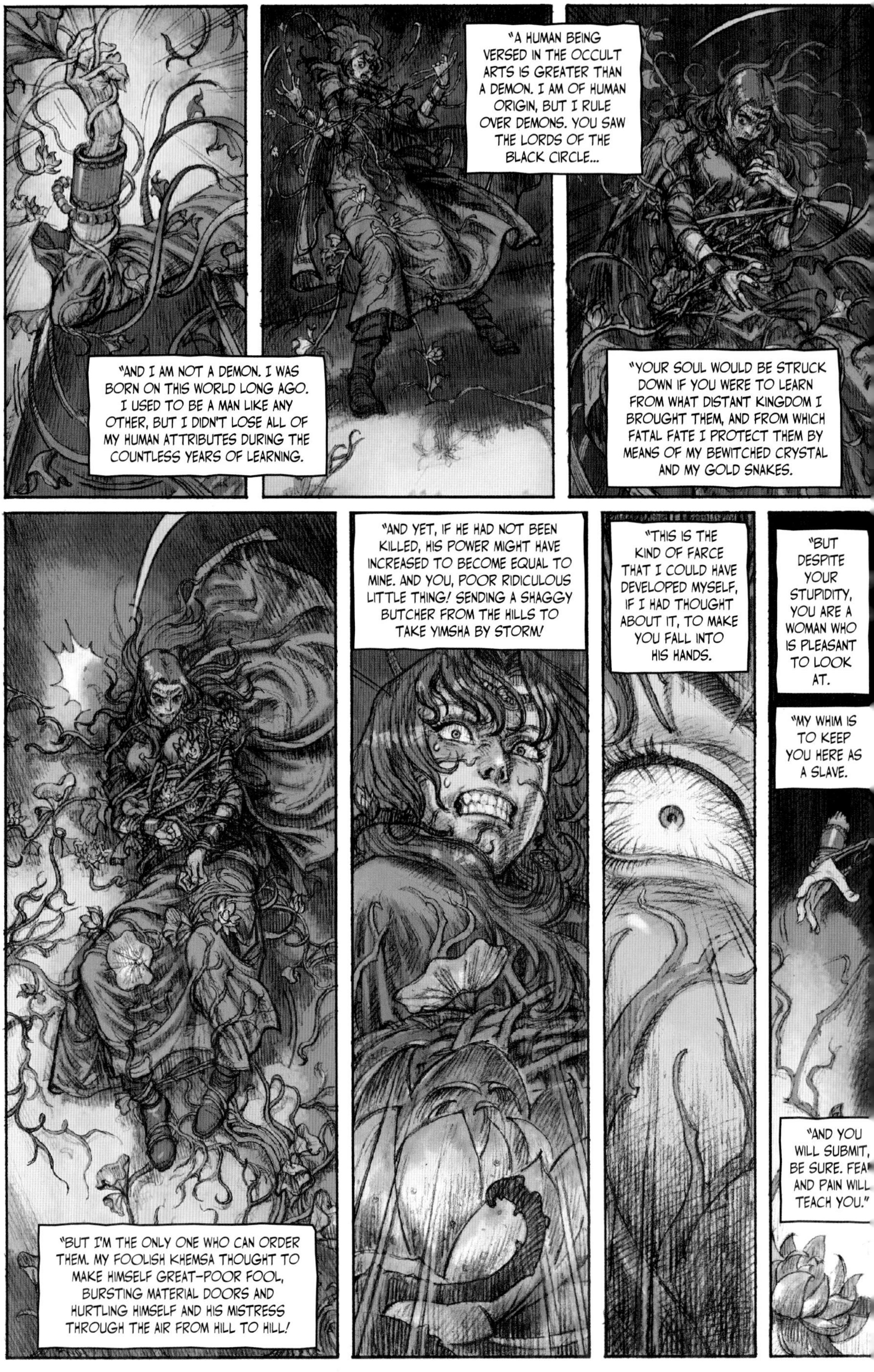
"AND I AM NOT A DEMON. I WAS BORN ON THIS WORLD LONG AGO. I USED TO BE A MAN LIKE ANY OTHER, BUT I DIDN'T LOSE ALL OF MY HUMAN ATTRIBUTES DURING THE COUNTLESS YEARS OF LEARNING.
"A HUMAN BEING VERSED IN THE OCCULT ARTS IS GREATER THAN A DEMON. I AM OF HUMAN ORIGIN, BUT I RULE OVER DEMONS. YOU SAW THE LORDS OF THE BLACK CIRCLE...
"YOUR SOUL WOULD BE STRUCK DOWN IF YOU WERE TO LEARN FROM WHAT DISTANT KINGDOM I BROUGHT THEM, AND FROM WHICH FATAL FATE I PROTECT THEM BY MEANS OF MY BEWITCHED CRYSTAL AND MY GOLD SNAKES.
"BUT I'M THE ONLY ONE WHO CAN ORDER THEM. MY FOOLISH KHEMSA THOUGHT TO MAKE HIMSELF GREAT—POOR FOOL, BURSTING MATERIAL DOORS AND HURTLING HIMSELF AND HIS MISTRESS THROUGH THE AIR FROM HILL TO HILL!
"AND YET, IF HE HAD NOT BEEN KILLED, HIS POWER MIGHT HAVE INCREASED TO BECOME EQUAL TO MINE. AND YOU, POOR RIDICULOUS LITTLE THING! SENDING A SHAGGY BUTCHER FROM THE HILLS TO TAKE YIMSHA BY STORM!
"THIS IS THE KIND OF FARCE THAT I COULD HAVE DEVELOPED MYSELF, IF I HAD THOUGHT ABOUT IT, TO MAKE YOU FALL INTO HIS HANDS.
"BUT DESPITE YOUR STUPIDITY, YOU ARE A WOMAN WHO IS PLEASANT TO LOOK AT.
"MY WHIM IS TO KEEP YOU HERE AS A SLAVE.
"AND YOU WILL SUBMIT, BE SURE. FEA AND PAIN WILL TEACH YOU."

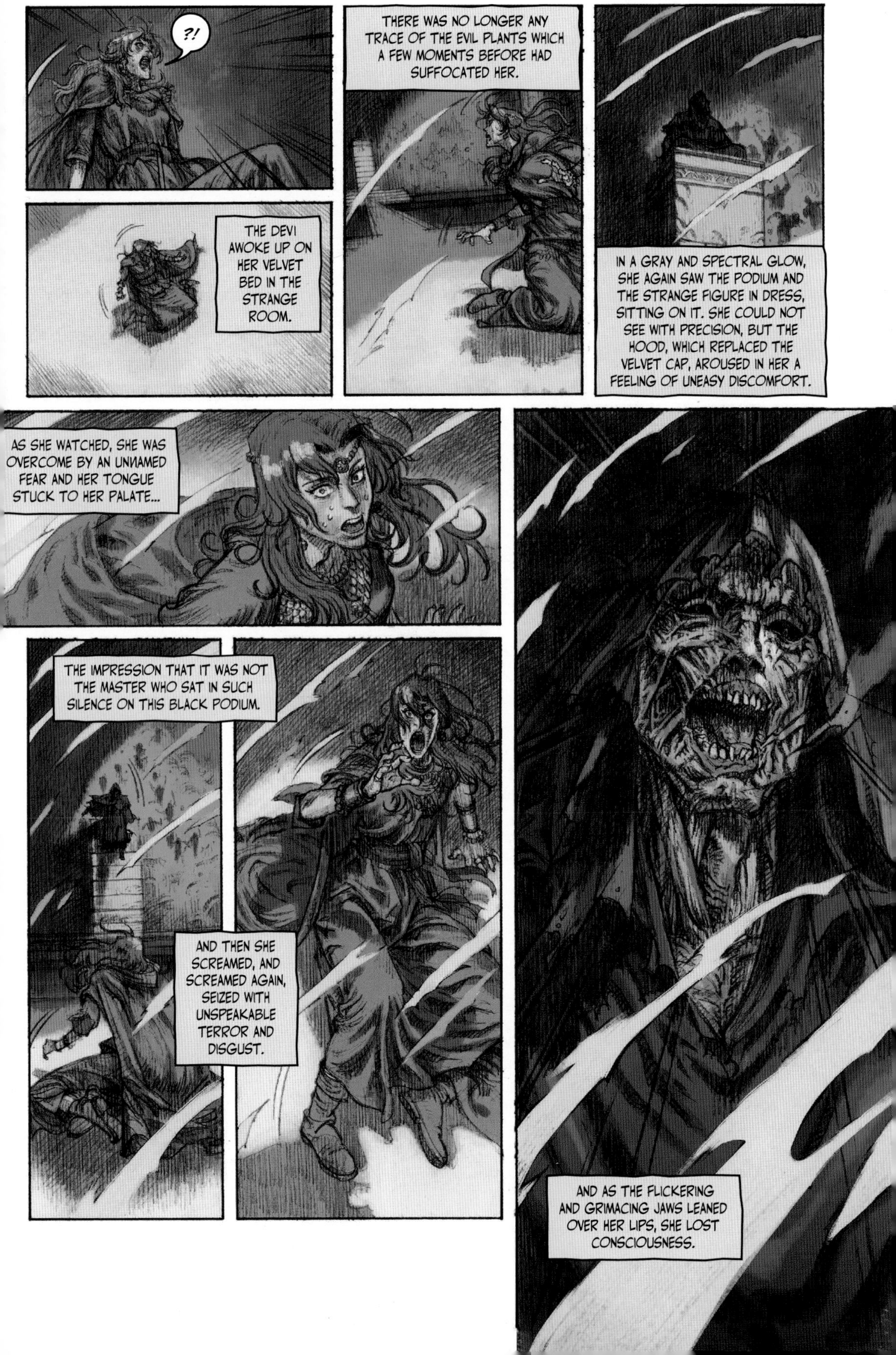
?!
THE DEVI AWOKE UP ON HER VELVET BED IN THE STRANGE ROOM.
THERE WAS NO LONGER ANY TRACE OF THE EVIL PLANTS WHICH A FEW MOMENTS BEFORE HAD SUFFOCATED HER.
IN A GRAY AND SPECTRAL GLOW, SHE AGAIN SAW THE PODIUM AND THE STRANGE FIGURE IN DRESS, SITTING ON IT. SHE COULD NOT SEE WITH PRECISION, BUT THE HOOD, WHICH REPLACED THE VELVET CAP, AROUSED IN HER A FEELING OF UNEASY DISCOMFORT.
AS SHE WATCHED, SHE WAS OVERCOME BY AN UNNAMED FEAR AND HER TONGUE STUCK TO HER PALATE...
THE IMPRESSION THAT IT WAS NOT THE MASTER WHO SAT IN SUCH SILENCE ON THIS BLACK PODIUM.
AND THEN SHE SCREAMED, AND SCREAMED AGAIN, SEIZED WITH UNSPEAKABLE TERROR AND DISGUST.
AND AS THE FLICKERING AND GRIMACING JAWS LEANED OVER HER LIPS, SHE LOST CONSCIOUSNESS.

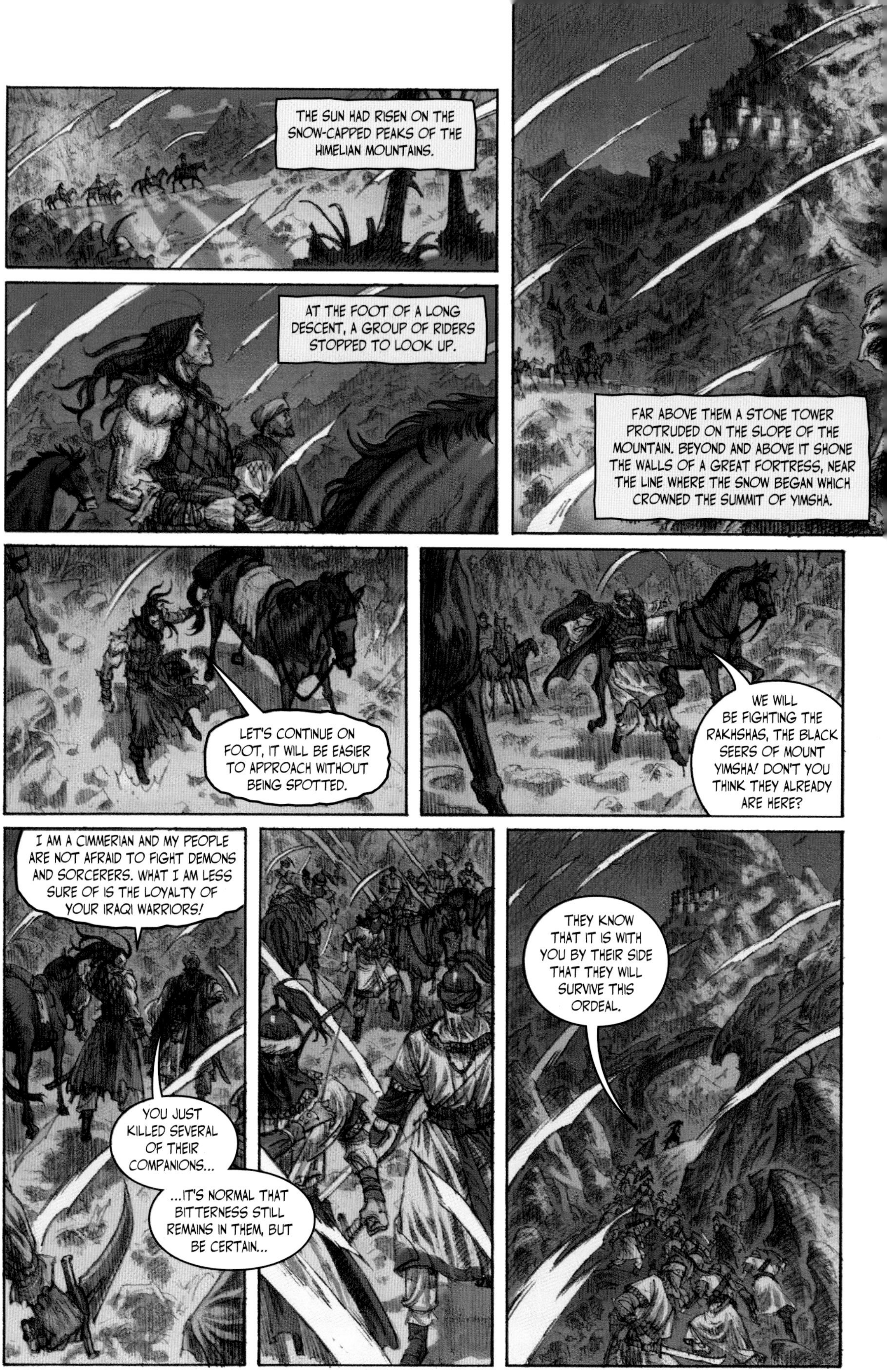
THE SUN HAD RISEN ON THE SNOW-CAPPED PEAKS OF THE HIMELIAN MOUNTAINS.
AT THE FOOT OF A LONG DESCENT, A GROUP OF RIDERS STOPPED TO LOOK UP.
FAR ABOVE THEM A STONE TOWER PROTRUDED ON THE SLOPE OF THE MOUNTAIN. BEYOND AND ABOVE IT SHONE THE WALLS OF A GREAT FORTRESS, NEAR THE LINE WHERE THE SNOW BEGAN WHICH CROWNED THE SUMMIT OF YIMSHA.
LET'S CONTINUE ON FOOT, IT WILL BE EASIER TO APPROACH WITHOUT BEING SPOTTED.
WE WILL BE FIGHTING THE RAKHSHAS, THE BLACK SEERS OF MOUNT YIMSHA! DON'T YOU THINK THEY ALREADY ARE HERE?
I AM A CIMMERIAN AND MY PEOPLE ARE NOT AFRAID TO FIGHT DEMONS AND SORCERERS. WHAT I AM LESS SURE OF IS THE LOYALTY OF YOUR IRAQI WARRIORS!
YOU JUST KILLED SEVERAL OF THEIR COMPANIONS...
...IT'S NORMAL THAT BITTERNESS STILL REMAINS IN THEM, BUT BE CERTAIN...
THEY KNOW THAT IT IS WITH YOU BY THEIR SIDE THAT THEY WILL SURVIVE THIS ORDEAL.

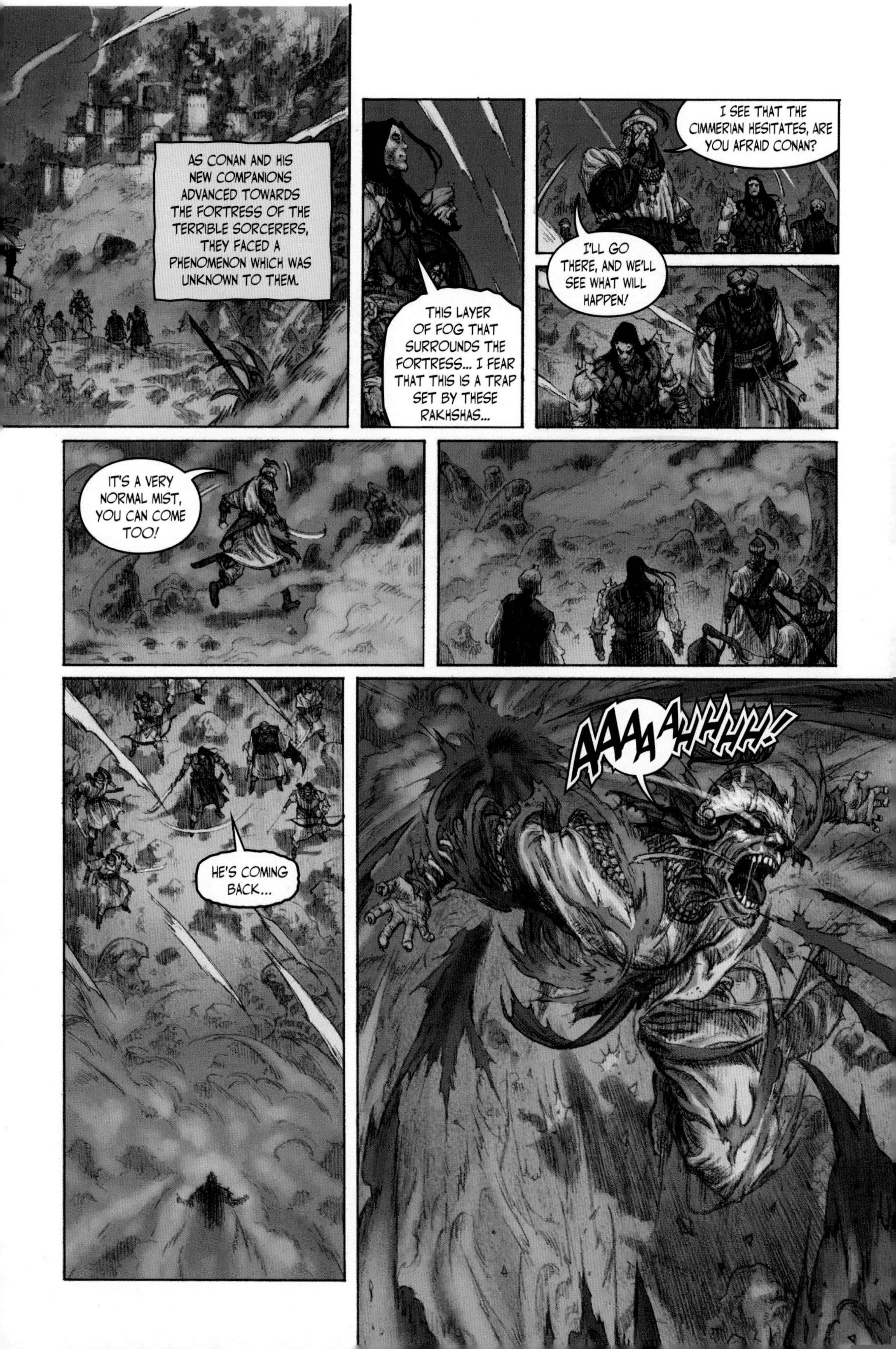

AS CONAN AND HIS NEW COMPANIONS ADVANCED TOWARDS THE FORTRESS OF THE TERRIBLE SORCERERS, THEY FACED A PHENOMENON WHICH WAS UNKNOWN TO THEM.
THIS LAYER OF FOG THAT SURROUNDS THE FORTRESS... I FEAR THAT THIS IS A TRAP SET BY THESE RAKHSHAS...
I SEE THAT THE CIMMERIAN HESITATES, ARE YOU AFRAID CONAN?
I'LL GO THERE, AND WE'LL SEE WHAT WILL HAPPEN!
IT'S A VERY NORMAL MIST, YOU CAN COME TOO!
HE'S COMING BACK...
AAAAAHHHH!

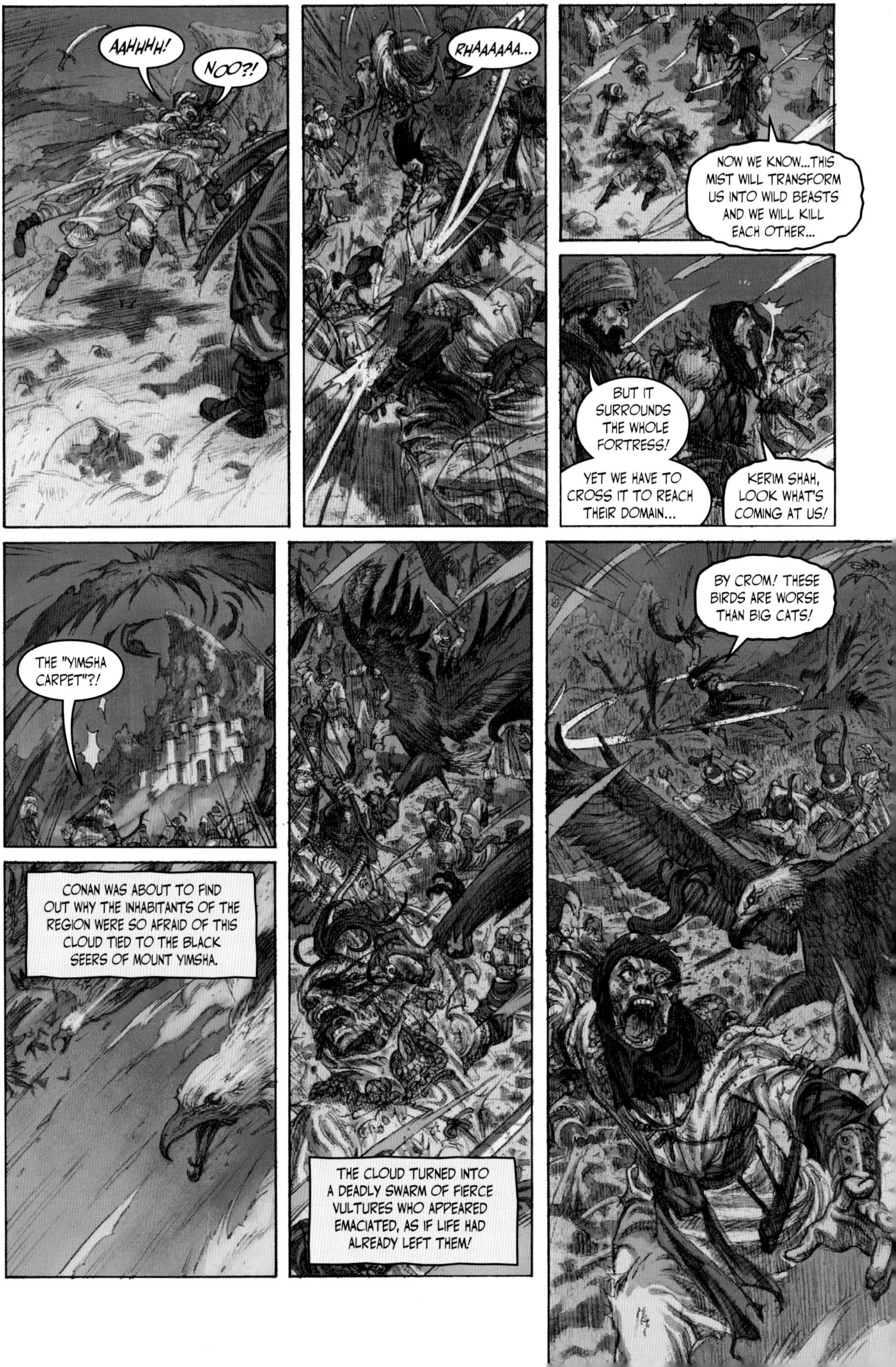

AAHHHH!
NOO?!
RHAAAAAA...
NOW WE KNOW...THIS MIST WILL TRANSFORM US INTO WILD BEASTS AND WE WILL KILL EACH OTHER...
BUT IT SURROUNDS THE WHOLE FORTRESS!
YET WE HAVE TO CROSS IT TO REACH THEIR DOMAIN...
KERIM SHAH, LOOK WHAT'S COMING AT US!
THE "YIMSHA CARPET"?!
CONAN WAS ABOUT TO FIND OUT WHY THE INHABITANTS OF THE REGION WERE SO AFRAID OF THIS CLOUD TIED TO THE BLACK SEERS OF MOUNT YIMSHA.
THE CLOUD TURNED INTO A DEADLY SWARM OF FIERCE VULTURES WHO APPEARED EMACIATED, AS IF LIFE HAD ALREADY LEFT THEM!
BY CROM! THESE BIRDS ARE WORSE THAN BIG CATS!

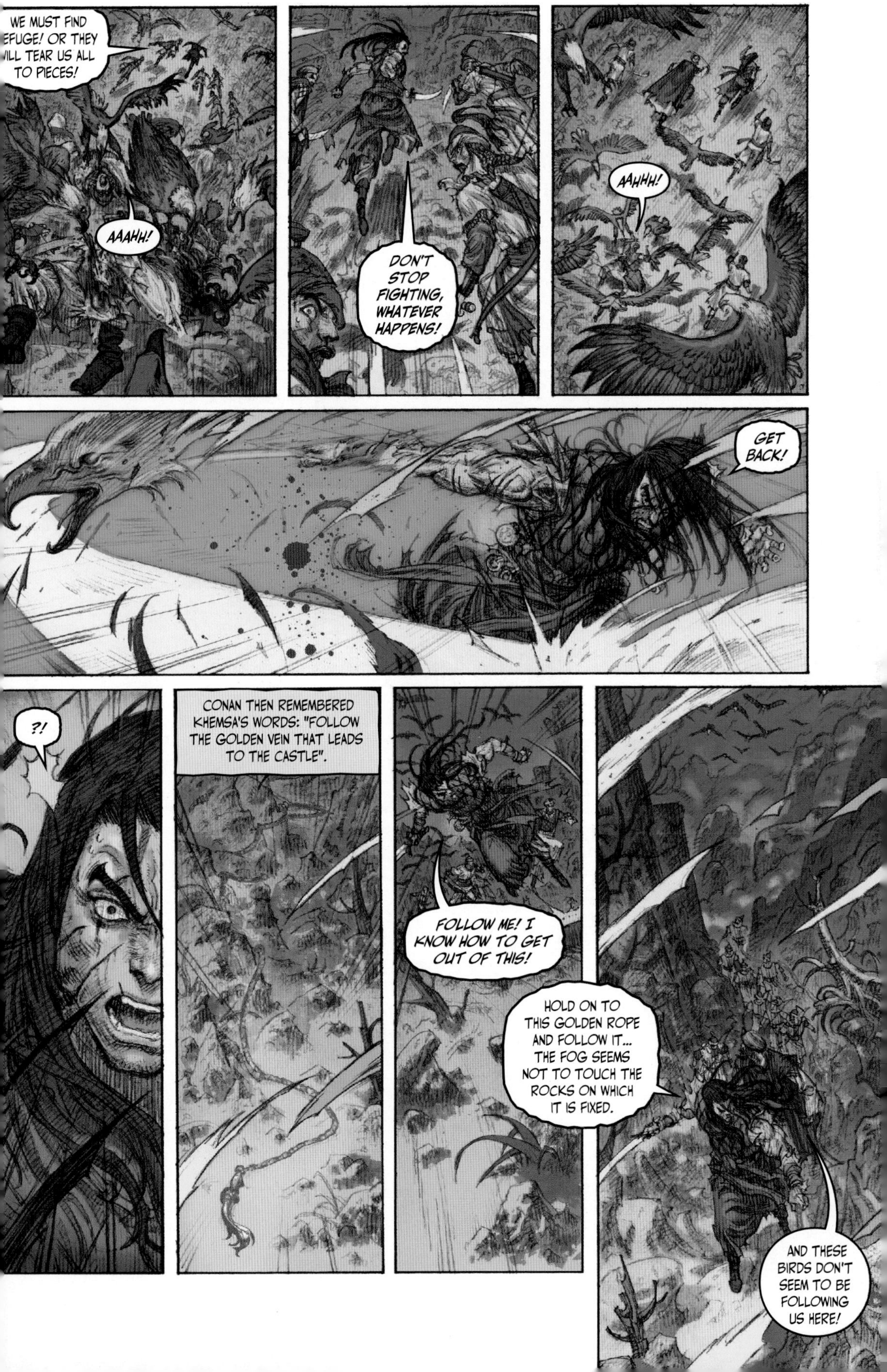
WE MUST FIND EFUGE! OR THEY WILL TEAR US ALL TO PIECES!
AAAHH!
DON'T STOP FIGHTING, WHATEVER HAPPENS!
AAHHH!
GET BACK!
?!
CONAN THEN REMEMBERED KHEMSA'S WORDS: "FOLLOW THE GOLDEN VEIN THAT LEADS TO THE CASTLE".
FOLLOW ME! I KNOW HOW TO GET OUT OF THIS!
HOLD ON TO THIS GOLDEN ROPE AND FOLLOW IT... THE FOG SEEMS NOT TO TOUCH THE ROCKS ON WHICH IT IS FIXED.
AND THESE BIRDS DON'T SEEM TO BE FOLLOWING US HERE!

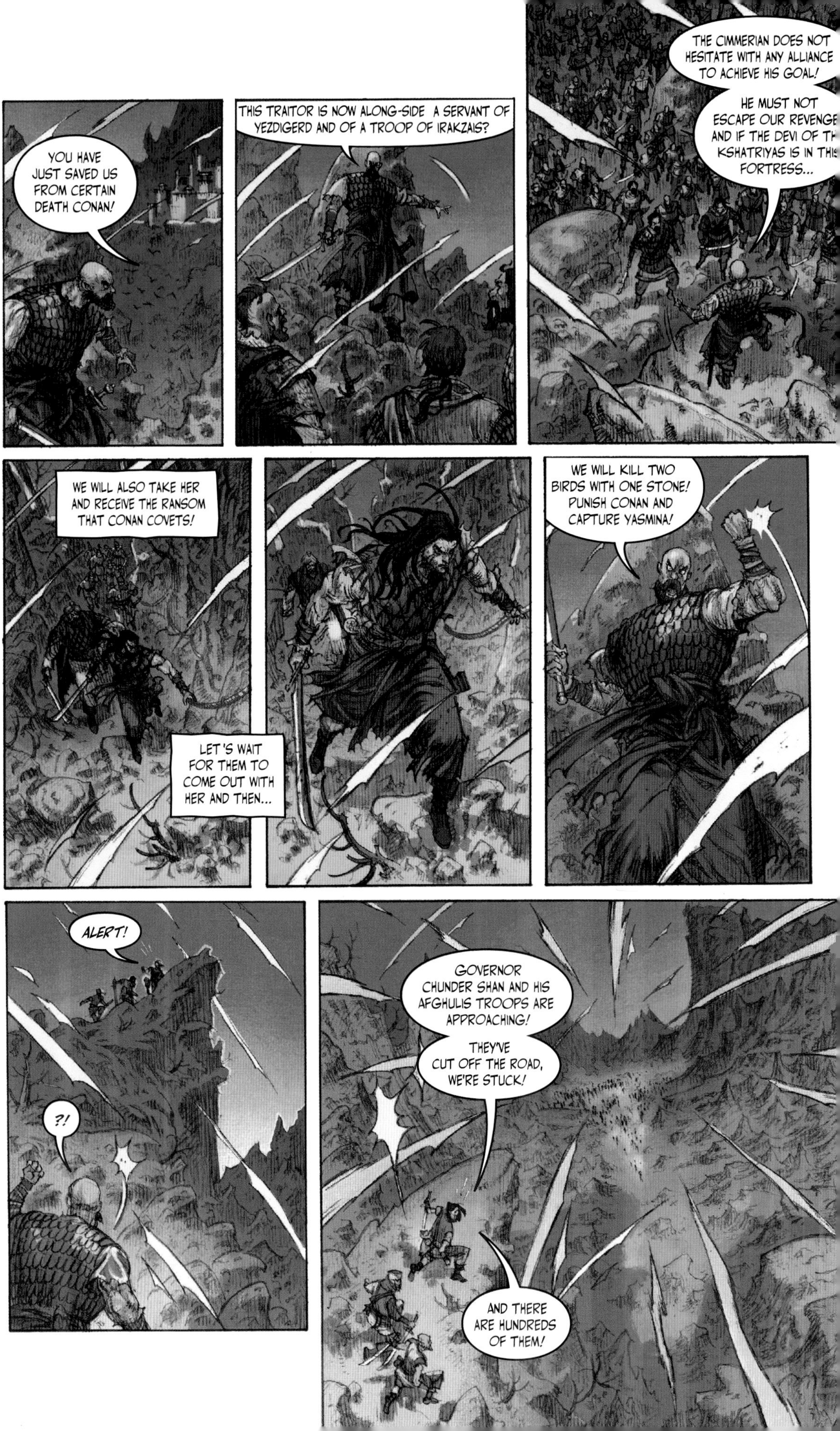
YOU HAVE JUST SAVED US FROM CERTAIN DEATH CONAN!
THIS TRAITOR IS NOW ALONG-SIDE A SERVANT OF YEZDIGERD AND OF A TROOP OF IRAKZAIS?
THE CIMMERIAN DOES NOT HESITATE WITH ANY ALLIANCE TO ACHIEVE HIS GOAL!
HE MUST NOT ESCAPE OUR REVENGE AND IF THE DEVI OF THE KSHATRIYAS IS IN THIS FORTRESS...
WE WILL ALSO TAKE HER AND RECEIVE THE RANSOM THAT CONAN COVETS!
LET'S WAIT FOR THEM TO COME OUT WITH HER AND THEN...
WE WILL KILL TWO BIRDS WITH ONE STONE! PUNISH CONAN AND CAPTURE YASMINA!
ALERT!
?!
GOVERNOR CHUNDER SHAN AND HIS AFGHULIS TROOPS ARE APPROACHING!
THEY'VE CUT OFF THE ROAD, WE'RE STUCK!
AND THERE ARE HUNDREDS OF THEM!

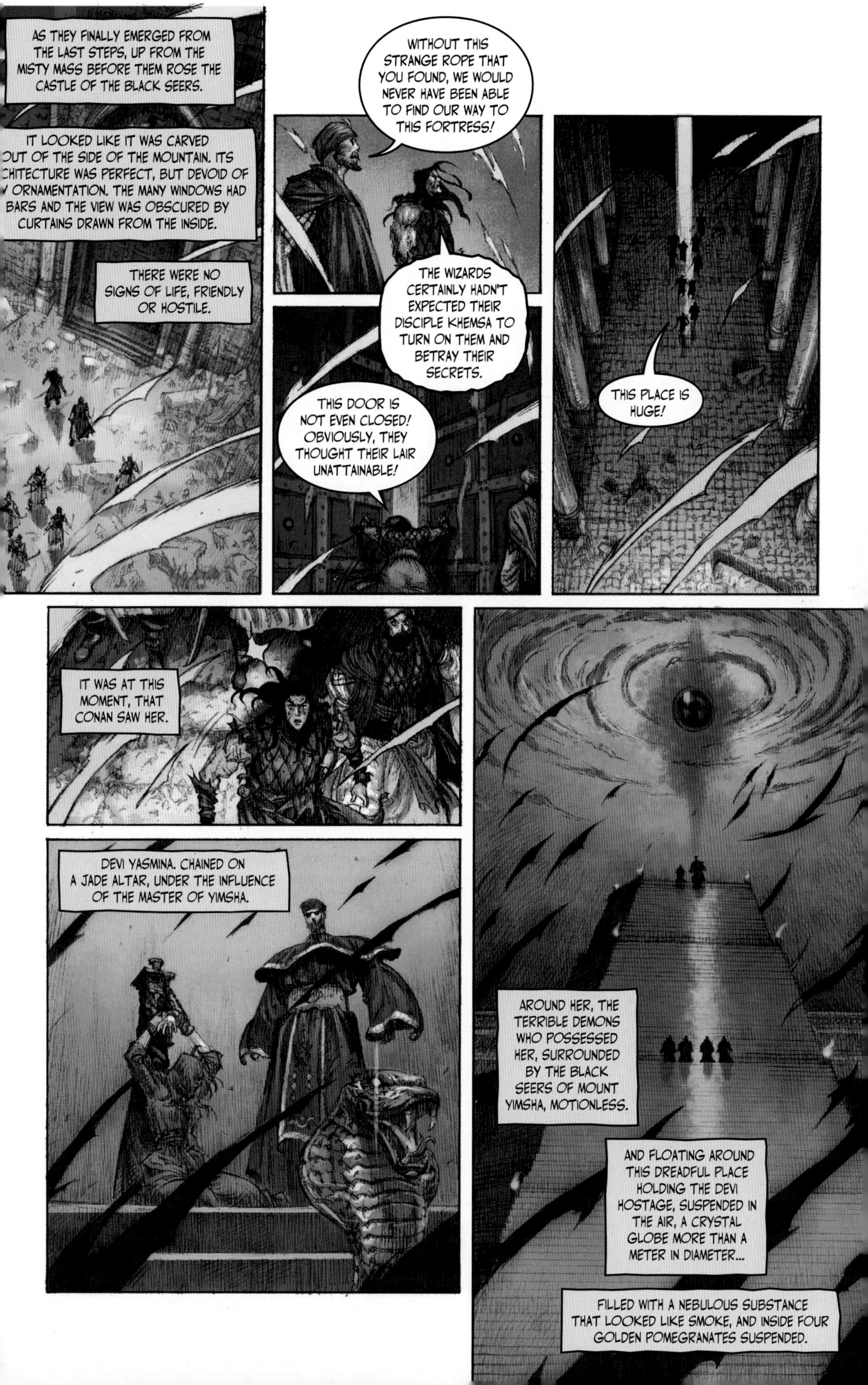

AS THEY FINALLY EMERGED FROM THE LAST STEPS, UP FROM THE MISTY MASS BEFORE THEM ROSE THE CASTLE OF THE BLACK SEERS.
IT LOOKED LIKE IT WAS CARVED OUT OF THE SIDE OF THE MOUNTAIN. ITS CHITECTURE WAS PERFECT, BUT DEVOID OF ORNAMENTATION. THE MANY WINDOWS HAD BARS AND THE VIEW WAS OBSCURED BY CURTAINS DRAWN FROM THE INSIDE.
THERE WERE NO SIGNS OF LIFE, FRIENDLY OR HOSTILE.
WITHOUT THIS STRANGE ROPE THAT YOU FOUND, WE WOULD NEVER HAVE BEEN ABLE TO FIND OUR WAY TO THIS FORTRESS!
THE WIZARDS CERTAINLY HADN'T EXPECTED THEIR DISCIPLE KHEMSA TO TURN ON THEM AND BETRAY THEIR SECRETS.
THIS DOOR IS NOT EVEN CLOSED! OBVIOUSLY, THEY THOUGHT THEIR LAIR UNATTAINABLE!
THIS PLACE IS HUGE!
IT WAS AT THIS MOMENT, THAT CONAN SAW HER.
DEVI YASMINA. CHAINED ON A JADE ALTAR, UNDER THE INFLUENCE OF THE MASTER OF YIMSHA.
AROUND HER, THE TERRIBLE DEMONS WHO POSSESSED HER, SURROUNDED BY THE BLACK SEERS OF MOUNT YIMSHA, MOTIONLESS.
AND FLOATING AROUND THIS DREADFUL PLACE HOLDING THE DEVI HOSTAGE, SUSPENDED IN THE AIR, A CRYSTAL GLOBE MORE THAN A METER IN DIAMETER...
FILLED WITH A NEBULOUS SUBSTANCE THAT LOOKED LIKE SMOKE, AND INSIDE FOUR GOLDEN POMEGRANATES SUSPENDED.

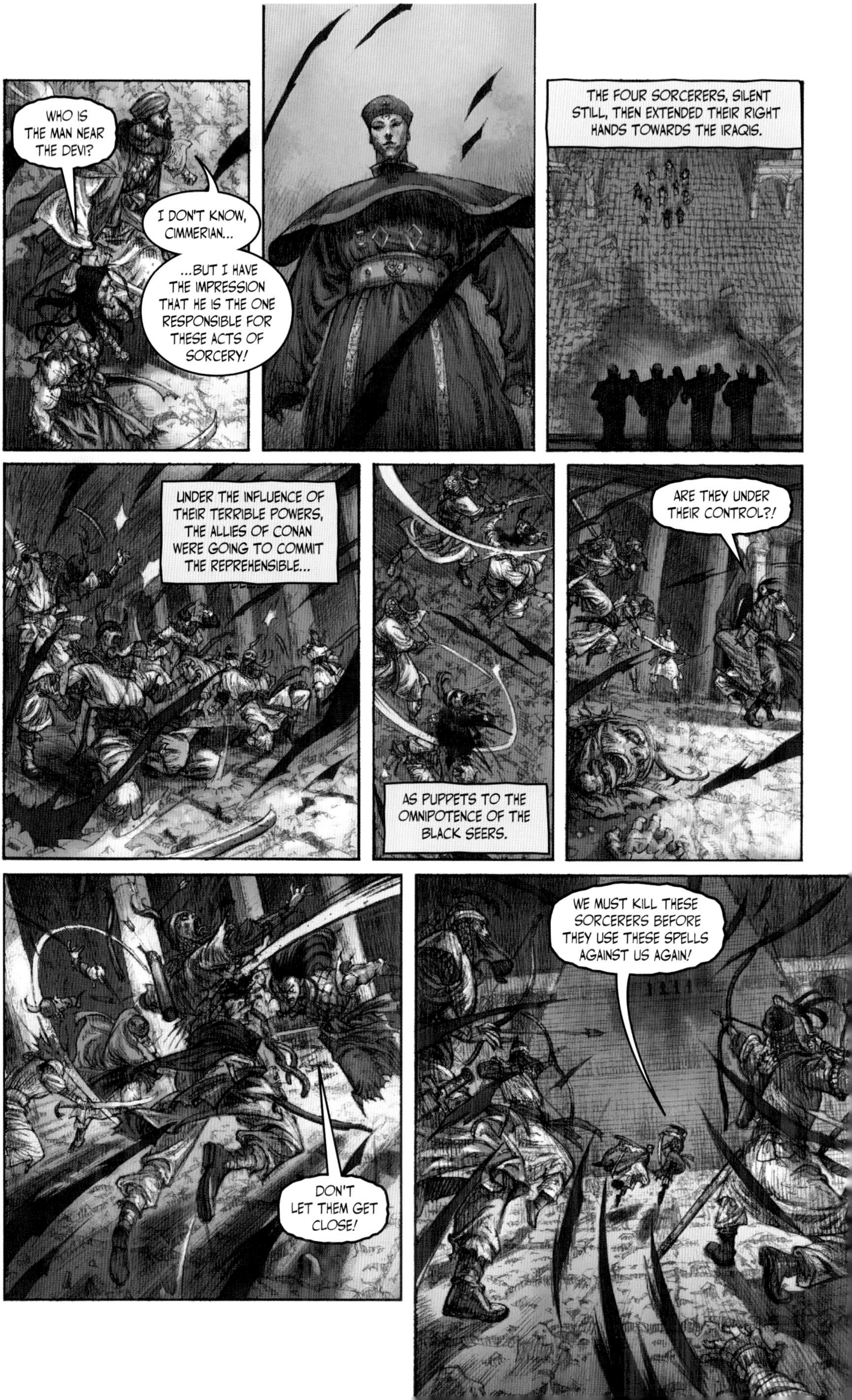
WHO IS THE MAN NEAR THE DEVI?
I DON'T KNOW, CIMMERIAN...
...BUT I HAVE THE IMPRESSION THAT HE IS THE ONE RESPONSIBLE FOR THESE ACTS OF SORCERY!
THE FOUR SORCERERS, SILENT STILL, THEN EXTENDED THEIR RIGHT HANDS TOWARDS THE IRAQIS.
UNDER THE INFLUENCE OF THEIR TERRIBLE POWERS, THE ALLIES OF CONAN WERE GOING TO COMMIT THE REPREHENSIBLE...
AS PUPPETS TO THE OMNIPOTENCE OF THE BLACK SEERS.
ARE THEY UNDER THEIR CONTROL?!
DON'T LET THEM GET CLOSE!
WE MUST KILL THESE SORCERERS BEFORE THEY USE THESE SPELLS AGAINST US AGAIN!

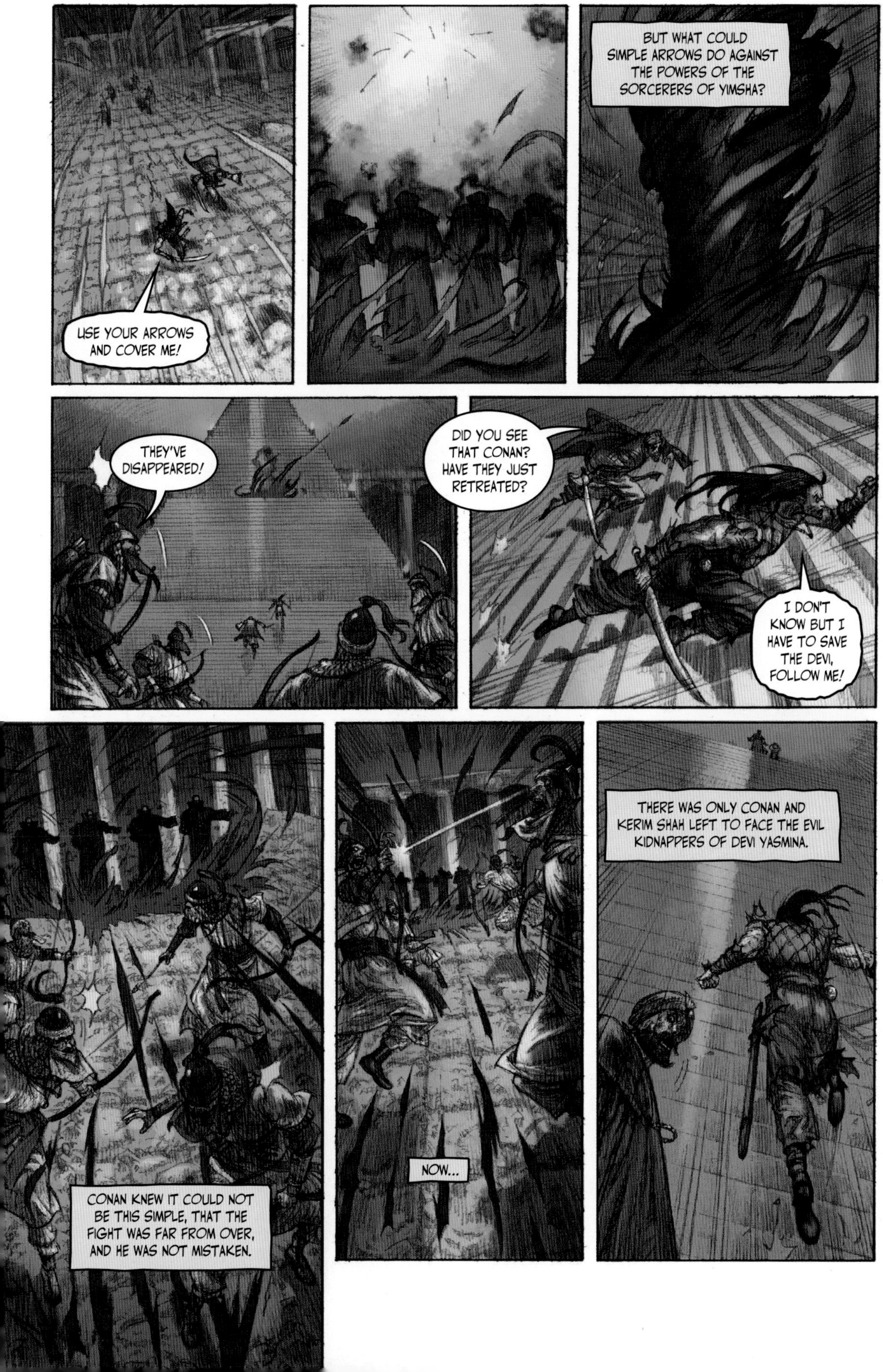
USE YOUR ARROWS AND COVER ME!
BUT WHAT COULD SIMPLE ARROWS DO AGAINST THE POWERS OF THE SORCERERS OF YIMSHA?
THEY'VE DISAPPEARED!
DID YOU SEE THAT CONAN? HAVE THEY JUST RETREATED?
I DON'T KNOW BUT I HAVE TO SAVE THE DEVI, FOLLOW ME!
CONAN KNEW IT COULD NOT BE THIS SIMPLE, THAT THE FIGHT WAS FAR FROM OVER, AND HE WAS NOT MISTAKEN.
NOW...
THERE WAS ONLY CONAN AND KERIM SHAH LEFT TO FACE THE EVIL KIDNAPPERS OF DEVI YASMINA.

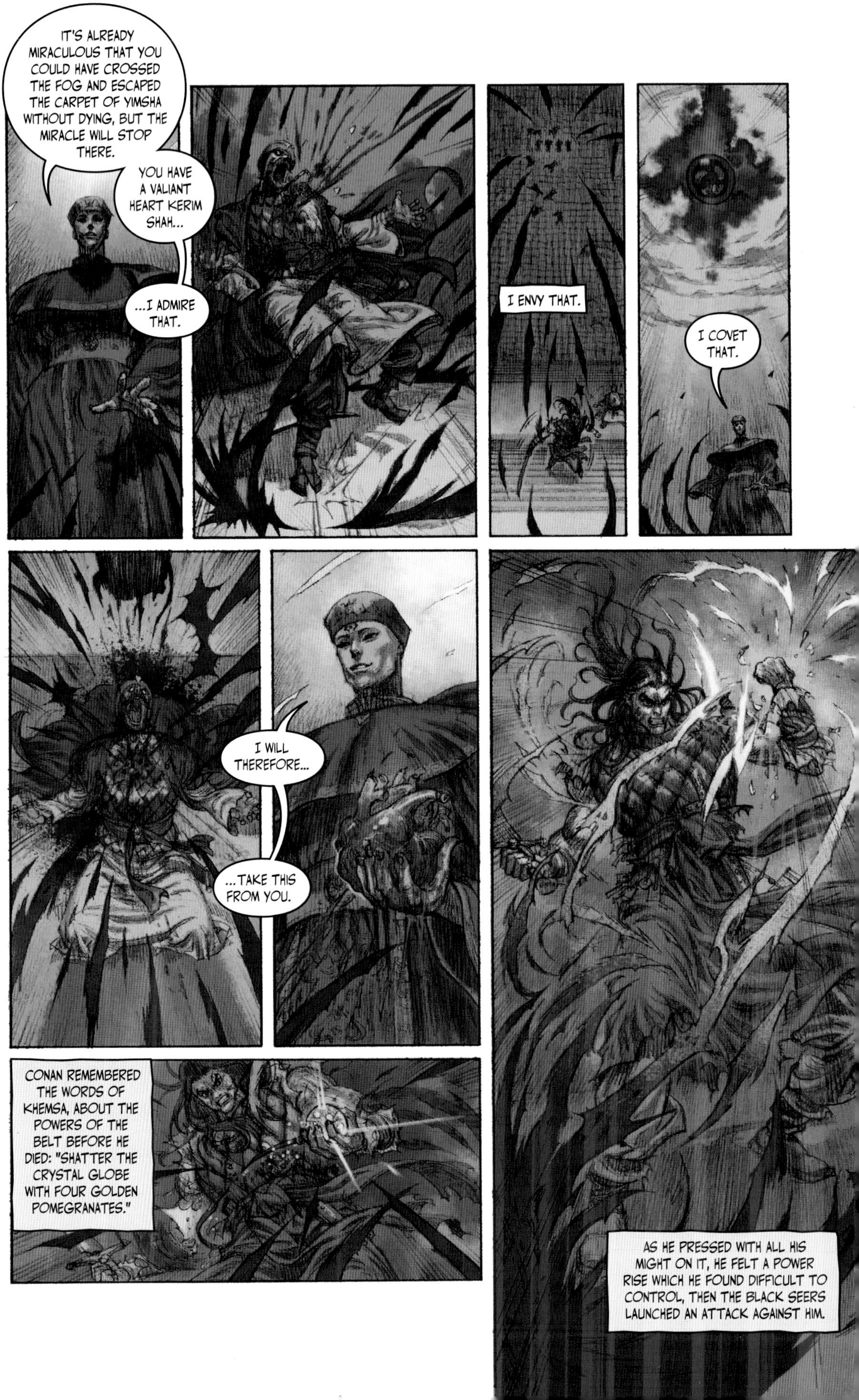
IT'S ALREADY MIRACULOUS THAT YOU COULD HAVE CROSSED THE FOG AND ESCAPED THE CARPET OF YIMSHA WITHOUT DYING, BUT THE MIRACLE WILL STOP THERE.
YOU HAVE A VALIANT HEART KERIM SHAH...
...I ADMIRE THAT.
I ENVY THAT.
I COVET THAT.
I WILL THEREFORE...
...TAKE THIS FROM YOU.
CONAN REMEMBERED THE WORDS OF KHEMSA, ABOUT THE POWERS OF THE BELT BEFORE HE DIED: "SHATTER THE CRYSTAL GLOBE WITH FOUR GOLDEN POMEGRANATES."
AS HE PRESSED WITH ALL HIS MIGHT ON IT, HE FELT A POWER RISE WHICH HE FOUND DIFFICULT TO CONTROL, THEN THE BLACK SEERS LAUNCHED AN ATTACK AGAINST HIM.

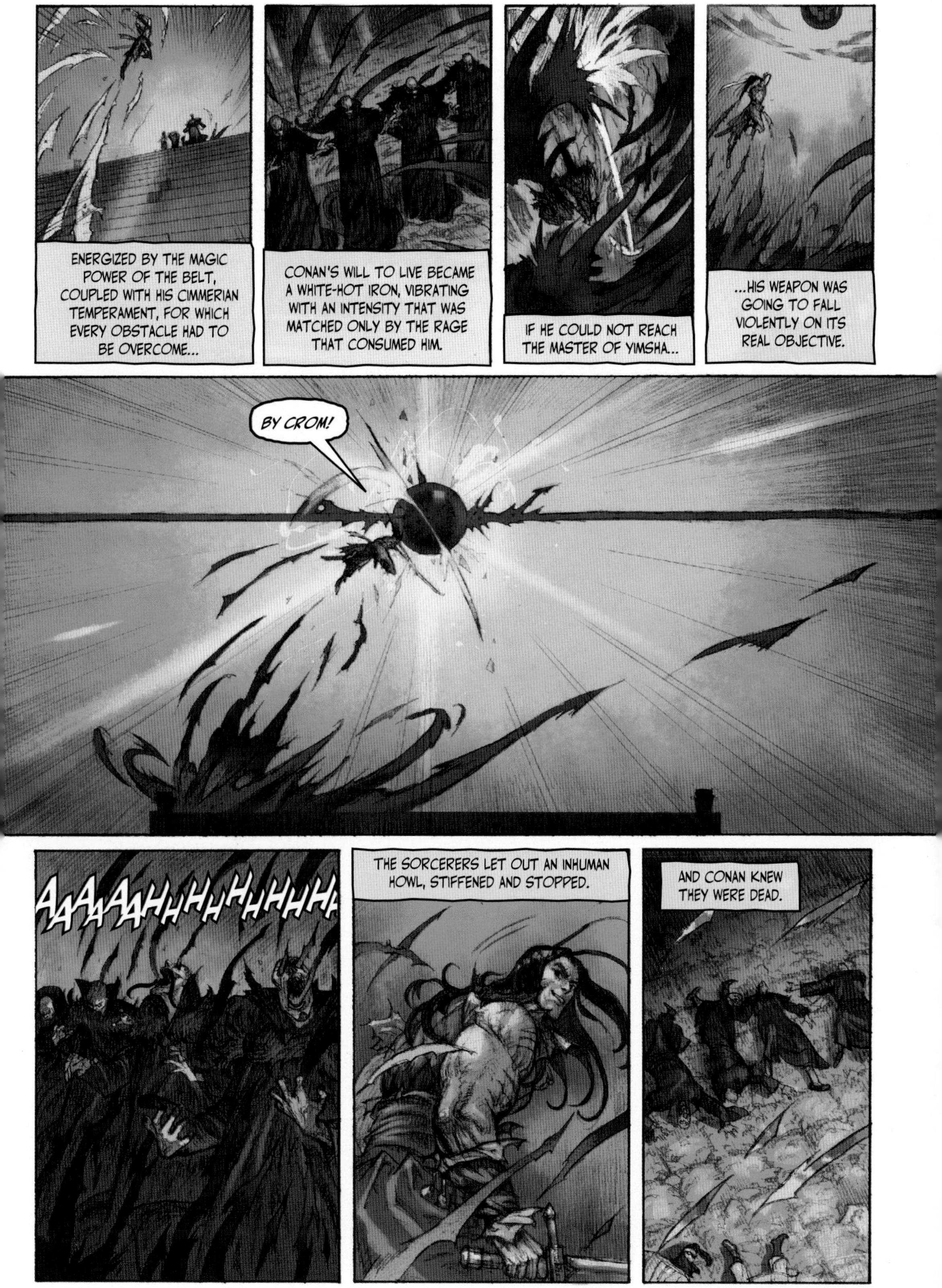
ENERGIZED BY THE MAGIC POWER OF THE BELT, COUPLED WITH HIS CIMMERIAN TEMPERAMENT, FOR WHICH EVERY OBSTACLE HAD TO BE OVERCOME...
CONAN'S WILL TO LIVE BECAME A WHITE-HOT IRON, VIBRATING WITH AN INTENSITY THAT WAS MATCHED ONLY BY THE RAGE THAT CONSUMED HIM.
IF HE COULD NOT REACH THE MASTER OF YIMSHA...
...HIS WEAPON WAS GOING TO FALL VIOLENTLY ON ITS REAL OBJECTIVE.
BY CROM!
AAAAAAHHHHHHHHHH
THE SORCERERS LET OUT AN INHUMAN HOWL, STIFFENED AND STOPPED.
AND CONAN KNEW THEY WERE DEAD.

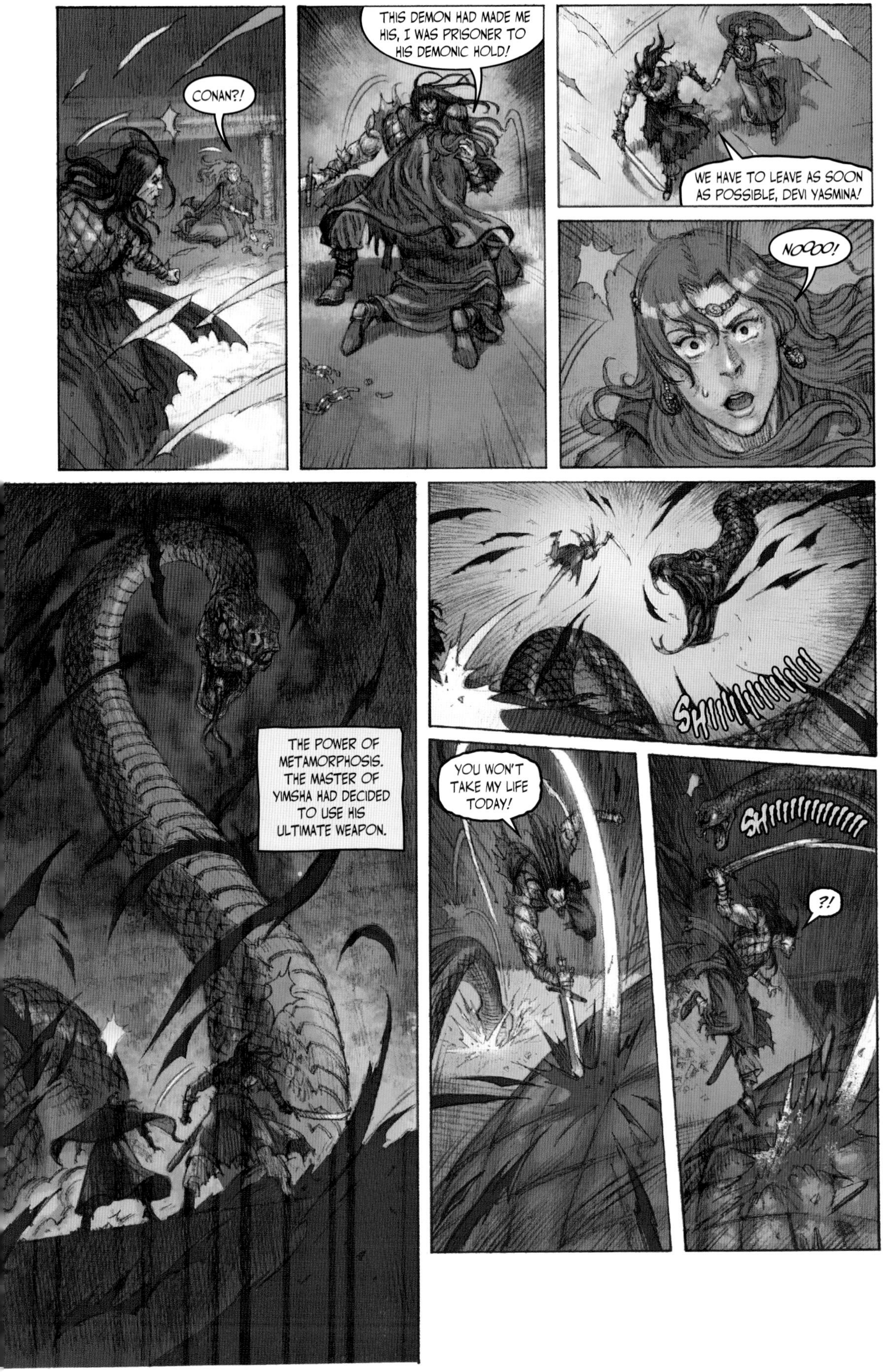
CONAN?!
THIS DEMON HAD MADE ME HIS, I WAS PRISONER TO HIS DEMONIC HOLD!
WE HAVE TO LEAVE AS SOON AS POSSIBLE, DEVI YASMINA!
NOOOO!
THE POWER OF METAMORPHOSIS. THE MASTER OF YIMSHA HAD DECIDED TO USE HIS ULTIMATE WEAPON.
SHHHHHHHHH
YOU WON'T TAKE MY LIFE TODAY!
SHHHHHHHHHH
?!

SHIIIIIIIIIIII

TCHACK

SHIIIIIIIIIIII

CONAN?!

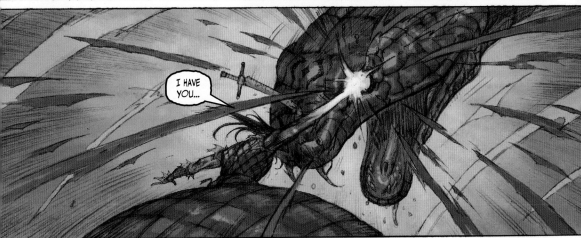

I HAVE YOU...

...AND...

...YOU'VE BEEN WARNED!

YOU WON'T TAKE MY LIFE TODAY.

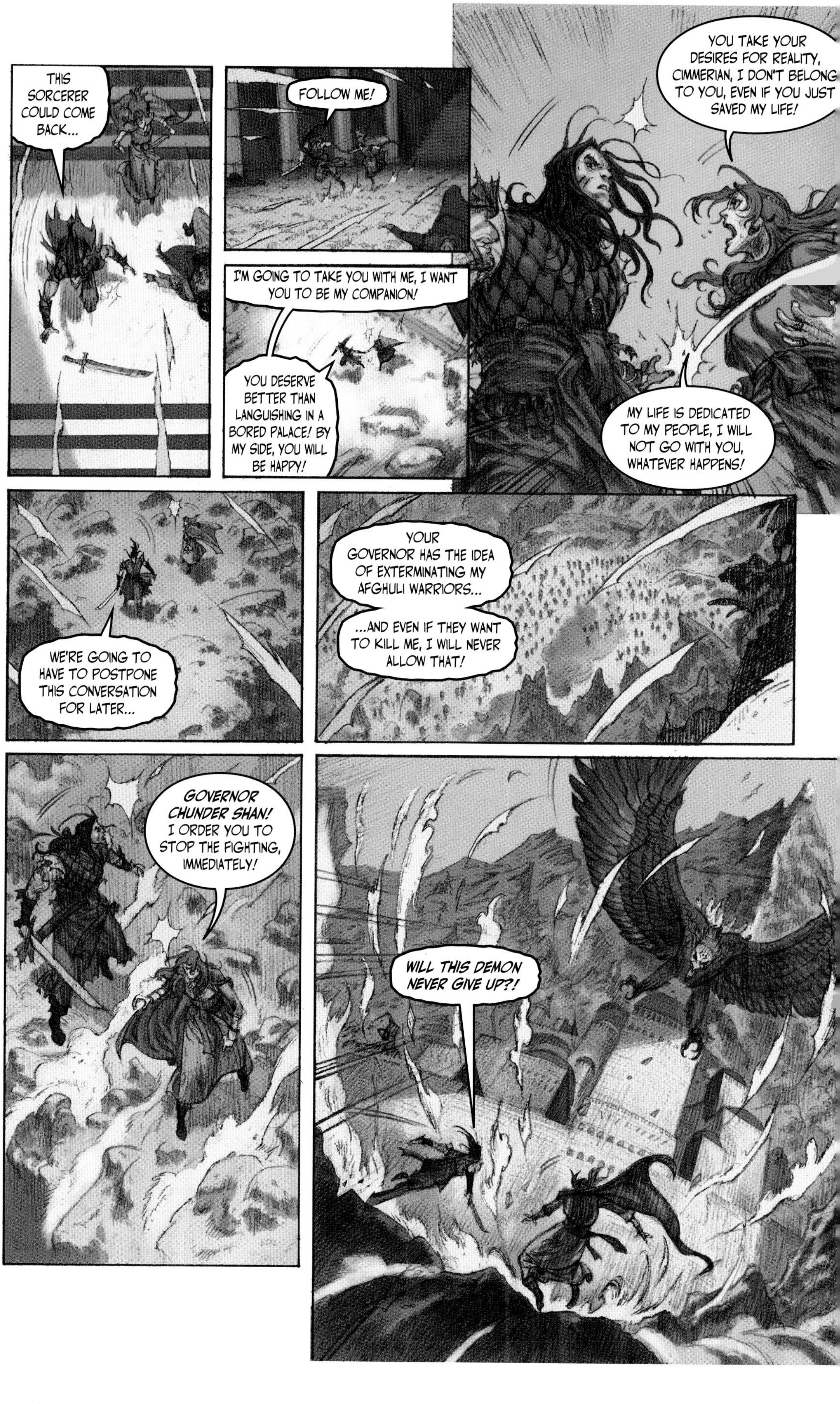

THIS SORCERER COULD COME BACK...
FOLLOW ME!
I'M GOING TO TAKE YOU WITH ME, I WANT YOU TO BE MY COMPANION!
YOU DESERVE BETTER THAN LANGUISHING IN A BORED PALACE! BY MY SIDE, YOU WILL BE HAPPY!
YOU TAKE YOUR DESIRES FOR REALITY, CIMMERIAN, I DON'T BELONG TO YOU, EVEN IF YOU JUST SAVED MY LIFE!
MY LIFE IS DEDICATED TO MY PEOPLE, I WILL NOT GO WITH YOU, WHATEVER HAPPENS!
WE'RE GOING TO HAVE TO POSTPONE THIS CONVERSATION FOR LATER...
YOUR GOVERNOR HAS THE IDEA OF EXTERMINATING MY AFGHULI WARRIORS...
...AND EVEN IF THEY WANT TO KILL ME, I WILL NEVER ALLOW THAT!
GOVERNOR CHUNDER SHAN! I ORDER YOU TO STOP THE FIGHTING, IMMEDIATELY!
WILL THIS DEMON NEVER GIVE UP?!

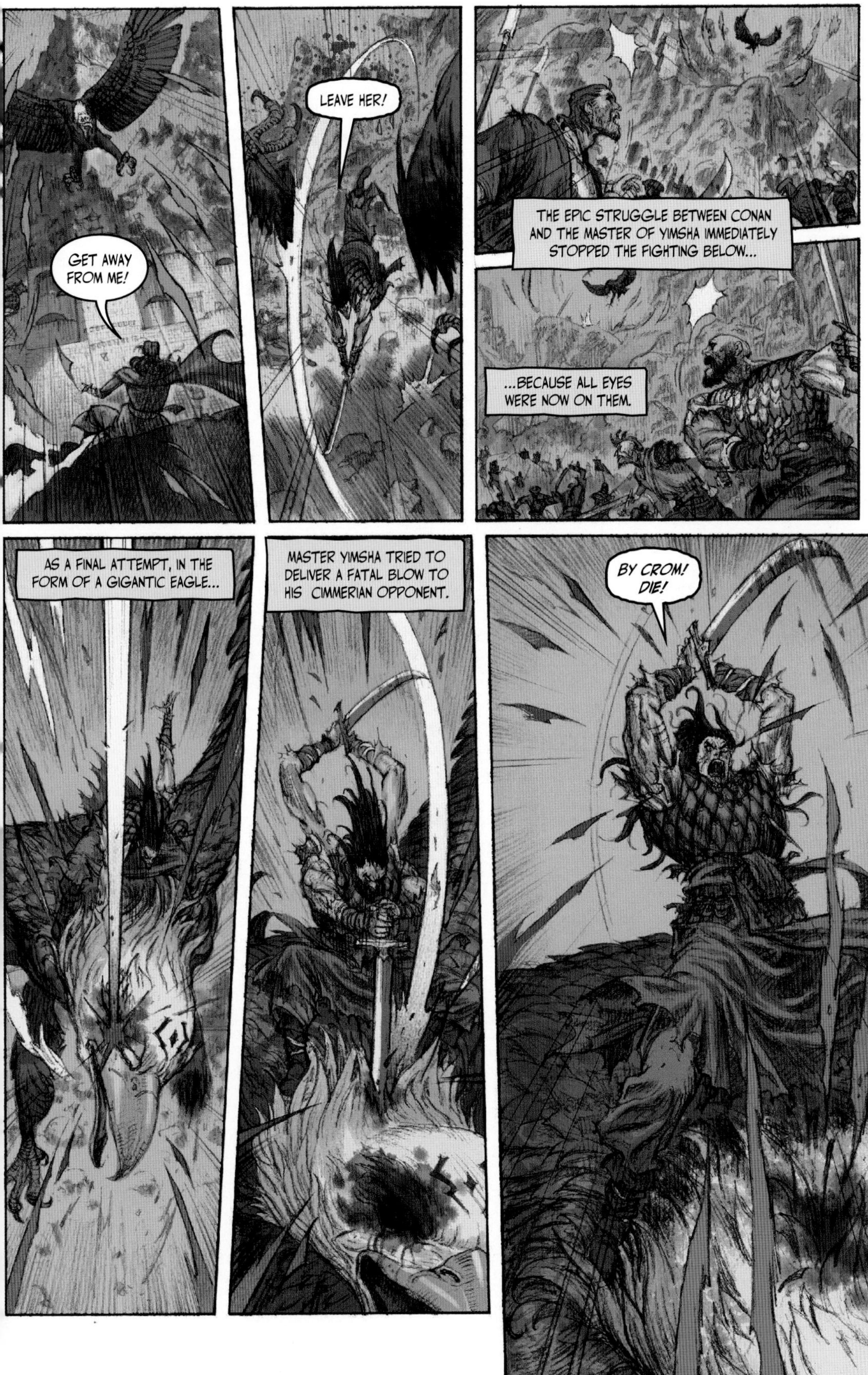
GET AWAY FROM ME!
LEAVE HER!
THE EPIC STRUGGLE BETWEEN CONAN AND THE MASTER OF YIMSHA IMMEDIATELY STOPPED THE FIGHTING BELOW...
...BECAUSE ALL EYES WERE NOW ON THEM.
AS A FINAL ATTEMPT, IN THE FORM OF A GIGANTIC EAGLE...
MASTER YIMSHA TRIED TO DELIVER A FATAL BLOW TO HIS CIMMERIAN OPPONENT.
BY CROM! DIE!

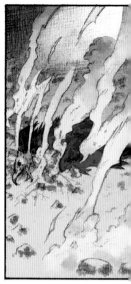

CONAN?! AREN'T YOU HURT?

MY INJURIES DON'T MATTER...

...I WON THE FIGHT.

AND IN THE END...

...THAT IS ALL THAT MATTERS.

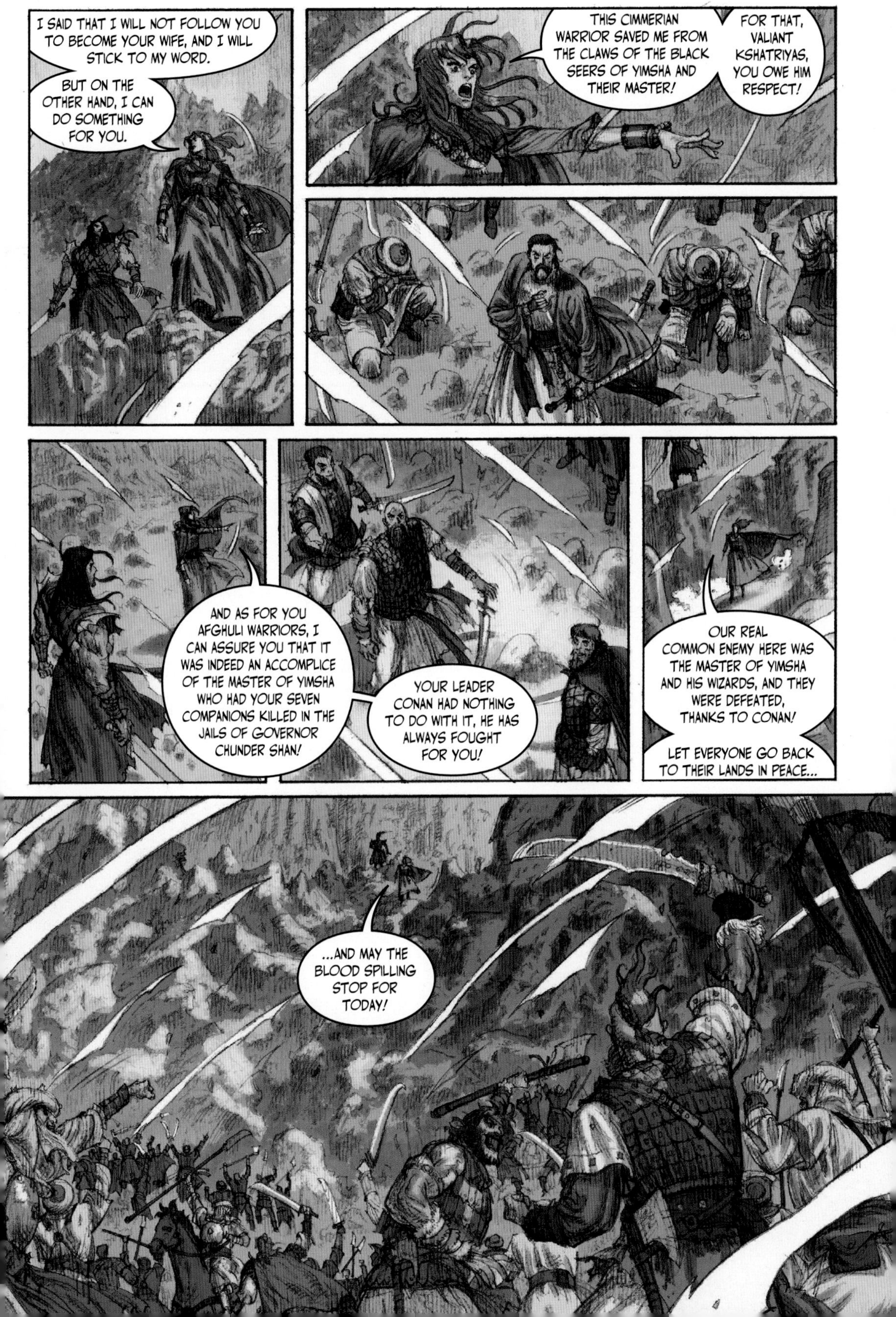
I SAID THAT I WILL NOT FOLLOW YOU TO BECOME YOUR WIFE, AND I WILL STICK TO MY WORD.
BUT ON THE OTHER HAND, I CAN DO SOMETHING FOR YOU.
THIS CIMMERIAN WARRIOR SAVED ME FROM THE CLAWS OF THE BLACK SEERS OF YIMSHA AND THEIR MASTER!
FOR THAT, VALIANT KSHATRIYAS, YOU OWE HIM RESPECT!
AND AS FOR YOU AFGHULI WARRIORS, I CAN ASSURE YOU THAT IT WAS INDEED AN ACCOMPLICE OF THE MASTER OF YIMSHA WHO HAD YOUR SEVEN COMPANIONS KILLED IN THE JAILS OF GOVERNOR CHUNDER SHAN!
YOUR LEADER CONAN HAD NOTHING TO DO WITH IT, HE HAS ALWAYS FOUGHT FOR YOU!
OUR REAL COMMON ENEMY HERE WAS THE MASTER OF YIMSHA AND HIS WIZARDS, AND THEY WERE DEFEATED, THANKS TO CONAN!
LET EVERYONE GO BACK TO THEIR LANDS IN PEACE...
...AND MAY THE BLOOD SPILLING STOP FOR TODAY!

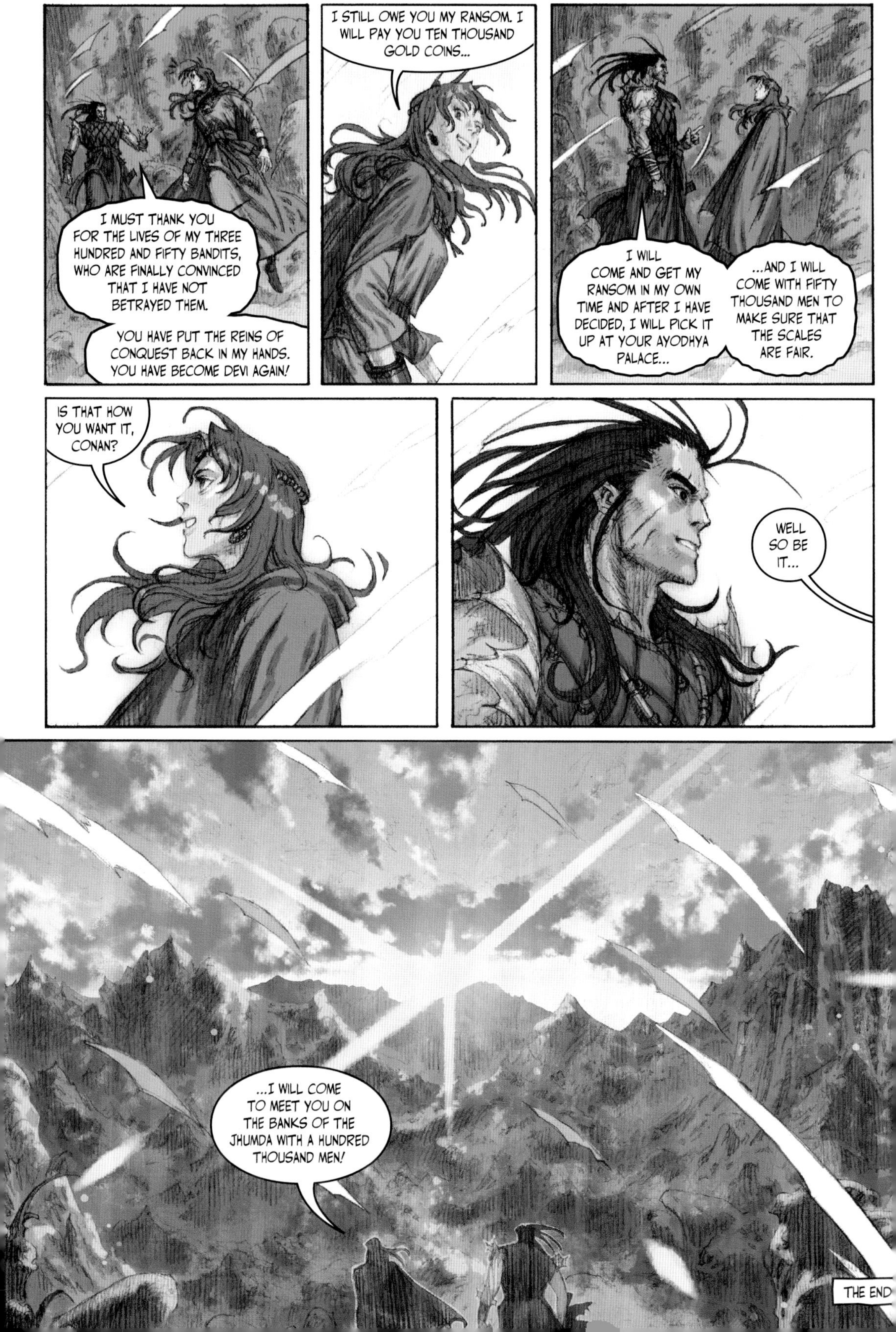

I MUST THANK YOU FOR THE LIVES OF MY THREE HUNDRED AND FIFTY BANDITS, WHO ARE FINALLY CONVINCED THAT I HAVE NOT BETRAYED THEM.
YOU HAVE PUT THE REINS OF CONQUEST BACK IN MY HANDS. YOU HAVE BECOME DEVI AGAIN!
I STILL OWE YOU MY RANSOM. I WILL PAY YOU TEN THOUSAND GOLD COINS...
I WILL COME AND GET MY RANSOM IN MY OWN TIME AND AFTER I HAVE DECIDED, I WILL PICK IT UP AT YOUR AYODHYA PALACE...
...AND I WILL COME WITH FIFTY THOUSAND MEN TO MAKE SURE THAT THE SCALES ARE FAIR.
IS THAT HOW YOU WANT IT, CONAN?
WELL SO BE IT...
...I WILL COME TO MEET YOU ON THE BANKS OF THE JHUMDA WITH A HUNDRED THOUSAND MEN!
THE END

THE PEOPLE OF THE BLACK CIRCLE

By Robert E. Howard

Weird Tales —September, October, November 1934.

1 DEATH STRIKES A KING

The king of Vendhya was dying. Through the hot, stifling night the temple gongs boomed and the conchs roared. Their clamor was a faint echo in the gold-domed chamber where Bunda Chand struggled on the velvet- cushioned dais. Beads of sweat glistened on his dark skin; his fingers twisted the gold-worked fabric beneath him. He was young; no spear had touched him, no poison lurked in his wine. But his veins stood out like blue cords on his temples, and his eyes dilated with the nearness of death. Trembling slave-girls knelt at the foot of the dais, and leaning down to him, watching him with passionate intensity, was his sister, the Devi Yasmina. With her was the *wazam*, a noble grown old in the royal court.

She threw up her head in a gusty gesture of wrath and despair as the thunder of the distant drums reached her ears. 'The priests and their clamor!' she exclaimed. 'They are no wiser than the leeches who are helpless! Nay, he dies and none can say why. He is dying now—and I stand here helpless, who would burn the whole city and spill the blood of thousands to save him.'

'Not a man of Ayodhya but would die in his place, if it might be, Devi,' answered the *wazam*. 'This poison—'

'I tell you it is not poison!' she cried. 'Since his birth he has been guarded so closely that the cleverest poisoners of the east could not reach him. Five skulls bleaching on the Tower of the Kites can testify to attempts which were made—and which failed. As you well know, there are ten men and ten women whose sole duty is to taste his food and wine, and fifty armed warriors guard his chamber as they guard it now. No, it is not poison; it is sorcery—black, ghastly magic—'

She ceased as the king spoke; his livid lips did not move, and there was no recognition in his glassy eyes. But his voice rose in an eery call, indistinct and far away, as if called to her from beyond vast, wind-blown gulfs. 'Yasmina! Yasmina! My sister, where are you? I can not find you. All is darkness, and the roaring of great winds!'

'Brother!' cried Yasmina, catching his limp hand in a convulsive grasp. 'I am here! Do you not know me—'

Her voice died at the utter vacancy of his face. A low confused moan waned from his mouth. The slave-girls at the foot of the dais whimpered with fear, and Yasmina beat her breast in anguish.

In another part of the city a man stood in a latticed balcony overlooking a long street in which torches tossed luridly, smokily revealing upturned dark faces and the whites of gleaming eyes. A long-drawn wailing rose from the multitude.

The man shrugged his broad shoulders and turned back into the arabesque chamber. He was a tall man, compactly built, and richly clad.

'The king is not yet dead, but the dirge is sounded,' he said to another man who sat cross-legged on a mat in a corner. This man was clad in a brown camel-hair robe and sandals, and a green turban was on his head. His expression was tranquil, his gaze impersonal.

'The people know he will never see another dawn,' this man answered. The first speaker favored him with a long, searching stare.

'What I can not understand,' he said, 'is why I have had to wait so long for your masters to strike. If they have slain the king now, why could they not have slain him months ago?'

'Even the arts you call sorcery are governed by cosmic laws,' answered the man in the green turban. 'The stars direct these actions, as in other affairs. Not even my masters can alter the stars. Not until the heavens were in the proper order could they perform this necromancy.' With a long, stained fingernail he mapped the constellations on the marble-tiled floor. 'The slant of the moon presaged evil for the king of Vendhya; the stars are in turmoil, the Serpent in the House of the Elephant. During such juxtaposition, the invisible guardians are removed from the spirit of Bhunda Chand. A path is opened in the unseen realms, and once a point of contact was established, mighty powers were put in play along that path.'

'Point of contact?' inquired the other. 'Do you mean that lock of Bhunda Chand's hair?'

'Yes. All discarded portions of the human body still remain part of it, attached to it by intangible connections. The priests of Asura have a dim inkling of this truth, and so all nail trimmings, hair and other waste products of the persons of the royal family are carefully reduced to ashes and the ashes hidden. But at the urgent entreaty of the princess of Khosala, who loved Bhunda Chand vainly, he gave her a lock of his long black hair as a token of remembrance. When my masters decided upon his doom, the lock, in its golden, jewel-encrusted case, was stolen from under her pillow while she slept, and another substituted, so like the first that she never knew the difference. Then the genuine lock travelled by camel-caravan up the long, long road to Peshkhauri, thence up the Zhaibar Pass, until it reached the hands of those for whom it was intended.'

'Only a lock of hair,' murmured the nobleman.

'By which a soul is drawn from its body and across gulfs of echoing space,' returned the man on the mat. The nobleman studied him curiously.

'I do not know if you are a man or a demon, Khemsa,' he said at last. 'Few of us are what we seem. I, whom the Kshatriyas know as Kerim Shah, a prince from Iranistan, am no greater a masquerader than most men. They are all traitors in one way or another, and half of them know not whom they serve. There at least I have no doubts; for I serve King Yezdigerd of Turan.'

'And I the Black Seers of Yimsha,' said Khemsa; 'and my masters are greater than yours, for they have accomplished by their arts what Yezdigerd could not with a hundred thousand swords.'

Outside, the moan of the tortured thousands shuddered up to the stars which crusted the sweating Vendhyan night, and the conchs bellowed like oxen in pain.

In the gardens of the palace the torches glinted on polished helmets and curved swords and gold-chased corselets. All the noble-born fighting-men of Ayodhya were gathered in the great palace or about it, and at each broad-arched gate and door fifty archers stood on guard, with bows in their hands. But Death stalked through the royal palace and none could stay his ghostly tread.

On the dais under the golden dome the king cried out again, racked by awful paroxysms. Again his voice came faintly and far away, and again the Devi bent to him, trembling with a fear that was darker than the terror of death.

'Yasmina!' Again that far, weirdly dreeing cry, from realms immeasurable. 'Aid me! I am far from my mortal house! Wizards have drawn my soul through the wind-blown darkness. They seek to snap the silver cord that binds me to my dying body. They cluster around me; their hands are taloned, their eyes are red like flame burning in darkness. *Aie*, save me, my sister! Their fingers sear me like fire! They would slay my body and damn my soul! What is this they bring before me?—*Aie!*'

At the terror in his hopeless cry Yasmina screamed uncontrollably and threw herself bodily upon him in the abandon of her anguish. He was torn by a terrible convulsion; foam flew from his contorted lips and his writhing fingers left their marks on the girl's shoulders. But the glassy blankness passed from his eyes like smoke blown from a fire, and he looked up at his sister with recognition.

'Brother!' she sobbed. 'Brother—'

'Swift!' he gasped, and his weakening voice was rational. 'I know now what brings me to the pyre. I have been on a far journey and I understand. I have been ensorcelled by the wizards of the Himelians. They drew my soul out of my body and far away, into a stone room. There they strove to break the silver cord of life, and thrust my soul into the body of a foul night-weird their sorcery summoned up from hell. Ah! I feel their pull upon me now! Your cry and the grip of your fingers brought me back, but I am going fast. My soul clings to my body, but its hold weakens. Quick—kill me, before they can trap my soul for ever!'

'I cannot!' she wailed, smiting her naked breasts.

'Swiftly, I command you!' There was the old imperious note in his failing whisper. 'You have never disobeyed me—obey my last command! Send my soul clean to Asura! Haste, lest you damn me to spend eternity as a filthy gaunt of darkness. Strike, I command you! *Strike!*'

Sobbing wildly, Yasmina plucked a jeweled dagger from her girdle and plunged it to the hilt in his breast. He stiffened and then went limp, a grim smile curving his dead lips. Yasmina hurled herself face-down on the rush-covered floor, beating the reeds with her clenched hands. Outside, the gongs and conchs brayed and thundered and the priests gashed themselves with copper knives.

2 A BARBARIAN FROM THE HILLS

Chunder Shan, governor of Peshkhauri, laid down his golden pen and carefully scanned that which he had written on parchment that bore his official seal. He had ruled Peshkhauri so long only because he weighed his every word, spoken or written. Danger breeds caution, and only a wary man lives long in that wild country where the hot Vendhyan plains meet the crags of the Himelians. An hour's ride westward or northward and one crossed the border and was among the Hills where men lived by the law of the knife.

The governor was alone in his chamber, seated at his ornately carven table of inlaid ebony. Through the wide window, open for the coolness, he could see a square of the blue Himelian night, dotted with great white stars. An adjacent parapet was a shadowy line, and further crenelles and embrasures were barely hinted at in the dim starlight. The governor's fortress was strong, and situated outside the walls of the city it guarded. The breeze that stirred the tapestries on the wall brought faint noises from the streets of Peshkhauri— occasional snatches of wailing song, or the thrum of a cithern.

The governor read what he had written, slowly, with his open hand shading his eyes from the bronze butterlamp, his lips moving. Absently, as he read, he heard the drum of horses' hoofs outside the barbican, the sharp staccato of the guards' challenge. He did not heed, intent upon his letter. It was addressed to the *wazam* of Vendhya, at the royal court of Ayodhya, and it stated, after the customary salutations:

'Let it be known to your excellency that I have faithfully carried out your excellency's instructions. The seven tribesmen are well guarded in their prison, and I have repeatedly sent word into the hills that their chief come in person to bargain for their release. But he has made no move, except to send word that unless they are freed he will burn Peshkhauri and cover his saddle with my hide, begging your excellency's indulgence. This he is quite capable of attempting, and I have tripled the numbers of the lance guards. The man is not a native of Ghulistan. I cannot with certainty predict his next move. But since it is the wish of the Devi—'

He was out of his ivory chair and on his feet facing the arched door, all in one instant. He snatched at the curved sword lying in its ornate scabbard on the table, and then checked the movement.

It was a woman who had entered unannounced, a woman whose gossamer robes did not conceal the rich garments beneath them any more than they concealed the suppleness and beauty of her tall, slender figure. A filmy veil fell below her breasts, supported by a flowing headdress bound about with a triple gold braid and adorned with a golden crescent. Her dark eyes regarded the astonished governor over the veil, and then with an imperious gesture of her white hand, she uncovered her face.

'Devi!' The governor dropped to his knees before her, surprize and confusion somewhat spoiling the stateliness of his obeisance. With a gesture she motioned him to rise, and he hastened to lead her to the ivory chair, all the while bowing level with his girdle. But his first words were of reproof.

'Your Majesty! This was most unwise! The border is unsettled. Raids from the hills are incessant. You came with a large attendance?' 'An ample retinue followed me to Peshkhaur. I lodged my people there and came on to the fort with my maid, Gitara.' Chunder Shan groaned in horror.

'Devi! You do not understand the peril. An hour's ride from this spot the hills swarm with barbarians who make profession of murder and rapine. Women have been stolen and men stabbed between the fort and the city. Peshkhauri is not like your southern provinces—'

'But I am here, and unharmed,' she interrupted with a trace of impatience. 'I showed my signet ring to the guard at the gate, and to the one outside your door, and they admitted me unannounced, not knowing me, but supposing me to be a secret courier from Ayodhya. Let us not now waste time.

'You have received no word from the chief of the barbarians?

'None save threats and curses, Devi. He is wary and suspicious. He deems it a trap, and perhaps he is not to be blamed. The Kshatriyas have not always kept their promise to the hill people.' 'He must be brought to terms!' broke in Yasmina, the knuckles of her clenched hands showing white.

'I do not understand.' The governor shook his head. 'When I chanced to capture these seven hill-men, I reported their capture to the *wazam*, as is the custom, and then, before I could hang them, there came an order to hold them and communicate with their chief. This I did, but the man holds aloof, as I have said. These men are of the tribe of Afghulis but he is a foreigner from the west, and he is called Conan. I have threatened to hang them tomorrow at dawn, if he does not come.'

'Good!' exclaimed the Devi. 'You have done well. And I will tell you why I have given these orders. My brother—' she faltered, choking, and the governor bowed his head, with the customary gesture of respect for a departed sovereign.

'The king of Vendhya was destroyed by magic,' she said at last. 'I have devoted my life to the destruction of his murderers. As he died he gave me a clue, and I have followed it. I have read the *Book of Skelos*, and talked with nameless hermits in the caves below Jhelai. I learned how, and by whom, he was destroyed. His enemies were the Black Seers of Mount Yimsha.'

'Asura!' whispered Chunder Shan, paling.

Her eyes knifed him through. 'Do you fear them?'

'Who does not, Your Majesty?' he replied. 'They are black devils, haunting the uninhabited hills beyond the Zhaibar. But the sages say that they seldom interfere in the lives of mortal men.'

'Why they slew my brother I do not know,' she answered. 'But I have sworn on the altar of Asura to destroy them! And I need the aid of a man beyond the border. A Kshatriya army, unaided, would never reach Yimsha.'

'Aye,' muttered Chunder Shan. 'You speak the truth there. It would be fight every step of the way, with hairy hill-men hurling down boulders from every height, and rushing us with their long knives in every valley. The Turanians fought their way through the Himelians once, but how many returned to Khurusun? Few of those who escaped the swords of the Kshatriyas, after the king, your brother, defeated their host on the Jhumda River, ever saw Secunderam again.'

'And so I must control men across the border,' she said, 'men who know the way to Mount Yimsha—' 'But the tribes fear the Black Seers and shun the unholy mountain,' broke in the governor.

'Does the chief, Conan, fear them?' she asked.

'Well, as to that,' muttered the governor, 'I doubt if there is anything that devil fears.'

'So I have been told. Therefore he is the man I must deal

with. He wishes the release of his seven men. Very well; their ransom shall be the heads of the Black Seers!' Her voice drummed with hate as she uttered the last words, and her hands clenched at her sides. She looked an image of incarnate passion as she stood there with her head thrown high and her bosom heaving.

Again the governor knelt, for part of his wisdom was the knowledge that a woman in such an emotional tempest is as perilous as a blind cobra to any about her.

'It shall be as you wish, Your Majesty.' Then as she presented a calmer aspect, he rose and ventured to drop a word of warning. 'I can not predict what the chief Conan's action will be. The tribesmen are always turbulent, and I have reason to believe that emissaries from the Turanians are stirring them up to raid our borders. As your majesty knows, the Turanians have established themselves in Secunderam and other northern cities, though the hill tribes remain unconquered. King Yezdigerd has long looked southward with greedy lust and perhaps is seeking to gain by treachery what he could not win by force of arms. I have thought that Conan might well be one of his spies.'

'We shall see,' she answered. 'If he loves his followers, he will be at the gates at dawn, to parley. I shall spend the night in the fortress. I came in disguise to Peshkhauri, and lodged my retinue at an inn instead of the palace. Besides my people, only yourself knows of my presence here.'

'I shall escort you to your quarters, Your Majesty,' said the governor, and as they emerged from the doorway, he beckoned the warrior on guard there, and the man fell in behind them, spear held at salute.

The maid waited, veiled like her mistress, outside the door, and the group traversed a wide, winding corridor, lighted by smoky torches, and reached the quarters reserved for visiting notables—generals and viceroys, mostly; none of the royal family had ever honored the fortress before. Chunder Shan had a perturbed feeling that the suite was not suitable to such an exalted personage as the Devi, and though she sought to make him feel at ease in her presence, he was glad when she dismissed him and he bowed himself out. All the menials of the fort had been summoned to serve his royal guest—though he did not divulge her identity—and he stationed a squad of spearmen before her doors, among them the warrior who had guarded his own chamber. In his preoccupation he forgot to replace the man.

The governor had not been long gone from her when Jasmina suddenly remembered something else which she had wished to discuss with him, but had forgotten until that moment. It concerned the past actions of one Kerim Shah, a nobleman from Iranistan, who had dwelt for a while in Peshkhauri before coming on to the court at Ayodhya. A vague suspicion concerning the man had been stirred by a glimpse of him in Peshkhauri that night. She wondered if he had followed her from Ayodhya. Being a truly remarkable Devi, she did not summon the governor to her again, but hurried out into the corridor alone, and hastened toward his chamber.

Chunder Shan, entering his chamber, closed the door and went to his table. There he took the letter he had been writing and tore it to bits. Scarcely had he finished when he heard something drop softly onto the parapet adjacent to the window. He looked up to see a figure loom briefly against the stars, and then a man dropped lightly into the room. The light glinted on a long sheen of steel in his hand.

'Shhhh!' he warned. 'Don't make a noise, or I'll send the devil a henchman!'

The governor checked his motion toward the sword on the table. He was within reach of the yard-long Zhaibar knife that glittered in the intruder's fist, and he knew the desperate quickness of a hillman.

The invader was a tall man, at once strong and supple. He was dressed like a hillman, but his dark features and blazing blue eyes did not match his garb. Chunder Shan had never seen a man like him; he was not an Easterner, but some barbarian from the West. But his aspect was as untamed and formidable as any of the hairy tribesmen who haunt the hills of Ghulistan.

'You come like a thief in the night,' commented the governor, recovering some of his composure, although he remembered that there was no guard within call. Still, the hillman could not know that. 'I climbed a bastion,' snarled the intruder. 'A guard thrust his head over the battlement in time for me to rap it with my knife-hilt.'

'You are Conan?'

'Who else? You sent word into the hills that you wished for me to come and parley with you. Well, by Crom, I've come! Keep away from that table or I'll gut you.'

'I merely wish to seat myself,' answered the governor, carefully sinking into the ivory chair, which he wheeled away from the table. Conan moved restlessly before him, glancing suspiciously at the door, thumbing the razor edge of his three-foot knife. He did not walk like an Afghuli, and was bluntly direct where the East is subtle.

'You have seven of my men,' he said abruptly. 'You refused the ransom I offered. What the devil do you want?' 'Let us discuss terms,' answered Chunder Shan cautiously.

'Terms?' There was a timbre of dangerous anger in his voice. 'What do you mean? Haven't I offered you gold?' Chunder Shan laughed.

'Gold? There is more gold in Peshkhauri than you ever saw.'

'You're a liar,' retorted Conan. 'I've seen the *suk* of the goldsmiths in Khurusun.'

'Well, more than an Afghuli ever saw,' amended Chunder Shan. 'And it is but a drop of all the treasure of Vendhya. Why should we desire gold? It would be more to our advantage to hang these seven thieves.' Conan ripped out a sulfurous oath and the long blade quivered in his grip as the muscles rose in ridges on his brown arm.

'I'll split your head like a ripe melon!'

A wild blue flame flickered in the hillman's eyes, but Chunder Shan shrugged his shoulders, though keeping an eye on the keen steel.

'You can kill me easily, and probably escape over the wall afterward. But that would not save the seven tribesmen. My men would surely hang them. And these men are headmen among the Afghulis.'

'I know it,' snarled Conan. 'The tribe is baying like wolves at my heels because I have not procured their release. Tell me in plain words what you want, because, by Crom! if there's no other way, I'll raise a horde and lead it to the very gates of Peshkhauri!'

Looking at the man as he stood squarely, knife in fist and eyes glaring, Chunder Shan did not doubt that he was capable of it. The governor did not believe any hill-horde could take Peshkhauri, but he did not wish a devastated countryside.

'There is a mission you must perform,' he said, choosing his words with as much care as if they had been razors. 'There—'

Conan had sprung back, wheeling to face the door at the same instant, lips asnarl. His barbarian ears had caught the quick tread of soft slippers outside the door. The next instant the door was thrown open and a slim, silk-robed form entered hastily, pulling the door shut—then stopping short at sight of the hillman.

Chunder Shan sprang up, his heart jumping into his mouth.

'Devi!' he cried involuntarily, losing his head momentarily in his fright.

'*Devi!*' It was like an explosive echo from the hillman's lips. Chunder Shan saw recognition and intent flame up in the fierce blue eyes.

The governor shouted desperately and caught at his sword, but the hillman moved with the devastating speed of a hurricane. He sprang, knocked the governor sprawling with a savage blow of his knife-hilt, swept up the astounded Devi in one brawny arm and leaped for the window. Chunder Shan, struggling frantically to his feet, saw the man poise an instant on the sill in a flutter of silken skirts and white limbs that was his royal captive, and heard his fierce, exultant snarl: '*Now* dare to hang my men!' and then Conan leaped to the parapet and was gone. A wild scream floated back to the governor's ears.

'Guard! *Guard!*' screamed the governor, struggling up and running drunkenly to the door. He tore it open and reeled into the hall. His shouts re-echoed along the corridors, and warriors came running, gaping to see the governor holding his broken head, from which the blood streamed.

'Turn out the lancers!' he roared. 'There has been an abduction!' Even in his frenzy he had enough sense left to withhold the full truth. He stopped short as he heard a sudden drum of hoofs outside, a frantic scream and a wild yell of barbaric exultation.

Followed by the bewildered guardsmen, the governor raced for the stair. In the courtyard of the fort a force of lancers stood by saddled steeds, ready to ride at an instant's notice. Chunder Shan led his squadron flying after the fugitive, though his head swam so he had to hold with both hands to the saddle. He did not divulge the identity of the victim, but said merely that the noblewoman who had borne the royal signet-ring had been carried away by the chief of the Afghulis. The abductor was out of sight and hearing, but they knew the path he would strike—the road that runs straight to the mouth of the Zhaibar. There was no moon; peasant huts rose dimly in the starlight. Behind them fell away the grim bastion of the fort, and the towers of Peshkhauri. Ahead of them loomed the black walls of the Himelians.

3 KHEMSA USES MAGIC

In the confusion that reigned in the fortress while the guard was being turned out, no one noticed that the girl who had accompanied the Devi slipped out the great arched gate and vanished in the darkness. She ran straight for the city, her garments tucked high. She did not follow the open road, but cut straight through fields and over slopes, avoiding fences and leaping irrigation ditches as surely as if it were broad daylight, and as easily as if she were a trained masculine runner. The hoof-drum of the guardsmen had faded away up the hill before she reached the city wall. She did not go to the great gate, beneath whose arch men leaned on spears and craned their necks into the darkness, discussing the unwonted activity about the fortress. She skirted the wall until she reached a certain point where the spire of the tower was visible above the battlements. Then she placed her hands to her mouth and voiced a low weird call that carried strangely.

Almost instantly a head appeared at an embrasure and a rope came wriggling down the wall. She seized it, placed a foot in the loop at the end, and waved her arm. Then quickly and smoothly she was drawn up the sheer stone curtain. An instant later she scrambled over the merlons and stood up on a flat roof which covered a house that was built against the wall. There was an open trap there, and a man in a camel-hair robe who silently coiled the rope, not showing in any way the strain of hauling a full-grown woman up a forty-foot wall.

'Where is Kerim Shah?' she gasped, panting after her long run. 'Asleep in the house below. You have news?'

'Conan has stolen the Devi out of the fortress and carried her away into the hills!' She blurted out her news in a rush, the words stumbling over one another. Khemsa showed no emotion, but merely nodded his turbaned head. 'Kerim Shah will be glad to hear that,' he said.

'Wait!' The girl threw her supple arms about his neck. She was panting hard, but not only from exertion. Her eyes blazed like black jewels in the starlight. Her upturned face was close to Khemsa's, but though he submitted to her embrace, he did not return it.

'Do not tell the Hyrkanian!' she panted. 'Let us use this knowledge ourselves! The governor has gone into the hills with his riders, but he might as well chase a ghost. He has not told anyone that it was the Devi who was kidnapped. None in Peshkhauri or the fort knows it except us.'

'But what good does it do us?' the man expostulated. 'M— masters sent me with Kerim Shah to aid him in every way— 'Aid yourself!' she cried fiercely. 'Shake off your yoke!'

'You mean—disobey my masters?' he gasped, and she fe his whole body turn cold under her arms.

'Aye!' she shook him in the fury of her emotion. 'You too a a magician! Why will you be a slave, using your powers only t elevate others? Use your arts for yourself!'

'That is forbidden!' He was shaking as if with an ague. 'I ar not one of the Black Circle. Only by the command of th masters do I dare to use the knowledge they have taught m

'But you *can* use it!' she argued passionately. 'Do as I be you! Of course Conan has taken the Devi to hold as hostag against the seven tribesmen in the governor's prison. Destro them, so Chunder Shan can not use them to buy back th Devi. Then let us go into the mountains and take her fro the Afghulis. They can not stand against your sorcery wit their knives. The treasure of the Vendhyan kings will be ou as ransom—and then when we have it in our hands, we ca trick them, and sell her to the king of Turan. We shall hav wealth beyond our maddest dreams. With it we can bu warriors. We will take Khorbhul, oust the Turanians from th hills, and send our hosts southward; become king and quee of an empire!'

Khemsa too was panting, shaking like a leaf in her grasp; h face showed gray in the starlight, beaded with great drops perspiration.

'I love you!' she cried fiercely, writhing her body against h almost strangling him in her wild embrace, shaking him in h abandon. 'I will make a king of you! For love of you I betraye my mistress; for love of me betray your masters! Why fear th Black Seers? By your love for me you have broken one of the laws already! Break the rest! You are as strong as they!'

A man of ice could not have withstood the searing heat her passion and fury. With an inarticulate cry he crushed h to him, bending her backward and showering gasping kiss on her eyes, face and lips. 'I'll do it!' His voice was thick wit laboring emotions. He staggered like a drunken man. 'The ar they have taught me shall work for me, not for my maste We shall be rulers of the world—of the world—' 'Come the Twisting lithely out of his embrace, she seized his hand ar led him toward the trap-door. 'First we must make sure th the governor does not exchange those seven Afghulis for th Devi.'

He moved like a man in a daze, until they had descende a ladder and she paused in the chamber below. Kerim Sha lay on a couch motionless, an arm across his face as thoug to shield his sleeping eyes from the soft light of a brass lam She plucked Khemsa's arm and made a quick gesture acro her own throat. Khemsa lifted his hand; then his expressio changed and he drew away.

'I have eaten his salt,' he muttered. 'Besides, he can n interfere with us.'

He led the girl through a door that opened on a windin stair. After their soft tread had faded into silence, the man o the couch sat up. Kerim Shah wiped the sweat from his fac A knife-thrust he did not dread, but he feared Khemsa as man fears a poisonous reptile.

'People who plot on roofs should remember to lower the voices,' he muttered. 'But as Khemsa has turned against h masters, and as he was my only contact between them, I ca count on their aid no longer. From now on I play the game my own way.'

Rising to his feet he went quickly to a table, drew pen ar parchment from his girdle and scribbled a few succinct line

'To Khosru Khan, governor of Secunderam: the Cimmeri Conan has carried the Devi Yasmina to the villages of th Afghulis. It is an opportunity to get the Devi into our hands, the king has so long desired. Send three thousand horseme at once. I will meet them in the valley of Gurashah with nati guides.'

And he signed it with a name that was not in the least li

erim Shah.

Then from a golden cage he drew forth a carrier pigeon, o whose leg he made fast the parchment, rolled into a tiny ylinder and secured with gold wire. Then he went quickly to casement and tossed the bird into the night. It wavered on uttering wings, balanced, and was gone like a flitting shadow. atching up helmet, sword and cloak, Kerim Shah hurried out f the chamber and down the winding stair.

The prison quarters of Peshkhauri were separated from the st of the city by a massive wall, in which was set a single on-bound door under an arch. Over the arch burned a lurid d cresset, and beside the door squatted a warrior with spear d shield.

This warrior, leaning on his spear, and yawning from time o time, started suddenly to his feet. He had not thought he ad dozed, but a man was standing before him, a man he had ot heard approach. The man wore a camel-hair robe and a een turban. In the flickering light of the cresset his features ere shadowy, but a pair of lambent eyes shone surprisingly the lurid glow.

'Who comes?' demanded the warrior, presenting his spear. Vho are you?'

The stranger did not seem perturbed, though the spear- oint touched his bosom. His eyes held the warrior's with range intensity. 'What are you obliged to do?' he asked, rangely.

'To guard the gate!' The warrior spoke thickly and echanically; he stood rigid as a statue, his eyes slowly glazing.

'You lie! You are obliged to obey me! You have looked into y eyes, and your soul is no longer your own. Open that oor!'

Stiffly, with the wooden features of an image, the guard heeled about, drew a great key from his girdle, turned it in e massive lock and swung open the door. Then he stood at tention, his unseeing stare straight ahead of him.

A woman glided from the shadows and laid an eager hand the mesmerist's arm. 'Bid him fetch us horses, Khemsa,' she hispered.

'No need of that,' answered the Rakhsha. Lifting his voice ghtly he spoke to the guardsman. 'I have no more use for ou. Kill yourself!'

Like a man in a trance the warrior thrust the butt of his ear against the base of the wall, and placed the keen head ainst his body, just below the ribs. Then slowly, stolidly, he aned against it with all his weight, so that it transfixed his ody and came out between his shoulders. Sliding down the aft he lay still, the spear jutting above him its full length, like horrible stalk growing out of his back.

The girl stared down at him in morbid fascination, until hemsa took her arm and led her through the gate. Torches hted a narrow space between the outer wall and a lower ner one, in which were arched doors at regular intervals. warrior paced this enclosure, and when the gate opened e came sauntering up, so secure in his knowledge of the ison's strength that he was not suspicious until Khemsa d the girl emerged from the archway. Then it was too late. e Rakhsha did not waste time in hypnotism, though his tion savored of magic to the girl. The guard lowered his ear threateningly, opening his mouth to shout an alarm at would bring spearmen swarming out of the guardrooms either end of the alleyway. Khemsa flicked the spear aside th his left hand, as a man might flick a straw, and his right shed out and back, seeming gently to caress the warrior's ck in passing. And the guard pitched on his face without a und, his head lolling on a broken neck.

Khemsa did not glance at him, but went straight to one of e arched doors and placed his open hand against the heavy onze lock. With a rending shudder the portal buckled ward. As the girl followed him through, she saw that the ick teakwood hung in splinters, the bronze bolts were bent d twisted from their sockets, and the great hinges broken d disjointed. A thousand-pound battering-ram with forty men to swing it could have shattered the barrier no more completely. Khemsa was drunk with freedom and the exercise of his power, glorying in his might and flinging his strength about as a young giant exercises his thews with unnecessary vigor in the exultant pride of his prowess.

The broken door let them into a small courtyard, lit by a cresset. Opposite the door was a wide grille of iron bars. A hairy hand was visible, gripping one of these bars, and in the darkness behind them glimmered the whites of eyes.

Khemsa stood silent for a space, gazing into the shadows from which those glimmering eyes gave back his stare with burning intensity. Then his hand went into his robe and came out again, and from his opening fingers a shimmering feather of sparkling dust sifted to the flags. Instantly a flare of green fire lighted the enclosure. In the brief glare the forms of seven men, standing motionless behind the bars, were limned in vivid detail; tall, hairy men in ragged hill-men's garments. They did not speak, but in their eyes blazed the fear of death, and their hairy fingers gripped the bars.

The fire died out but the glow remained, a quivering ball of lambent green that pulsed and shimmered on the flags before Khemsa's feet. The wide gaze of the tribesmen was fixed upon it. It wavered, elongated; it turned into a luminous greensmoke spiraling upward. It twisted and writhed like a great shadowy serpent, then broadened and billowed out in shining folds and whirls. It grew to a cloud moving silently over the flags—straight toward the grille. The men watched its coming with dilated eyes; the bars quivered with the grip of their desperate fingers. Bearded lips parted but no sound came forth. The green cloud rolled on the bars and blotted them from sight; like a fog it oozed through the grille and hid the men within. From the enveloping folds came a strangled gasp, as of a man plunged suddenly under the surface of water. That was all.

Khemsa touched the girl's arm, as she stood with parted lips and dilated eyes. Mechanically she turned away with him, looking back over her shoulder. Already the mist was thinning; close to the bars she saw a pair of sandalled feet, the toes turned upward—she glimpsed the indistinct outlines of seven still, prostrate shapes.

'And now for a steed swifter than the fastest horse ever bred in a mortal stable,' Khemsa was saying. 'We will be in Afghulistan before dawn.'

4 AN ENCOUNTER IN THE PASS

Yasmina Devi could never clearly remember the details of her abduction. The unexpectedness and violence stunned her; she had only a confused impression of a whirl of happenings—the terrifying grip of a mighty arm, the blazing eyes of her abductor, and his hot breath burning on her flesh. The leap through the window to the parapet, the mad race across battlements and roofs when the fear of falling froze her, the reckless descent of a rope bound to a merlon—he went down almost at a run, his captive folded limply over his brawny shoulder—all this was a befuddled tangle in the Devi's mind. She retained a more vivid memory of him running fleetly into the shadows of the trees, carrying her like a child, and vaulting into the saddle of a fierce Bhalkhana stallion which reared and snorted. Then there was a sensation of flying, and the racing hoofs were striking sparks of fire from the flinty road as the stallion swept up the slopes.

As the girl's mind cleared, her first sensations were furious rage and shame. She was appalled. The rulers of the golden kingdoms south of the Himelians were considered little short of divine; and she was the Devi of Vendhya! Fright was submerged in regal wrath. She cried out furiously and began struggling. She, Yasmina, to be carried on the saddle-bow of a hill chief, like a common wench of the market-place! He merely hardened his massive thews slightly against her writhings, and for the first time in her life she experienced the coercion of superior physical strength. His arms felt like iron about her slender limbs. He glanced down at her and grinned hugely. His teeth glimmered whitely in the starlight. The reins lay loose on the stallion's flowing mane, and every thew and fiber of the great beast strained as he hurtled along the boulder-strewn trail. But Conan sat easily, almost carelessly, in the saddle, riding like a centaur.

'You hill-bred dog!' she panted, quivering with the impact of shame, anger, and the realization of helplessness. 'You dare— you *dare*! Your life shall pay for this! Where are you taking me?'

'To the villages of Afghulistan,' he answered, casting a glance over his shoulder.

Behind them, beyond the slopes they had traversed, torches were tossing on the walls of the fortress, and he glimpsed a flare of light that meant the great gate had been opened. And he laughed, a deep-throated boom gusty as the hill wind.

'The governor has sent his riders after us,' he laughed. 'By Crom, we will lead him a merry chase! What do you think, Devi—will they pay seven lives for a Kshatriya princess?' 'They will send an army to hang you and your spawn of devils,' she promised him with conviction.

He laughed gustily and shifted her to a more comfortable position in his arms. But she took this as a fresh outrage, and renewed her vain struggle, until she saw that her efforts were only amusing him. Besides, her light silken garments, floating on the wind, were being outrageously disarranged by her struggles. She concluded that a scornful submission was the better part of dignity, and lapsed into a smoldering quiescence.

She felt even her anger being submerged by awe as they entered the mouth of the Pass, lowering like a black well mouth in the blacker walls that rose like colossal ramparts to bar their way. It was as if a gigantic knife had cut the Zhaibar out of walls of solid rock. On either hand sheer slopes pitched up for thousands of feet, and the mouth of the Pass was dark as hate. Even Conan could not see with any accuracy, but he knew the road, even by night. And knowing that armed men were racing through the starlight after him, he did not check the stallion's speed. The great brute was not yet showing fatigue. He thundered along the road that followed the valley bed, labored up a slope, swept along a low ridge where treacherous shale on either hand lurked for the unwary, and came upon a trail that followed the lap of the left-hand wall.

Not even Conan could spy, in that darkness, an ambush set by Zhaibar tribesmen. As they swept past the black mouth of a gorge that opened into the Pass, a javelin swished through the air and thudded home behind the stallion's straining shoulder. The great beast let out his life in a shuddering sob and stumbled, going headlong in mid-stride. But Conan had recognized the flight and stroke of the javelin, and he acted with spring-steel quickness.

As the horse fell he leaped clear, holding the girl aloft to guard her from striking boulders. He lit on his feet like a cat, thrust her into a cleft of rock, and wheeled toward the outer darkness, drawing his knife.

Yasmina, confused by the rapidity of events, not quite sure just what had happened, saw a vague shape rush out of the darkness, bare feet slapping softly on the rock, ragged garments whipping on the wind of his haste. She glimpsed the flicker of steel, heard the lightning crack of stroke, parry and counter-stroke, and the crunch of bone as Conan's long knife split the other's skull.

Conan sprang back, crouching in the shelter of the rocks. Out in the night men were moving and a stentorian voice roared: 'What, you dogs! Do you flinch? In, curse you, and take them!' Conan started, peered into the darkness and lifted his voice.

'Yar Afzal! Is it you?'

There sounded a startled imprecation, and the voice called warily. 'Conan? Is it you, Conan?'

'Aye!' the Cimmerian laughed. 'Come forth, you old war-dog. I've slain one of your men.'

There was movement among the rocks, a light flared dimly, and then a flame appeared and came bobbing toward him,

and as it approached, a fierce bearded countenance grew o of the darkness. The man who carried it held it high, thru forward, and craned his neck to peer among the boulders lighted; the other hand gripped a great curved tulwar. Cona stepped forward, sheathing his knife, and the other roared greeting.

'Aye, it is Conan! Come out of your rocks, dogs! It is Cona

Others pressed into the wavering circle of light—wi ragged, bearded men, with eyes like wolves, and long blad in their fists. They did not see Yasmina, for she was hidden b Conan's massive body. But peeping from her covert, she kne icy fear for the first time that night. These men were more li wolves than human beings.

'What are you hunting in the Zhaibar by night, Yar Afza Conan demanded of the burly chief, who grinned like bearded ghoul. 'Who knows what might come up the Pa after dark? We Wazulis are night-hawks. But what of yo Conan?'

'I have a prisoner,' answered the Cimmerian. And movir aside he disclosed the cowering girl. Reaching a long arm in the crevice he drew her trembling forth.

Her imperious bearing was gone. She stared timidly at th ring of bearded faces that hemmed her in, and was gratef for the strong arm that clasped her possessively. The torc was thrust close to her, and there was a sucking intake breath about the ring.

'She is my captive,' Conan warned, glancing pointedly at th feet of the man he had slain, just visible within the ring light. 'I was taking her to Afghulistan, but now you have sla my horse, and the Kshatriyas are close behind me.'

'Come with us to my village,' suggested Yar Afzal. 'We hav horses hidden in the gorge. They can never follow us in th darkness. They are close behind you, you say?' 'So close th I hear now the clink of their hoofs on the flint,' answere Conan grimly.

Instantly there was movement; the torch was dashe out and the ragged shapes melted like phantoms into th darkness. Conan swept up the Devi in his arms, and she d not resist. The rocky ground hurt her slim feet in their sc slippers and she felt very small and helpless in that brutis primordial blackness among those colossal, nighted crags.

Feeling her shiver in the wind that moaned down the defil Conan jerked a ragged cloak from its owner's shoulders ar wrapped it about her. He also hissed a warning in her e ordering her to make no sound. She did not hear the dista clink of shod hoofs on rock that warned the keen-eared hi men; but she was far too frightened to disobey, in any even

She could see nothing but a few faint stars far above, b she knew by the deepening darkness when they entere the gorge mouth. There was a stir about them, the unea movement of horses. A few muttered words, and Cona mounted the horse of the man he had killed, lifting the g up in front of him. Like phantoms except for the click of th hoofs, the band swept away up the shadowy gorge. Behir them on the trail they left the dead horse and the dead ma which were found less than half an hour later by the ride from the fortress, who recognized the man as a Wazuli ar drew their own conclusions accordingly.

Yasmina, snuggled warmly in her captor's arms, gre drowsy in spite of herself. The motion of the horse, though was uneven, uphill and down, yet possessed a certain rhyth which combined with weariness and emotional exhaustic to force sleep upon her. She had lost all sense of time direction. They moved in soft thick darkness, in which s sometimes glimpsed vaguely gigantic walls sweeping up li black ramparts, or great crags shouldering the stars; at tim she sensed echoing depths beneath them, or felt the wind dizzy heights blowing cold about her. Gradually these thin faded into a dreamy unwakefulness in which the clink hoofs and the creak of saddles were like the irrelevant soun in a dream.

She was vaguely aware when the motion ceased and s

as lifted down and carried a few steps. Then she was laid own on something soft and rustling, and something—a lded coat perhaps—was thrust under her head, and the oak in which she was wrapped was carefully tucked about er. She heard Yar Afzal laugh.

'A rare prize, Conan; fit mate for a chief of the Afghulis.'

'Not for me,' came Conan's answering rumble. 'This wench ill buy the lives of my seven headmen, blast their souls.' That as the last she heard as she sank into dreamless slumber.

She slept while armed men rode through the dark hills, nd the fate of kingdoms hung in the balance. Through the adowy gorges and defiles that night there rang the hoofs f galloping horses, and the starlight glimmered on helmets nd curved blades, until the ghoulish shapes that haunt the ags stared into the darkness from ravine and boulder and ondered what things were afoot.

A band of these sat gaunt horses in the black pitmouth f a gorge as the hurrying hoofs swept past. Their leader, a ell-built man in a helmet and gilt-braided cloak, held up his and warningly, until the riders had sped on. Then he laughed oftly.

'They must have lost the trail! Or else they have found that onan has already reached the Afghuli villages. It will take any riders to smoke out that hive. There will be squadrons ding up the Zhaibar by dawn.' 'If there is fighting in the hills ere will be looting,' muttered a voice behind him, in the alect of the Irakzai.

'There will be looting,' answered the man with the helmet. ut first it is our business to reach the valley of Gurashah nd await the riders that will be galloping southward from ecunderam before daylight.' He lifted his reins and rode out f the defile, his men falling in behind him—thirty ragged hantoms in the starlight.

5 THE BLACK STALLION

The sun was well up when Yasmina awoke. She did not start nd stare blankly, wondering where she was. She awoke with ull knowledge of all that had occurred. Her supple limbs were tiff from her long ride, and her firm flesh seemed to feel the ontact of the muscular arm that had borne her so far.

She was lying on a sheepskin covering a pallet of leaves on hard-beaten dirt floor. A folded sheepskin coat was under er head, and she was wrapped in a ragged cloak. She was a large room, the walls of which were crudely but strongly uilt of uncut rocks, plastered with sun-baked mud. Heavy eams supported a roof of the same kind, in which showed a rap-door up to which led a ladder. There were no windows the thick walls, only loop-holes. There was one door, a turdy bronze affair that must have been looted from some endhyan border tower. Opposite it was a wide opening the wall, with no door, but several strong wooden bars place. Beyond them Yasmina saw a magnificent black tallion munching a pile of dried grass. The building was fort, welling-place and stable in one.

At the other end of the room a girl in the vest and baggy rousers of a hill-woman squatted beside a small fire, cooking trips of meat on an iron grid laid over blocks of stone. There as a sooty cleft in the wall a few feet from the floor, and ome of the smoke found its way out there. The rest floated n blue wisps about the room.

The hill-girl glanced at Yasmina over her shoulder, displaying bold, handsome face, and then continued her cooking. oices boomed outside; then the door was kicked open, and onan strode in. He looked more enormous than ever with he morning sunlight behind him, and Yasmina noted some etails that had escaped her the night before. His garments ere clean and not ragged. The broad Bakhariot girdle that upported his knife in its ornamented scabbard would have natched the robes of a prince, and there was a glint of fine uranian mail under his shirt.

'Your captive is awake, Conan,' said the Wazuli girl, and he runted, strode up to the fire and swept the strips of mutton off into a stone dish.

The squatting girl laughed up at him, with some spicy jest, and he grinned wolfishly, and hooking a toe under her haunches, tumbled her sprawling onto the floor. She seemed to derive considerable amusement from this bit of rough horse-play, but Conan paid no more heed to her. Producing a great hunk of bread from somewhere, with a copper jug of wine, he carried the lot to Yasmina, who had risen from her pallet and was regarding him doubtfully.

'Rough fare for a Devi, girl, but our best,' he grunted. 'It will fill your belly, at least.'

He set the platter on the floor, and she was suddenly aware of a ravenous hunger. Making no comment, she seated herself cross-legged on the floor, and taking the dish in her lap, she began to eat, using her fingers, which were all she had in the way of table utensils. After all, adaptability is one of the tests of true aristocracy. Conan stood looking down at her, his thumbs hooked in his girdle. He never sat cross-legged, after the Eastern fashion.

'Where am I?' she asked abruptly.

'In the hut of Yar Afzal, the chief of the Khurum Wazulis,' he answered. 'Afghulistan lies a good many miles farther on to the west. We'll hide here awhile. The Kshatriyas are beating up the hills for you—several of their squads have been cut up by the tribes already.'

'What are you going to do?' she asked.

'Keep you until Chunder Shan is willing to trade back my seven cow-thieves,' he grunted. 'Women of the Wazulis are crushing ink out of *shoki* leaves, and after a while you can write a letter to the governor.'

A touch of her old imperious wrath shook her, as she thought how maddeningly her plans had gone awry, leaving her captive of the very man she had plotted to get into her power. She flung down the dish, with the remnants of her meal, and sprang to her feet, tense with anger.

'I will not write a letter! If you do not take me back, they will hang your seven men, and a thousand more besides!'

The Wazuli girl laughed mockingly, Conan scowled, and then the door opened and Yar Afzal came swaggering in. The Wazuli chief was as tall as Conan, and of greater girth, but he looked fat and slow beside the hard compactness of the Cimmerian. He plucked his red-stained beard and stared meaningly at the Wazuli girl, and that wench rose and scurried out without delay. Then Yar Afzal turned to his guest.

'The damnable people murmur, Conan,' quoth he. 'They wish me to murder you and take the girl to hold for ransom. They say that anyone can tell by her garments that she is a noble lady. They say why should the Afghuli dogs profit by her, when it is the people who take the risk of guarding her?'

'Lend me your horse,' said Conan. 'I'll take her and go.'

'Pish!' boomed Yar Afzal. 'Do you think I can't handle my own people? I'll have them dancing in their shirts if they cross me! They don't love you—or any other outlander—but you saved my life once, and I will not forget. Come out, though, Conan; a scout has returned.'

Conan hitched at his girdle and followed the chief outside. They closed the door after them, and Yasmina peeped through a loop-hole. She looked out on a level space before the hut. At the farther end of that space there was a cluster of mud and stone huts, and she saw naked children playing among the boulders, and the slim erect women of the hills going about their tasks.

Directly before the chief's hut a circle of hairy, ragged men squatted, facing the door. Conan and Yar Afzal stood a few paces before the door, and between them and the ring of warriors another man sat cross-legged. This one was addressing his chief in the harsh accents of the Wazuli which Yasmina could scarcely understand, though as part of her royal education she had been taught the languages of Iranistan and the kindred tongues of Ghulistan.

'I talked with a Dagozai who saw the riders last night,' said the scout. 'He was lurking near when they came to the spot where we ambushed the lord Conan. He overheard their speech. Chunder Shan was with them. They found the dead horse, and one of the men recognized it as Conan's. Then they found the man Conan slew, and knew him for a Wazuli. It seemed to them that Conan had been slain and the girl taken by the Wazuli; so they turned aside from their purpose of following to Afghulistan. But they did not know from which village the dead man was come, and we had left no trail a Kshatriya could follow.

'So they rode to the nearest Wazuli village, which was the village of Jugra, and burnt it and slew many of the people. But the men of Khojur came upon them in darkness and slew some of them, and wounded the governor. So the survivors retired down the Zhaibar in the darkness before dawn, but they returned with reinforcements before sunrise, and there has been skirmishing and fighting in the hills all morning. It is said that a great army is being raised to sweep the hills about the Zhaibar. The tribes are whetting their knives and laying ambushes in every pass from here to Gurashah valley. Moreover, Kerim Shah has returned to the hills.'

A grunt went around the circle, and Yasmina leaned closer to the loop-hole at the name she had begun to mistrust. 'Where went he?' demanded Yar Afzal.

'The Dagozai did not know; with him were thirty Irakzai of the lower villages. They rode into the hills and disappeared.'

'These Irakzai are jackals that follow a lion for crumbs,' growled Yar Afzal. 'They have been lapping up the coins Kerim Shah scatters among the border tribes to buy men like horses. I like him not, for all he is our kinsman from Iranistan.'

'He's not even that,' said Conan. 'I know him of old. He's an Hyrkanian, a spy of Yezdigerd's. If I catch him I'll hang his hide to a tamarisk.'

'But the Kshatriyas!' clamored the men in the semicircle. 'Are we to squat on our haunches until they smoke us out? They will learn at last in which Wazuli village the wench is held. We are not loved by the Zhaibari; they will help the Kshatriyas hunt us out.'

'Let them come,' grunted Yar Afzal. 'We can hold the defiles against a host.' One of the men leaped up and shook his fist at Conan.

'Are we to take all the risks while he reaps the rewards?' he howled. 'Are we to fight his battles for him?'

With a stride Conan reached him and bent slightly to stare full into his hairy face. The Cimmerian had not drawn his long knife, but his left hand grasped the scabbard, jutting the hilt suggestively forward. 'I ask no man to fight my battles,' he said softly. 'Draw your blade if you dare, you yapping dog!'

The Wazuli started back, snarling like a cat.

'Dare to touch me and here are fifty men to rend you apart!' he screeched.

'What!' roared Yar Afzal, his face purpling with wrath. His whiskers bristled, his belly swelled with his rage. 'Are you chief of Khurum? Do the Wazulis take orders from Yar Afzal, or from a low-bred cur?'

The man cringed before his invincible chief, and Yar Afzal, striding up to him, seized him by the throat and choked him until his face was turning black. Then he hurled the man savagely against the ground and stood over him with his tulwar in his hand.

'Is there any who questions my authority?' he roared, and his warriors looked down sullenly as his bellicose glare swept their semicircle. Yar Afzal grunted scornfully and sheathed his weapon with a gesture that was the apex of insult. Then he kicked the fallen agitator with a concentrated vindictiveness that brought howls from his victim.

'Get down the valley to the watchers on the heights and bring word if they have seen anything,' commanded Yar Afzal, and the man went, shaking with fear and grinding his teeth with fury.

Yar Afzal then seated himself ponderously on a stone, growling in his beard. Conan stood near him, legs braced apart, thumbs hooked in his girdle, narrowly watching the assembled warriors. They stared at him sullenly, not daring to brave Yar Afzal's fury, but hating the foreigner as only a hillman can hate.

'Now listen to me, you sons of nameless dogs, while I t you what the lord Conan and I have planned to fool th Kshatriyas.' The boom of Yar Afzal's bull-like voice followe the discomfited warrior as he slunk away from the assembl

The man passed by the cluster of huts, where wome who had seen his defeat laughed at him and called stingir comments, and hastened on along the trail that wour among spurs and rocks toward the valley head.

Just as he rounded the first turn that took him out of sigh of the village, he stopped short, gaping stupidly. He ha not believed it possible for a stranger to enter the valley Khurum without being detected by the hawk-eyed watche along the heights; yet a man sat cross-legged on a low ledg beside the path—a man in a camel-hair robe and a gree turban.

The Wazuli's mouth gaped for a yell, and his hand leape to his knife-hilt. But at that instant his eyes met those of th stranger and the cry died in his throat, his fingers went lim He stood like a statue, his own eyes glazed and vacant.

For minutes the scene held motionless; then the man o the ledge drew a cryptic symbol in the dust on the rock wi his forefinger. The Wazuli did not see him place anythir within the compass of that emblem, but presently somethir gleamed there—a round, shiny black ball that looked lik polished jade. The man in the green turban took this up ar tossed it to the Wazuli, who mechanically caught it.

'Carry this to Yar Afzal,' he said, and the Wazuli turned lik an automaton and went back along the path, holding th black jade ball in his outstretched hand. He did not even tur his head to the renewed jeers of the women as he passed th huts. He did not seem to hear.

The man on the ledge gazed after him with a cryptic smil A girl's head rose above the rim of the ledge and she looke at him with admiration and a touch of fear that had not bee present the night before. 'Why did you do that?' she asked.

He ran his fingers through her dark locks caressingly.

'Are you still dizzy from your flight on the horse-of-air, tha you doubt my wisdom?' he laughed. 'As long as Yar Afzal live Conan will bide safe among the Wazuli fighting-men. The knives are sharp, and there are many of them. What I plo will be safer, even for me, than to seek to slay him and tak her from among them. It takes no wizard to predict what th Wazulis will do, and what Conan will do, when my victir hands the globe of Yezud to the chief of Khurum.'

Back before the hut, Yar Afzal halted in the midst of som tirade, surprized and displeased to see the man he had ser up the valley, pushing his way through the throng. 'I bade yo go to the watchers!' the chief bellowed. 'You have not ha time to come from them.'

The other did not reply; he stood woodenly, staring vacant into the chief's face, his palm outstretched holding the jad ball. Conan, looking over Yar Afzal's shoulder, murmure something and reached to touch the chief's arm, but as h did so, Yar Afzal, in a paroxysm of anger, struck the man wit his clenched fist and felled him like an ox. As he fell, the jad sphere rolled to Yar Afzal's foot, and the chief, seeming to se it for the first time, bent and picked it up. The men, starin perplexedly at their senseless comrade, saw their chief ben but they did not see what he picked up from the ground.

Yar Afzal straightened, glanced at the jade, and made motion to thrust it into his girdle.

'Carry that fool to his hut,' he growled. 'He has the look of lotus-eater. He returned me a blank stare. I—aie!'

In his right hand, moving toward his girdle, he had suddenl felt movement where movement should not be. His voic died away as he stood and glared at nothing; and insid his clenched right hand he felt the quivering of change, o motion, of life. He no longer held a smooth shining spher in his fingers. And he dared not look; his tongue clove to he roof of his mouth, and he could not open his hand. His astonished warriors saw Yar Afzal's eyes distend, the color ebb from his face. Then suddenly a bellow of agony burst from his bearded lips; he swayed and fell as if struck by lightning, his right arm tossed out in front of him. Face down he lay, and from between his opening fingers crawled a spider—a hideous, black, hairy-legged monster whose body shone like black jade. The men yelled and gave back suddenly, and the creature scuttled into a crevice of the rocks and disappeared.

The warriors started up, glaring wildly, and a voice rose above their clamor, a far-carrying voice of command which came from none knew where. Afterward each man there—who still lived—denied that he had shouted, but all there heard it.

'Yar Afzal is dead! Kill the outlander!'

That shout focused their whirling minds as one. Doubt, bewilderment and fear vanished in the uproaring surge of the blood-lust. A furious yell rent the skies as the tribesmen responded instantly to the suggestion. They came headlong across the open space, cloaks flapping, eyes blazing, knives lifted.

Conan's action was as quick as theirs. As the voice shouted he sprang for the hut door. But they were closer to him than he was to the door, and with one foot on the sill he had to wheel and parry the swipe of a yard-long blade. He split the man's skull—ducked another swinging knife and gutted the wielder—felled a man with his left fist and stabbed another in the belly—and heaved back mightily against the closed door with his shoulders. Hacking blades were nicking chips out of the jambs about his ears, but the door flew open under the impact of his shoulders, and he went stumbling backward into the room. A bearded tribesman, thrusting with all his fury as Conan sprang back, overreached and pitched head-first through the doorway. Conan stopped, grasped the slack of his garments and hauled him clear, and slammed the door in the faces of the men who came surging into it. Bones snapped under the impact, and the next instant Conan slammed the bolts into place and whirled with desperate haste to meet the man who sprang from the floor and tore into action like a madman.

Yasmina cowered in a corner, staring in horror as the two men fought back and forth across the room, almost trampling her at times; the flash and clangor of their blades filled the room, and outside the mob clamored like a wolf-pack, hacking deafeningly at the bronze door with their long knives, and dashing huge rocks against it. Somebody fetched a tree trunk, and the door began to stagger under the thunderous assault. Yasmina clasped her ears, staring wildly. Violence and fury within, cataclysmic madness without. The stallion in his stall neighed and reared, thundering with his heels against the walls. He wheeled and launched his hoofs through the bars just as the tribesman, backing away from Conan's murderous swipes, stumbled against them. His spine cracked in three places like a rotten branch and he was hurled headlong against the Cimmerian, bearing him backward so that they both crashed to the beaten floor.

Yasmina cried out and ran forward; to her dazed sight it seemed that both were slain. She reached them just as Conan threw aside the corpse and rose. She caught his arm, trembling from head to foot. 'Oh, you live! I thought—I thought you were dead!'

He glanced down at her quickly, into the pale, upturned face and the wide staring dark eyes. 'Why are you trembling?' he demanded. 'Why should you care if I live or die?'

A vestige of her poise returned to her, and she drew away, making a rather pitiful attempt at playing the Devi.

'You are preferable to those wolves howling without,' she answered, gesturing toward the door, the stone sill of which was beginning to splinter away. 'That won't hold long,' he muttered, then turned and went swiftly to the stall of the stallion.

Yasmina clenched her hands and caught her breath as she saw him tear aside the splintered bars and go into the stall with the maddened beast. The stallion reared above him, neighing terribly, hoofs lifted, eyes and teeth flashing and ears laid back, but Conan leaped and caught his mane with a display of sheer strength that seemed impossible, and dragged the beast down on his forelegs. The steed snorted and quivered, but stood still while the man bridled him and clapped on the gold-worked saddle, with the wide silver stirrups.

Wheeling the beast around in the stall, Conan called quickly to Yasmina, and the girl came, sidling nervously past the stallion's heels. Conan was working at the stone wall, talking swiftly as he worked. 'A secret door in the wall here, that not even the Wazuli know about. Yar Afzal showed it to me once when he was drunk. It opens out into the mouth of the ravine behind the hut. Ha!'

As he tugged at a projection that seemed casual, a whole section of the wall slid back on oiled iron runners. Looking through, the girl saw a narrow defile opening in a sheer stone cliff within a few feet of the hut's back wall. Then Conan sprang into the saddle and hauled her up before him. Behind them the great door groaned like a living thing and crashed in, and a yell rang to the roof as the entrance was instantly flooded with hairy faces and knives in hairy fists. And then the great stallion went through the wall like a javelin from a catapult, and thundered into the defile, running low, foam flying from the bit-rings.

That move came as an absolute surprize to the Wazulis. It was a surprize, too, to those stealing down the ravine. It happened so quickly—the hurricane-like charge of the great horse—that a man in a green turban was unable to get out of the way. He went down under the frantic hoofs, and a girl screamed. Conan got one glimpse of her as they thundered by—a slim, dark girl in silk trousers and a jeweled breast-band, flattening herself against the ravine wall. Then the black horse and his riders were gone up the gorge like the spume blown before a storm, and the men who came tumbling through the wall into the defile after them met that which changed their yells of blood-lust to shrill screams of fear and death.

6 THE MOUNTAIN OF THE BLACK SEERS

'Where now?' Yasmina was trying to sit erect on the rocking saddle-bow, clutching her captor. She was conscious of a recognition of shame that she should not find unpleasant the feel of his muscular flesh under her fingers.

'To Afghulistan,' he answered. 'It's a perilous road, but the stallion will carry us easily, unless we fall in with some of your friends, or my tribal enemies. Now that Yar Afzal is dead, those damned Wazulis will be on our heels. I'm surprised we haven't sighted them behind us already.'

'Who was that man you rode down?' she asked.

'I don't know. I never saw him before. He's no Ghuli, that's certain. What the devil he was doing there is more than I can say. There was a girl with him, too.'

'Yes.' Her gaze was shadowed. 'I can not understand that. That girl was my maid, Gitara. Do you suppose she was coming to aid me? That the man was a friend? If so, the Wazulis have captured them both.'

'Well,' he answered, 'there's nothing we can do. If we go back, they'll skin us both. I can't understand how a girl like that could get this far into the mountains with only one man—and he a robed scholar, for that's what he looked like. There's something infernally queer in all this. That fellow Yar Afzal beat and sent away—he moved like a man walking in his sleep. I've seen the priests of Zamora perform their abominable rituals in their forbidden temples, and their victims had a stare like that man. The priests looked into their eyes and muttered incantations, and then the people became the walking dead men, with glassy eyes, doing as they were ordered.

'And then I saw what the fellow had in his hand, which Yar Afzal picked up. It was like a big black jade bead, such as the temple girls of Yezud wear when they dance before the black stone spider which is their god. Yar Afzal held it in his hand,

and he didn't pick up anything else. Yet when he fell dead, a spider, like the god at Yezud, only smaller, ran out of his fingers. And then, when the Wazulis stood uncertain there, a voice cried out for them to kill me, and I know that voice didn't come from any of the warriors, nor from the women who watched by the huts. It seemed to come from *above*.'

Yasmina did not reply. She glanced at the stark outlines of the mountains all about them and shuddered. Her soul shrank from their gaunt brutality. This was a grim, naked land where anything might happen. Age-old traditions invested it with shuddery horror for anyone born in the hot, luxuriant southern plains.

The sun was high, beating down with fierce heat, yet the wind that blew in fitful gusts seemed to sweep off slopes of ice. Once she heard a strange rushing above them that was not the sweep of the wind, and from the way Conan looked up, she knew it was not a common sound to him, either. She thought that a strip of the cold blue sky was momentarily blurred, as if some all but invisible object had swept between it and herself, but she could not be sure. Neither made any comment, but Conan loosened his knife in his scabbard.

They were following a faintly marked path dipping down into ravines so deep the sun never struck bottom, laboring up steep slopes where loose shale threatened to slide from beneath their feet, and following knife-edge ridges with blue-hazed echoing depths on either hand.

The sun had passed its zenith when they crossed a narrow trail winding among the crags. Conan reined the horse aside and followed it southward, going almost at right angles to their former course. 'A Galzai village is at one end of this trail,' he explained. 'Their women follow it to a well, for water. You need new garments.'

Glancing down at her filmy attire, Yasmina agreed with him. Her cloth-of-gold slippers were in tatters, her robes and silken under-garments torn to shreds that scarcely held together decently. Garments meant for the streets of Peshkhauri were scarcely appropriate for the crags of the Himelians.

Coming to a crook in the trail, Conan dismounted, helped Yasmina down and waited. Presently he nodded, though she heard nothing. 'A woman coming along the trail,' he remarked. In sudden panic she clutched his arm.

'You will not—not kill her?'

'I don't kill women ordinarily,' he grunted; 'though some of the hill-women are she-wolves. No,' he grinned as at a huge jest. 'By Crom, I'll *pay* for her clothes! How is that?' He displayed a large handful of gold coins, and replaced all but the largest. She nodded, much relieved. It was perhaps natural for men to slay and die; her flesh crawled at the thought of watching the butchery of a woman.

Presently a woman appeared around the crook of the trail—a tall, slim Galzai girl, straight as a young sapling, bearing a great empty gourd. She stopped short and the gourd fell from her hands when she saw them; she wavered as though to run, then realized that Conan was too close to her to allow her to escape, and so stood still, staring at them with a mixed expression of fear and curiosity.

Conan displayed the gold coin.

'If you will give this woman your garments,' he said, 'I will give you this money.'

The response was instant. The girl smiled broadly with surprize and delight, and, with the disdain of a hill-woman for prudish conventions, promptly yanked off her sleeveless embroidered vest, slipped down her wide trousers and stepped out of them, twitched off her wide-sleeved shirt, and kicked off her sandals. Bundling them all in a bunch, she proffered them to Conan, who handed them to the astonished Devi.

'Get behind that rock and put these on,' he directed, further proving himself no native hillman. 'Fold your robes up into a bundle and bring them to me when you come out.' 'The money!' clamored the hill-girl, stretching out her hands eagerly. 'The gold you promised me!'

Conan flipped the coin to her, she caught it, bit, then thrust it into her hair, bent and caught up the gourd and went on down the path, as devoid of self-consciousness as of garment. Conan waited with some impatience while the Devi, for the first time in her pampered life, dressed herself. When she stepped from behind the rock he swore in surprize, and she felt a curious rush of emotions at the unrestrained admiration burning in his fierce blue eyes. She felt shame, embarrassment, yet a stimulation of vanity she had never before experienced, and a tingling when meeting the impact of his eyes. He laid a heavy hand on her shoulder and turned her about, staring avidly at her from all angles.

'By Crom!' said he. 'In those smoky, mystic robes you were aloof and cold and far off as a star! Now you are a woman of warm flesh and blood! You went behind that rock as the Devi of Vendhya; you come out as a hill-girl—though a thousand times more beautiful than any wench of the Zhaibar! You were a goddess—now you are real!'

He spanked her resoundingly, and she, recognizing this as merely another expression of admiration, did not feel outraged. It was indeed as if the changing of her garment had wrought a change in her personality. The feelings and sensations she had suppressed rose to domination in her now, as if the queenly robes she had cast off had been material shackles and inhibitions.

But Conan, in his renewed admiration, did not forget that peril lurked all about them. The farther they drew away from the region of the Zhaibar, the less likely he was to encounter any Kshatriya troops. On the other hand he had been listening all throughout their flight for sounds that would tell him the vengeful Wazulis of Khurum were on their heels.

Swinging the Devi up, he followed her into the saddle and again reined the stallion westward. The bundle of garments she had given him, he hurled over a cliff, to fall into the depths of a thousand-foot gorge. 'Why did you do that?' she asked. 'Why did you not give them to the girl?'

'The riders from Peshkhauri are combing these hills,' he said. 'They'll be ambushed and harried at every turn, and by way of reprisal they'll destroy every village they can take. They may turn westward any time. If they found a girl wearing your garments, they'd torture her into talking, and she might put them on my trail.'

'What will she do?' asked Yasmina.

'Go back to her village and tell her people that a stranger attacked her,' he answered. 'She'll have them on our track, all right. But she had to go on and get the water first; if she dared go back without it, they'd whip the skin off her. That gives us a long start. They'll never catch us. By nightfall we'll cross the Afghuli border.'

'There are no paths or signs of human habitation in these parts,' she commented. 'Even for the Himelians this region seems singularly deserted. We have not seen a trail since we left the one where we met the Galzai woman.'

For answer he pointed to the northwest, where she glimpsed a peak in a notch of the crags. 'Yimsha,' grunted Conan. 'The tribes build their villages as far from the mountain as they can.' She was instantly rigid with attention.

'Yimsha!' she whispered. 'The mountain of the Black Seers!'

'So they say,' he answered. 'This is as near as I ever approached it. I have swung north to avoid any Kshatriya troops that might be prowling through the hills. The regular trail from Khurum to Afghulistan lies farther south. This is an ancient one, and seldom used.'

She was staring intently at the distant peak. Her nails bit into her pink palms. 'How long would it take to reach Yimsha from this point?'

'All the rest of the day, and all night,' he answered, and grinned. 'Do you want to go there? By Crom, it's no place for an ordinary human, from what the hill-people say.' 'Why do they not gather and destroy the devils that inhabit it?' she demanded.

'Wipe out wizards with swords? Anyway, they never

interfere with people, unless the people interfere with them. I never saw one of them, though I've talked with men who wore they had. They say they've glimpsed people from the ower among the crags at sunset or sunrise—tall, silent men n black robes.'

'Would you be afraid to attack them?'

'I?' The idea seemed a new one to him. 'Why, if they imposed pon me, it would be my life or theirs. But I have nothing to o with them. I came to these mountains to raise a following f human beings, not to war with wizards.'

Yasmina did not at once reply. She stared at the peak as at human enemy, feeling all her anger and hatred stir in her osom anew. And another feeling began to take dim shape. he had plotted to hurl against the masters of Yimsha the an in whose arms she was now carried. Perhaps there as another way, besides the method she had planned, to ccomplish her purpose. She could not mistake the look that as beginning to dawn in this wild man's eyes as they rested n her. Kingdoms have fallen when a woman's slim white ands pulled the strings of destiny. Suddenly she stiffened, ointing.

'Look!'

Just visible on the distant peak there hung a cloud of eculiar aspect. It was a frosty crimson in color, veined with parkling gold. This cloud was in motion; it rotated, and as whirled it contracted. It dwindled to a spinning taper that ashed in the sun. And suddenly it detached itself from the now-tipped peak, floated out over the void like a gay-hued eather, and became invisible against the cerulean sky.

'What could that have been?' asked the girl uneasily, as a noulder of rock shut the distant mountain from view; the henomenon had been disturbing, even in its beauty.

'The hill-men call it Yimsha's Carpet, whatever that means,' nswered Conan. 'I've seen five hundred of them running as if ne devil were at their heels, to hide themselves in caves and rags, because they saw that crimson cloud float up from the eak. What in—'

They had advanced through a narrow, knife-cut gash etween turreted walls and emerged upon a broad ledge, anked by a series of rugged slopes on one hand, and a igantic precipice on the other. The dim trail followed this dge, bent around a shoulder and reappeared at intervals r below, working a tedious way downward. And emerging om the cut that opened upon the ledge, the black stallion alted short, snorting. Conan urged him on impatiently, and ne horse snorted and threw his head up and down, quivering nd straining as if against an invisible barrier.

Conan swore and swung off, lifting Yasmina down with im. He went forward, with a hand thrown out before him s if expecting to encounter unseen resistance, but there was othing to hinder him, though when he tried to lead the orse, it neighed shrilly and jerked back. Then Yasmina cried ut, and Conan wheeled, hand starting to knife-hilt.

Neither of them had seen him come, but he stood there, vith his arms folded, a man in a camel-hair robe and a green urban. Conan grunted with surprize to recognize the man ne stallion had spurned in the ravine outside the Wazuli llage.

'Who the devil are you?' he demanded.

The man did not answer. Conan noticed that his eyes were vide, fixed, and of a peculiar luminous quality. And those eyes eld his like a magnet.

Khemsa's sorcery was based on hypnotism, as is the case vith most Eastern magic. The way has been prepared for ne hypnotist for untold centuries of generations who have ved and died in the firm conviction of the reality and power f hypnotism, building up, by mass thought and practise, a olossal though intangible atmosphere against which the individual, steeped in the traditions of the land, finds himself elpless.

But Conan was not a son of the East. Its traditions were neaningless to him; he was the product of an utterly alien atmosphere. Hypnotism was not even a myth in Cimmeria. The heritage that prepared a native of the East for submission to the mesmerist was not his.

He was aware of what Khemsa was trying to do to him; but he felt the impact of the man's uncanny power only as a vague impulsion, a tugging and pulling that he could shake off as a man shakes spiderwebs from his garments.

Aware of hostility and black magic, he ripped out his long knife and lunged, as quick on his feet as a mountain lion.

But hypnotism was not all of Khemsa's magic. Yasmina, watching, did not see by what roguery of movement or illusion the man in the green turban avoided the terrible disembowelling thrust. But the keen blade whickered between side and lifted arm, and to Yasmina it seemed that Khemsa merely brushed his open palm lightly against Conan's bull-neck. But the Cimmerian went down like a slain ox.

Yet Conan was not dead; breaking his fall with his left hand, he slashed at Khemsa's legs even as he went down, and the Rakhsha avoided the scythe-like swipe only by a most unwizardly bound backward. Then Yasmina cried out sharply as she saw a woman she recognized as Gitara glide out from among the rocks and come up to the man. The greeting died in the Devi's throat as she saw the malevolence in the girl's beautiful face.

Conan was rising slowly, shaken and dazed by the cruel craft of that blow which, delivered with an art forgotten of men before Atlantis sank, would have broken like a rotten twig the neck of a lesser man. Khemsa gazed at him cautiously and a trifle uncertainly. The Rakhsha had learned the full flood of his own power when he faced at bay the knives of the maddened Wazulis in the ravine behind Khurum village; but the Cimmerian's resistance had perhaps shaken his new-found confidence a trifle. Sorcery thrives on success, not on failure.

He stepped forward, lifting his hand—then halted as if frozen, head tilted back, eyes wide open, hand raised. In spite of himself Conan followed his gaze, and so did the women—the girl cowering by the trembling stallion, and the girl beside Khemsa.

Down the mountain slopes, like a whirl of shining dust blown before the wind, a crimson, conoid cloud came dancing. Khemsa's dark face turned ashen; his hand began to tremble, then sank to his side. The girl beside him, sensing the change in him, stared at him inquiringly.

The crimson shape left the mountain slope and came down in a long arching sweep. It struck the ledge between Conan and Khemsa, and the Rakhsha gave back with a stifled cry. He backed away, pushing the girl Gitara back with groping, fending hands.

The crimson cloud balanced like a spinning top for an instant, whirling in a dazzling sheen on its point. Then without warning it was gone, vanished as a bubble vanishes when burst. There on the ledge stood four men. It was miraculous, incredible, impossible, yet it was true. They were not ghosts or phantoms. They were four tall men, with shaven, vulture-like heads, and black robes that hid their feet. Their hands were concealed by their wide sleeves. They stood in silence, their naked heads nodding slightly in unison. They were facing Khemsa, but behind them Conan felt his own blood turning to ice in his veins. Rising, he backed stealthily away, until he could feel the stallion's shoulder trembling against his back, and the Devi crept into the shelter of his arm. There was no word spoken. Silence hung like a stifling pall.

All four of the men in black robes stared at Khemsa. Their vulture-like faces were immobile, their eyes introspective and contemplative. But Khemsa shook like a man in an ague. His feet were braced on the rock, his calves straining as if in physical combat. Sweat ran in streams down his dark face. His right hand locked on something under his brown robe so desperately that the blood ebbed from that hand and left it white. His left hand fell on the shoulder of Gitara and clutched in agony like the grasp of a drowning man. She did not flinch or whimper, though his fingers dug like talons into her firm flesh.

Conan had witnessed hundreds of battles in his wild life, but never one like this, wherein four diabolical wills sought to beat down one lesser but equally devilish will that opposed them. But he only faintly sensed the monstrous quality of that hideous struggle. With his back to the wall, driven to bay by his former masters, Khemsa was fighting for his life with all the dark power, all the frightful knowledge they had taught him through long, grim years of neophytism and vassalage.

He was stronger than even he had guessed, and the free exercise of his powers in his own behalf had tapped unsuspected reservoirs of forces. And he was nerved to super-energy by frantic fear and desperation. He reeled before the merciless impact of those hypnotic eyes, but he held his ground. His features were distorted into a bestial grin of agony, and his limbs were twisted as on a rack. It was a war of souls, of frightful brains steeped in lore forbidden to men for a million years, of mentalities which had plumbed the abysses and explored the dark stars where spawn the shadows.

Yasmina understood this better than did Conan. And she dimly understood why Khemsa could withstand the concentrated impact of those four hellish wills which might have blasted into atoms the very rock on which he stood. The reason was the girl that he clutched with the strength of his despair. She was like an anchor to his staggering soul, battered by the waves of those psychic emanations. His weakness was now his strength. His love for the girl, violent and evil though it might be, was yet a tie that bound him to the rest of humanity, providing an earthly leverage for his will, a chain that his inhuman enemies could not break; at least not break through Khemsa.

They realized that before he did. And one of them turned his gaze from the Rakhsha full upon Gitara. There was no battle there. The girl shrank and wilted like a leaf in the drought. Irresistibly impelled, she tore herself from her lover's arms before he realized what was happening. Then a hideous thing came to pass. She began to back toward the precipice, facing her tormentors, her eyes wide and blank as dark gleaming glass from behind which a lamp has been blown out. Khemsa groaned and staggered toward her, falling into the trap set for him. A divided mind could not maintain the unequal battle. He was beaten, a straw in their hands. The girl went backward, walking like an automaton, and Khemsa reeled drunkenly after her, hands vainly outstretched, groaning, slobbering in his pain, his feet moving heavily like dead things.

On the very brink she paused, standing stiffly, her heels on the edge, and he fell on his knees and crawled whimpering toward her, groping for her, to drag her back from destruction. And just before his clumsy fingers touched her, one of the wizards laughed, like the sudden, bronze note of a bell in hell. The girl reeled suddenly and, consummate climax of exquisite cruelty, reason and understanding flooded back into her eyes, which flared with awful fear. She screamed, clutched wildly at her lover's straining hand, and then, unable to save herself, fell headlong with a moaning cry.

Khemsa hauled himself to the edge and stared over, haggardly, his lips working as he mumbled to himself. Then he turned and stared for a long minute at his torturers, with wide eyes that held no human light. And then with a cry that almost burst the rocks, he reeled up and came rushing toward them, a knife lifted in his hand.

One of the Rakhshas stepped forward and stamped his foot, and as he stamped, there came a rumbling that grew swiftly to a grinding roar. Where his foot struck, a crevice opened in the solid rock that widened instantly. Then, with a deafening crash, a whole section of the ledge gave way. There was a last glimpse of Khemsa, with arms wildly upflung, and then he vanished amidst the roar of the avalanche that thundered down into the abyss.

The four looked contemplatively at the ragged edge of rock that formed the new rim of the precipice, and then turned

suddenly. Conan, thrown off his feet by the shudder of th[e] mountain, was rising, lifting Yasmina. He seemed to move [as] slowly as his brain was working. He was befogged and stupi[d.] He realized that there was a desperate need for him to li[ft] the Devi on the black stallion and ride like the wind, but a[n] unaccountable sluggishness weighted his every thought an[d] action.

And now the wizards had turned toward him; they raise[d] their arms, and to his horrified sight, he saw their outline[s] fading, dimming, becoming hazy and nebulous, as a crimso[n] smoke billowed around their feet and rose about them. The[y] were blotted out by a sudden whirling cloud—and then h[e] realized that he too was enveloped in a blinding crimso[n] mist—he heard Yasmina scream, and the stallion cried ou[t] like a woman in pain. The Devi was torn from his arm, an[d] as he lashed out with his knife blindly, a terrific blow like [a] gust of storm wind knocked him sprawling against a roc[k.] Dazedly he saw a crimson conoid cloud spinning up and ove[r] the mountain slopes. Yasmina was gone, and so were the fou[r] men in black. Only the terrified stallion shared the ledge wit[h] him.

7 ON TO YIMSHA

As mists vanish before a strong wind, the cobwebs vanishe[d] from Conan's brain. With a searing curse he leaped into th[e] saddle and the stallion reared neighing beneath him. He glare[d] up the slopes, hesitated, and then turned down the trail i[n] the direction he had been going when halted by Khemsa[s] trickery. But now he did not ride at a measured gait. He shoo[k] loose the reins and the stallion went like a thunderbolt, a[s] if frantic to lose hysteria in violent physical exertion. Acros[s] the ledge and around the crag and down the narrow tra[il] threading the great steep they plunged at breakneck spee[d.] The path followed a fold of rock, winding interminably dow[n] from tier to tier of striated escarpment, and once, far belo[w,] Conan got a glimpse of the ruin that had fallen—a might[y] pile of broken stone and boulders at the foot of a gigantic clif[f.]

The valley floor was still far below him when he reached [a] long and lofty ridge that led out from the slope like a natura[l] causeway. Out upon this he rode, with an almost sheer dro[p] on either hand. He could trace ahead of him the trail an[d] made a great horseshoe back into the river-bed at his le[ft] hand. He cursed the necessity of traversing those miles, bu[t] it was the only way. To try to descend to the lower lap of th[e] trail here would be to attempt the impossible. Only a bir[d] could get to the river-bed with a whole neck.

So he urged on the wearying stallion, until a clink of hoof[s] reached his ears, welling up from below. Pulling up short an[d] reining to the lip of the cliff, he stared down into the dry rive[r-] bed that wound along the foot of the ridge. Along that gorg[e] rode a motley throng—bearded men on half-wild horses, fiv[e] hundred strong, bristling with weapons. And Conan shoute[d] suddenly, leaning over the edge of the cliff, three hundred fee[t] above them.

At his shout they reined back, and five hundred bearde[d] faces were tilted up towards him; a deep, clamorous roa[r] filled the canyon. Conan did not waste words. 'I was ridin[g] for Ghor!' he roared. 'I had not hoped to meet you dogs o[n] the trail. Follow me as fast as your nags can push! I'm going t[o] Yimsha, and—' 'Traitor!' The howl was like a dash of ice-wate[r] in his face.

'What?' He glared down at them, jolted speechless. He saw [the] wild eyes blazing up at him, faces contorted with fury, fist[s] brandishing blades. 'Traitor!' they roared back, wholehearted[ly.] 'Where are the seven chiefs held captive in Peshkhauri?'

'Why, in the governor's prison, I suppose,' he answered.

A bloodthirsty yell from a hundred throats answered hi[m] with such a waving of weapons and a clamor that he coul[d] not understand what they were saying. He beat down the di[n] with a bull-like roar, and bellowed: 'What devil's play is this[?] Let one of you speak, so I can understand what you mean!'

A gaunt old chief elected himself to this position, shoo[k]

tulwar at Conan as a preamble, and shouted accusingly: ou would not let us go raiding Peshkhauri to rescue our others!' 'No, you fools!' roared the exasperated Cimmerian. ven if you'd breached the wall, which is unlikely, they'd have nged the prisoners before you could reach them.'

'And you went alone to traffic with the governor!' yelled the ghuli, working himself into a frothing frenzy. 'Well?'

'Where are the seven chiefs?' howled the old chief, making s tulwar into a glimmering wheel of steel about his head. /here are they? Dead!' 'What!' Conan nearly fell off his horse his surprize.

'Aye, dead!' five hundred bloodthirsty voices assured him. The old chief brandished his arms and got the floor again. hey were not hanged!' he screeched. 'A Wazuli in another ll saw them die! The governor sent a wizard to slay them by aft!' 'That must be a lie,' said Conan. 'The governor would t dare. Last night I talked with him—'

The admission was unfortunate. A yell of hate and cusation split the skies.

Aye! You went to him alone! To betray us! It is no lie. e Wazuli escaped through the doors the wizard burst in s entry, and told the tale to our scouts whom he met in haibar. They had been sent forth to search for you, when u did not return. When they heard the Wazuli's tale, they turned with all haste to Ghor, and we saddled our steeds d girt our swords!'

And what do you fools mean to do?' demanded the mmerian.

To avenge our brothers!' they howled. 'Death to the hatriyas! Slay him, brothers, he is a traitor!'

Arrows began to rattle around him. Conan rose in his rrups, striving to make himself heard above the tumult, d then, with a roar of mingled rage, defiance and disgust, wheeled and galloped back up the trail. Behind him and low him the Afghulis came pelting, mouthing their rage, o furious even to remember that the only way they could ach the height whereon he rode was to traverse the river- d in the other direction, make the broad bend and follow e twisting trail up over the ridge. When they did remember is, and turned back, their repudiated chief had almost ached the point where the ridge joined the escarpment.

At the cliff he did not take the trail by which he had scended, but turned off on another, a mere trace along a ck-fault, where the stallion scrambled for footing. He had t ridden far when the stallion snorted and shied back om something lying in the trail. Conan stared down on e travesty of a man, a broken, shredded, bloody heap that obered and gnashed splintered teeth.

Impelled by some obscure reason, Conan dismounted and od looking down at the ghastly shape, knowing that he as witness of a thing miraculous and opposed to nature. e Rakhsha lifted his gory head, and his strange eyes, glazed th agony and approaching death, rested on Conan with cognition.

'Where are they?' It was a racking croak not even remotely sembling a human voice.

'Gone back to their damnable castle on Yimsha,' grunted onan. 'They took the Devi with them.'

I will go!' muttered the man. 'I will follow them! They killed tara; I will kill them—the acolytes, the Four of the Black rcle, the Master himself! Kill—kill them all!' He strove to ag his mutilated frame along the rock, but not even his domitable will could animate that gory mass longer, where e splintered bones hung together only by torn tissue and ptured fibre.

'Follow them!' raved Khemsa, drooling a bloody slaver. ollow!'

'I'm going to,' growled Conan. 'I went to fetch my Afghulis, it they've turned on me. I'm going on to Yimsha alone. have the Devi back if I have to tear down that damned ountain with my bare hands. I didn't think the governor ould dare kill my headmen, when I had the Devi, but it

seems he did. I'll have his head for that. She's no use to me now as a hostage, but—'

'The curse of Yizil on them!' gasped Khemsa. 'Go! I am dying. Wait—take my girdle.'

He tried to fumble with a mangled hand at his tatters, and Conan, understanding what he sought to convey, bent and drew from about his gory waist a girdle of curious aspect.

'Follow the golden vein through the abyss,' muttered Khemsa. 'Wear the girdle. I had it from a Stygian priest. It will aid you, though it failed me at last. Break the crystal globe with the four golden pomegranates. Beware of the Master's transmutations—I am going to Gitara—she is waiting for me in hell—aie, ya Skelos yar!' And so he died.

Conan stared down at the girdle. The hair of which it was woven was not horsehair. He was convinced that it was woven of the thick black tresses of a woman. Set in the thick mesh were tiny jewels such as he had never seen before. The buckle was strangely made, in the form of a golden serpent-head, flat, wedge-shaped and scaled with curious art. A strong shudder shook Conan as he handled it, and he turned as though to cast it over the precipice; then he hesitated, and finally buckled it about his waist, under the Bakhariot girdle. Then he mounted and pushed on.

The sun had sunk behind the crags. He climbed the trail in the vast shadow of the cliffs that was thrown out like a dark blue mantle over valleys and ridges far below. He was not far from the crest when, edging around the shoulder of a jutting crag, he heard the clink of shod hoofs ahead of him. He did not turn back. Indeed, so narrow was the path that the stallion could not have wheeled his great body upon it. He rounded the jut of the rock and came upon a portion of the path that broadened somewhat. A chorus of threatening yells broke on his ear, but his stallion pinned a terrified horse hard against the rock, and Conan caught the arm of the rider in an iron grip, checking the lifted sword in midair.

'Kerim Shah!' muttered Conan, red glints smoldering luridly in his eyes. The Turanian did not struggle; they sat their horses almost breast to breast, Conan's fingers locking the other's sword-arm. Behind Kerim Shah filed a group of lean Irakzai on gaunt horses. They glared like wolves, fingering bows and knives, but rendered uncertain because of the narrowness of the path and the perilous proximity of the abyss that yawned beneath them.

'Where is the Devi?' demanded Kerim Shah.

'What's it to you, you Hyrkanian spy?' snarled Conan.

'I know you have her,' answered Kerim Shah. 'I was on my way northward with some tribesmen when we were ambushed by enemies in Shalizah Pass. Many of my men were slain, and the rest of us harried through the hills like jackals. When we had beaten off our pursuers, we turned westward, toward Amir Jehun Pass, and this morning we came upon a Wazuli wandering through the hills. He was quite mad, but I learned much from his incoherent gibberings before he died. I learned that he was the sole survivor of a band which followed a chief of the Afghulis and a captive Kshatriya woman into a gorge behind Khurum village. He babbled much of a man in a green turban whom the Afghuli rode down, but who, when attacked by the Wazulis who pursued, smote them with a nameless doom that wiped them out as a gust of wind-driven fire wipes out a cluster of locusts.

'How that one man escaped, I do not know, nor did he; but I knew from his maunderings that Conan of Ghor had been in Khurum with his royal captive. And as we made our way through the hills, we overtook a naked Galzai girl bearing a gourd of water, who told us a tale of having been stripped and ravished by a giant foreigner in the garb of an Afghuli chief, who, she said, gave her garments to a Vendhyan woman who accompanied him. She said you rode westward.'

Kerim Shah did not consider it necessary to explain that he had been on his way to keep his rendezvous with the expected troops from Secunderam when he found his way barred by hostile tribesmen. The road to Gurashah valley through Shalizah Pass was longer than the road that wound through Amir Jehun Pass, but the latter traversed part of the Afghuli country, which Kerim Shah had been anxious to avoid until he came with an army. Barred from the Shalizah road, however, he had turned to the forbidden route, until news that Conan had not yet reached Afghulistan with his captive had caused him to turn southward and push on recklessly in the hope of overtaking the Cimmerian in the hills.

'So you had better tell me where the Devi is,' suggested Kerim Shah. 'We outnumber you—'

'Let one of your dogs nock a shaft and I'll throw you over the cliff,' Conan promised. 'It wouldn't do you any good to kill me, anyhow. Five hundred Afghulis are on my trail, and if they find you've cheated them, they'll flay you alive. Anyway, I haven't got the Devi. She's in the hands of the Black Seers of Yimsha.'

'Tarim!' swore Kerim Shah softly, shaken out of his poise for the first time. 'Khemsa—'

'Khemsa's dead,' grunted Conan. 'His masters sent him to hell on a landslide. And now get out of my way. I'd be glad to kill you if I had the time, but I'm on my way to Yimsha.' 'I'll go with you,' said the Turanian abruptly.

Conan laughed at him. 'Do you think I'd trust you, you Hyrkanian dog?'

'I don't ask you to,' returned Kerim Shah. 'We both want the Devi. You know my reason; King Yezdigerd desires to add her kingdom to his empire, and herself in his seraglio. And I knew you, in the days when you were a hetman of the kozak steppes; so I know your ambition is wholesale plunder. You want to loot Vendhya, and to twist out a huge ransom for Yasmina. Well, let us for the time being, without any illusion about each other, unite our forces, and try to rescue the Devi from the Seers. If we succeed, and live, we can fight it out to see who keeps her.'

Conan narrowly scrutinized the other for a moment, and then nodded, releasing the Turanian's arm. 'Agreed; what about your men?'

Kerim Shah turned to the silent Irakzai and spoke briefly: 'This chief and I are going to Yimsha to fight the wizards. Will you go with us, or stay here to be flayed by the Afghulis who are following this man?'

They looked at him with eyes grimly fatalistic. They were doomed and they knew it—had known it ever since the singing arrows of the ambushed Dagozai had driven them back from the pass of Shalizah. The men of the lower Zhaibar had too many reeking bloodfeuds among the crag-dwellers. They were too small a band to fight their way back through the hills to the villages of the border, without the guidance of the crafty Turanian. They counted themselves as dead already, so they made the reply that only dead men would make: 'We will go with thee and die on Yimsha.'

'Then in Crom's name let us be gone,' grunted Conan, fidgeting with impatience as he started into the blue gulfs of the deepening twilight. 'My wolves were hours behind me, but we've lost a devilish lot of time.'

Kerim Shah backed his steed from between the black stallion and the cliff, sheathed his sword and cautiously turned the horse. Presently the band was filing up the path as swiftly as they dared. They came out upon the crest nearly a mile east of the spot where Khemsa had halted the Cimmerian and the Devi. The path they had traversed was a perilous one, even for hill-men, and for that reason Conan had avoided it that day when carrying Yasmina, though Kerim Shah, following him, had taken it supposing the Cimmerian had done likewise. Even Conan sighed with relief when the horses scrambled up over the last rim. They moved like phantom riders through an enchanted realm of shadows. The soft creak of leather, the clink of steel marked their passing, then again the dark mountain slopes lay naked and silent in the starlight.

8 YASMINA KNOWS STARK TERROR

Yasmina had time but for one scream when she felt herself enveloped in that crimson whirl and torn from her protect with appalling force. She screamed once, and then she had n breath to scream. She was blinded, deafened, rendered mu and eventually senseless by the terrific rushing of the air abo her. There was a dazed consciousness of dizzy height a numbing speed, a confused impression of natural sensatio gone mad, and then vertigo and oblivion.

A vestige of these sensations clung to her as she recover consciousness; so she cried out and clutched wildly as thou to stay a headlong and involuntary flight. Her fingers clos on soft fabric, and a relieving sense of stability pervaded h She took cognizance of her surroundings.

She was lying on a dais covered with black velvet. Th dais stood in a great, dim room whose walls were hung wi dusky tapestries across which crawled dragons reproduce with repellent realism. Floating shadows merely hinted at tl lofty ceiling, and gloom that lent itself to illusion lurked the corners. There seemed to be neither windows nor doo in the walls, or else they were concealed by the nightc tapestries. Where the dim light came from, Yasmina cou not determine. The great room was a realm of mysteries, shadows, and shadowy shapes in which she could not ha sworn to observe movement, yet which invaded her min with a dim and formless terror.

But her gaze fixed itself on a tangible object. On anoth smaller dais of jet, a few feet away, a man sat cross-legge gazing contemplatively at her. His long black velvet rob embroidered with gold thread, fell loosely about hi masking his figure. His hands were folded in his sleeves. The was a velvet cap upon his head. His face was calm, plac not unhandsome, his eyes lambent and slightly oblique. H did not move a muscle as he sat regarding her, nor did h expression alter when he saw she was conscious.

Yasmina felt fear crawl like a trickle of ice-water down h supple spine. She lifted herself on her elbows and stare apprehensively at the stranger. 'Who are you?' she demande Her voice sounded brittle and inadequate.

'I am the Master of Yimsha.' The tone was rich and resona like the mellow tones of a temple bell. 'Why did you bring n here?' she demanded.

'Were you not seeking me?'

'If you are one of the Black Seers—yes!' she answere recklessly, believing that he could read her thoughts anyw. He laughed softly, and chills crawled up and down her spi again.

'You would turn the wild children of the hills against tl Seers of Yimsha!' He smiled. 'I have read it in your min princess. Your weak, human mind, filled with petty dreams hate and revenge.'

'You slew my brother!' A rising tide of anger was vying wi her fear; her hands were clenched, her lithe body rigid. 'Wl did you persecute him? He never harmed you. The priests s the Seers are above meddling in human affairs. Why did yc destroy the king of Vendhya?'

'How can an ordinary human understand the motives of Seer?' returned the Master calmly. 'My acolytes in the templ of Turan, who are the priests behind the priests of Tarin urged me to bestir myself in behalf of Yezdigerd. For reaso of my own, I complied. How can I explain my mystic reaso to your puny intellect? You could not understand.'

'I understand this: that my brother died!' Tears of grief an rage shook in her voice. She rose upon her knees and stare at him with wide blazing eyes, as supple and dangerous that moment as a she-panther. 'As Yezdigerd desired,' agree the Master calmly. 'For a while it was my whim to further h ambitions.'

'Is Yezdigerd your vassal?' Yasmina tried to keep the timbre her voice unaltered. She had felt her knee pressing somethin hard and symmetrical under a fold of velvet. Subtly she shifte her position, moving her hand under the fold.

'Is the dog that licks up the offal in the temple yard th vassal of the god?' returned the Master.

He did not seem to notice the actions she sought to ssemble. Concealed by the velvet, her fingers closed on what e knew was the golden hilt of a dagger. She bent her head to de the light of triumph in her eyes. 'I am weary of Yezdigerd,' id the Master. 'I have turned to other amusements—ha!'

With a fierce cry Yasmina sprang like a jungle cat, stabbing urderously. Then she stumbled and slid to the floor, where e cowered, staring up at the man on the dais. He had not oved; his cryptic smile was unchanged. Tremblingly she ted her hand and stared at it with dilated eyes. There was dagger in her fingers; they grasped a stalk of golden lotus, e crushed blossoms drooping on the bruised stem.

She dropped it as if it had been a viper, and scrambled away om the proximity of her tormentor. She returned to her own is, because that was at least more dignified for a queen than oveling on the floor at the feet of a sorcerer, and eyed him prehensively, expecting reprisals.

But the Master made no move.

'All substance is one to him who holds the key of the cosmos,' e said cryptically. 'To an adept nothing is immutable. At will, eel blossoms bloom in unnamed gardens, or flower-swords sh in the moonlight.' 'You are a devil,' she sobbed.

'Not I!' he laughed. 'I was born on this planet, long ago. Once was a common man, nor have I lost all human attributes the numberless eons of my adeptship. A human steeped the dark arts is greater than a devil. I am of human origin, t I rule demons. You have seen the Lords of the Black rcle—it would blast your soul to hear from what far realm ummoned them and from what doom I guard them with sorcelled crystal and golden serpents.

'But only I can rule them. My foolish Khemsa thought to ake himself great—poor fool, bursting material doors and urtling himself and his mistress through the air from hill to l! Yet if he had not been destroyed his power might have own to rival mine.'

He laughed again. 'And you, poor, silly thing! Plotting to nd a hairy hill chief to storm Yimsha! It was such a jest that myself could have designed, had it occurred to me, that you ould fall in his hands. And I read in your childish mind an tention to seduce by your feminine wiles to attempt your rpose, anyway.

'But for all your stupidity, you are a woman fair to look on. It is my whim to keep you for my slave.' The daughter a thousand proud emperors gasped with shame and fury the word.

'You dare not!'

His mocking laughter cut her like a whip across her naked oulders.

'The king dares not trample a worm in the road? Little fool, you not realize that your royal pride is no more than a aw blown on the wind? I, who have known the kisses of the eens of Hell! You have seen how I deal with a rebel!'

Cowed and awed, the girl crouched on the velvet-covered is. The light grew dimmer and more phantom-like. The tures of the Master became shadowy. His voice took on a wer tone of command. 'I will never yield to you!' Her voice mbled with fear but it carried a ring of resolution.

'You will yield,' he answered with horrible conviction. 'Fear d pain shall teach you. I will lash you with horror and ony to the last quivering ounce of your endurance, until u become as melted wax to be bent and molded in my nds as I desire. You shall know such discipline as no mortal man ever knew, until my slightest command is to you as e unalterable will of the gods. And first, to humble your de, you shall travel back through the lost ages, and view all e shapes that have been you. Aie, yil la khosa!'

At these words the shadowy room swam before Yasmina's righted gaze. The roots of her hair prickled her scalp, and r tongue clove to her palate. Somewhere a gong sounded eep, ominous note. The dragons on the tapestries glowed blue fire, and then faded out. The Master on his dais was a shapeless shadow. The dim light gave way to soft, thick

darkness, almost tangible, that pulsed with strange radiations. She could no longer see the Master. She could see nothing. She had a strange sensation that the walls and ceiling had withdrawn immensely from her.

Then somewhere in the darkness a glow began, like a firefly that rhythmically dimmed and quickened. It grew to a golden ball, and as it expanded its light grew more intense, flaming whitely. It burst suddenly, showering the darkness with white sparks that did not illumine the shadows. But like an impression left in the gloom, a faint luminance remained, and revealed a slender dusky shaft shooting up from the shadowy floor. Under the girl's dilated gaze it spread, took shape; stems and broad leaves appeared, and great black poisonous blossoms that towered above her as she cringed against the velvet. A subtle perfume pervaded the atmosphere. It was the dread figure of the black lotus that had grown up as she watched, as it grows in the haunted, forbidden jungles of Khitai.

The broad leaves were murmurous with evil life. The blossoms bent toward her like sentient things, nodding serpent-like on pliant stems. Etched against soft, impenetrable darkness it loomed over her, gigantic, blackly visible in some mad way. Her brain reeled with the drugging scent and she sought to crawl from the dais. Then she clung to it as it seemed to be pitching at an impossible slant. She cried out with terror and clung to the velvet, but she felt her fingers ruthlessly torn away. There was a sensation as of all sanity and stability crumbling and vanishing. She was a quivering atom of sentiency driven through a black, roaring, icy void by a thundering wind that threatened to extinguish her feeble flicker of animate life like a candle blown out in a storm.

Then there came a period of blind impulse and movement, when the atom that was she mingled and merged with myriad other atoms of spawning life in the yeasty morass of existence, molded by formative forces until she emerged again a conscious individual, whirling down an endless spiral of lives.

In a mist of terror she relived all her former existences, recognized and was again all the bodies that had carried her ego throughout the changing ages. She bruised her feet again over the long, weary road of life that stretched out behind her into the immemorial past. Back beyond the dimmest dawns of Time she crouched shuddering in primordial jungles, hunted by slavering beasts of prey. Skin-clad, she waded thigh-deep in rice swamps, battling with squawking water-fowl for the precious grains. She labored with the oxen to drag the pointed stick through the stubborn soil, and she crouched endlessly over looms in peasant huts.

She saw walled cities burst into flame, and fled screaming before the slayers. She reeled naked and bleeding over burning sands, dragged at the slaver's stirrup, and she knew the grip of hot, fierce hands on her writhing flesh, the shame and agony of brutal lust. She screamed under the bite of the lash, and moaned on the rack; mad with terror she fought against the hands that forced her head inexorably down on the bloody block.

She knew the agonies of childbirth, and the bitterness of love betrayed. She suffered all the woes and wrongs and brutalities that man has inflicted on woman throughout the eons; and she endured all the spite and malice of women for woman. And like the flick of a fiery whip throughout was the consciousness she retained of her Devi-ship. She was all the women she had ever been, yet in her knowing she was Yasmina. This consciousness was not lost in the throes of reincarnation. At one and the same time she was a naked slave-wench groveling under the whip, and the proud Devi of Vendhya. And she suffered not only as the slave-girl suffered, but as Yasmina, to whose pride the whip was like a white-hot brand.

Life merged into life in flying chaos, each with its burden of woe and shame and agony, until she dimly heard her own voice screaming unbearably, like one long-drawn cry of suffering echoing down the ages. Then she awakened on the velvet-covered dais in the mystic room.

In a ghostly gray light she saw again the dais and the cryptic robed figure seated upon it. The hooded head was bent, the high shoulders faintly etched against the uncertain dimness. She could make out no details clearly, but the hood, where the velvet cap had been, stirred a formless uneasiness in her. As she stared, there stole over her a nameless fear that froze her tongue to her palate—a feeling that it was not the Master who sat so silently on that black dais.

Then the figure moved and rose upright, towering above her. It stooped over her and the long arms in their wide black sleeves bent about her. She fought against them in speechless fright, surprized by their lean hardness. The hooded head bent down toward her averted face. And she screamed, and screamed again in poignant fear and loathing. Bony arms gripped her lithe body, and from that hood looked forth a countenance of death and decay—features like rotting parchment on a moldering skull.

She screamed again, and then, as those champing, grinning jaws bent toward her lips, she lost consciousness....

9 THE CASTLE OF THE WIZARDS

The sun had risen over the white Himelian peaks. At the foot of a long slope a group of horsemen halted and stared upward. High above them a stone tower poised on the pitch of the mountainside. Beyond and above that gleamed the walls of a greater keep, near the line where the snow began that capped Yimsha's pinnacle. There was a touch of unreality about the whole—purple slopes pitching up to that fantastic castle, toy-like with distance, and above it the white glistening peak shouldering the cold blue.

'We'll leave the horses here,' grunted Conan. 'That treacherous slope is safer for a man on foot. Besides, they're done.'

He swung down from the black stallion which stood with wide-braced legs and drooping head. They had pushed hard throughout the night, gnawing at scraps from saddle-bags, and pausing only to give the horses the rests they had to have.

'That first tower is held by the acolytes of the Black Seers,' said Conan. 'Or so men say; watch-dogs for their masters—lesser sorcerers. They won't sit sucking their thumbs as we climb this slope.'

Kerim Shah glanced up the mountain, then back the way they had come; they were already far up Yimsha's side, and a vast expanse of lesser peaks and crags spread out beneath them. Among these labyrinths the Turanian sought in vain for a movement of color that would betray men. Evidently the pursuing Afghulis had lost their chief's trail in the night.

'Let us go, then.' They tied the weary horses in a clump of tamarisk and without further comment turned up the slope. There was no cover. It was a naked incline, strewn with boulders not big enough to conceal a man. But they did conceal something else.

The party had not gone fifty steps when a snarling shape burst from behind a rock. It was one of the gaunt savage dogs that infested the hill villages, and its eyes glared redly, its jaws dripped foam. Conan was leading, but it did not attack him. It dashed past him and leaped at Kerim Shah. The Turanian leaped aside, and the great dog flung itself upon the Irakzai behind him. The man yelled and threw up his arm, which was torn by the brute's fangs as it bore him backward, and the next instant half a dozen tulwars were hacking at the beast. Yet not until it was literally dismembered did the hideous creature cease its efforts to seize and rend its attackers.

Kerim Shah bound up the wounded warrior's gashed arm, looked at him narrowly, and then turned away without a word. He rejoined Conan, and they renewed the climb in silence. Presently Kerim Shah said: 'Strange to find a village dog in this place.'

'There's no offal here,' grunted Conan.

Both turned their heads to glance back at the wounded warrior toiling after them among his companions. Sweat glistened on his dark face and his lips were drawn back fro[m] his teeth in a grimace of pain. Then both looked again at th[e] stone tower squatting above them.

A slumberous quiet lay over the uplands. The tower showe[d] no sign of life, nor did the strange pyramidal structure beyon[d] it. But the men who toiled upward went with the tenseness [of] men walking on the edge of a crater. Kerim Shah had unslun[g] the powerful Turanian bow that killed at five hundred pace[s] and the Irakzai looked to their own lighter and less leth[al] bows.

But they were not within bow-shot of the tower whe[n] something shot down out of the sky without warning. [It] passed so close to Conan that he felt the wind of rushin[g] wings, but it was an Irakzai who staggered and fell, blood jettin[g] from a severed jugular. A hawk with wings like burnished ste[el] shot up again, blood dripping from the scimitar-beak, to re[el] against the sky as Kerim Shah's bowstring twanged. It droppe[d] like a plummet, but no man saw where it struck the earth.

Conan bent over the victim of the attack, but the man wa[s] already dead. No one spoke; useless to comment on the fa[ct] that never before had a hawk been known to swoop on [a] man. Red rage began to vie with fatalistic lethargy in the wil[d] souls of the Irakzai. Hairy fingers nocked arrows and me[n] glared vengefully at the tower whose very silence mocke[d] them.

But the next attack came swiftly. They all saw it—a whi[te] puffball of smoke that tumbled over the tower-rim and cam[e] drifting and rolling down the slope toward them. Othe[rs] followed it. They seemed harmless, mere woolly globes [of] cloudy foam, but Conan stepped aside to avoid contact wi[th] the first. Behind him one of the Irakzai reached out and thru[st] his sword into the unstable mass. Instantly a sharp repo[rt] shook the mountainside. There was a burst of blinding flam[e] and then the puffball had vanished, and the too-curiou[s] warrior remained only a heap of charred and blackene[d] bones. The crisped hand still gripped the ivory sword-h[ilt] but the blade was gone—melted and destroyed by that awf[ul] heat. Yet men standing almost within reach of the victim ha[d] not suffered except to be dazzled and half blinded by th[e] sudden flare.

'Steel touches it off,' grunted Conan. 'Look out—here th[ey] come!'

The slope above them was almost covered by the billowi[ng] spheres. Kerim Shah bent his bow and sent a shaft into t[he] mass, and those touched by the arrow burst like bubbles spurting flame. His men followed his example and for t[he] next few minutes it was as if a thunderstorm raged on t[he] mountain slope, with bolts of lightning striking and bursti[ng] in showers of flame. When the barrage ceased, only a fe[w] arrows were left in the quivers of the archers.

They pushed on grimly, over soil charred and blackene[d] where the naked rock had in places been turned to lava [by] the explosion of those diabolical bombs. Now they we[re] almost within arrow-flight of the silent tower, and th[ey] spread their line, nerves taut, ready for any horror that mig[ht] descend upon them.

On the tower appeared a single figure, lifting a ten-fo[ot] bronze horn. Its strident bellow roared out across the echoi[ng] slopes, like the blare of trumpets on Judgment Day. And [it] began to be fearfully answered. The ground trembled und[er] the feet of the invaders, and rumblings and grindings well[ed] up from the subterranean depths.

The Irakzai screamed, reeling like drunken men on t[he] shuddering slope, and Conan, eyes glaring, charged reckles[sly] up the incline, knife in hand, straight at the door that show[ed] in the tower-wall. Above him the great horn roared a[nd] bellowed in brutish mockery. And then Kerim Shah dre[w a] shaft to his ear and loosed.

Only a Turanian could have made that shot. The bellow[ing] of the horn ceased suddenly, and a high, thin scream shrill[ed] in its place. The green-robed figure on the tower stagger[ed]

utching at the long shaft which quivered in its bosom, and
hen pitched across the parapet. The great horn tumbled
pon the battlement and hung precariously, and another
obed figure rushed to seize it, shrieking in horror. Again the
uranian bow twanged, and again it was answered by a death-
owl. The second acolyte, in falling, struck the horn with his
bow and knocked it clattering over the parapet to shatter
n the rocks far below.

At such headlong speed had Conan covered the ground
at before the clattering echoes of that fall had died away,
e was hacking at the door. Warned by his savage instinct, he
ave back suddenly as a tide of molten lead splashed down
om above. But the next instant he was back again, attacking
e panels with redoubled fury. He was galvanized by the fact
at his enemies had resorted to earthly weapons. The sorcery
f the acolytes was limited. Their necromantic resources
ight well be exhausted.

Kerim Shah was hurrying up the slope, his hill-men behind
m in a straggling crescent. They loosed as they ran, their
rows splintering against the walls or arching over the
arapet.

The heavy teak portal gave way beneath the Cimmerian's
sault, and he peered inside warily, expecting anything. He
as looking into a circular chamber from which a stair wound
ward. On the opposite side of the chamber a door gaped
en, revealing the outer slope—and the backs of half a
zen green-robed figures in full retreat.

Conan yelled, took a step into the tower, and then native
ution jerked him back, just as a great block of stone fell
ashing to the floor where his foot had been an instant
fore. Shouting to his followers, he raced around the tower.
The acolytes had evacuated their first line of defence. As
onan rounded the tower he saw their green robes twinkling
o the mountain ahead of him. He gave chase, panting with
rnest blood-lust, and behind him Kerim Shah and the
kzai came pelting, the latter yelling like wolves at the flight
their enemies, their fatalism momentarily submerged by
mporary triumph.

The tower stood on the lower edge of a narrow plateau
nose upward slant was barely perceptible. A few hundred
rds away this plateau ended abruptly in a chasm which had
en invisible farther down the mountain. Into this chasm
e acolytes apparently leaped without checking their speed.
heir pursuers saw the green robes flutter and disappear over
e edge.

A few moments later they themselves were standing on the
ink of the mighty moat that cut them off from the castle
the Black Seers. It was a sheer-walled ravine that extended
either direction as far as they could see, apparently girdling
e mountain, some four hundred yards in width and five
ndred feet deep. And in it, from rim to rim, a strange,
anslucent mist sparkled and shimmered.

Looking down, Conan grunted. Far below him, moving
ross the glimmering floor, which shone like burnished silver,
saw the forms of the green-robed acolytes. Their outline
s wavering and indistinct, like figures seen under deep
ater. They walked in single file, moving toward the opposite
ll.

Kerim Shah nocked an arrow and sent it singing downward.
t when it struck the mist that filled the chasm it seemed
lose momentum and direction, wandering widely from its
urse. 'If they went down, so can we!' grunted Conan, while
rim Shah stared after his shaft in amazement. 'I saw them
t at this spot—'

quinting down he saw something shining like a golden
ead across the canyon floor far below. The acolytes
emed to be following this thread, and there suddenly came
him Khemsa's cryptic words—'Follow the golden vein!' On
e brink, under his very hand as he crouched, he found it, a
n vein of sparkling gold running from an outcropping of
to the edge and down across the silvery floor. And he
nd something else, which had before been invisible to him

because of the peculiar refraction of the light. The gold vein
followed a narrow ramp which slanted down into the ravine,
fitted with niches for hand and foot hold.

'Here's where they went down,' he grunted to Kerim Shah.
'They're no adepts, to waft themselves through the air! We'll
follow them—'

It was at that instant that the man who had been bitten
by the mad dog cried out horribly and leaped at Kerim Shah,
foaming and gnashing his teeth. The Turanian, quick as a cat
on his feet, sprang aside and the madman pitched head-first
over the brink. The others rushed to the edge and glared
after him in amazement. The maniac did not fall plummet-
like. He floated slowly down through the rosy haze like a man
sinking in deep water. His limbs moved like a man trying to
swim, and his features were purple and convulsed beyond the
contortions of his madness. Far down at last on the shining
floor his body settled and lay still.

'There's death in that chasm,' muttered Kerim Shah, drawing
back from the rosy mist that shimmered almost at his feet.
'What now, Conan?' 'On!' answered the Cimmerian grimly.
'Those acolytes are human; if the mist doesn't kill them, it
won't kill me.'

He hitched his belt, and his hands touched the girdle
Khemsa had given him; he scowled, then smiled bleakly. He
had forgotten that girdle; yet thrice had death passed him by
to strike another victim.

The acolytes had reached the farther wall and were moving
up it like great green flies. Letting himself upon the ramp, he
descended warily. The rosy cloud lapped about his ankles,
ascending as he lowered himself. It reached his knees, his
thighs, his waist, his arm-pits. He felt as one feels a thick
heavy fog on a damp night. With it lapping about his chin he
hesitated, and then ducked under. Instantly his breath ceased;
all air was shut off from him and he felt his ribs caving in on
his vitals. With a frantic effort he heaved himself up, fighting
for life. His head rose above the surface and he drank air in
great gulps.

Kerim Shah leaned down toward him, spoke to him, but
Conan neither heard nor heeded. Stubbornly, his mind fixed
on what the dying Khemsa had told him, the Cimmerian
groped for the gold vein, and found that he had moved off
it in his descent. Several series of hand-holds were niched
in the ramp. Placing himself directly over the thread, he
began climbing down once more. The rosy mist rose about
him, engulfed him. Now his head was under, but he was
still drinking pure air. Above him he saw his companions
staring down at him, their features blurred by the haze that
shimmered over his head. He gestured for them to follow,
and went down swiftly, without waiting to see whether they
complied or not.

Kerim Shah sheathed his sword without comment and
followed, and the Irakzai, more fearful of being left alone
than of the terrors that might lurk below, scrambled after
him. Each man clung to the golden thread as they saw the
Cimmerian do.

Down the slanting ramp they went to the ravine floor and
moved out across the shining level, treading the gold vein like
rope-walkers. It was as if they walked along an invisible tunnel
through which air circulated freely. They felt death pressing
in on them above and on either hand, but it did not touch
them.

The vein crawled up a similar ramp on the other wall up
which the acolytes had disappeared, and up it they went with
taut nerves, not knowing what might be waiting for them
among the jutting spurs of rock that fanged the lip of the
precipice.

It was the green-robed acolytes who awaited them, with
knives in their hands. Perhaps they had reached the limits to
which they could retreat. Perhaps the Stygian girdle about
Conan's waist could have told why their necromantic spells
had proven so weak and so quickly exhausted. Perhaps it was
knowledge of death decreed for failure that sent them leaping

from among the rocks, eyes glaring and knives glittering, resorting in their desperation to material weapons.

There among the rocky fangs on the precipice lip was no war of wizard craft. It was a whirl of blades, where real steel bit and real blood spurted, where sinewy arms dealt forthright blows that severed quivering flesh, and men went down to be trodden under foot as the fight raged over them.

One of the Irakzai bled to death among the rocks, but the acolytes were down—slashed and hacked asunder or hurled over the edge to float sluggishly down to the silver floor that shone so far below. Then the conquerors shook blood and sweat from their eyes, and looked at one another. Conan and Kerim Shah still stood upright, and four of the Irakzai.

They stood among the rocky teeth that serrated the precipice brink, and from that spot a path wound up a gentle slope to a broad stair, consisting of half a dozen steps, a hundred feet across, cut out of a green jade-like substance. They led up to a broad stage or roofless gallery of the same polished stone, and above it rose, tier upon tier, the castle of the Black Seers. It seemed to have been carved out of the sheer stone of the mountain. The architecture was faultless, but unadorned. The many casements were barred and masked with curtains within. There was no sign of life, friendly or hostile.

They went up the path in silence, and warily as men treading the lair of a serpent. The Irakzai were dumb, like men marching to a certain doom. Even Kerim Shah was silent. Only Conan seemed unaware what a monstrous dislocating and uprooting of accepted thought and action their invasion constituted, what an unprecedented violation of tradition. He was not of the East; and he came of a breed who fought devils and wizards as promptly and matter-of-factly as they battled human foes.

He strode up the shining stairs and across the wide green gallery straight toward the great golden-bound teak door that opened upon it. He cast but a single glance upward at the higher tiers of the great pyramidal structure towering above him. He reached a hand for the bronze prong that jutted like a handle from the door—then checked himself, grinning hardly. The handle was made in the shape of a serpent, head lifted on arched neck; and Conan had a suspicion that that metal head would come to grisly life under his hand.

He struck it from the door with one blow, and its bronze clink on the glassy floor did not lessen his caution. He flipped it aside with his knife-point, and again turned to the door. Utter silence reigned over the towers. Far below them the mountain slopes fell away into a purple haze of distance. The sun glittered on snow-clad peaks on either hand. High above, a vulture hung like a black dot in the cold blue of the sky. But for it, the men before the gold-bound door were the only evidence of life, tiny figures on a green jade gallery poised on the dizzy height, with that fantastic pile of stone towering above them.

A sharp wind off the snow slashed them, whipping their tatters about. Conan's long knife splintering through the teak panels roused the startled echoes. Again and again he struck, hewing through polished wood and metal bands alike. Through the sundered ruins he glared into the interior, alert and suspicious as a wolf. He saw a broad chamber, the polished stone walls untapestried, the mosaic floor uncarpeted. Square, polished ebon stools and a stone dais formed the only furnishings. The room was empty of human life. Another door showed in the opposite wall.

'Leave a man on guard outside,' grunted Conan. 'I'm going in.'

Kerim Shah designated a warrior for that duty, and the man fell back toward the middle of the gallery, bow in hand. Conan strode into the castle, followed by the Turanian and the three remaining Irakzai. The one outside spat, grumbled in his beard, and started suddenly as a low mocking laugh reached his ears.

He lifted his head and saw, on the tier above him, a tall, black-robed figure, naked head nodding slightly as he stared

down. His whole attitude suggested mockery and malignit Quick as a flash the Irakzai bent his bow and loosed, and th arrow streaked upward to strike full in the black-robed brea The mocking smile did not alter. The Seer plucked out th missile and threw it back at the bowman, not as a weapon hurled, but with a contemptuous gesture. The Irakzai dodge instinctively throwing up his arm. His fingers closed on th revolving shaft.

Then he shrieked. In his hand the wooden shaft sudden *writhed*. Its rigid outline became pliant, melting in his gras He tried to throw it from him, but it was too late. He he a living serpent in his naked hand, and already it had coile about his wrist and its wicked wedge-shaped head darte his muscular arm. He screamed again and his eyes becam distended, his features purple. He went to his knees shaken b an awful convulsion, and then lay still.

The men inside had wheeled at his first cry. Conan took swift stride toward the open doorway, and then halted sho baffled. To the men behind him it seemed that he straine against empty air. But though he could see nothing, there w a slick, smooth, hard surface under his hands, and he kne that a sheet of crystal had been let down in the doorwa Through it he saw the Irakzai lying motionless on the glas gallery, an ordinary arrow sticking in his arm.

Conan lifted his knife and smote, and the watchers we dumbfounded to see his blow checked apparently midair, with the loud clang of steel that meets an unyieldi substance. He wasted no more effort. He knew that not eve the legendary tulwar of Amir Khurum could shatter th invisible curtain.

In a few words he explained the matter to Kerim Shah, an the Turanian shrugged his shoulders. 'Well, if our exit is barre we must find another. In the meanwhile our way lies forwa does it not?'

With a grunt the Cimmerian turned and strode across t chamber to the opposite door, with a feeling of treadi on the threshold of doom. As he lifted his knife to shatt the door, it swung silently open as if of its own accord. H strode into the great hall, flanked with tall glassy colum A hundred feet from the door began the broad jade-gre steps of a stair that tapered toward the top like the side a pyramid. What lay beyond that stair he could not tell. B between him and its shimmering foot stood a curious alt of gleaming black jade. Four great golden serpents twin their tails about this altar and reared their wedge-shap heads in the air, facing the four quarters of the compass li the enchanted guardians of a fabled treasure. But on the alt between the arching necks, stood only a crystal globe fill with a cloudy smoke-like substance, in which floated fo golden pomegranates.

The sight stirred some dim recollection in his mind; th Conan heeded the altar no longer, for on the lower ste of the stair stood four black-robed figures. He had not se them come. They were simply there, tall, gaunt, their vultu heads nodding in unison, their feet and hands hidden by th flowing garments.

One lifted his arm and the sleeve fell away revealing hand—and it was not a hand at all. Conan halted in m stride, compelled against his will. He had encountered a for differing subtly from Khemsa's mesmerism, and he could r advance, though he felt it in his power to retreat if he wishe His companions had likewise halted, and they seemed eve more helpless than he, unable to move in either direction.

The seer whose arm was lifted beckoned to one of t Irakzai, and the man moved toward him like one in a tran eyes staring and fixed, blade hanging in limp fingers. As pushed past Conan, the Cimmerian threw an arm across breast to arrest him. Conan was so much stronger than t Irakzai that in ordinary circumstances he could have brok his spine between his hands. But now the muscular arm w brushed aside like straw and the Irakzai moved toward stair, treading jerkily and mechanically. He reached the ste nd knelt stiffly, proffering his blade and bending his head. he Seer took the sword. It flashed as he swung it up and own. The Irakzai's head tumbled from his shoulders and udded heavily on the black marble floor. An arch of blood tted from the severed arteries and the body slumped over nd lay with arms spread wide.

Again a malformed hand lifted and beckoned, and another akzai stumbled stiffly to his doom. The ghastly drama was -enacted and another headless form lay beside the first.

As the third tribesman clumped his way past Conan to his eath, the Cimmerian, his veins bulging in his temples with is efforts to break past the unseen barrier that held him, was uddenly aware of allied forces, unseen, but waking into life out him. This realization came without warning, but so owerfully that he could not doubt his instinct. His left hand id involuntarily under his Bakhariot belt and closed on the rygian girdle. And as he gripped it he felt new strength flood is numbed limbs; the will to live was a pulsing white-hot fire, atched by the intensity of his burning rage.

The third Irakzai was a decapitated corpse, and the hideous nger was lifting again when Conan felt the bursting of the visible barrier. A fierce, involuntary cry burst from his lips as e leaped with the explosive suddenness of pent-up ferocity. lis left hand gripped the sorcerer's girdle as a drowning an grips a floating log, and the long knife was a sheen of ght in his right. The men on the steps did not move. They atched calmly, cynically; if they felt surprise they did not how it. Conan did not allow himself to think what might hance when he came within knife-reach of them. His blood vas pounding in his temples, a mist of crimson swam before is sight. He was afire with the urge to kill—to drive his knife eep into flesh and bone, and twist the blade in blood and ntrails.

Another dozen strides would carry him to the steps where he sneering demons stood. He drew his breath deep, his ary rising redly as his charge gathered momentum. He was urtling past the altar with its golden serpents when like a evin-flash there shot across his mind again as vividly as if poken in his external ear, the cryptic words of Khemsa: 'Break he crystal ball!'

His reaction was almost without his own volition. Execution ollowed impulse so spontaneously that the greatest sorcerer f the age would not have had time to read his mind and revent his action. Wheeling like a cat from his headlong harge, he brought his knife crashing down upon the crystal. nstantly the air vibrated with a peal of terror, whether from he stairs, the altar, or the crystal itself he could not tell. Hisses lled his ears as the golden serpents, suddenly vibrant with ideous life, writhed and smote at him. But he was fired to the peed of a maddened tiger. A whirl of steel sheared through he hideous trunks that waved toward him, and he smote he crystal sphere again and yet again. And the globe burst vith a noise like a thunderclap, raining fiery shards on the lack marble, and the gold pomegranates, as if released from aptivity, shot upward toward the lofty roof and were gone.

A mad screaming, bestial and ghastly, was echoing through he great hall. On the steps writhed four black-robed figures, wisting in convulsions, froth dripping from their livid mouths. hen with one frenzied crescendo of inhuman ululation they tiffened and lay still, and Conan knew that they were dead. le stared down at the altar and the crystal shards. Four eadless golden serpents still coiled about the altar, but no lien life now animated the dully gleaming metal.

Kerim Shah was rising slowly from his knees, whither he had een dashed by some unseen force. He shook his head to lear the ringing from his ears.

'Did you hear that crash when you struck? It was as if a housand crystal panels shattered all over the castle as that lobe burst. Were the souls of the wizards imprisoned in hose golden balls?—Ha!' Conan wheeled as Kerim Shah drew is sword and pointed.

Another figure stood at the head of the stair. His robe, too, was black, but of richly embroidered velvet, and there was a velvet cap on his head. His face was calm, and not unhandsome. 'Who the devil are you?' demanded Conan, staring up at him, knife in hand.

'I am the Master of Yimsha!' His voice was like the chime of a temple bell, but a note of cruel mirth ran through it. 'Where is Yasmina?' demanded Kerim Shah.

The Master laughed down at him.

'What is that to you, dead man? Have you so quickly forgotten my strength, once lent to you, that you come armed against me, you poor fool? I think I will take your heart, Kerim Shah!'

He held out his hand as if to receive something, and the Turanian cried out sharply like a man in mortal agony. He reeled drunkenly, and then, with a splintering of bones, a rending of flesh and muscle and a snapping of mail-links, his breast burst outward with a shower of blood, and through the ghastly aperture something red and dripping shot through the air into the Master's outstretched hand, as a bit of steel leaps to the magnet. The Turanian slumped to the floor and lay motionless, and the Master laughed and hurled the object to fall before Conan's feet—a still-quivering human heart.

With a roar and a curse Conan charged the stair. From Khemsa's girdle he felt strength and deathless hate flow into him to combat the terrible emanation of power that met him on the steps. The air filled with a shimmering steely haze through which he plunged like a swimmer, head lowered, left arm bent about his face, knife gripped low in his right hand. His half-blinded eyes, glaring over the crook of his elbow, made out the hated shape of the Seer before and above him, the outline wavering as a reflection wavers in disturbed water.

He was racked and torn by forces beyond his comprehension, but he felt a driving power outside and beyond his own lifting him inexorably upward and onward, despite the wizard's strength and his own agony.

Now he had reached the head of the stairs, and the Master's face floated in the steely haze before him, and a strange fear shadowed the inscrutable eyes. Conan waded through the mist as through a surf, and his knife lunged upward like a live thing. The keen point ripped the Master's robe as he sprang back with a low cry. Then before Conan's gaze, the wizard vanished—simply disappeared like a burst bubble, and something long and undulating darted up one of the smaller stairs that led up to left and right from the landing.

Conan charged after it, up the left-hand stair, uncertain as to just what he had seen whip up those steps, but in a berserk mood that drowned the nausea and horror whispering at the back of his consciousness.

He plunged out into a broad corridor whose uncarpeted floor and untapestried walls were of polished jade, and something long and swift whisked down the corridor ahead of him, and into a curtained door. From within the chamber rose a scream of urgent terror. The sound lent wings to Conan's flying feet and he hurtled through the curtains and headlong into the chamber within.

A frightful scene met his glare. Yasmina cowered on the farther edge of a velvet-covered dais, screaming her loathing and horror, an arm lifted as if to ward off attack, while before her swayed the hideous head of a giant serpent, shining neck arching up from dark-gleaming coils. With a choked cry Conan threw his knife.

Instantly the monster whirled and was upon him like the rush of wind through tall grass. The long knife quivered in its neck, point and a foot of blade showing on one side, and the hilt and a hand's-breadth of steel on the other, but it only seemed to madden the giant reptile. The great head towered above the man who faced it, and then darted down, the venom-dripping jaws gaping wide. But Conan had plucked a dagger from his girdle and he stabbed upward as the head dipped down. The point tore through the lower jaw and transfixed the upper, pinning them together. The next instant the great trunk had looped itself about the Cimmerian as the snake, unable to use its fangs, employed its remaining form of attack.

Conan's left arm was pinioned among the bone-crushing folds, but his right was free. Bracing his feet to keep upright, he stretched forth his hand, gripped the hilt of the long knife jutting from the serpent's neck, and tore it free in a shower of blood. As if divining his purpose with more than bestial intelligence, the snake writhed and knotted, seeking to cast its loops about his right arm. But with the speed of light the long knife rose and fell, shearing halfway through the reptile's giant trunk.

Before he could strike again, the great pliant loops fell from him and the monster dragged itself across the floor, gushing blood from its ghastly wounds. Conan sprang after it, knife lifted, but his vicious swipe cut empty air as the serpent writhed away from him and struck its blunt nose against a paneled screen of sandalwood. One of the panels gave inward and the long, bleeding barrel whipped through it and was gone.

Conan instantly attacked the screen. A few blows rent it apart and he glared into the dim alcove beyond. No horrific shape coiled there; there was blood on the marble floor, and bloody tracks led to a cryptic arched door. Those tracks were of a man's bare feet....

'Conan!' He wheeled back into the chamber just in time to catch the Devi of Vendhya in his arms as she rushed across the room and threw herself upon him, catching him about the neck with a frantic clasp, half hysterical with terror and gratitude and relief.

His wild blood had been stirred to its uttermost by all that had passed. He caught her to him in a grasp that would have made her wince at another time, and crushed her lips with his. She made no resistance; the Devi was drowned in the elemental woman. She closed her eyes and drank in his fierce, hot, lawless kisses with all the abandon of passionate thirst. She was panting with his violence when he ceased for breath, and glared down at her lying limp in his mighty arms.

'I knew you'd come for me,' she murmured. 'You would not leave me in this den of devils.'

At her words recollection of their environment came to him suddenly. He lifted his head and listened intently. Silence reigned over the castle of Yimsha, but it was a silence impregnated with menace. Peril crouched in every corner, leered invisibly from every hanging.

'We'd better go while we can,' he muttered. 'Those cuts were enough to kill any common beast—or *man*—but a wizard has a dozen lives. Wound one, and he writhes away like a crippled snake to soak up fresh venom from some source of sorcery.'

He picked up the girl and carrying her in his arms like a child, he strode out into the gleaming jade corridor and down the stairs, nerves tautly alert for any sign or sound.

'I met the Master,' she whispered, clinging to him and shuddering. 'He worked his spells on me to break my will. The most awful thing was a moldering corpse which seized me in its arms—I fainted then and lay as one dead, I do not know how long. Shortly after I regained consciousness I heard sounds of strife below, and cries, and then that snake came slithering through the curtains—ah!' She shook at the memory of that horror. 'I knew somehow that it was not an illusion, but a real serpent that sought my life.'

'It was not a shadow, at least,' answered Conan cryptically. 'He knew he was beaten, and chose to slay you rather than let you be rescued.'

'What do you mean, *he*?' she asked uneasily, and then shrank against him, crying out, and forgetting her question. She had seen the corpses at the foot of the stairs. Those of the Seers were not good to look at; as they lay twisted and contorted, their hands and feet were exposed to view, and at the sight Yasmina went livid and hid her face against Conan's powerful shoulder.

10 YASMINA AND CONAN

Conan passed through the hall quickly enough, traverse the outer chamber and approached the door that led upo the gallery. Then he saw the floor sprinkled with tiny, glitterin shards. The crystal sheet that had covered the doorway ha been shivered to bits, and he remembered the crash that ha accompanied the shattering of the crystal globe. He believe that every piece of crystal in the castle had broken at tha instant, and some dim instinct or memory of esoteric lor vaguely suggested the truth of the monstrous connectio between the Lords of the Black Circle and the golde pomegranates. He felt the short hair bristle chilly at the bac of his neck and put the matter hastily out of his mind.

He breathed a deep sigh of relief as he stepped out upo the green jade gallery. There was still the gorge to cross, but a least he could see the white peaks glistening in the sun, an the long slopes falling away into the distant blue hazes.

The Irakzai lay where he had fallen, an ugly blotch on th glassy smoothness. As Conan strode down the winding patl he was surprised to note the position of the sun. It had no yet passed its zenith; and yet it seemed to him that hours ha passed since he plunged into the castle of the Black Seers.

He felt an urge to hasten, not a mere blind panic, but a instinct of peril growing behind his back. He said nothing t Yasmina, and she seemed content to nestle her dark hea against his arching breast and find security in the clasp of h iron arms. He paused an instant on the brink of the chasm frowning down. The haze which danced in the gorge was n longer rose-hued and sparkling. It was smoky, dim, ghostl like the life-tide that flickered thinly in a wounded man. Th thought came vaguely to Conan that the spells of magiciar were more closely bound to their personal beings than wer the actions of common men to the actors.

But far below, the floor shone like tarnished silver, and th gold thread sparkled undimmed. Conan shifted Yasmin across his shoulder, where she lay docilely, and began th descent. Hurriedly he descended the ramp, and hurriedl he fled across the echoing floor. He had a conviction tha they were racing with time, that their chances of surviva depended upon crossing that gorge of horrors before th wounded Master of the castle should regain enough powe to loose some other doom upon them.

When he toiled up the farther ramp and came out upo the crest, he breathed a gusty sigh of relief and stood Yasmin upon her feet. 'You walk from here,' he told her; 'it's downh. all the way.'

She stole a glance at the gleaming pyramid across th chasm; it reared up against the snowy slope like the citadel c silence and immemorial evil.

'Are you a magician, that you have conquered the Blac Seers of Yimsha, Conan of Ghor?' she asked, as they wer down the path, with his heavy arm about her supple waist.

'It was a girdle Khemsa gave me before he died,' Cona answered. 'Yes, I found him on the trail. It is a curious one which I'll show you when I have time. Against some spells i was weak, but against others it was strong, and a good knife i always a hearty incantation.'

'But if the girdle aided you in conquering the Master,' sh argued, 'why did it not aid Khemsa?'

He shook his head. 'Who knows? But Khemsa had bee the Master's slave; perhaps that weakened its magic. He ha no hold on me as he had on Khemsa. Yet I can't say that conquered him. He retreated, but I have a feeling that w haven't seen the last of him. I want to put as many mile between us and his lair as we can.'

He was further relieved to find horses tethered among th tamarisks as he had left them. He loosed them swiftly an mounted the black stallion, swinging the girl up before hin The others followed, freshened by their rest.

'And what now?' she asked. 'To Afghulistan?'

'Not just now!' He grinned hardly. 'Somebody—maybe th governor—killed my seven headmen. My idiotic follower think I had something to do with it, and unless I am able to convince them otherwise, they'll hunt me like a wounded jackal.'

'Then what of me? If the headmen are dead, I am useless to you as a hostage. Will you slay me, to avenge them?' He looked down at her, with eyes fiercely aglow, and laughed at the suggestion.

'Then let us ride to the border,' she said. 'You'll be safe from the Afghulis there—' 'Yes, on a Vendhyan gibbet.'

'I am Queen of Vendhya,' she reminded him with a touch of her old imperiousness. 'You have saved my life. You shall be rewarded.' She did not intend it as it sounded, but he growled in his throat, ill pleased.

'Keep your bounty for your city-bred dogs, princess! If you're a queen of the plains, I'm a chief of the hills, and not one foot toward the border will I take you!' 'But you would be safe—' she began bewilderedly.

'And you'd be the Devi again,' he broke in. 'No, girl; I prefer you as you are now—a woman of flesh and blood, riding on my saddle-bow.' 'But you can't *keep* me!' she cried. 'You can't—'

'Watch and see!' he advised grimly. 'But I will pay you a vast ransom—'

'Devil take your ransom!' he answered roughly, his arms hardening about her supple figure. 'The kingdom of Vendhya could give me nothing I desire half so much as I desire you. I took you at the risk of my neck; if your courtiers want you back, let them come up the Zhaibar and fight for you.'

'But you have no followers now!' she protested. 'You are hunted! How can you preserve your own life, much less mine?'

'I still have friends in the hills,' he answered. 'There is a chief of the Khurakzai who will keep you safely while I bicker with the Afghulis. If they will have none of me, by Crom! I will ride northward with you to the steppes of the *kozaki*. I was a hetman among the Free Companions before I rode southward. I'll make you a queen on the Zaporoska River!'

'But I can not!' she objected. 'You must not hold me—'

'If the idea's so repulsive,' he demanded, 'why did you yield your lips to me so willingly?'

'Even a queen is human,' she answered, coloring. 'But because I am a queen, I must consider my kingdom. Do not carry me away into some foreign country. Come back to Vendhya with me!' 'Would you make me your king?' he asked sardonically.

'Well, there are customs—' she stammered, and he interrupted her with a hard laugh.

'Yes, civilized customs that won't let you do as you wish. You'll marry some withered old king of the plains, and I can go my way with only the memory of a few kisses snatched from your lips. Ha!' 'But I must return to my kingdom!' she repeated helplessly.

'Why?' he demanded angrily. 'To chafe your rump on cold thrones, and listen to the plaudits of smirking, velvet-skirted fools? Where is the gain? Listen: I was born in the Cimmerian hills where the people are all barbarians. I have been a mercenary soldier, a corsair, a *kozak*, and a hundred other things. What king has roamed the countries, fought the battles, loved the women, and won the plunder that I have?

'I came into Ghulistan to raise a horde and plunder the kingdoms to the south—your own among them. Being chief of the Afghulis was only a start. If I can conciliate them, I'll have a dozen tribes following me within a year. But if I can't I'll ride back to the steppes and loot the Turanian borders with the *kozaki*. And you'll go with me. To the devil with your kingdom; they fended for themselves before you were born.'

She lay in his arms looking up at him, and she felt a tug at her spirit, a lawless, reckless urge that matched his own and was by it called into being. But a thousand generations of sovereignship rode heavy upon her. 'I can't! I can't!' she repeated helplessly.

'You haven't any choice,' he assured her. 'You—what the devil!'

They had left Yimsha some miles behind them, and were riding along a high ridge that separated two deep valleys. They had just topped a steep crest where they could gaze down into the valley on their right hand. And there was a running fight in progress. A strong wind was blowing away from them, carrying the sound from their ears, but even so the clashing of steel and thunder of hoofs welled up from far below.

They saw the glint of the sun on lance-tip and spired helmet. Three thousand mailed horsemen were driving before them a ragged band of turbaned riders, who fled snarling and striking like fleeing wolves. 'Turanians,' muttered Conan. 'Squadrons from Secunderam. What the devil are they doing here?'

'Who are the men they pursue?' asked Yasmina. 'And why do they fall back so stubbornly? They can not stand against such odds.'

'Five hundred of my mad Afghulis,' he growled, scowling down into the vale. 'They're in a trap, and they know it.'

The valley was indeed a cul-de-sac at that end. It narrowed to a high-walled gorge, opening out further into a round bowl, completely rimmed with lofty, unscalable walls.

The turbaned riders were being forced into this gorge, because there was nowhere else for them to go, and they went reluctantly, in a shower of arrows and a whirl of swords. The helmeted riders harried them, but did not press in too rashly. They knew the desperate fury of the hill tribes, and they knew too that they had their prey in a trap from which there was no escape. They had recognized the hill-men as Afghulis, and they wished to hem them in and force a surrender. They needed hostages for the purpose they had in mind.

Their emir was a man of decision and initiative. When he reached the Gurashah valley, and found neither guides nor emissary waiting for him, he pushed on, trusting to his own knowledge of the country. All the way from Secunderam there had been fighting, and tribesmen were licking their wounds in many a crag-perched village. He knew there was a good chance that neither he nor any of his helmeted spearmen would ever ride through the gates of Secunderam again, for the tribes would all be up behind him now, but he was determined to carry out his orders—which were to take Yasmina Devi from the Afghulis at all costs, and to bring her captive to Secunderam, or if confronted by impossibility, to strike off her head before he himself died.

Of all this, of course, the watchers on the ridge were not aware. But Conan fidgeted with nervousness.

'Why the devil did they get themselves trapped?' he demanded of the universe at large. 'I know what they're doing in these parts—they were hunting me, the dogs! Poking into every valley—and found themselves penned in before they knew it. The poor fools! They're making a stand in the gorge, but they can't hold out for long. When the Turanians have pushed them back into the bowl, they'll slaughter them at their leisure.'

The din welling up from below increased in volume and intensity. In the strait of the narrow gut, the Afghulis, fighting desperately, were for the time holding their own against the mailed riders, who could not throw their whole weight against them.

Conan scowled darkly, moved restlessly, fingering his hilt, and finally spoke bluntly: 'Devi, I must go down to them. I'll find a place for you to hide until I come back to you. You spoke of your kingdom—well, I don't pretend to look on those hairy devils as my children, but after all, such as they are, they're my henchmen. A chief should never desert his followers, even if they desert him first. They think they were right in kicking me out—hell, I won't be cast off! I'm still chief of the Afghulis, and I'll prove it! I can climb down on foot into the gorge.'

'But what of me?' she queried. 'You carried me away forcibly from *my* people; now will you leave me to die in the hills alone while you go down and sacrifice yourself uselessly?' His veins swelled with the conflict of his emotions.

'That's right,' he muttered helplessly. 'Crom knows what I *can* do.'

She turned her head slightly, a curious expression dawning on her beautiful face. Then:

'Listen!' she cried. 'Listen!'

A distant fanfare of trumpets was borne faintly to their ears. They stared into the deep valley on the left, and caught a glint of steel on the farther side. A long line of lances and polished helmets moved along the vale, gleaming in the sunlight.

'The riders of Vendhya!' she cried exultingly.

'There are thousands of them!' muttered Conan. 'It has been long since a Kshatriya host has ridden this far into the hills.'

'They are searching for me!' she exclaimed. 'Give me your horse! I will ride to my warriors! The ridge is not so precipitous on the left, and I can reach the valley floor. I will lead my horsemen into the valley at the upper end and fall upon the Turanians! We will crush them in the vise! Quick, Conan! Will you sacrifice your men to your own desire?'

The burning hunger of the steppes and the wintry forests glared out of his eyes, but he shook his head and swung off the stallion, placing the reins in her hands. 'You win!' he grunted. 'Ride like the devil!'

She wheeled away down the left-hand slope and he ran swiftly along the ridge until he reached the long ragged cleft that was the defile in which the fight raged. Down the rugged wall he scrambled like an ape, clinging to projections and crevices, to fall at last, feet first, into the mêlée that raged in the mouth of the gorge. Blades were whickering and clanging about him, horses rearing and stamping, helmet plumes nodding among turbans that were stained crimson.

As he hit, he yelled like a wolf, caught a gold-worked rein, and dodging the sweep of a scimitar, drove his long knife upward through the rider's vitals. In another instant he was in the saddle, yelling ferocious orders to the Afghulis. They stared at him stupidly for an instant; then as they saw the havoc his steel was wreaking among their enemies, they fell to their work again, accepting him without comment. In that inferno of licking blades and spurting blood there was no time to ask or answer questions.

The riders in their spired helmets and gold-worked hauberks swarmed about the gorge mouth, thrusting and slashing, and the narrow defile was packed and jammed with horses and men, the warriors crushed breast to breast, stabbing with shortened blades, slashing murderously when there was an instant's room to swing a sword. When a man went down he did not get up from beneath the stamping, swirling hoofs. Weight and sheer strength counted heavily there, and the chief of the Afghulis did the work of ten. At such times accustomed habits sway men strongly, and the warriors, who were used to seeing Conan in their vanguard, were heartened mightily, despite their distrust of him.

But superior numbers counted too. The pressure of the men behind forced the horsemen of Turan deeper and deeper into the gorge, in the teeth of the flickering tulwars. Foot by foot the Afghulis were shoved back, leaving the defile-floor carpeted with dead, on which the riders trampled. As he hacked and smote like a man possessed, Conan had time for some chilling doubts—would Yasmina keep her word? She had but to join her warriors, turn southward and leave him and his band to perish.

But at last, after what seemed centuries of desperate battling, in the valley outside there rose another sound above the clash of steel and yells of slaughter. And then with a burst of trumpets that shook the walls, and rushing thunder of hoofs, five thousand riders of Vendhya smote the hosts of Secunderam.

That stroke split the Turanian squadrons asunder, shattered, tore and rent them and scattered their fragments all over the valley. In an instant the surge had ebbed back out of the gorge; there was a chaotic, confused swirl of fighting, horsemen wheeling and smiting singly and in clusters, and then the emir went down with a Kshatriya lance through his breast, and the

riders in their spired helmets turned their horses down the valley, spurring like mad and seeking to slash a way through the swarms which had come upon them from the rear. As they scattered in flight, the conquerors scattered in pursuit and all across the valley floor, and up on the slopes near the mouth and over the crests streamed the fugitives and the pursuers. The Afghulis, those left to ride, rushed out of the gorge and joined in the harrying of their foes, accepting the unexpected alliance as unquestioningly as they had accepted the return of their repudiated chief.

The sun was sinking toward the distant crags when Conan, his garments hacked to tatters and the mail under them reeking and clotted with blood, his knife dripping and crusted to the hilt, strode over the corpses to where Yasmina Devi sat her horse among her nobles on the crest of the ridge, near a lofty precipice.

'You kept your word, Devi!' he roared. 'By Crom, though, I had some bad seconds down in that gorge—*look out!*'

Down from the sky swooped a vulture of tremendous size, with a thunder of wings that knocked men sprawling from their horses.

The scimitar-like beak was slashing for the Devi's soft neck, but Conan was quicker—a short run, a tigerish leap, the savage thrust of a dripping knife, and the vulture voiced a horribly human cry, pitched sideways and went tumbling down the cliffs to the rocks and river a thousand feet below. As it dropped, its black wings thrashing the air, it took on the semblance, not of a bird, but of a black-robed human body that fell, arms in wide black sleeves thrown abroad.

Conan turned to Yasmina, his red knife still in his hand, his blue eyes smoldering, blood oozing from wounds on his thickly muscled arms and thighs.

'You are the Devi again,' he said, grinning fiercely at the gold-clasped gossamer robe she had donned over her hill-girl attire, and awed not at all by the imposing array of chivalry about him. 'I have you to thank for the lives of some three hundred and fifty of my rogues, who are at least convinced that I didn't betray them. You have put my hands on the reins of conquest again.'

'I still owe you my ransom,' she said, her dark eyes glowing as they swept over him. 'Ten thousand pieces of gold I will pay you—' He made a savage, impatient gesture, shook the blood from his knife and thrust it back in its scabbard, wiping his hands on his mail.

'I will collect your ransom in my own way, at my own time,' he said. 'I will collect it in your palace at Ayodhya, and I will come with fifty thousand men to see that the scales are fair.' She laughed, gathering her reins into her hands. 'And I will meet you on the shores of the Jhumda with a hundred thousand!'

His eyes shone with fierce appreciation and admiration, and stepping back, he lifted his hand with a gesture that was like the assumption of kingship, indicating that her road was clear before her.

THE END

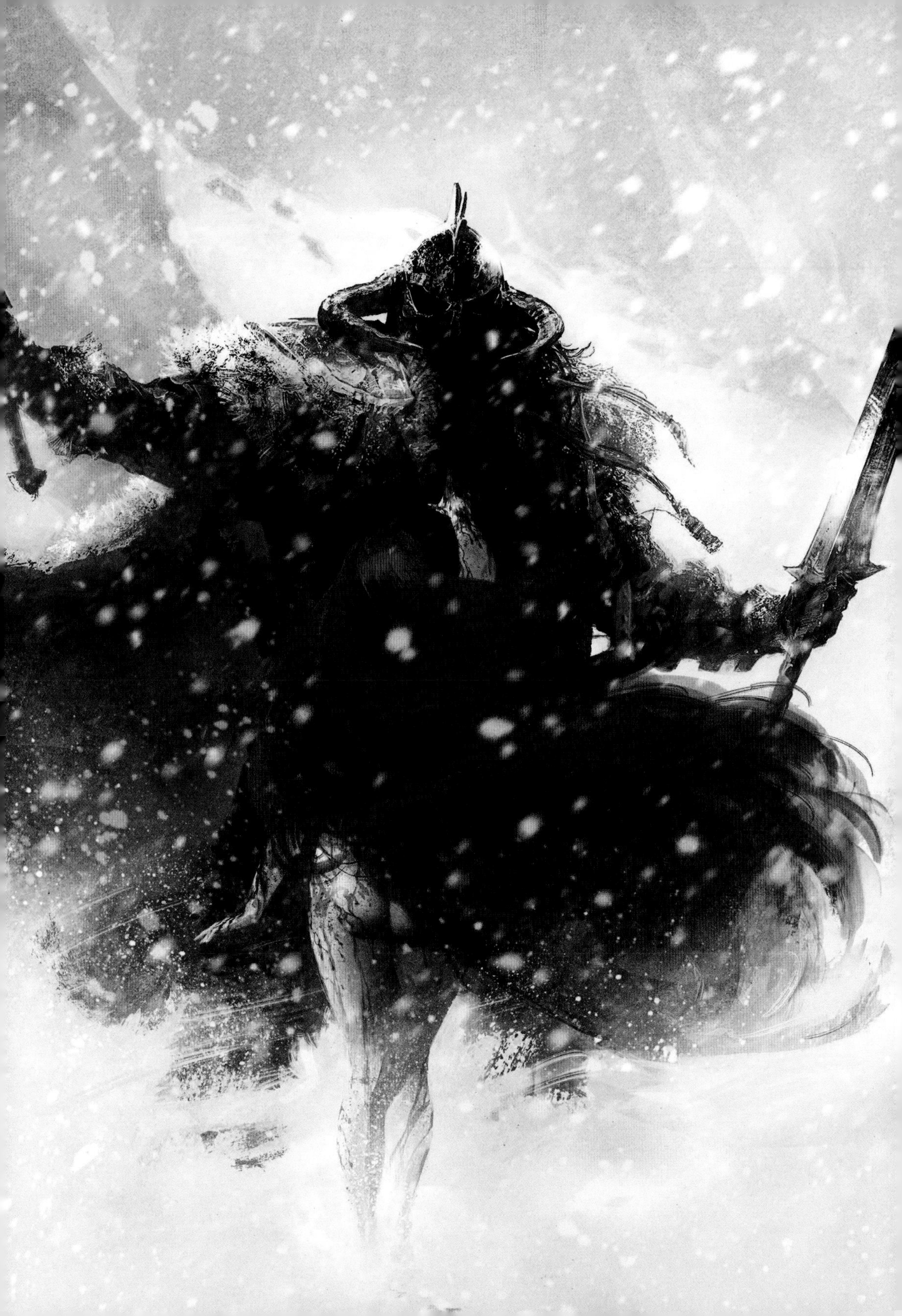

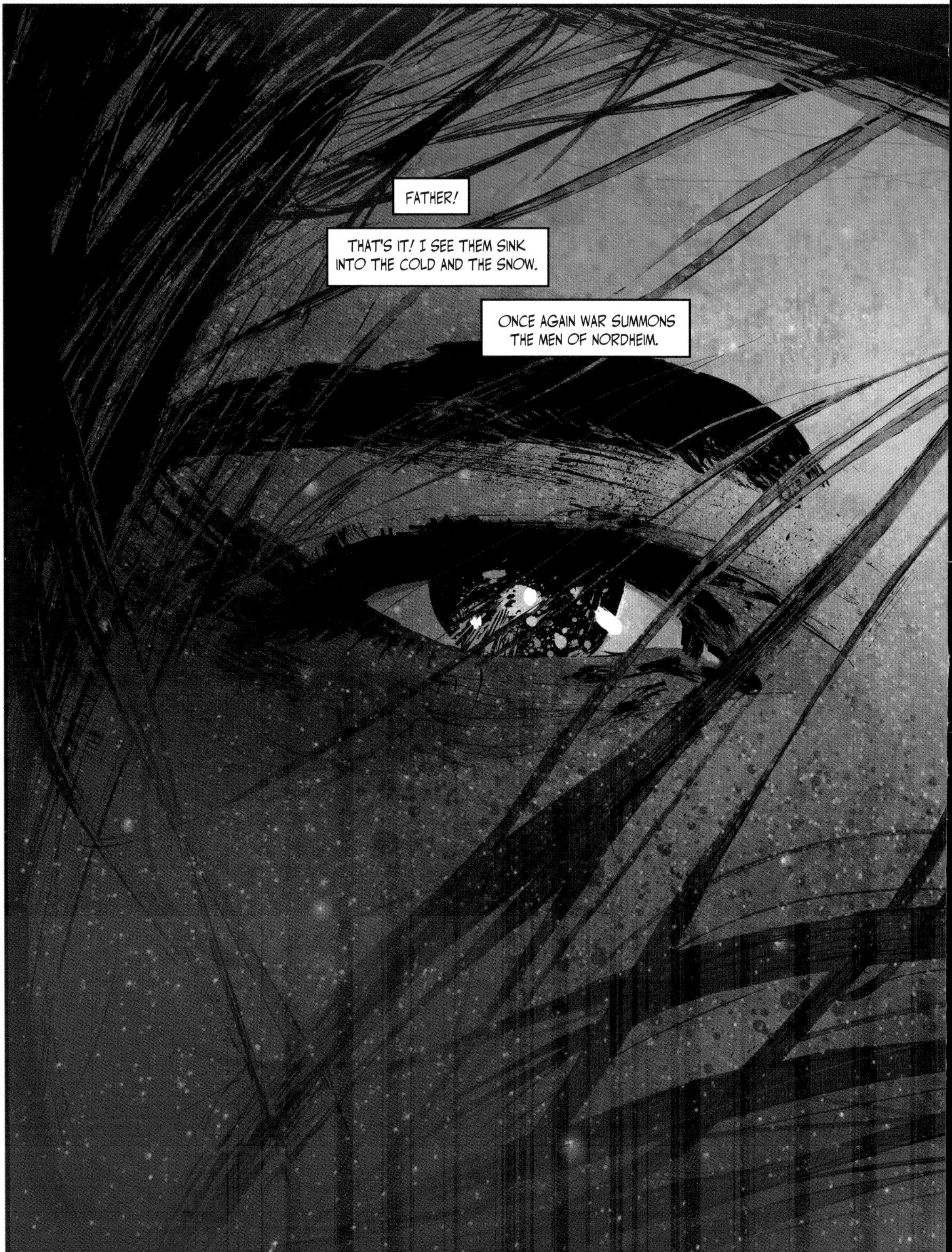
FATHER!
THAT'S IT! I SEE THEM SINK INTO THE COLD AND THE SNOW.
ONCE AGAIN WAR SUMMONS THE MEN OF NORDHEIM.

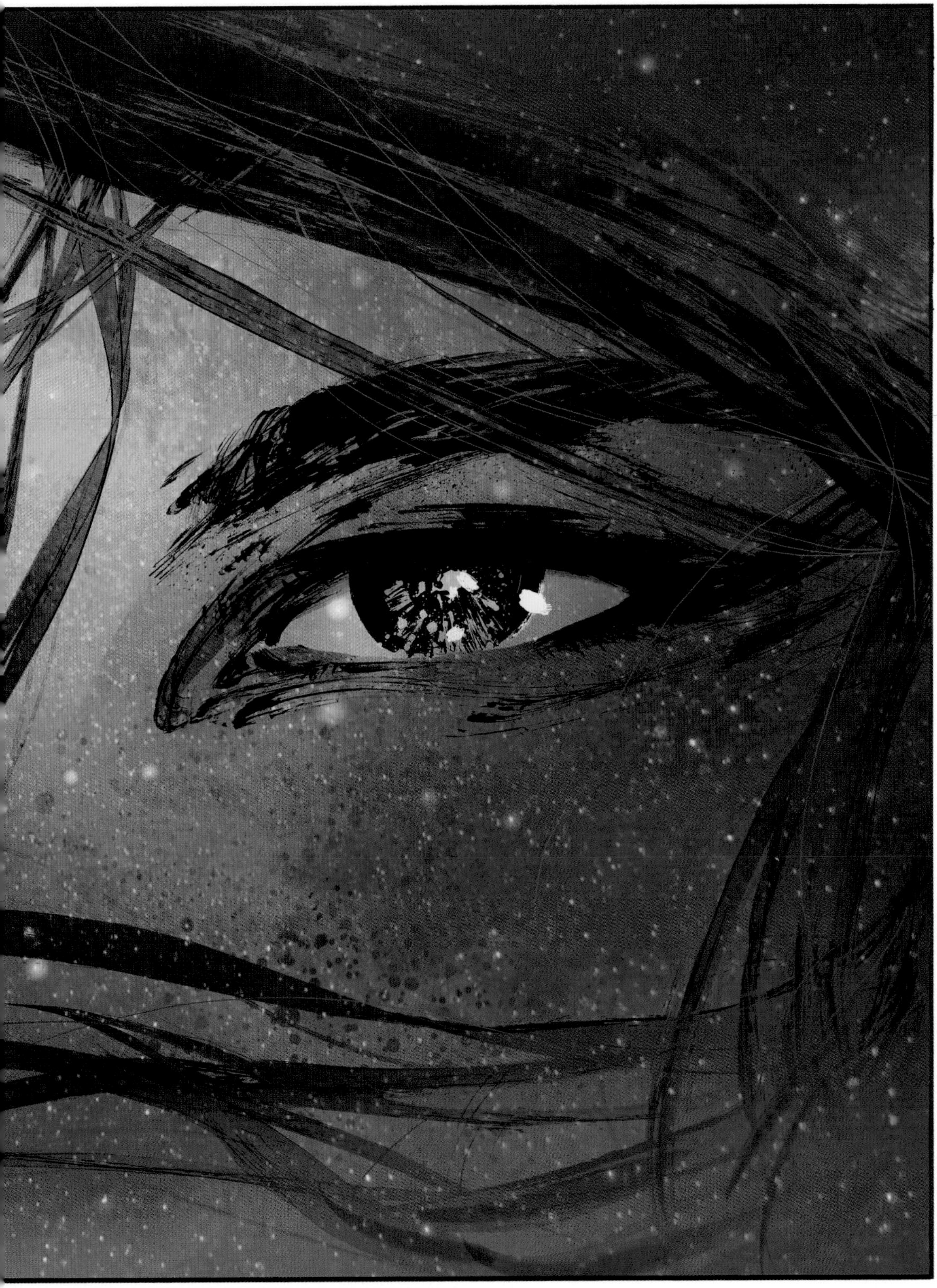

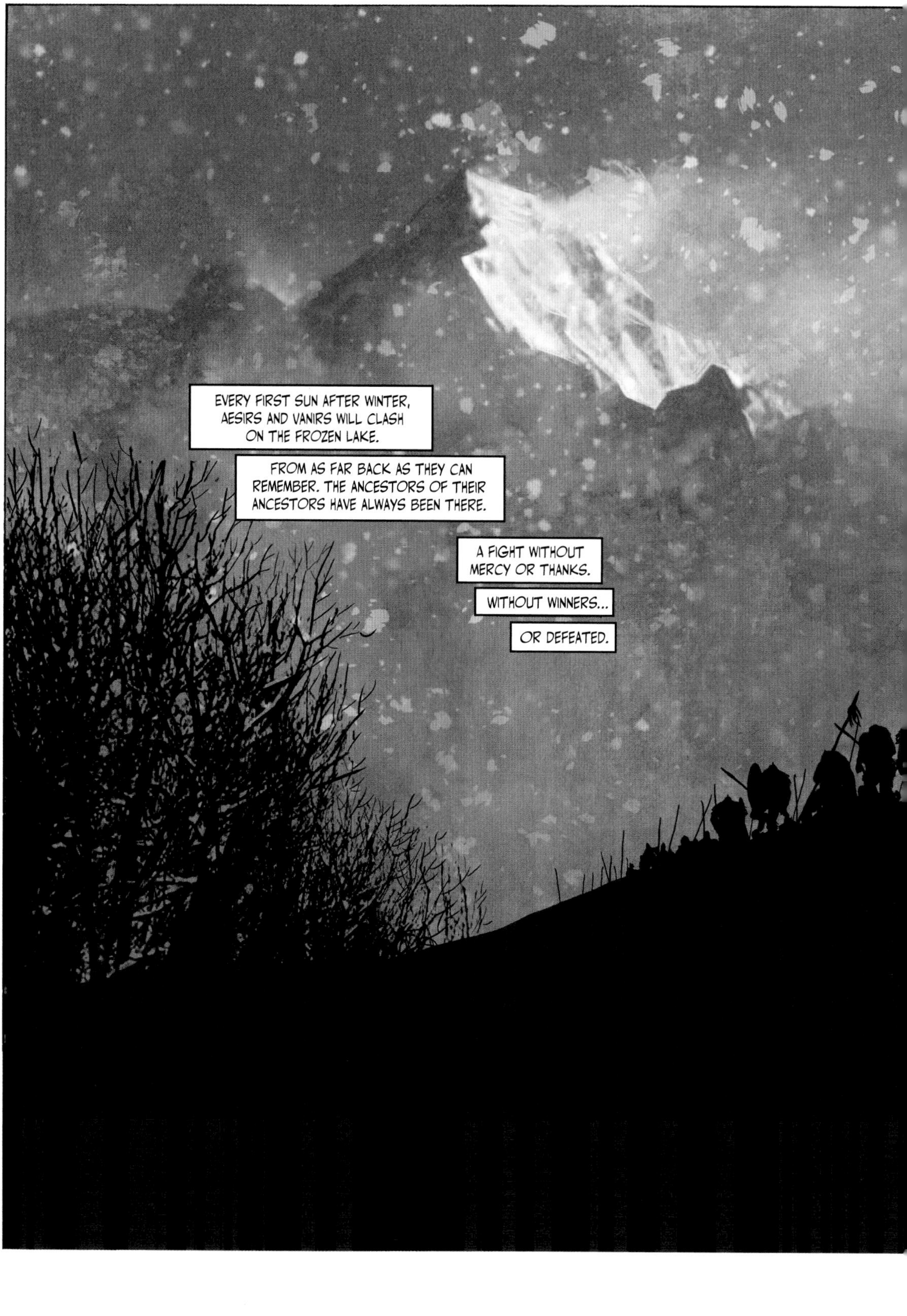
EVERY FIRST SUN AFTER WINTER, AESIRS AND VANIRS WILL CLASH ON THE FROZEN LAKE.
FROM AS FAR BACK AS THEY CAN REMEMBER. THE ANCESTORS OF THEIR ANCESTORS HAVE ALWAYS BEEN THERE.
A FIGHT WITHOUT MERCY OR THANKS.
WITHOUT WINNERS...
OR DEFEATED.

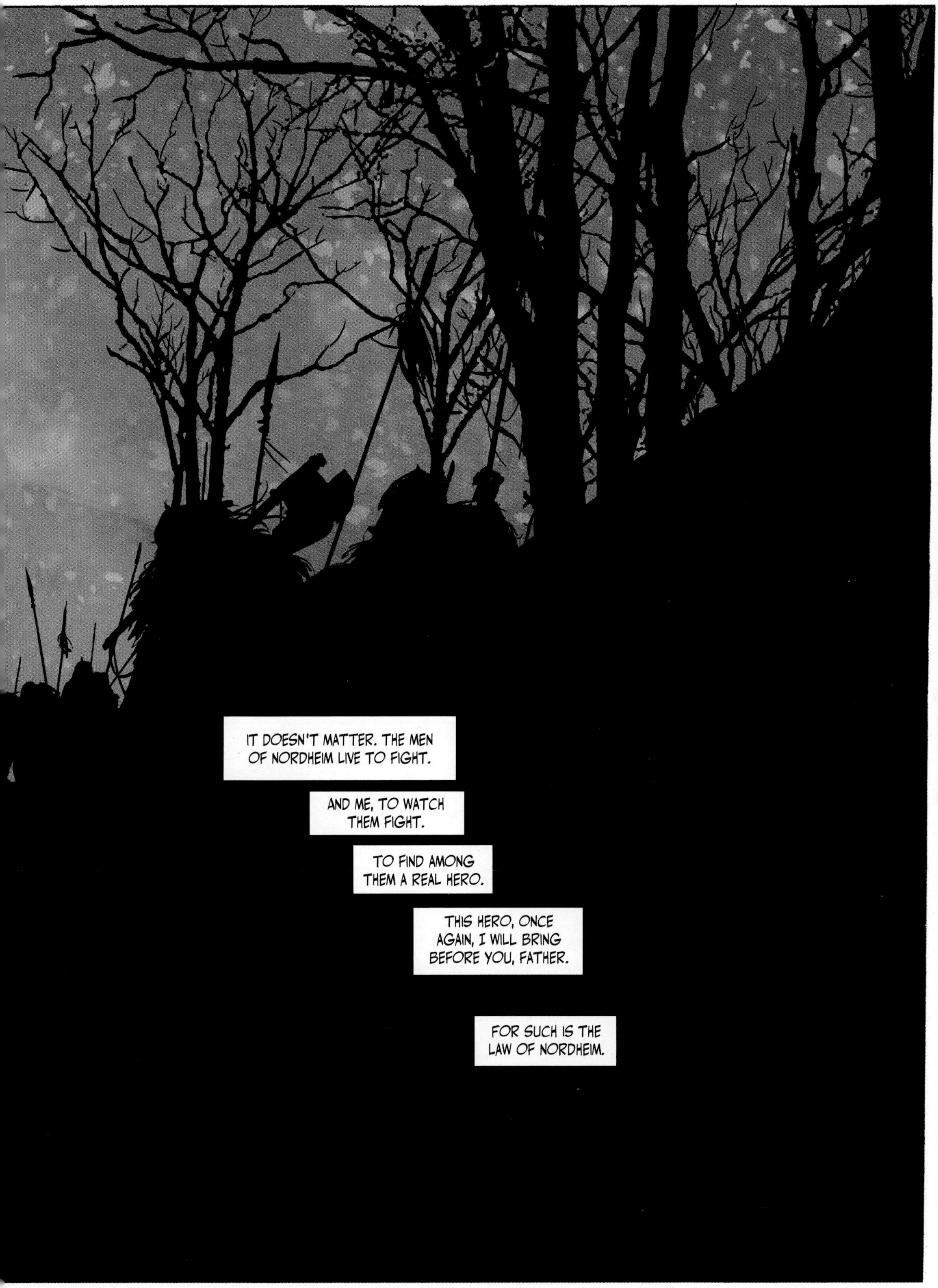
IT DOESN'T MATTER. THE MEN OF NORDHEIM LIVE TO FIGHT.
AND ME, TO WATCH THEM FIGHT.
TO FIND AMONG THEM A REAL HERO.
THIS HERO, ONCE AGAIN, I WILL BRING BEFORE YOU, FATHER.
FOR SUCH IS THE LAW OF NORDHEIM.

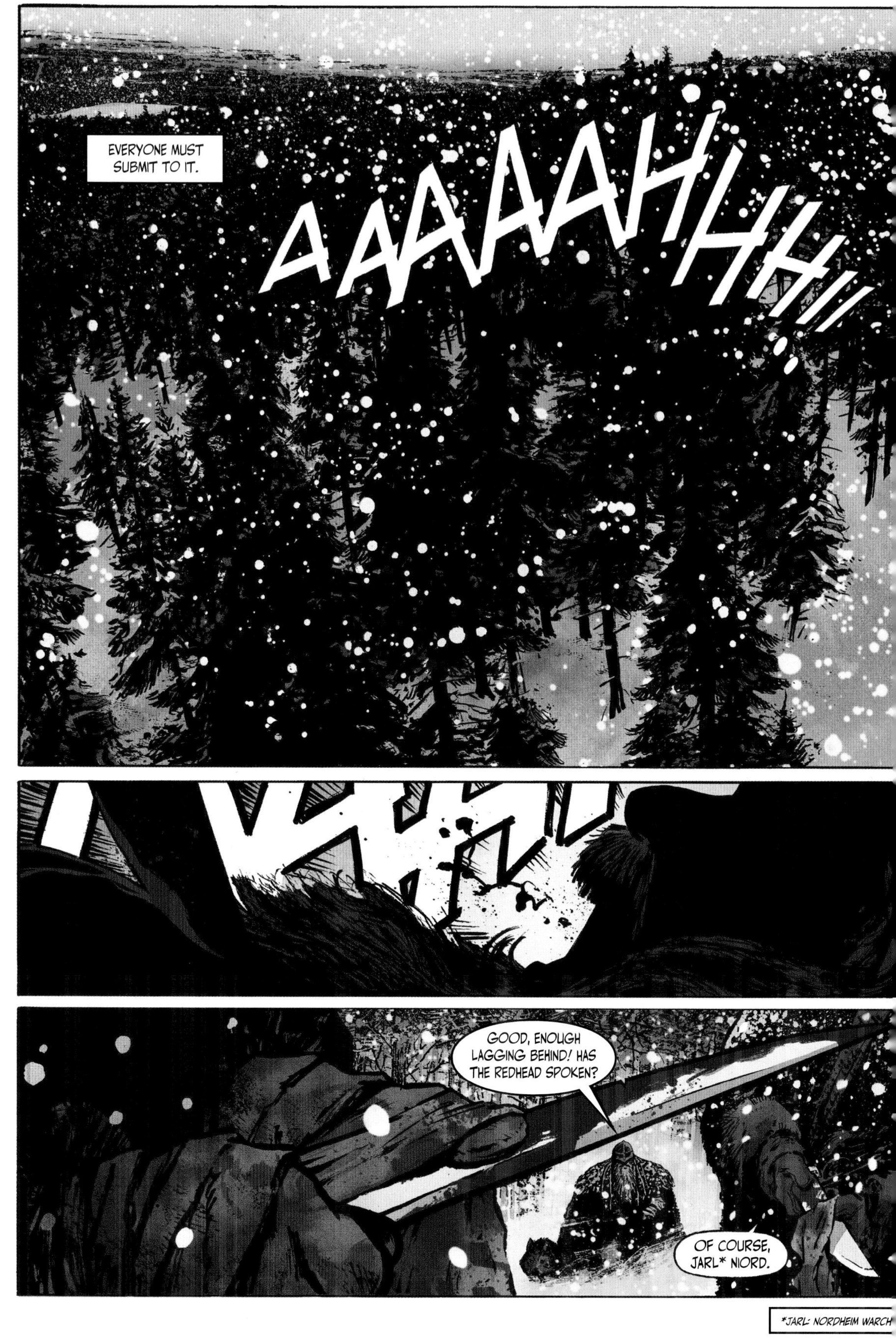
EVERYONE MUST SUBMIT TO IT.
AAAAAHHHH!!
GOOD, ENOUGH LAGGING BEHIND! HAS THE REDHEAD SPOKEN?
OF COURSE, JARL* NIORD.

*JARL: NORDHEIM WARCH

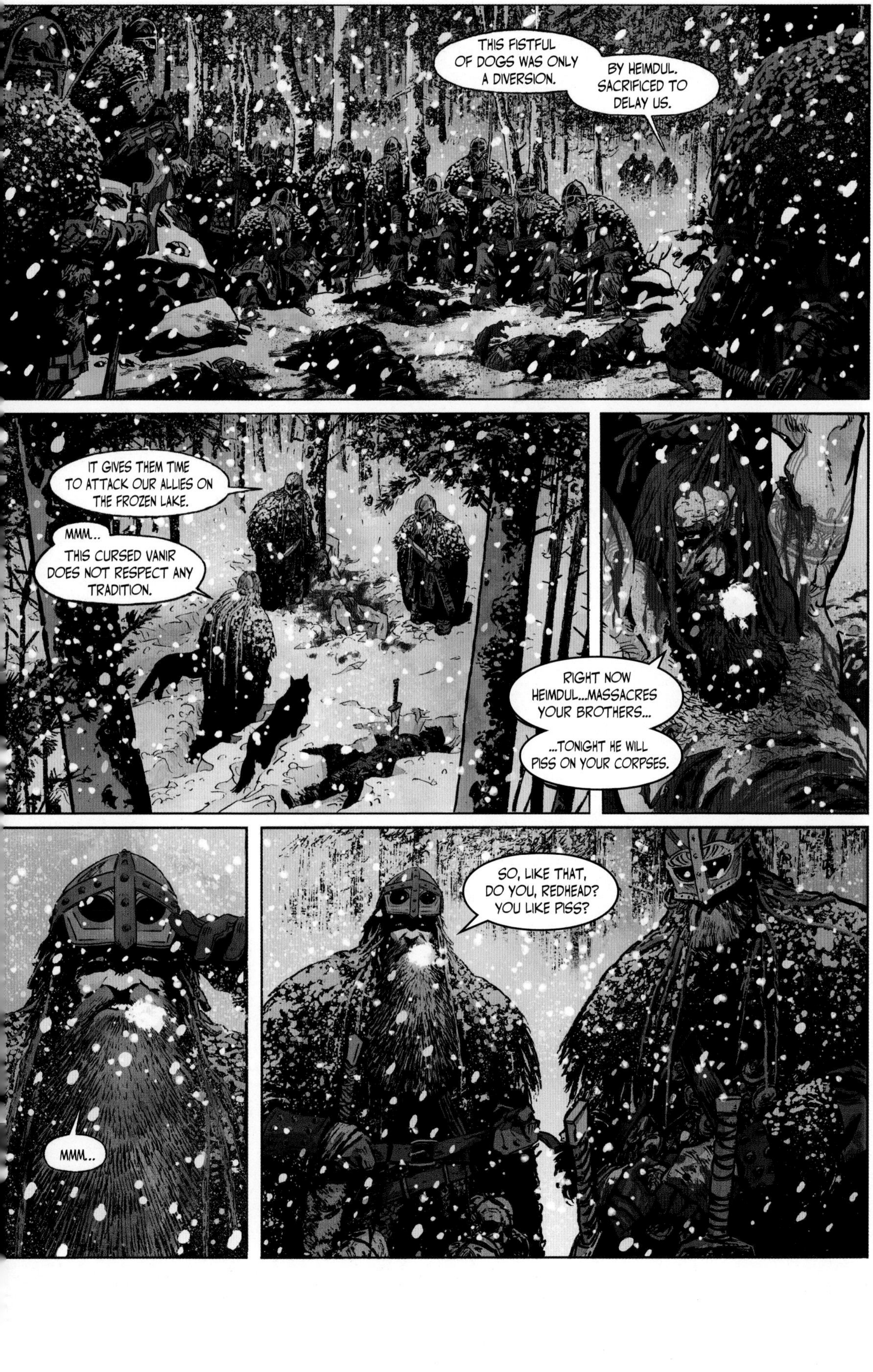
THIS FISTFUL OF DOGS WAS ONLY A DIVERSION.
BY HEIMDUL. SACRIFICED TO DELAY US.
IT GIVES THEM TIME TO ATTACK OUR ALLIES ON THE FROZEN LAKE.
MMM...
THIS CURSED VANIR DOES NOT RESPECT ANY TRADITION.
RIGHT NOW HEIMDUL...MASSACRES YOUR BROTHERS...
...TONIGHT HE WILL PISS ON YOUR CORPSES.
MMM...
SO, LIKE THAT, DO YOU, REDHEAD? YOU LIKE PISS?

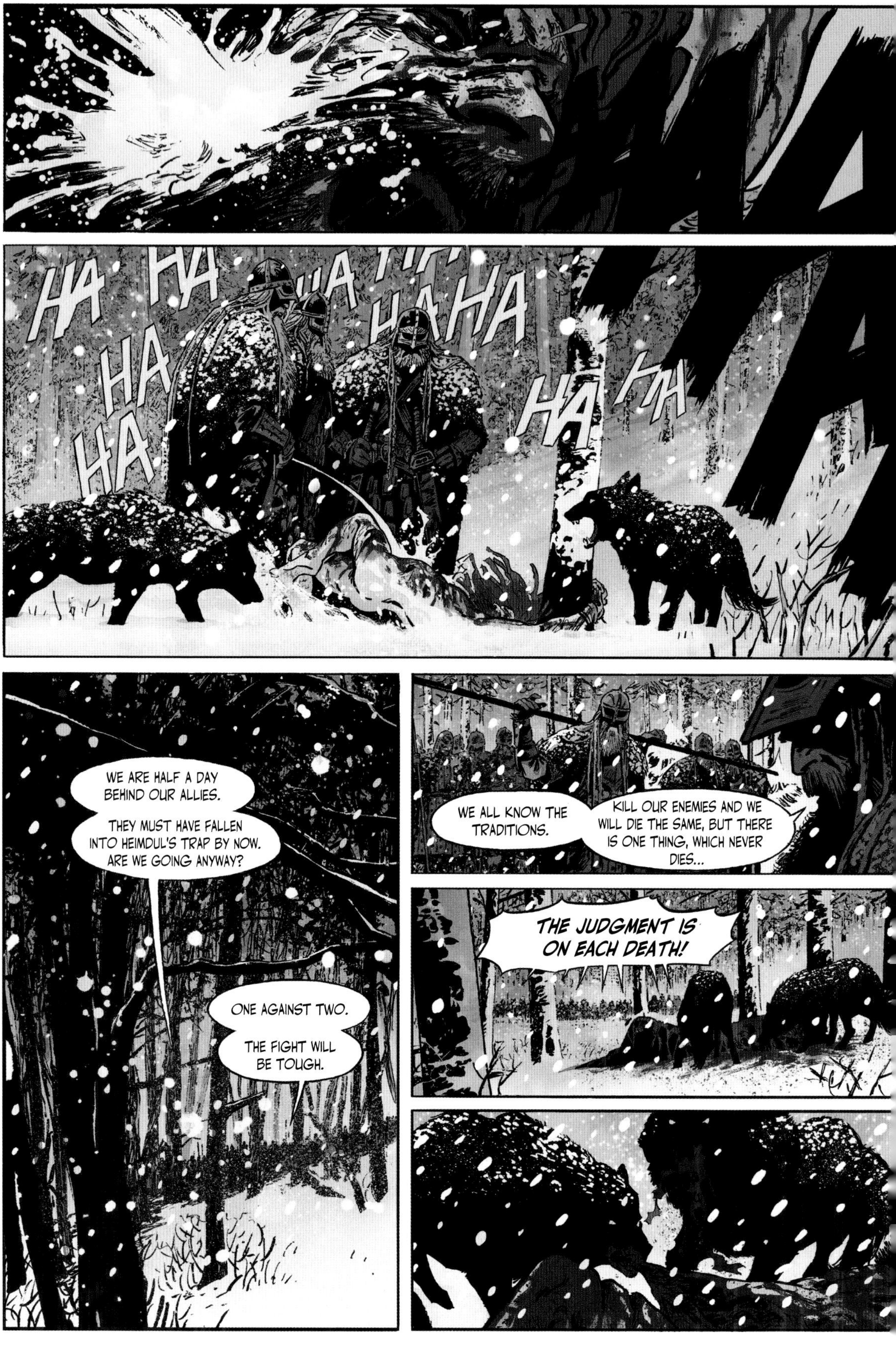
HA HA HA HA HA HA HA HAHA HA HA
WE ARE HALF A DAY BEHIND OUR ALLIES.
THEY MUST HAVE FALLEN INTO HEIMDUL'S TRAP BY NOW. ARE WE GOING ANYWAY?
ONE AGAINST TWO.
THE FIGHT WILL BE TOUGH.
WE ALL KNOW THE TRADITIONS.
KILL OUR ENEMIES AND WE WILL DIE THE SAME, BUT THERE IS ONE THING, WHICH NEVER DIES...
THE JUDGMENT IS ON EACH DEATH!

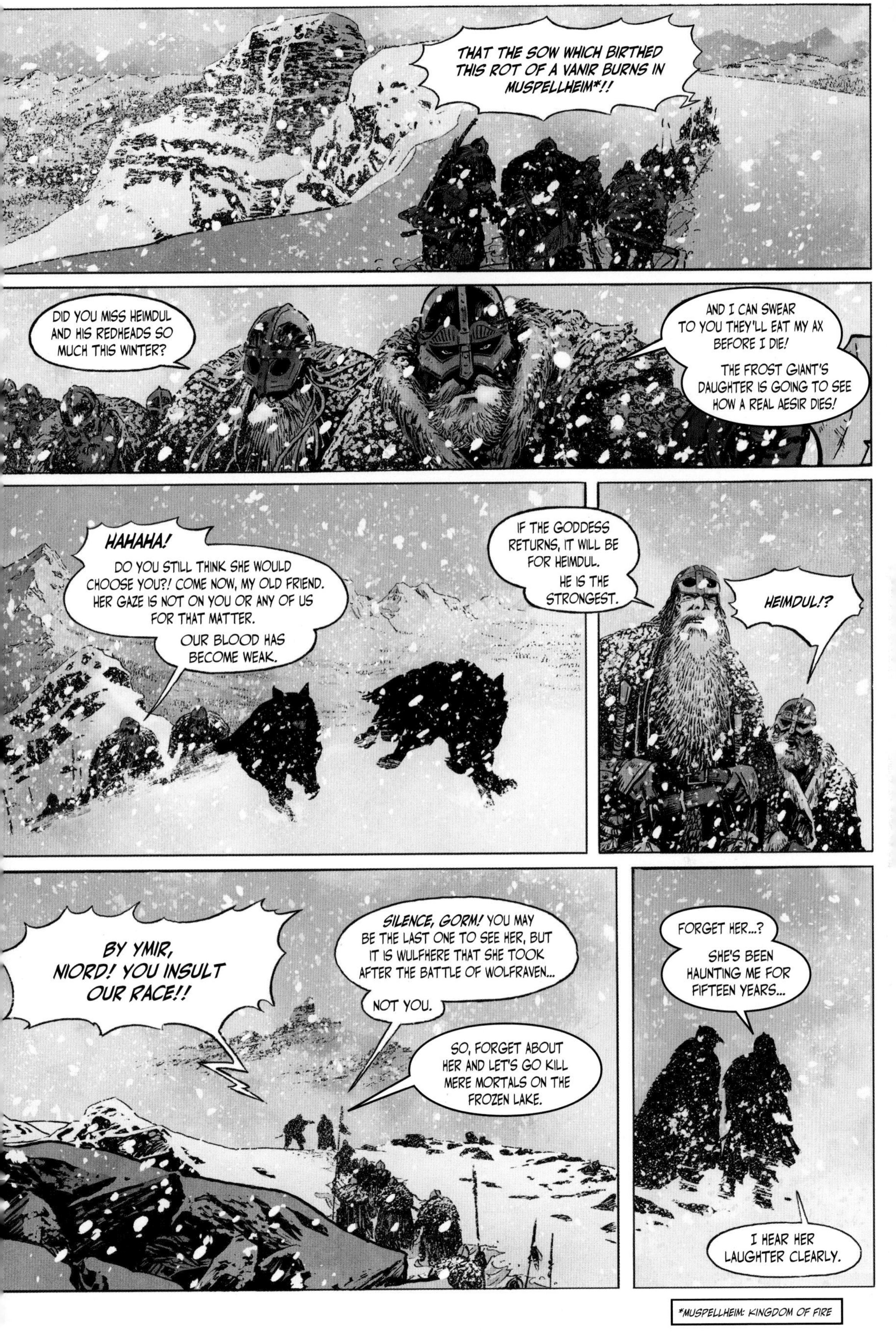
THAT THE SOW WHICH BIRTHED THIS ROT OF A VANIR BURNS IN MUSPELLHEIM*!!
DID YOU MISS HEIMDUL AND HIS REDHEADS SO MUCH THIS WINTER?
AND I CAN SWEAR TO YOU THEY'LL EAT MY AX BEFORE I DIE!
THE FROST GIANT'S DAUGHTER IS GOING TO SEE HOW A REAL AESIR DIES!
HAHAHA!
DO YOU STILL THINK SHE WOULD CHOOSE YOU?! COME NOW, MY OLD FRIEND. HER GAZE IS NOT ON YOU OR ANY OF US FOR THAT MATTER.
OUR BLOOD HAS BECOME WEAK.
IF THE GODDESS RETURNS, IT WILL BE FOR HEIMDUL.
HE IS THE STRONGEST.
HEIMDUL!?
BY YMIR, NIORD! YOU INSULT OUR RACE!!
SILENCE, GORM! YOU MAY BE THE LAST ONE TO SEE HER, BUT IT IS WULFHERE THAT SHE TOOK AFTER THE BATTLE OF WOLFRAVEN...
NOT YOU.
SO, FORGET ABOUT HER AND LET'S GO KILL MERE MORTALS ON THE FROZEN LAKE.
FORGET HER...?
SHE'S BEEN HAUNTING ME FOR FIFTEEN YEARS...
I HEAR HER LAUGHTER CLEARLY.

*MUSPELLHEIM: KINGDOM OF FIRE

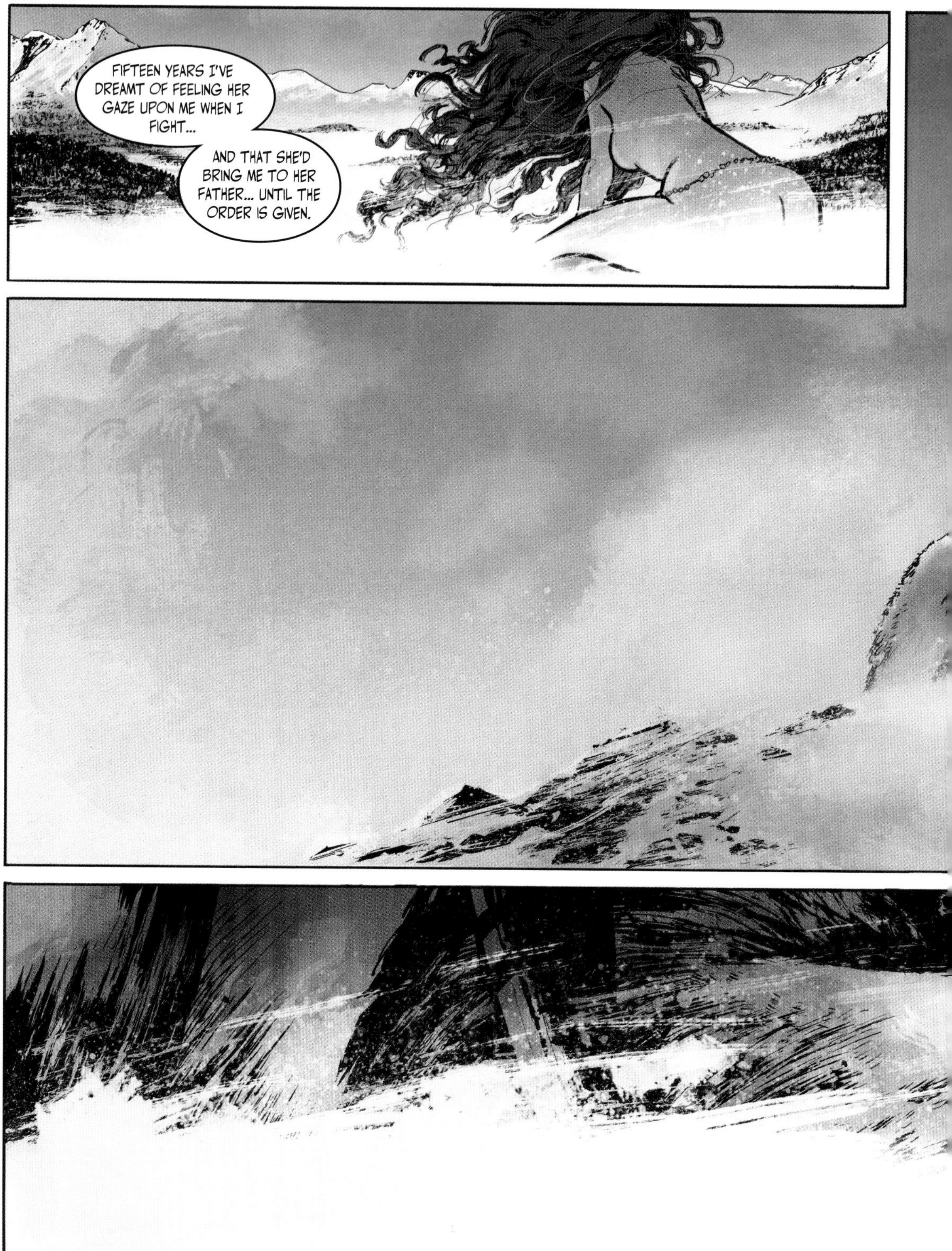
FIFTEEN YEARS I'VE DREAMT OF FEELING HER GAZE UPON ME WHEN I FIGHT...
AND THAT SHE'D BRING ME TO HER FATHER... UNTIL THE ORDER IS GIVEN.

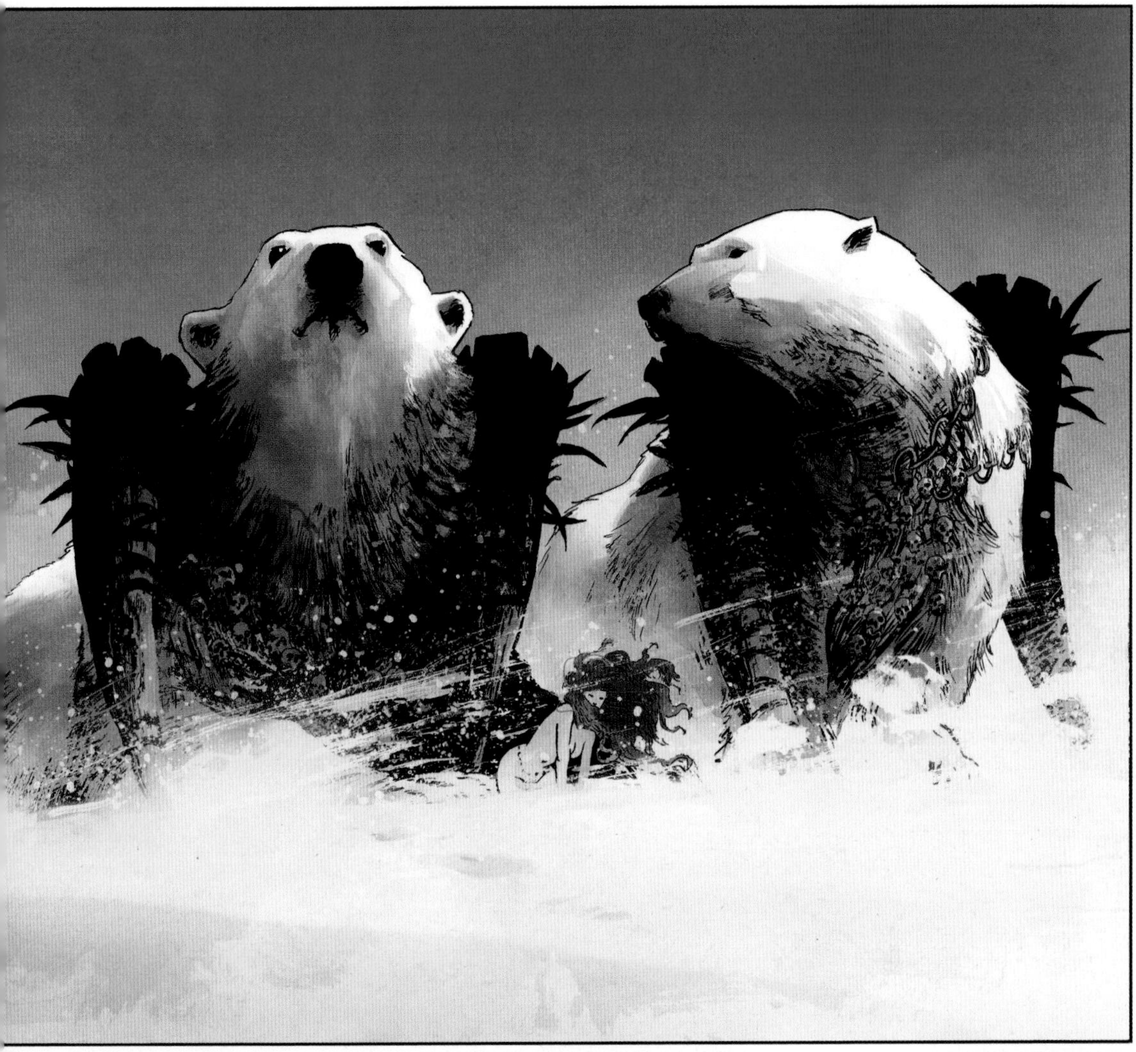

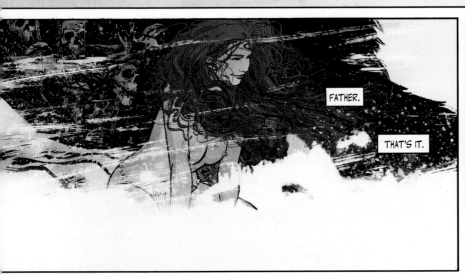

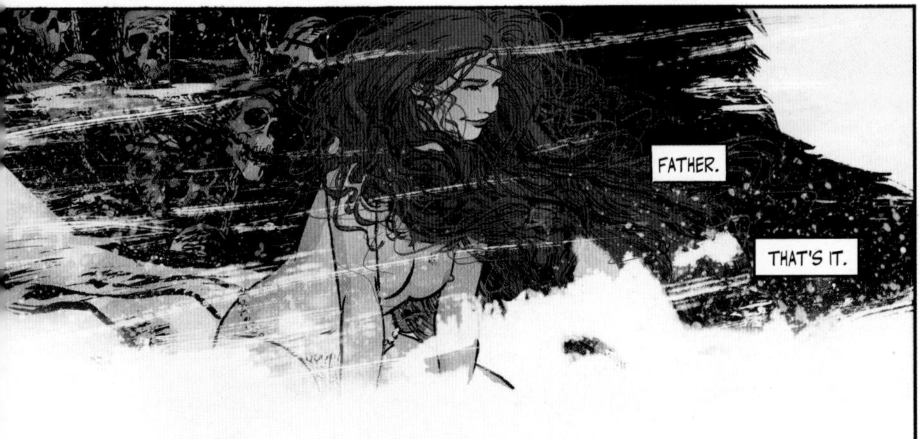
FATHER.
THAT'S IT.

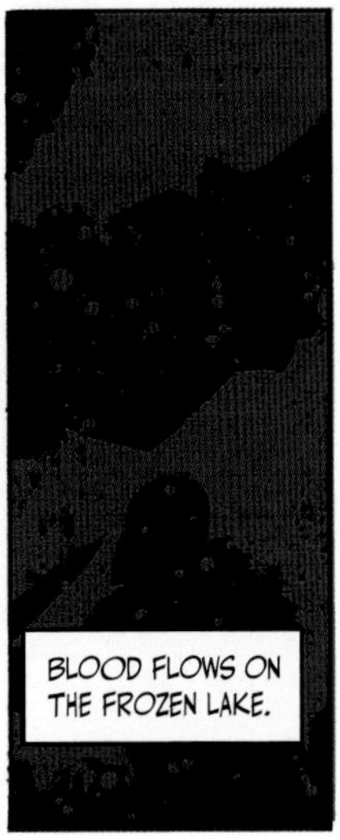
BLOOD FLOWS ON THE FROZEN LAKE.

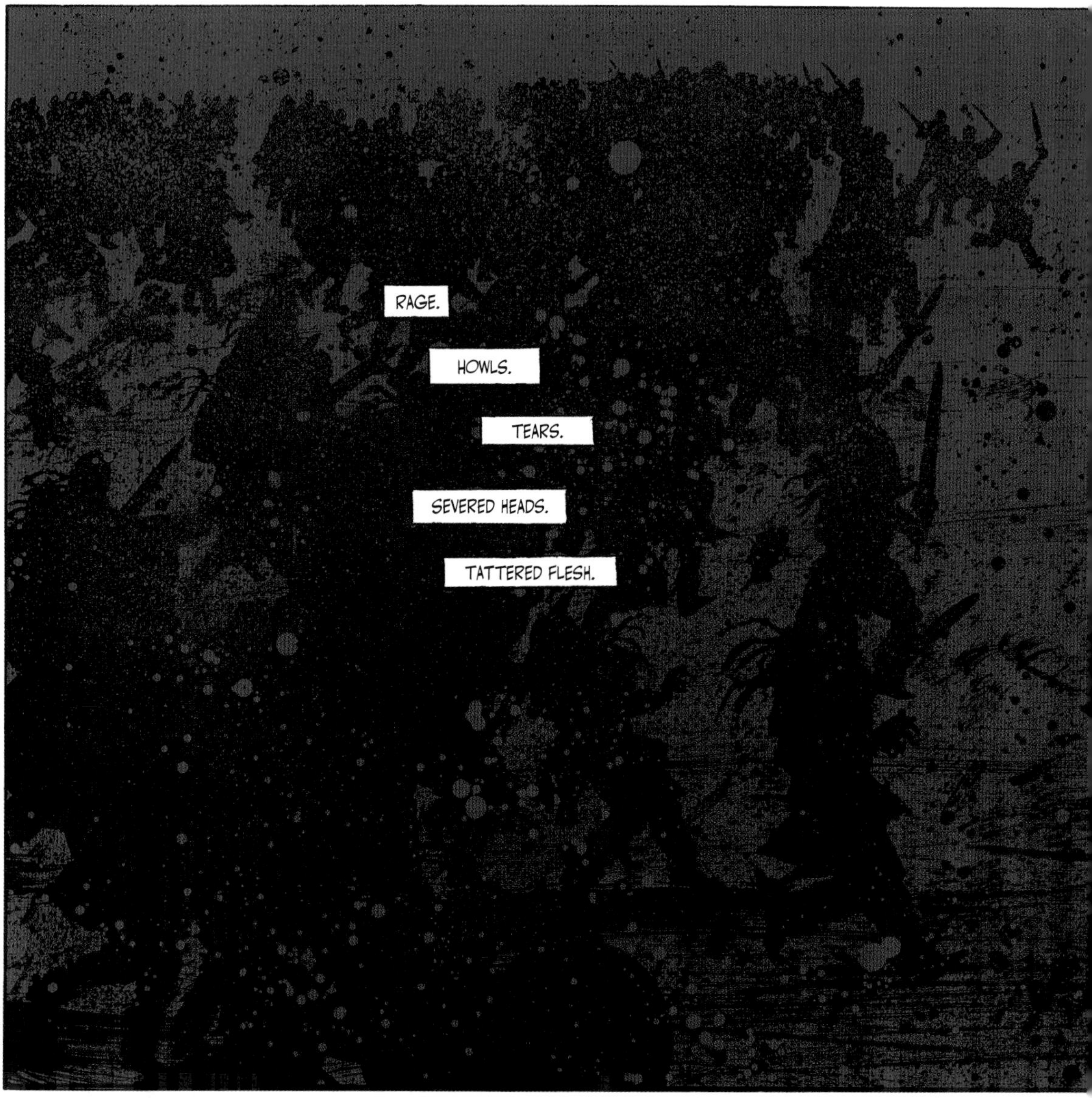
RAGE.
HOWLS.
TEARS.
SEVERED HEADS.
TATTERED FLESH.
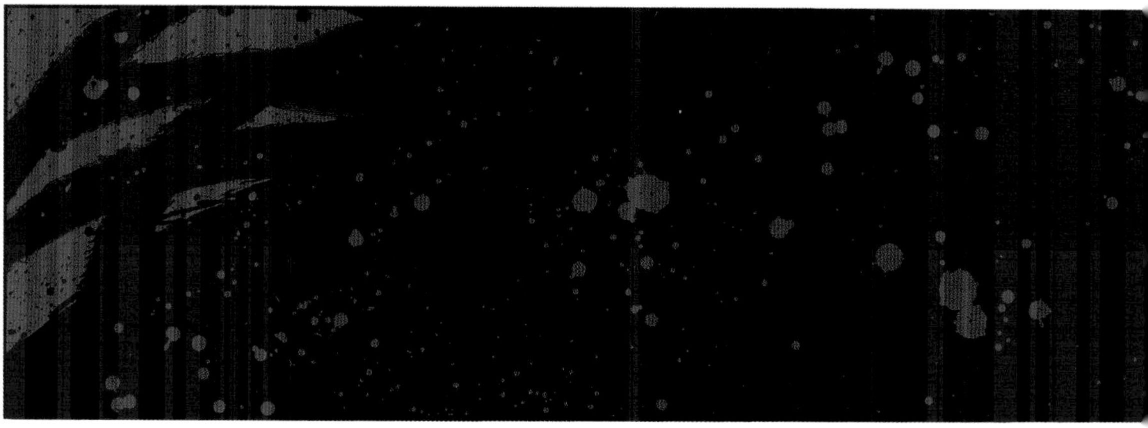

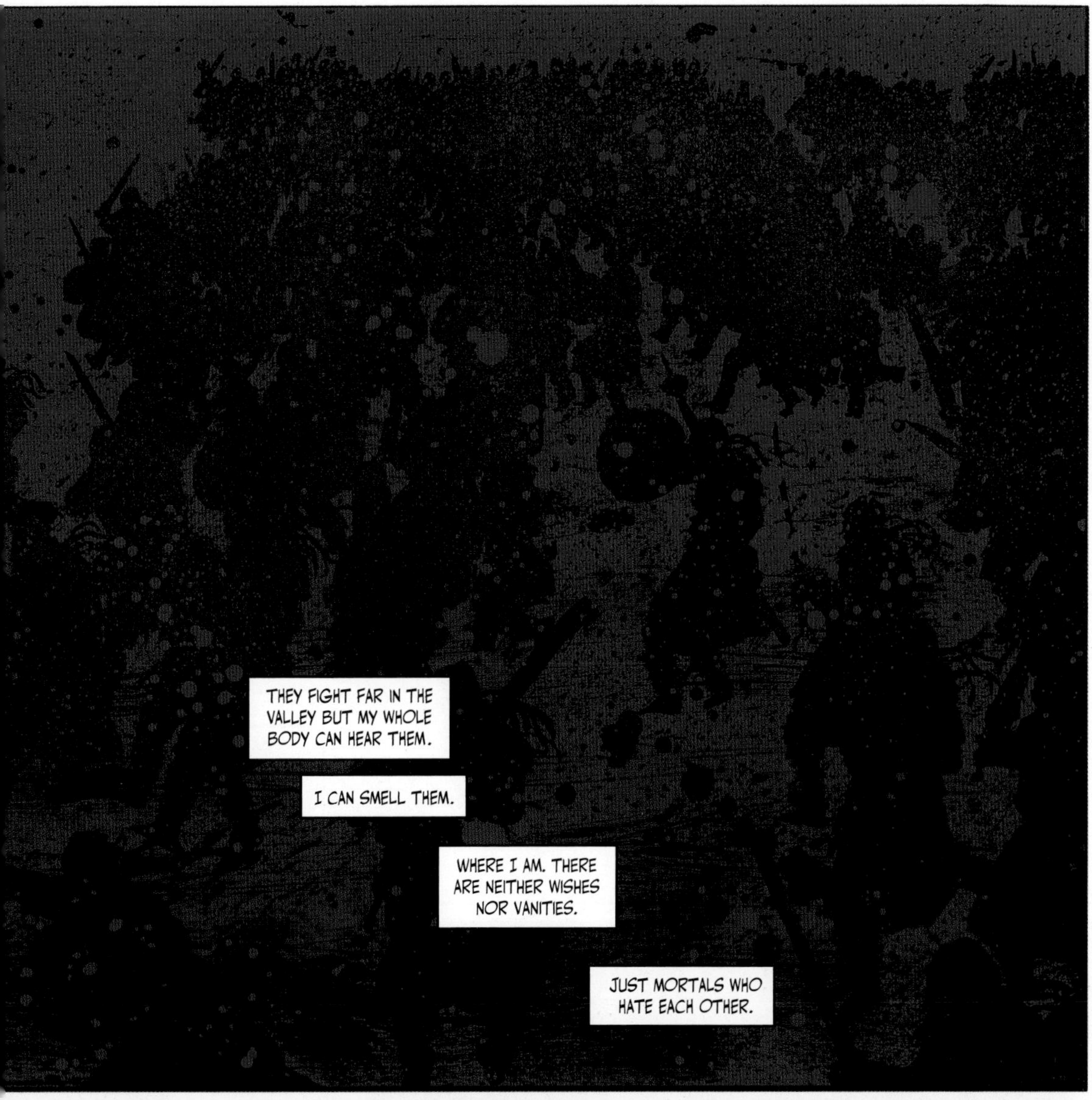
THEY FIGHT FAR IN THE VALLEY BUT MY WHOLE BODY CAN HEAR THEM.
I CAN SMELL THEM.
WHERE I AM. THERE ARE NEITHER WISHES NOR VANITIES.
JUST MORTALS WHO HATE EACH OTHER.

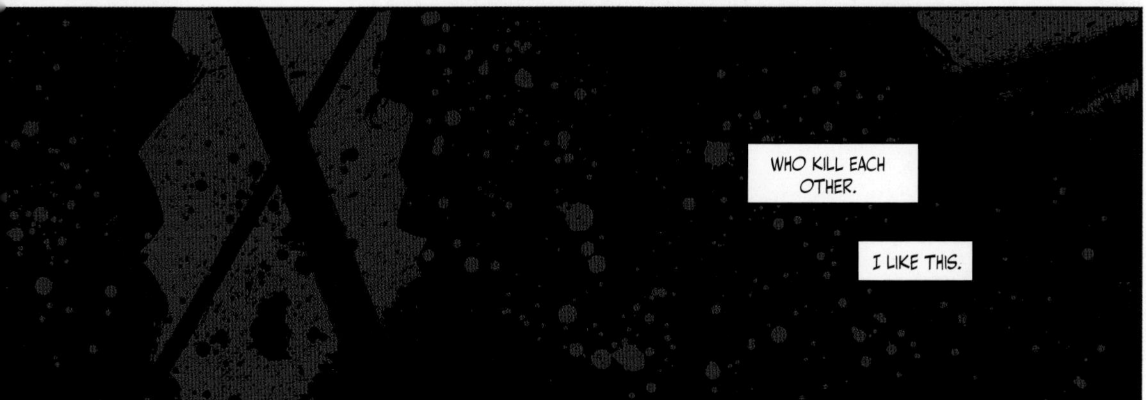
WHO KILL EACH OTHER.
I LIKE THIS.

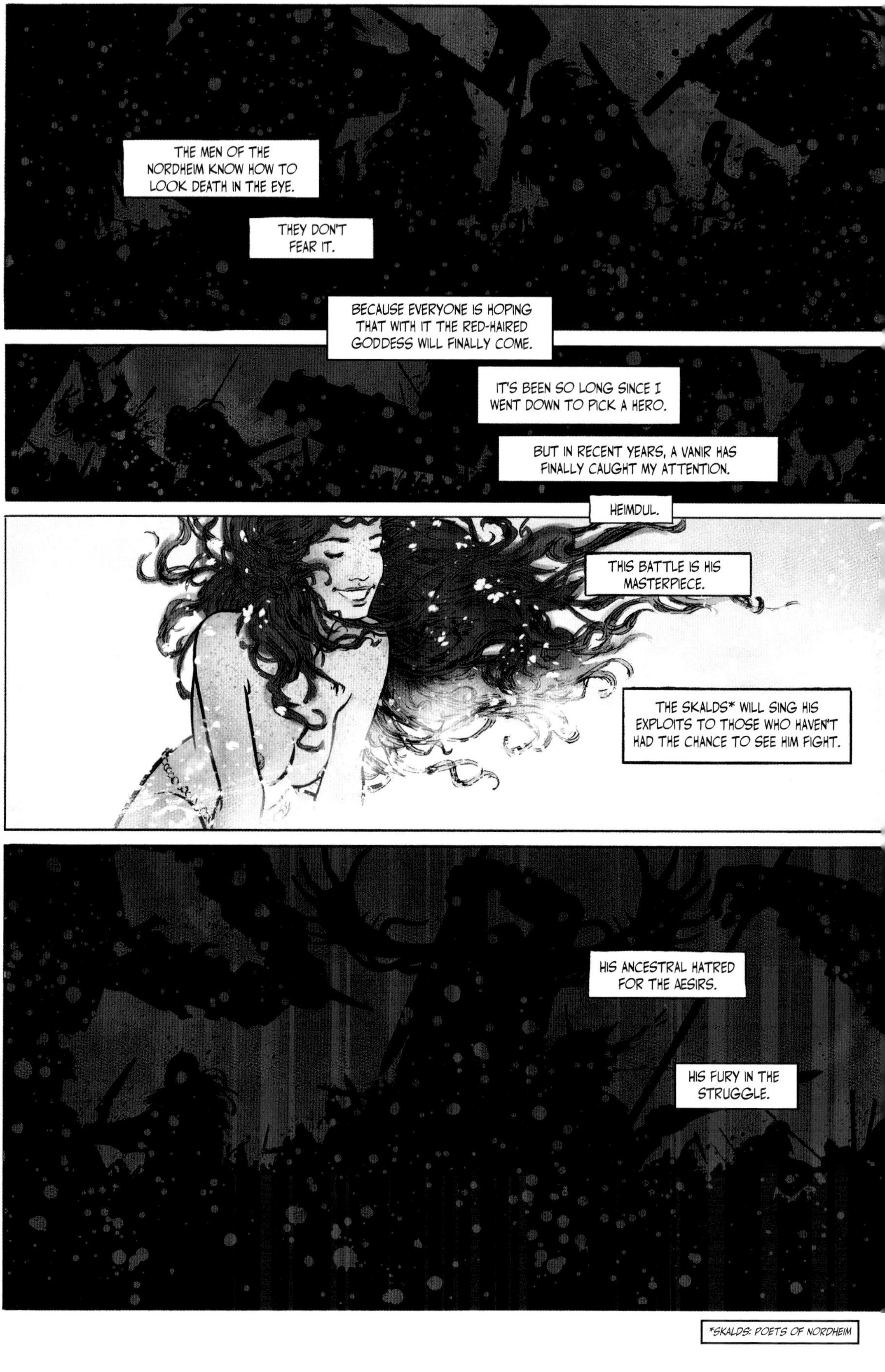
THE MEN OF THE NORDHEIM KNOW HOW TO LOOK DEATH IN THE EYE.
THEY DON'T FEAR IT.
BECAUSE EVERYONE IS HOPING THAT WITH IT THE RED-HAIRED GODDESS WILL FINALLY COME.
IT'S BEEN SO LONG SINCE I WENT DOWN TO PICK A HERO.
BUT IN RECENT YEARS, A VANIR HAS FINALLY CAUGHT MY ATTENTION.
HEIMDUL.
THIS BATTLE IS HIS MASTERPIECE.
THE SKALDS* WILL SING HIS EXPLOITS TO THOSE WHO HAVEN'T HAD THE CHANCE TO SEE HIM FIGHT.
HIS ANCESTRAL HATRED FOR THE AESIRS.
HIS FURY IN THE STRUGGLE.

*SKALDS: POETS OF NORDHEIM

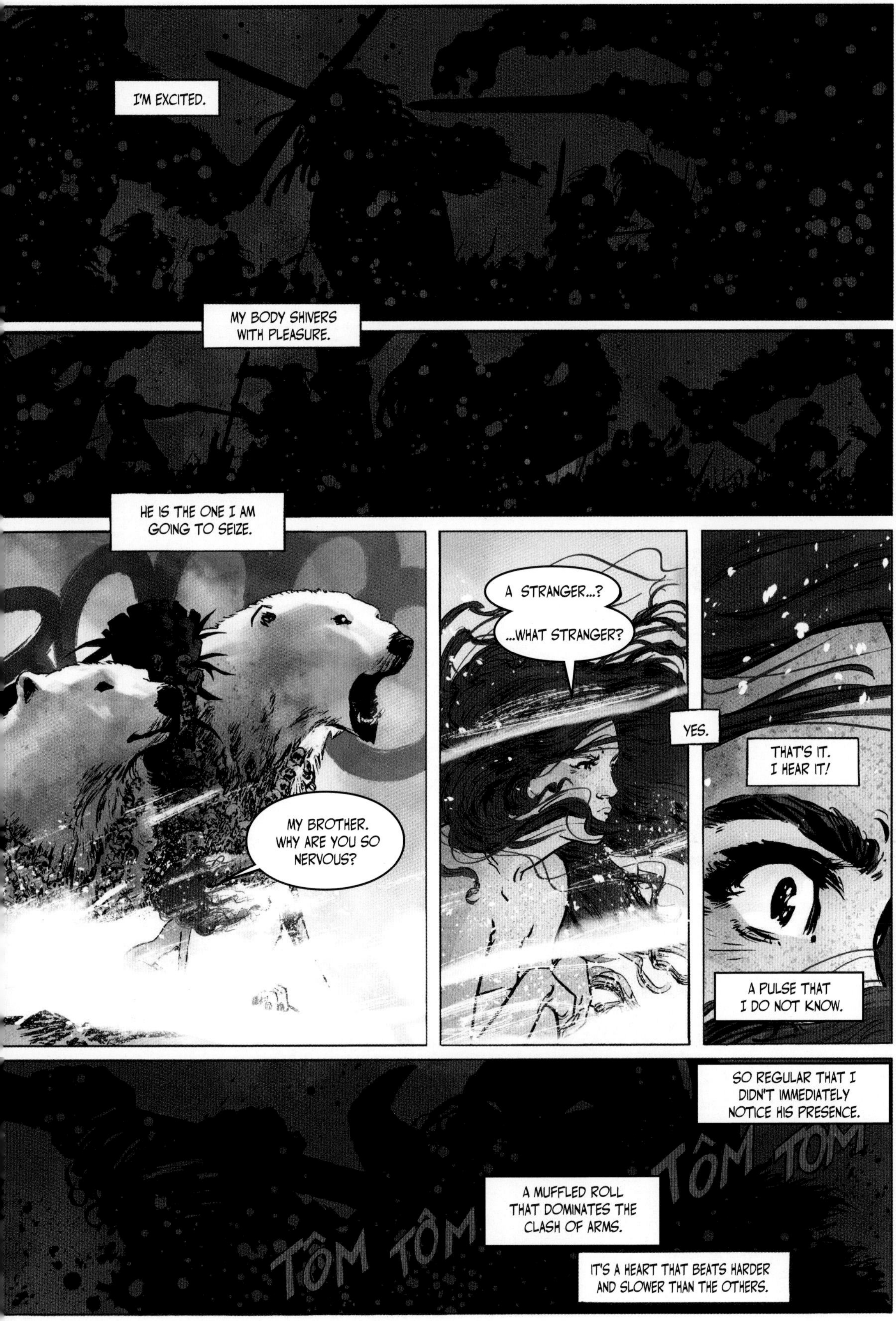
I'M EXCITED.
MY BODY SHIVERS WITH PLEASURE.
HE IS THE ONE I AM GOING TO SEIZE.
MY BROTHER. WHY ARE YOU SO NERVOUS?
A STRANGER...?
...WHAT STRANGER?
YES.
THAT'S IT. I HEAR IT!
A PULSE THAT I DO NOT KNOW.
SO REGULAR THAT I DIDN'T IMMEDIATELY NOTICE HIS PRESENCE.
TÔM TOM
A MUFFLED ROLL THAT DOMINATES THE CLASH OF ARMS.
TÔM TÔM
IT'S A HEART THAT BEATS HARDER AND SLOWER THAN THE OTHERS.

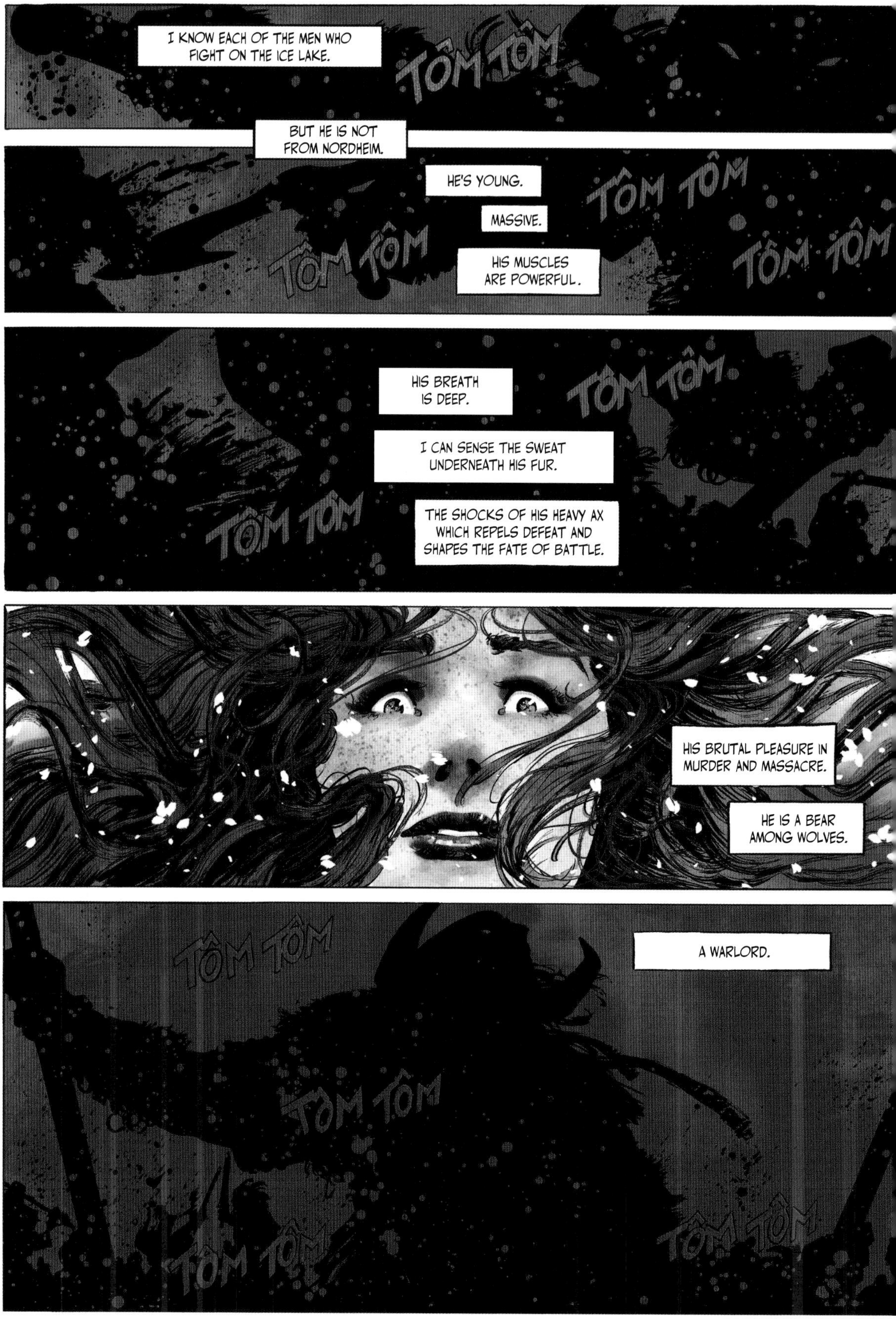

I KNOW EACH OF THE MEN WHO FIGHT ON THE ICE LAKE.
TÔM TÔM
BUT HE IS NOT FROM NORDHEIM.
HE'S YOUNG.
MASSIVE.
HIS MUSCLES ARE POWERFUL.
TÔM TÔM
TÔM TÔM
TÔM TÔM
HIS BREATH IS DEEP.
I CAN SENSE THE SWEAT UNDERNEATH HIS FUR.
THE SHOCKS OF HIS HEAVY AX WHICH REPELS DEFEAT AND SHAPES THE FATE OF BATTLE.
TÔM TÔM
TÔM TÔM
HIS BRUTAL PLEASURE IN MURDER AND MASSACRE.
HE IS A BEAR AMONG WOLVES.
A WARLORD.
TÔM TÔM
TÔM TÔM
TÔM TÔM
TÔM TÔM

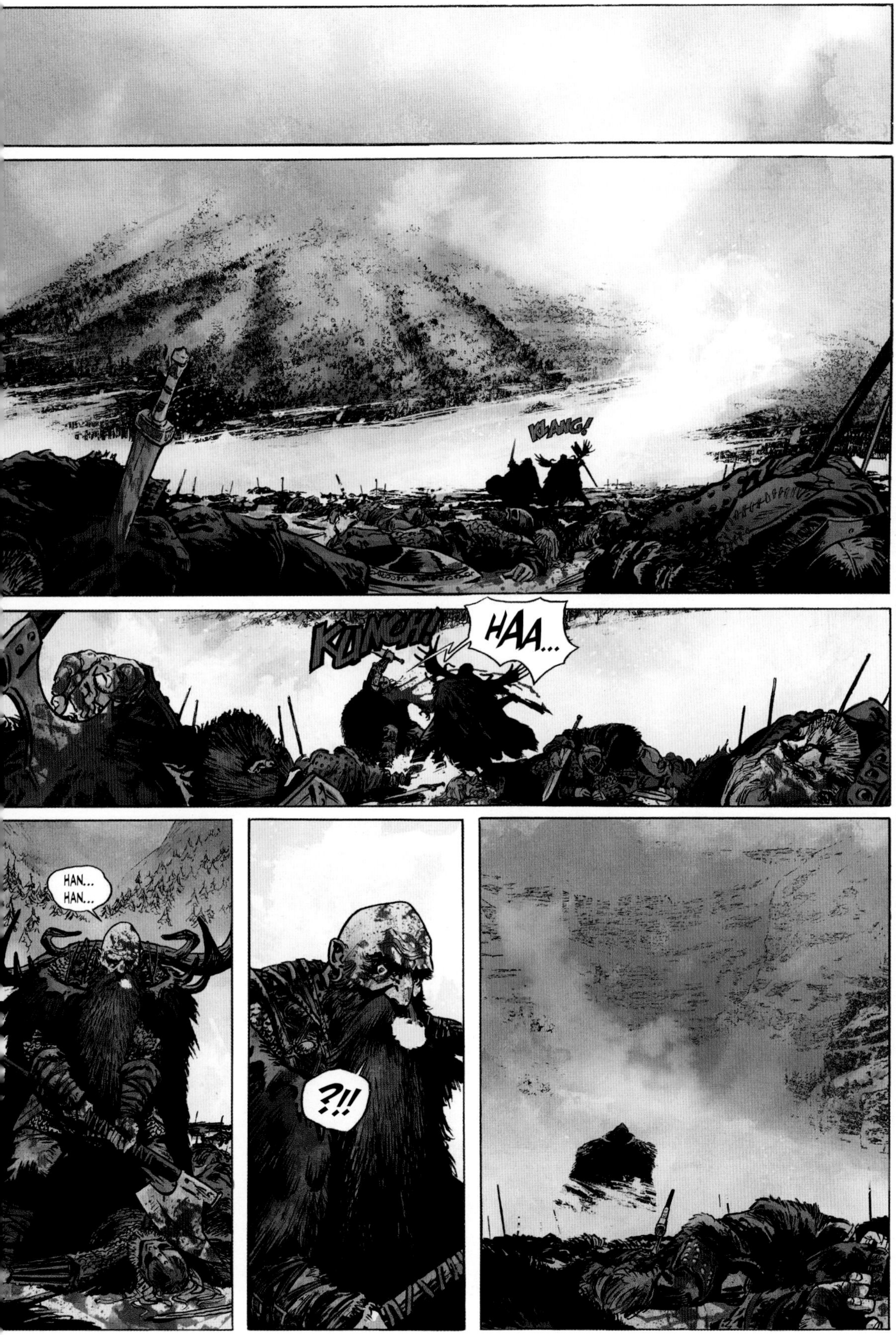
KLANG!
KLINCH!
HAA...
HAN...
HAN...
?!!

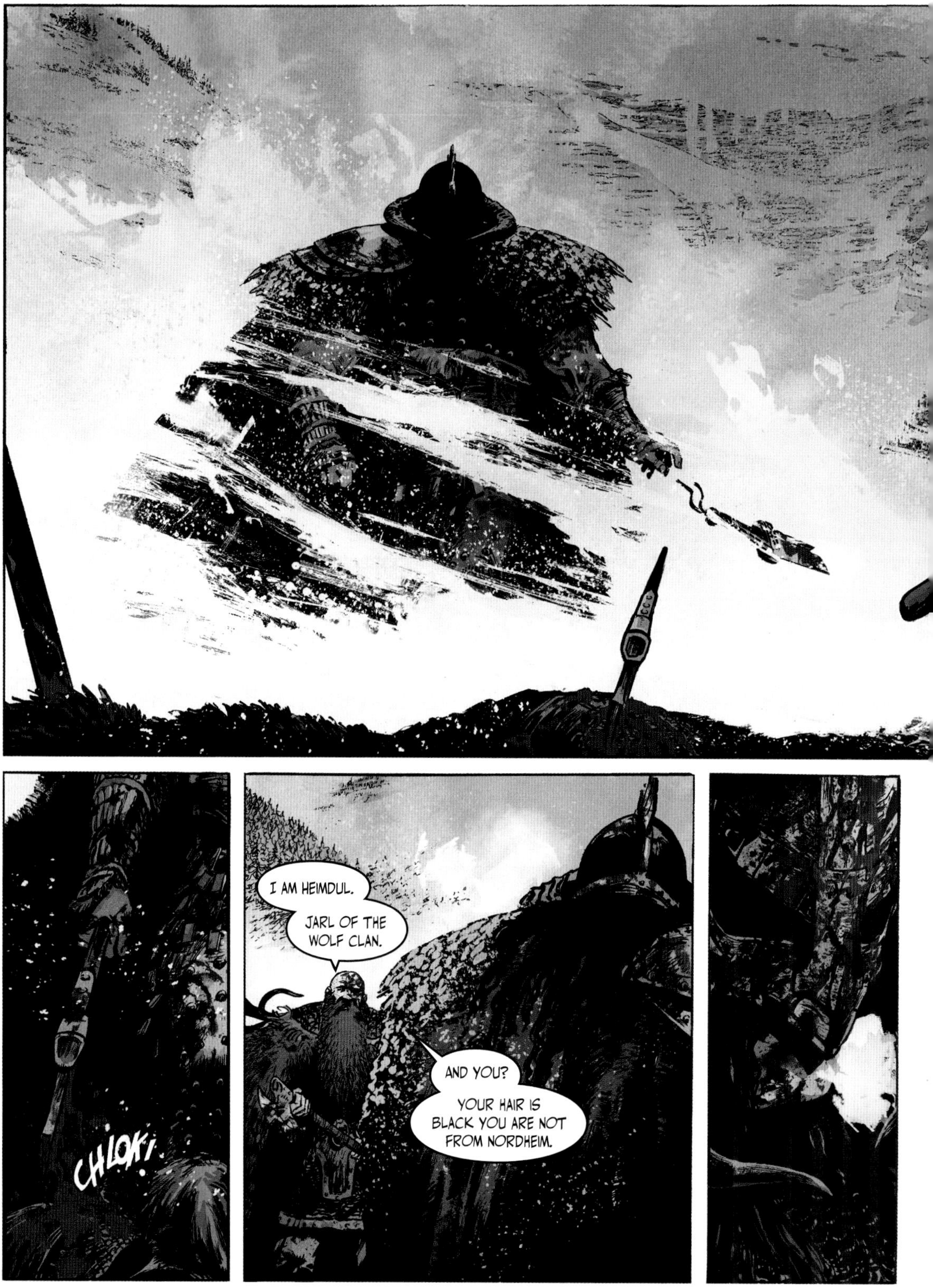

CHLOK!
I AM HEIMDUL.
JARL OF THE WOLF CLAN.
AND YOU?
YOUR HAIR IS BLACK YOU ARE NOT FROM NORDHEIM.

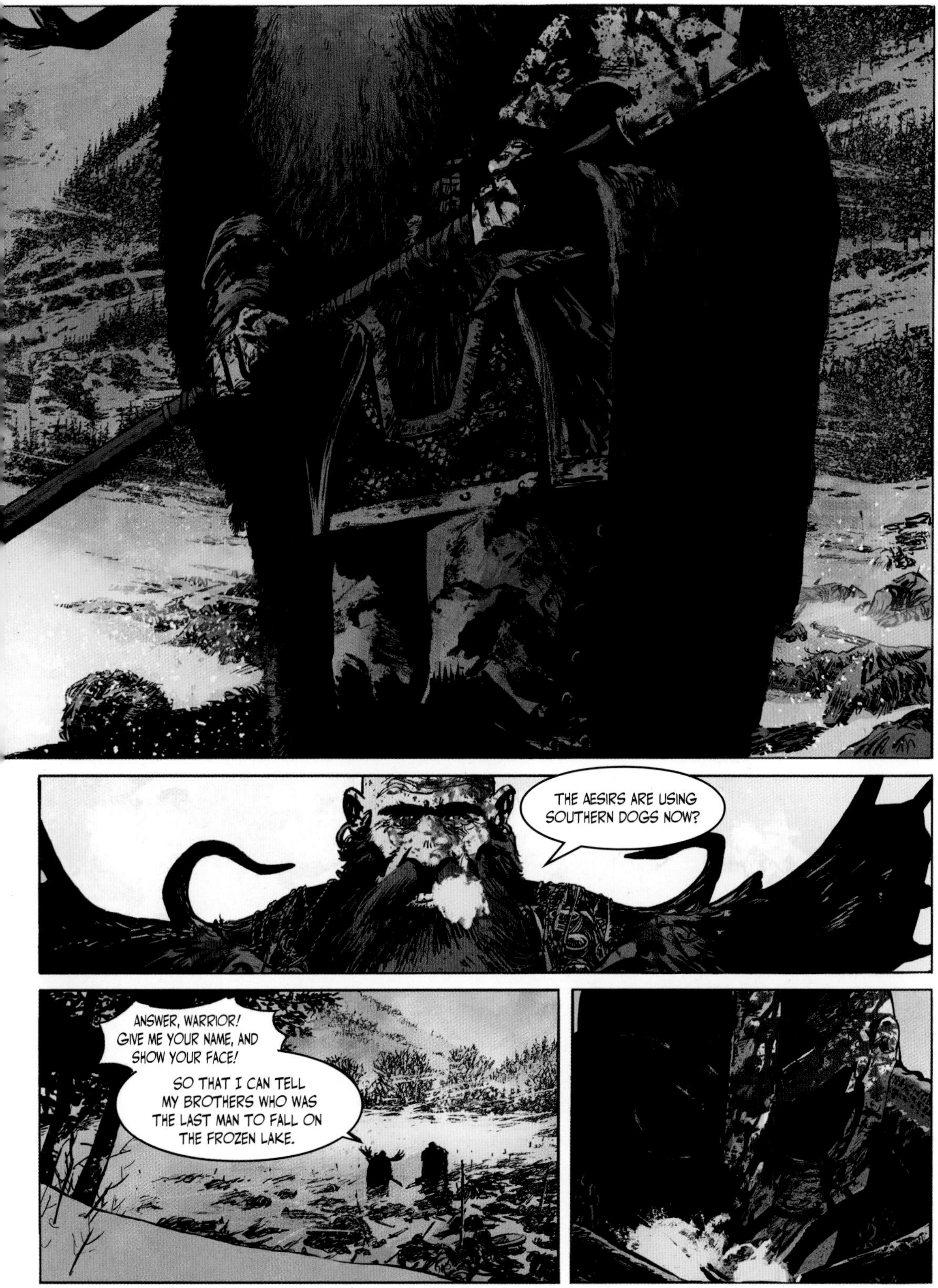
THE AESIRS ARE USING SOUTHERN DOGS NOW?
ANSWER, WARRIOR! GIVE ME YOUR NAME, AND SHOW YOUR FACE!
SO THAT I CAN TELL MY BROTHERS WHO WAS THE LAST MAN TO FALL ON THE FROZEN LAKE.

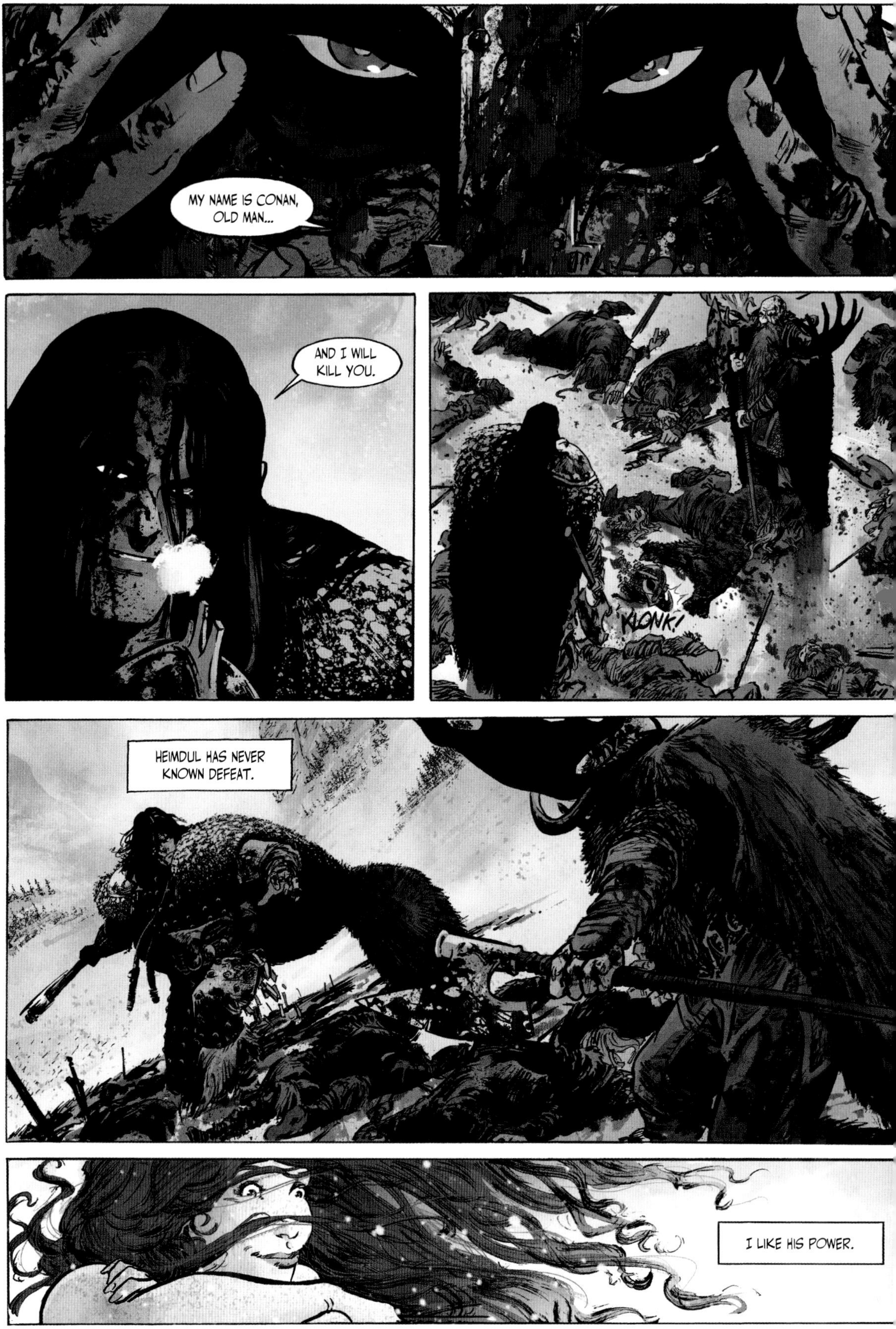
MY NAME IS CONAN, OLD MAN...
AND I WILL KILL YOU.
KLONK!
HEIMDUL HAS NEVER KNOWN DEFEAT.
I LIKE HIS POWER.

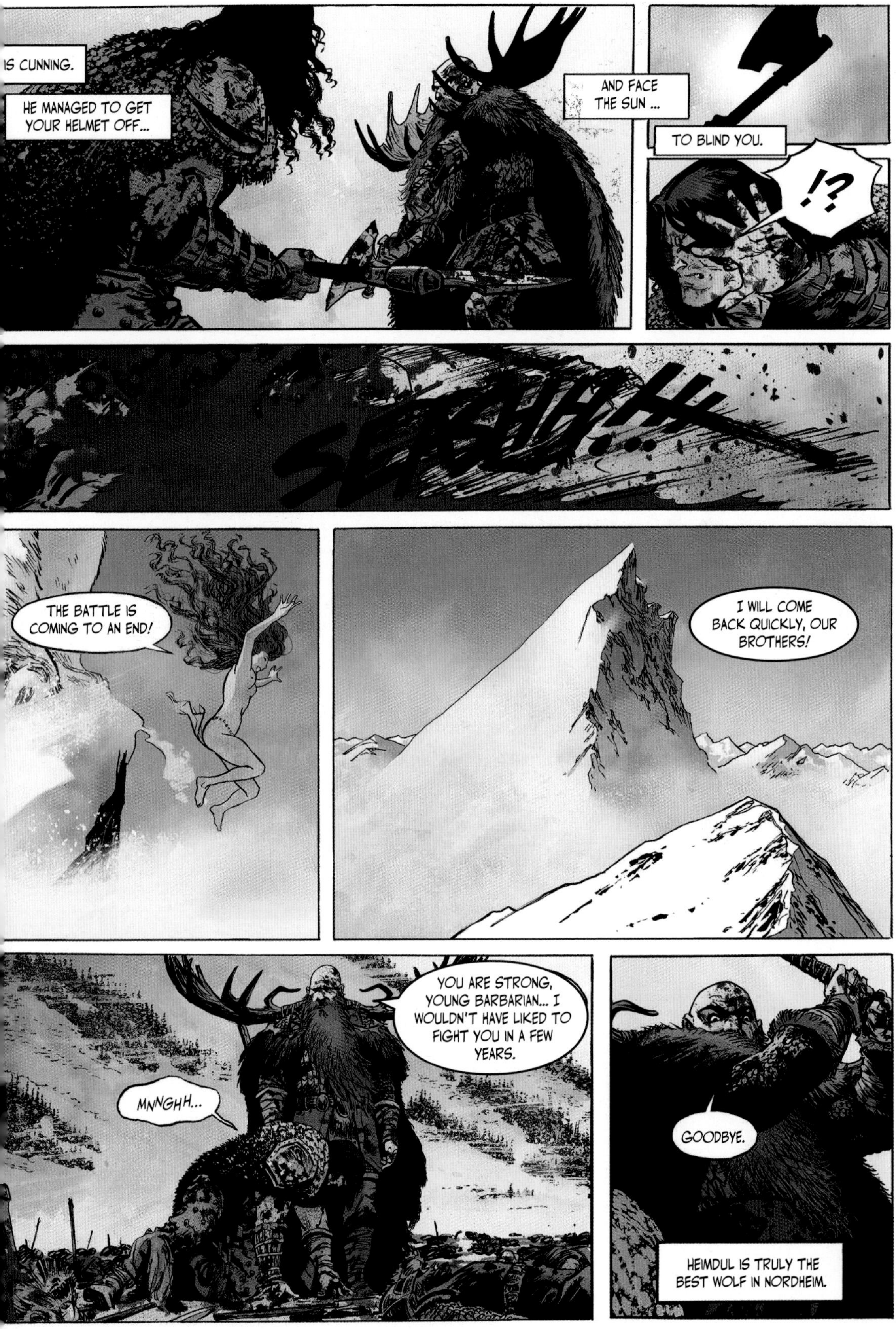

IS CUNNING.
HE MANAGED TO GET YOUR HELMET OFF...
AND FACE THE SUN ...
TO BLIND YOU.
!?
THE BATTLE IS COMING TO AN END!
I WILL COME BACK QUICKLY, OUR BROTHERS!
YOU ARE STRONG, YOUNG BARBARIAN... I WOULDN'T HAVE LIKED TO FIGHT YOU IN A FEW YEARS.
MNNGHH...
GOODBYE.
HEIMDUL IS TRULY THE BEST WOLF IN NORDHEIM.

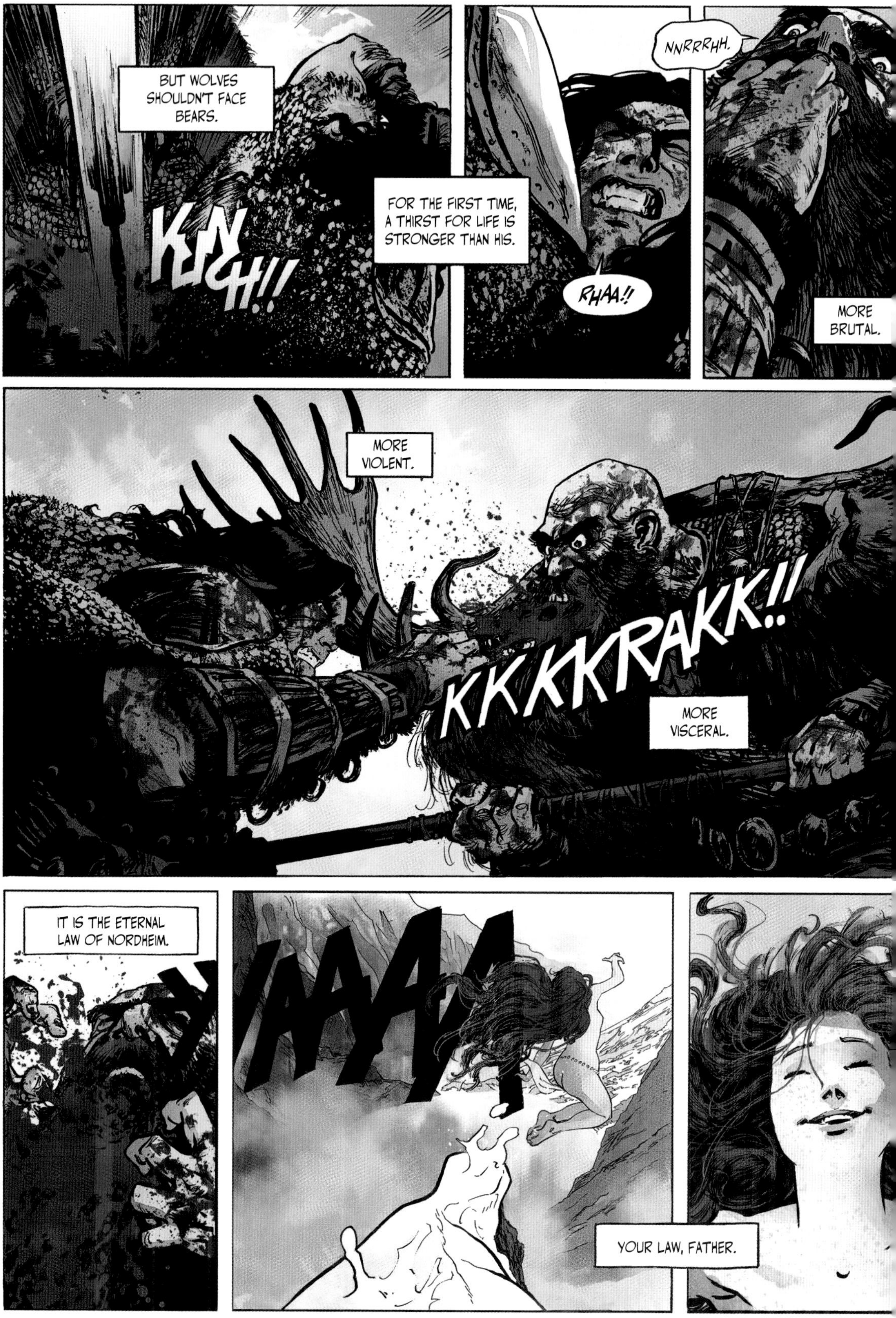
BUT WOLVES SHOULDN'T FACE BEARS.
KLUNCH!!
FOR THE FIRST TIME, A THIRST FOR LIFE IS STRONGER THAN HIS.
RHAA!!
NNRRRHH.
MORE BRUTAL.
MORE VIOLENT.
KKKKRAKK!!
MORE VISCERAL.
IT IS THE ETERNAL LAW OF NORDHEIM.
YOUR LAW, FATHER.

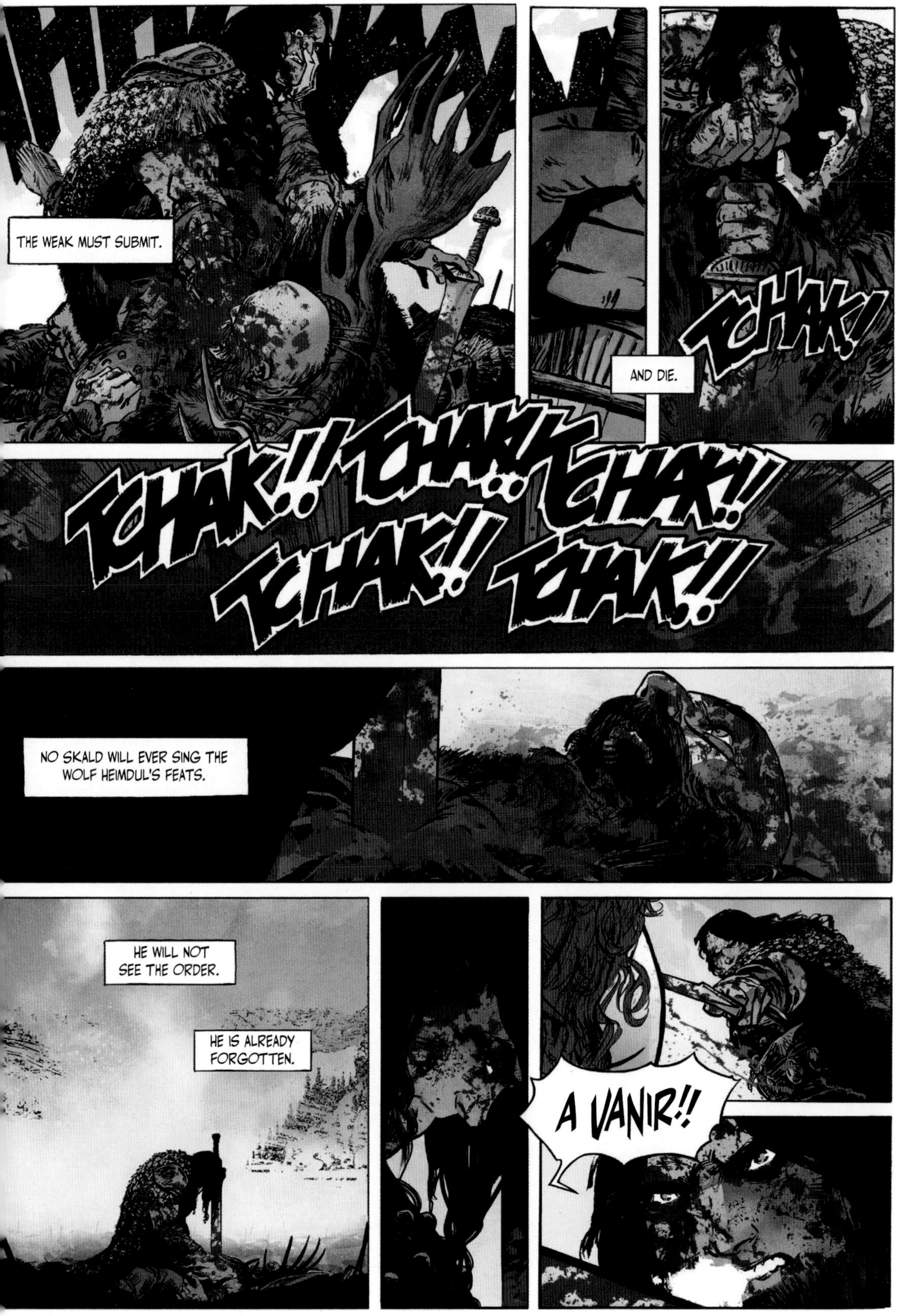
THE WEAK MUST SUBMIT.
AND DIE.
TCHAK!!
TCHAK!! TCHAK!! TCHAK!!
TCHAK!! TCHAK!!
NO SKALD WILL EVER SING THE WOLF HEIMDUL'S FEATS.
HE WILL NOT SEE THE ORDER.
HE IS ALREADY FORGOTTEN.
A VANIR!!

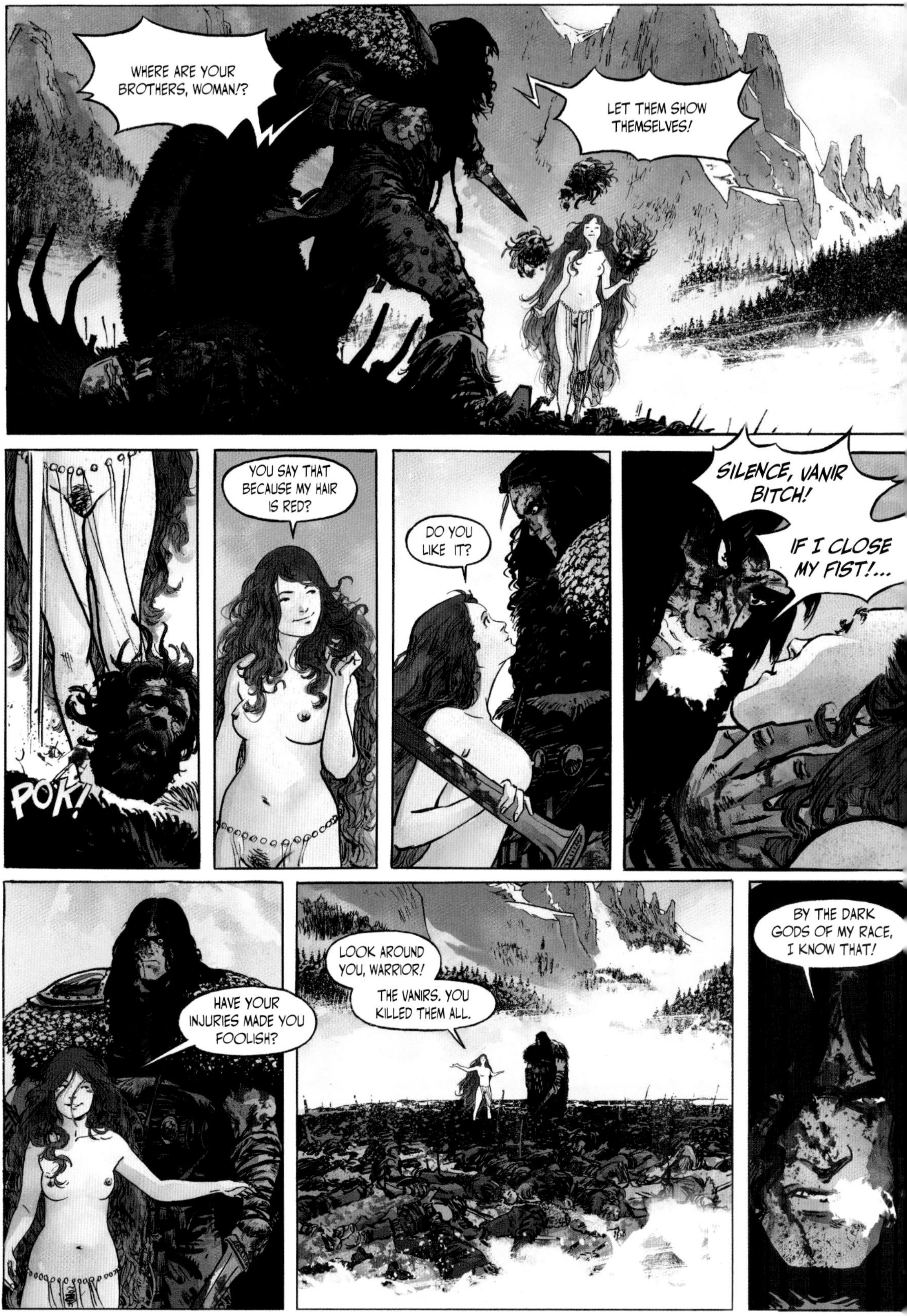
WHERE ARE YOUR BROTHERS, WOMAN!?
LET THEM SHOW THEMSELVES!
POK!
YOU SAY THAT BECAUSE MY HAIR IS RED?
DO YOU LIKE IT?
SILENCE, VANIR BITCH!
IF I CLOSE MY FIST!...
HAVE YOUR INJURIES MADE YOU FOOLISH?
LOOK AROUND YOU, WARRIOR!
THE VANIRS. YOU KILLED THEM ALL.
BY THE DARK GODS OF MY RACE, I KNOW THAT!

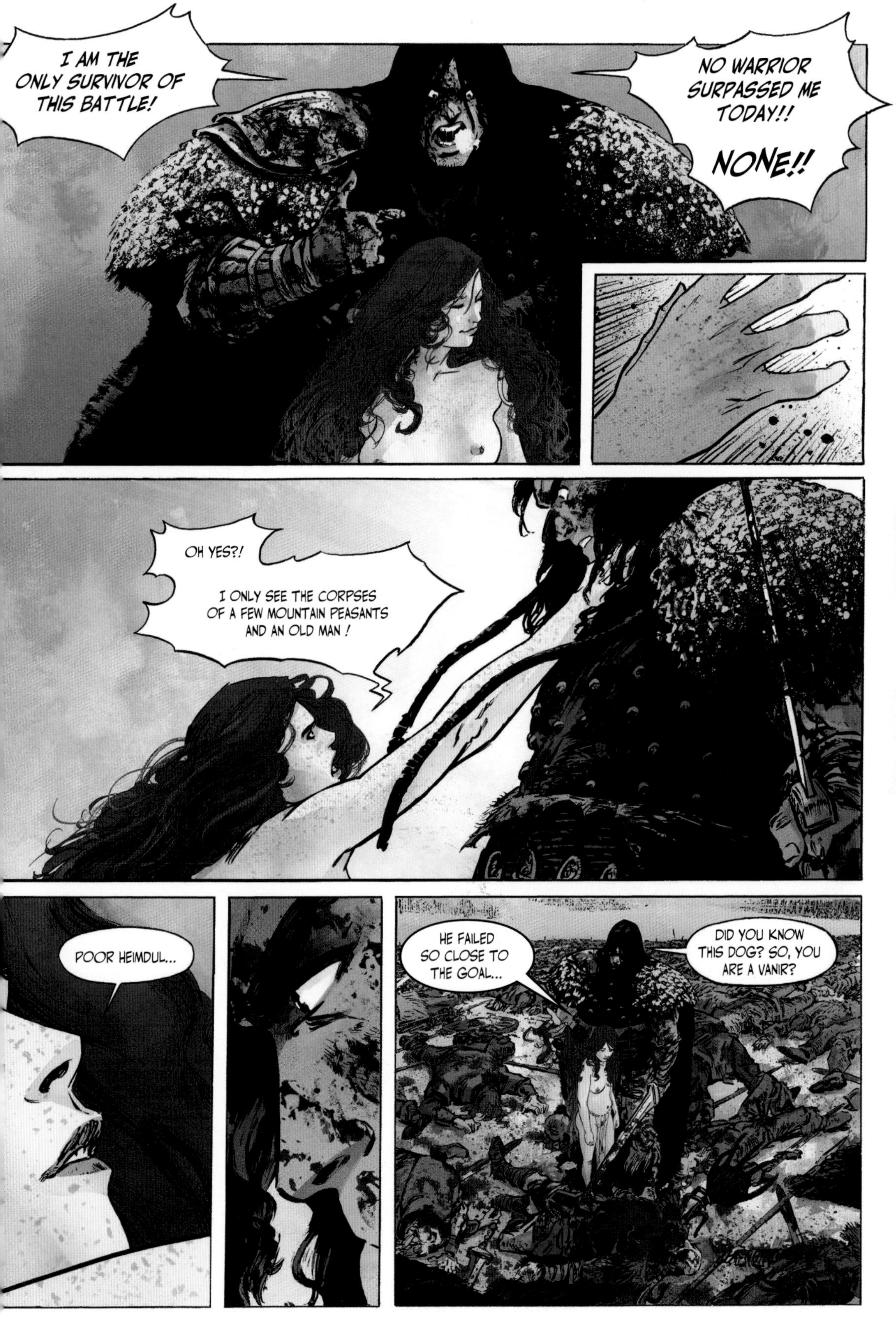
I AM THE ONLY SURVIVOR OF THIS BATTLE!
NO WARRIOR SURPASSED ME TODAY!!
NONE!!
OH YES?!
I ONLY SEE THE CORPSES OF A FEW MOUNTAIN PEASANTS AND AN OLD MAN !
POOR HEIMDUL...
HE FAILED SO CLOSE TO THE GOAL...
DID YOU KNOW THIS DOG? SO, YOU ARE A VANIR?

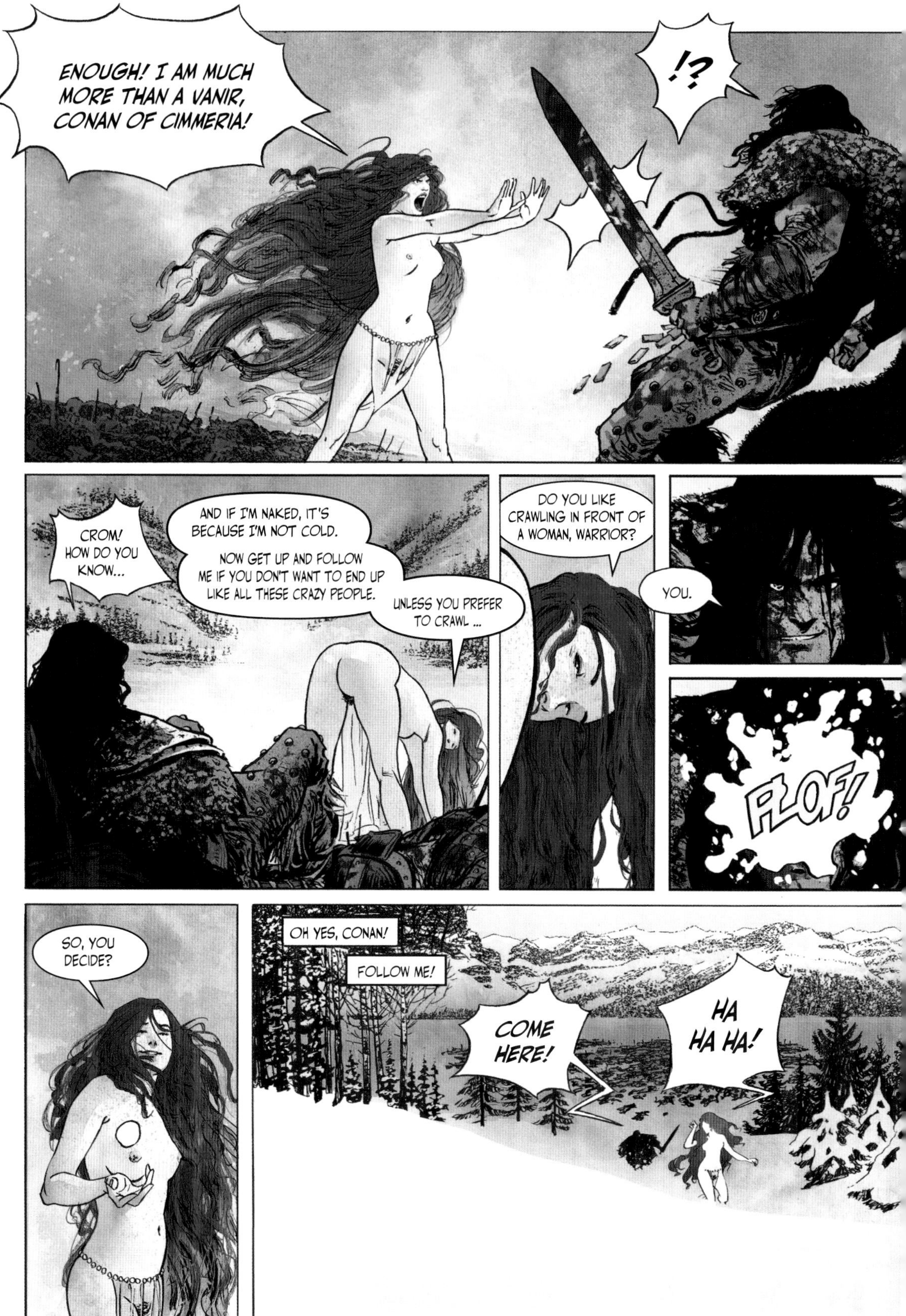
ENOUGH! I AM MUCH MORE THAN A VANIR, CONAN OF CIMMERIA!
!?
CROM! HOW DO YOU KNOW...
AND IF I'M NAKED, IT'S BECAUSE I'M NOT COLD.
NOW GET UP AND FOLLOW ME IF YOU DON'T WANT TO END UP LIKE ALL THESE CRAZY PEOPLE.
UNLESS YOU PREFER TO CRAWL ...
DO YOU LIKE CRAWLING IN FRONT OF A WOMAN, WARRIOR?
YOU.
PLOF!
SO, YOU DECIDE?
OH YES, CONAN!
FOLLOW ME!
COME HERE!
HA HA HA!

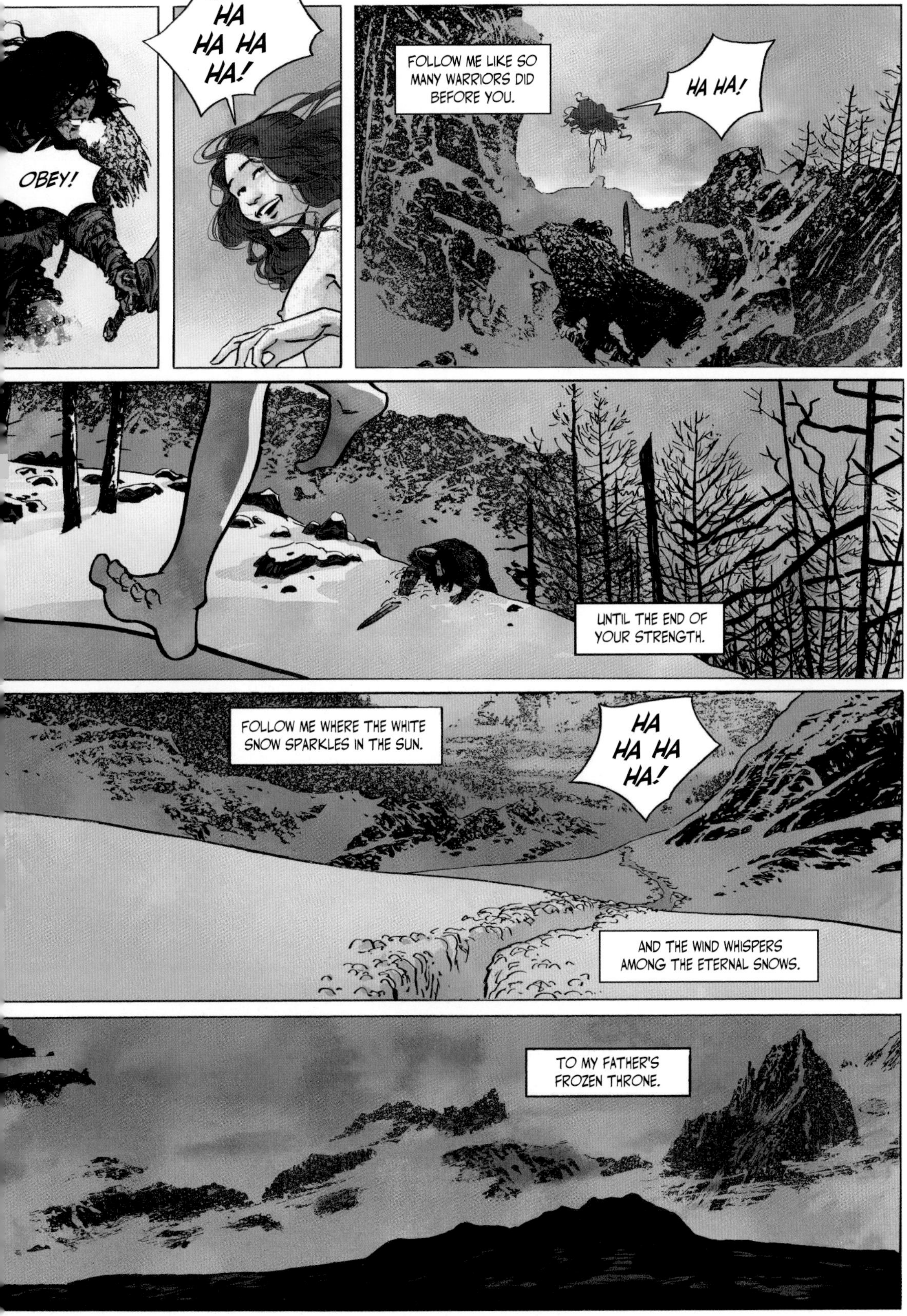
OBEY!
HA HA HA HA!
FOLLOW ME LIKE SO MANY WARRIORS DID BEFORE YOU.
HA HA!
UNTIL THE END OF YOUR STRENGTH.
FOLLOW ME WHERE THE WHITE SNOW SPARKLES IN THE SUN.
HA HA HA HA!
AND THE WIND WHISPERS AMONG THE ETERNAL SNOWS.
TO MY FATHER'S FROZEN THRONE.

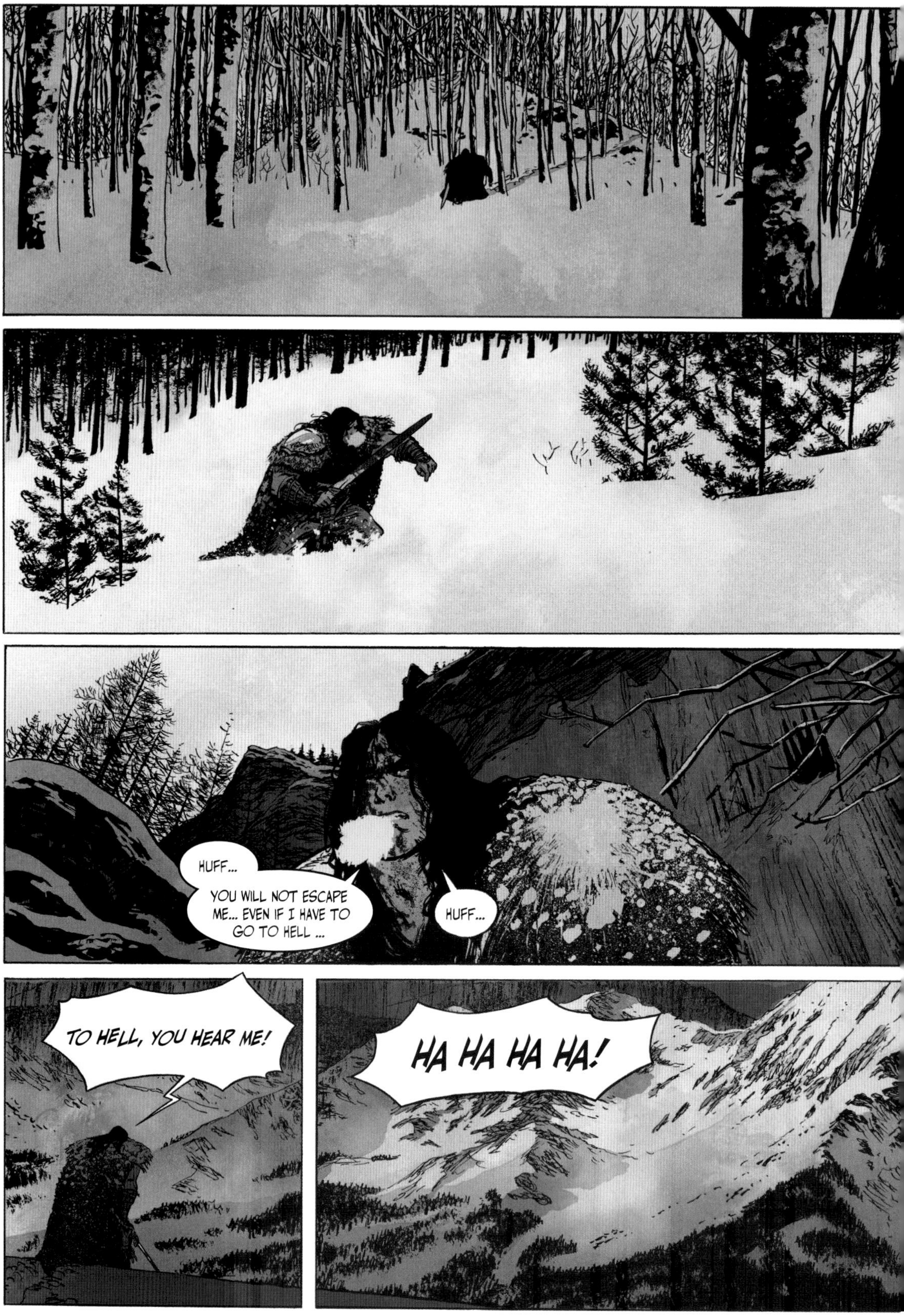
HUFF...
YOU WILL NOT ESCAPE ME... EVEN IF I HAVE TO GO TO HELL ...
HUFF...
TO HELL, YOU HEAR ME!
HA HA HA HA!

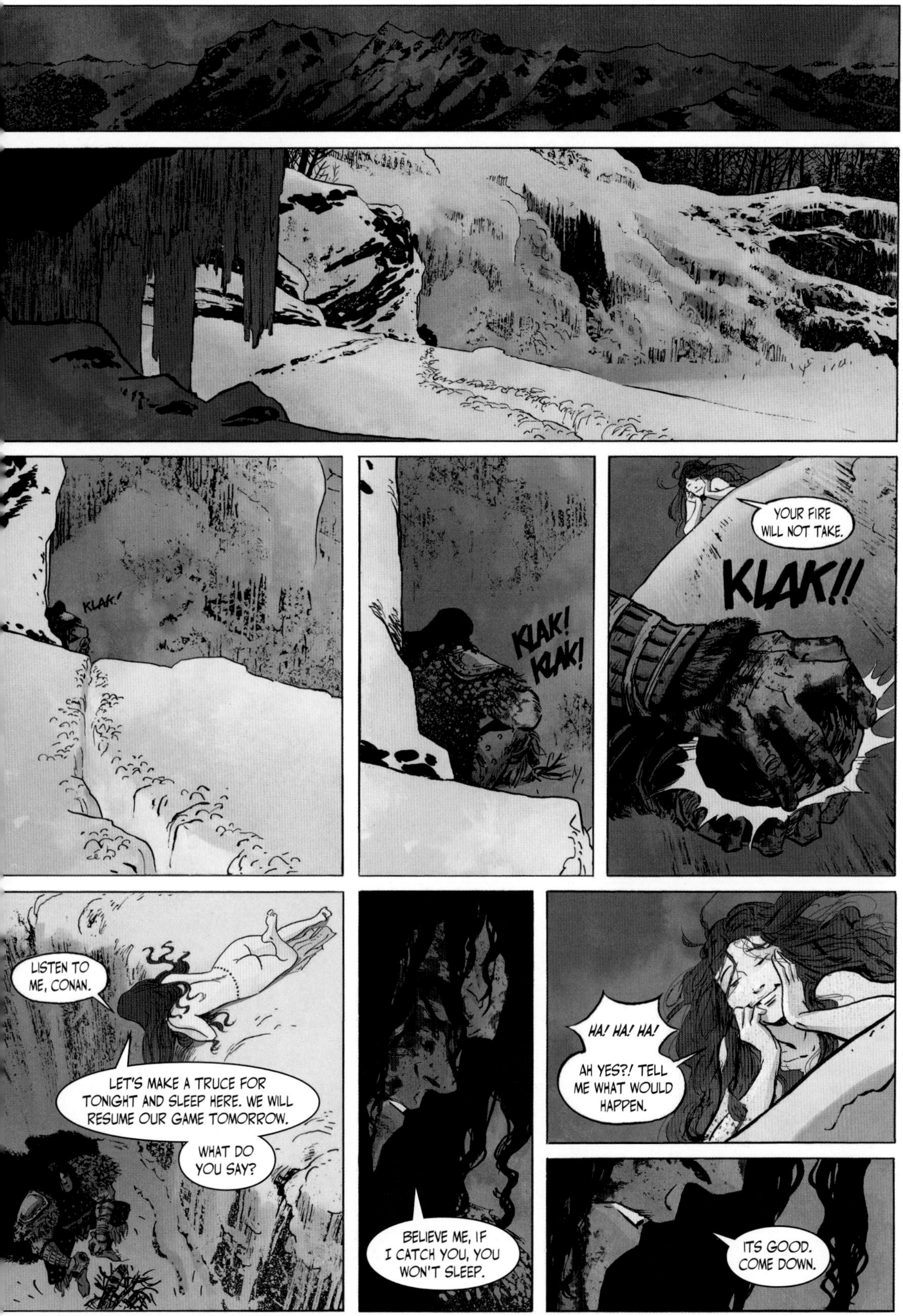
KLAK!
KLAK! KLAK!
YOUR FIRE WILL NOT TAKE.
KLAK!!
LISTEN TO ME, CONAN.
LET'S MAKE A TRUCE FOR TONIGHT AND SLEEP HERE. WE WILL RESUME OUR GAME TOMORROW.
WHAT DO YOU SAY?
BELIEVE ME, IF I CATCH YOU, YOU WON'T SLEEP.
HA! HA! HA!
AH YES?! TELL ME WHAT WOULD HAPPEN.
ITS GOOD. COME DOWN.

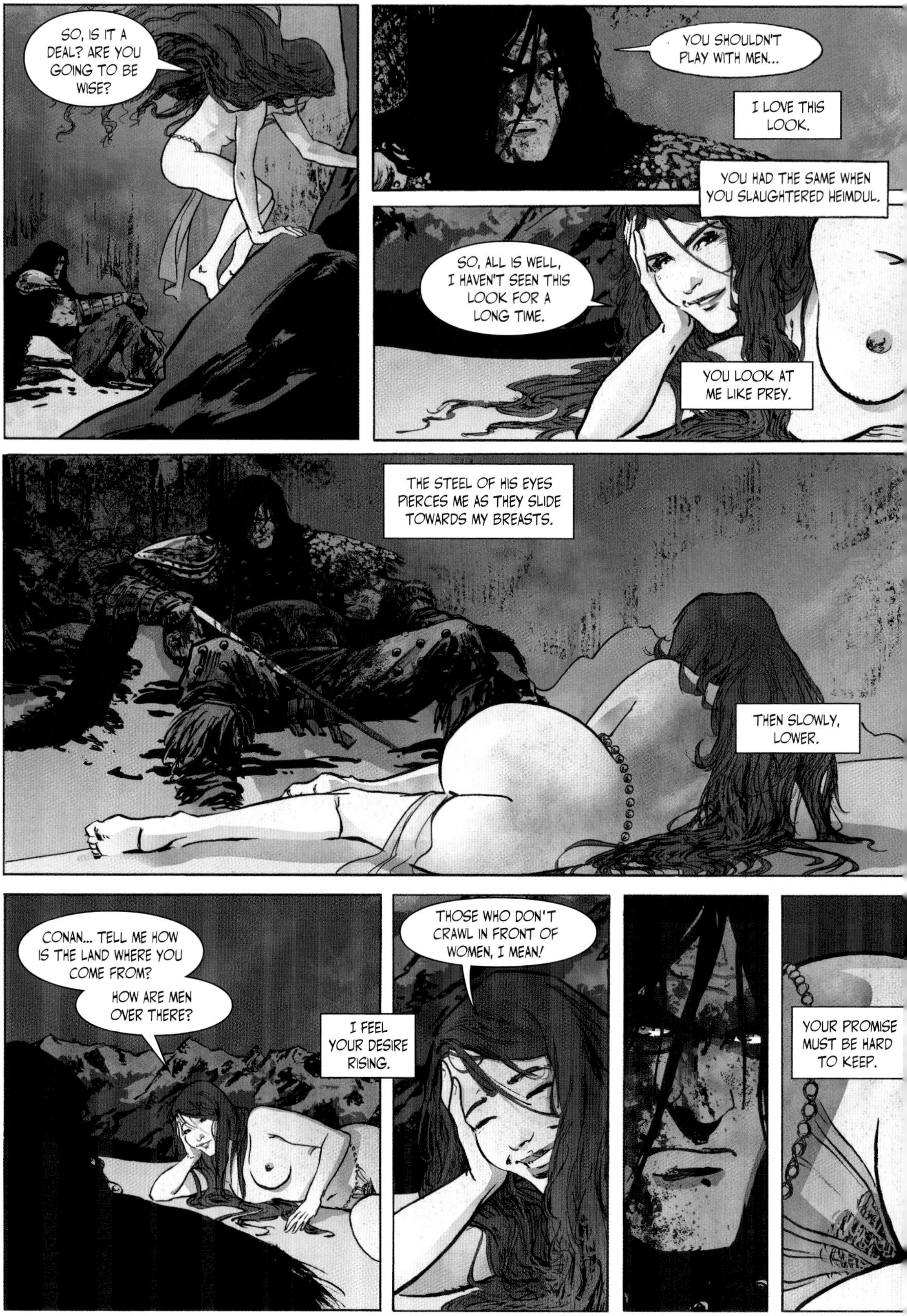
SO, IS IT A DEAL? ARE YOU GOING TO BE WISE?
YOU SHOULDN'T PLAY WITH MEN...
I LOVE THIS LOOK.
YOU HAD THE SAME WHEN YOU SLAUGHTERED HEIMDUL.
SO, ALL IS WELL, I HAVEN'T SEEN THIS LOOK FOR A LONG TIME.
YOU LOOK AT ME LIKE PREY.
THE STEEL OF HIS EYES PIERCES ME AS THEY SLIDE TOWARDS MY BREASTS.
THEN SLOWLY, LOWER.
CONAN... TELL ME HOW IS THE LAND WHERE YOU COME FROM?
HOW ARE MEN OVER THERE?
I FEEL YOUR DESIRE RISING.
THOSE WHO DON'T CRAWL IN FRONT OF WOMEN, I MEAN!
YOUR PROMISE MUST BE HARD TO KEEP.

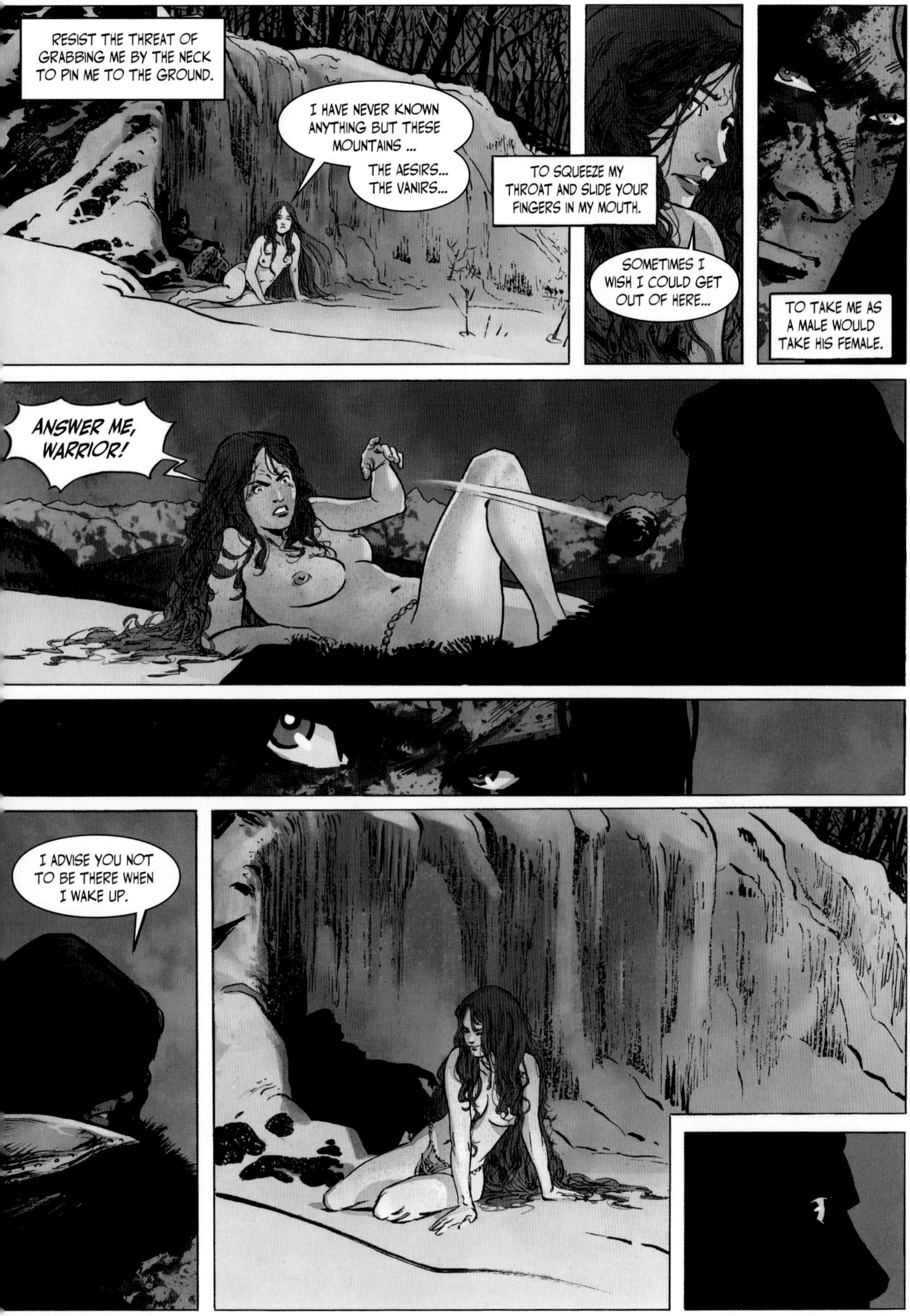
RESIST THE THREAT OF GRABBING ME BY THE NECK TO PIN ME TO THE GROUND.
I HAVE NEVER KNOWN ANYTHING BUT THESE MOUNTAINS ...
THE AESIRS... THE VANIRS...
TO SQUEEZE MY THROAT AND SLIDE YOUR FINGERS IN MY MOUTH.
SOMETIMES I WISH I COULD GET OUT OF HERE...
TO TAKE ME AS A MALE WOULD TAKE HIS FEMALE.
ANSWER ME, WARRIOR!
I ADVISE YOU NOT TO BE THERE WHEN I WAKE UP.

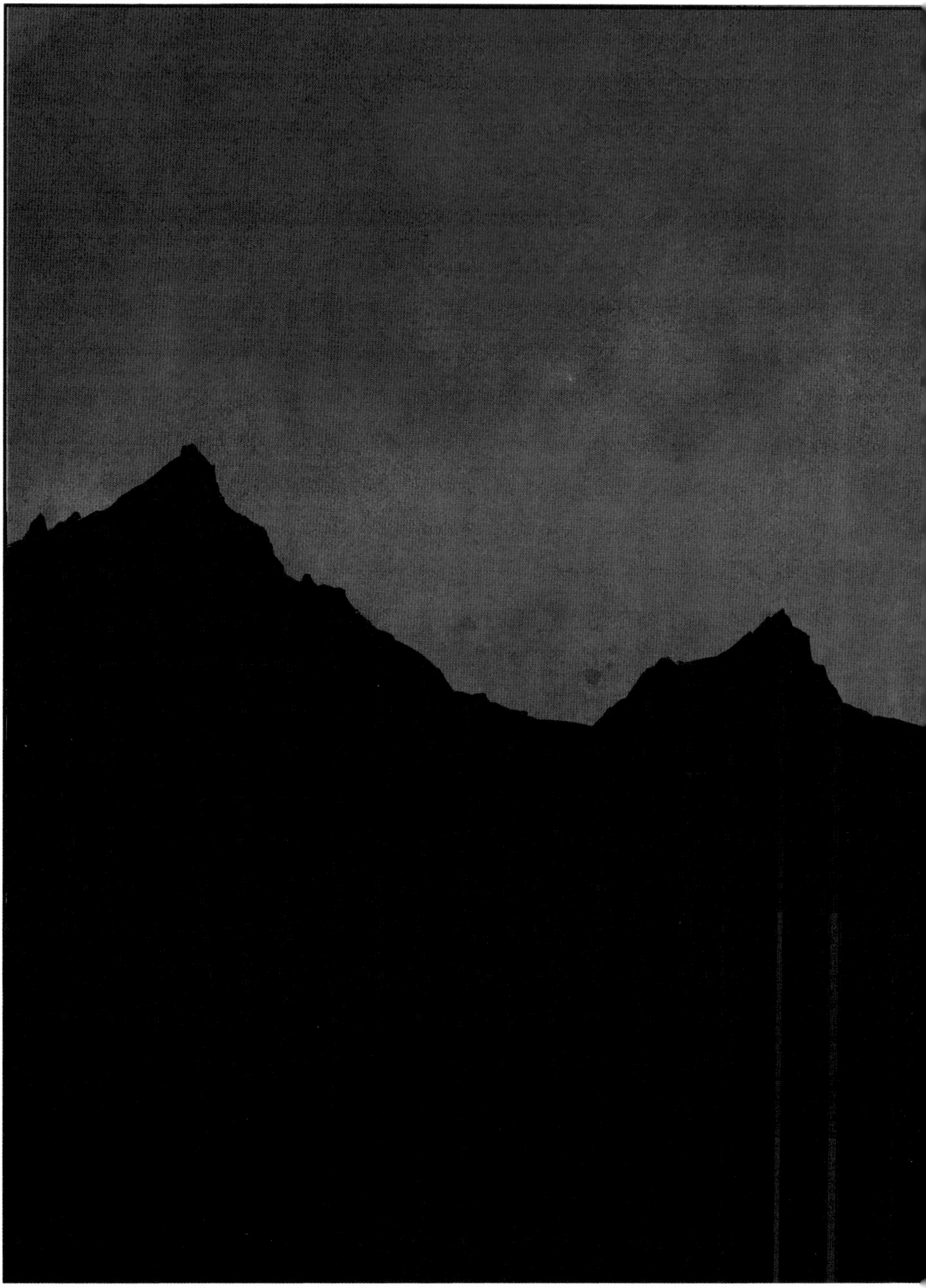

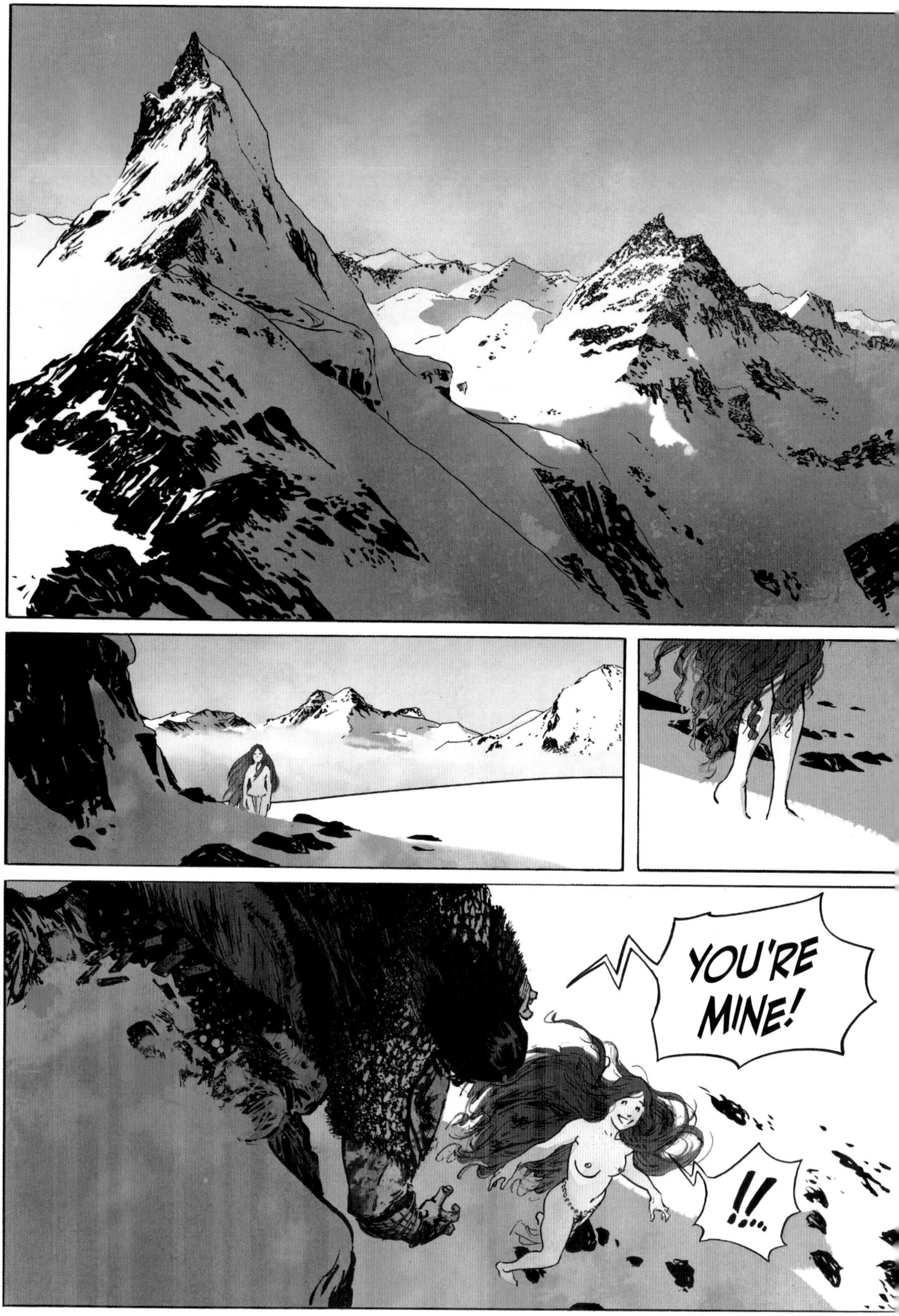

YOU'RE MINE!
!!...

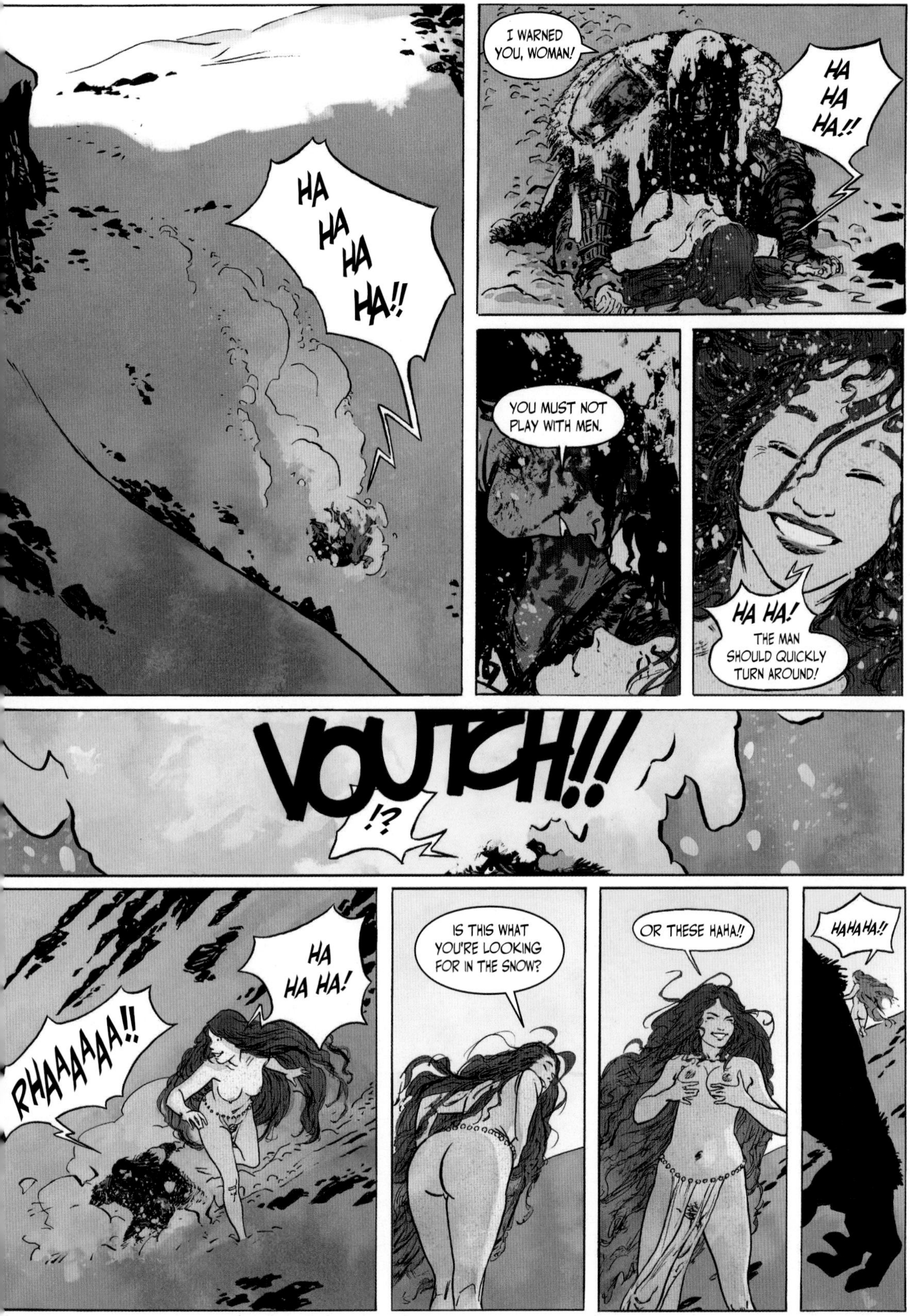

HA HA HA HA!!
I WARNED YOU, WOMAN!
HA HA HA!!
YOU MUST NOT PLAY WITH MEN.
HA HA! THE MAN SHOULD QUICKLY TURN AROUND!
VOUTCH!!
!?
RHAAAAA!!
HA HA HA!
IS THIS WHAT YOU'RE LOOKING FOR IN THE SNOW?
OR THESE HAHA!!
HAHAHA!!

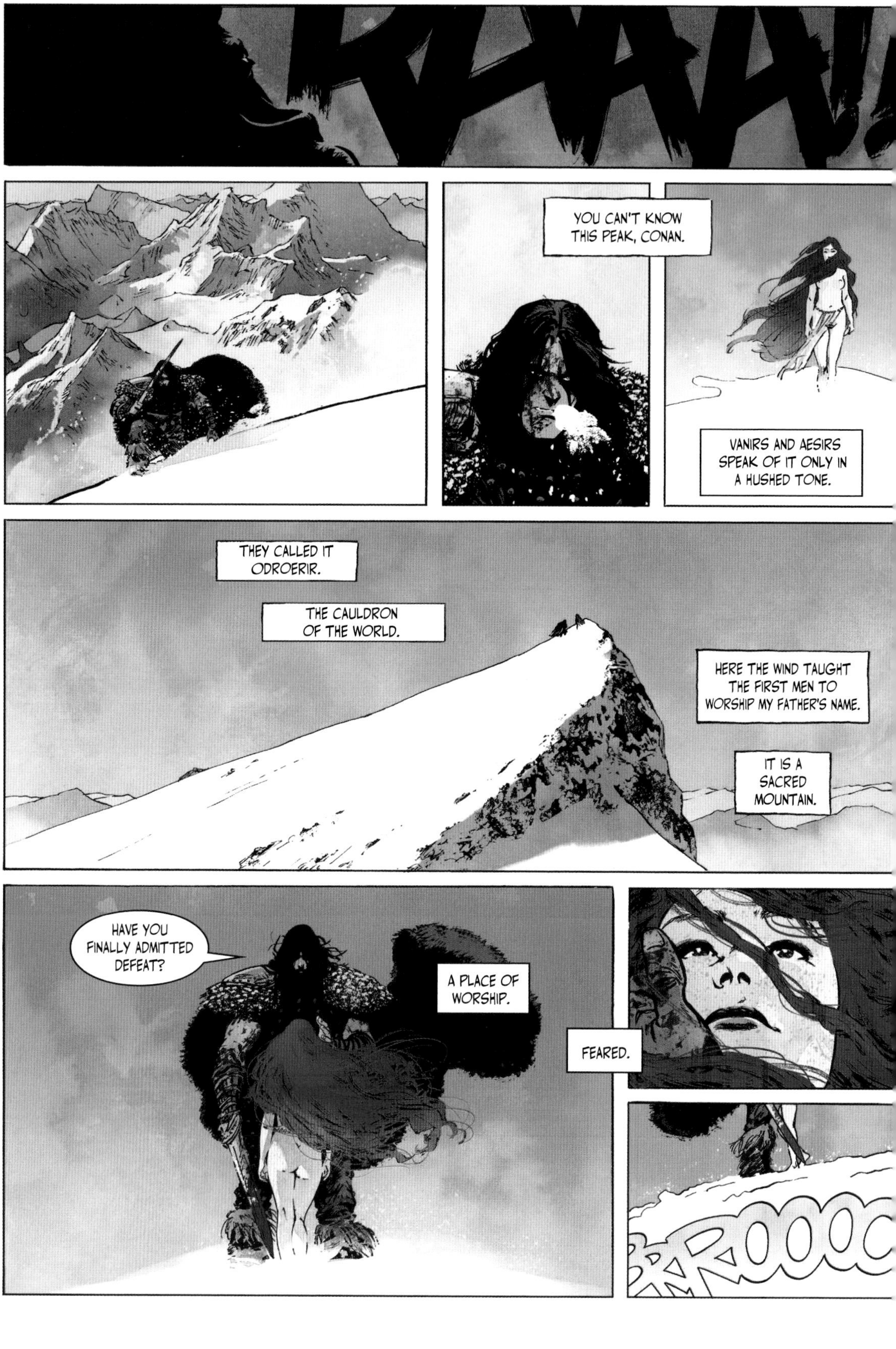
RAAA!!
YOU CAN'T KNOW THIS PEAK, CONAN.
VANIRS AND AESIRS SPEAK OF IT ONLY IN A HUSHED TONE.
THEY CALLED IT ODROERIR.
THE CAULDRON OF THE WORLD.
HERE THE WIND TAUGHT THE FIRST MEN TO WORSHIP MY FATHER'S NAME.
IT IS A SACRED MOUNTAIN.
HAVE YOU FINALLY ADMITTED DEFEAT?
A PLACE OF WORSHIP.
FEARED.
BRROOOO

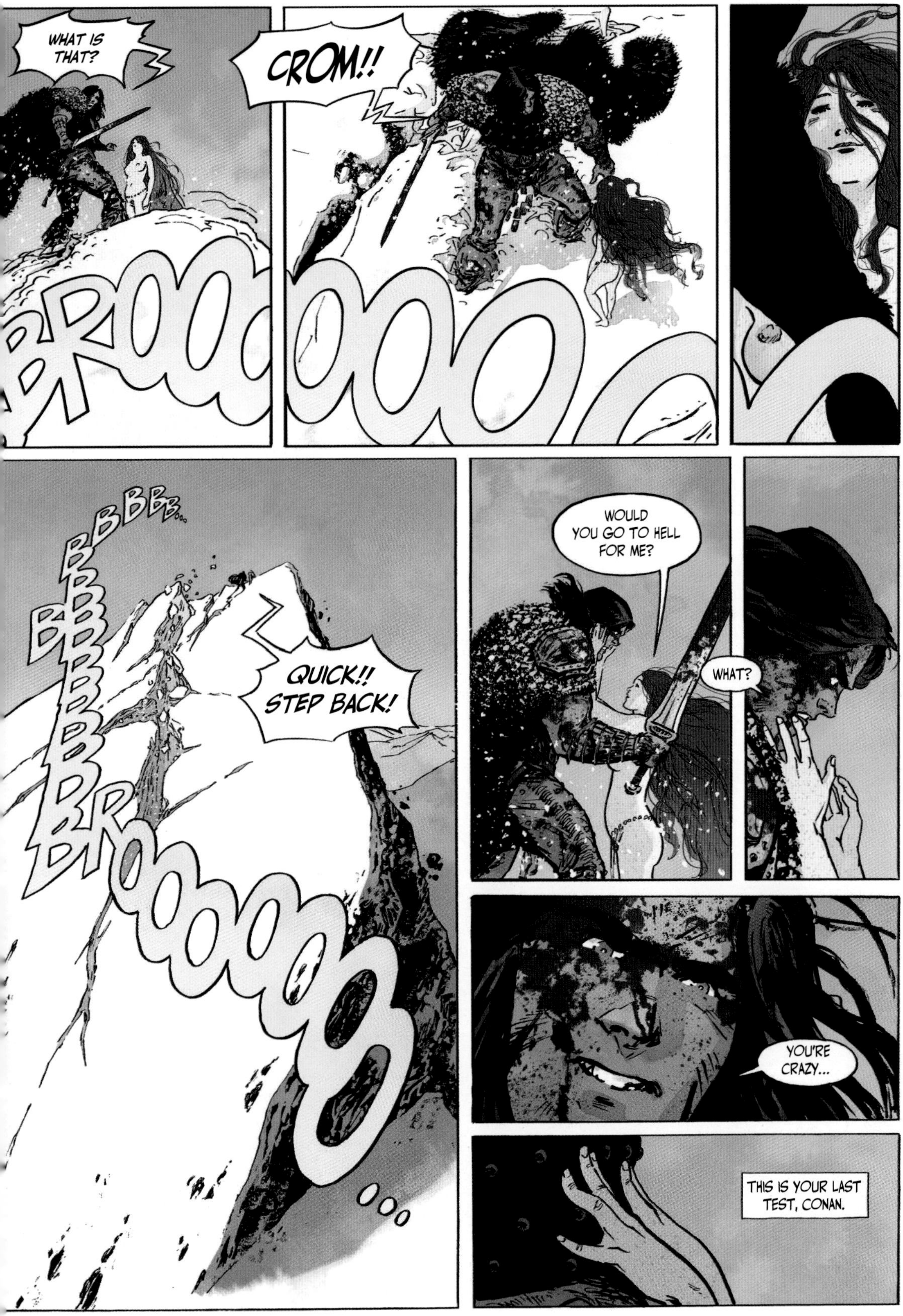
WHAT IS THAT?
CROM!!
BROOOOOOOO
BBBBB...
BBBBBBBBBBBROOOOOOOO...
QUICK!! STEP BACK!
WOULD YOU GO TO HELL FOR ME?
WHAT?
YOU'RE CRAZY...
THIS IS YOUR LAST TEST, CONAN.

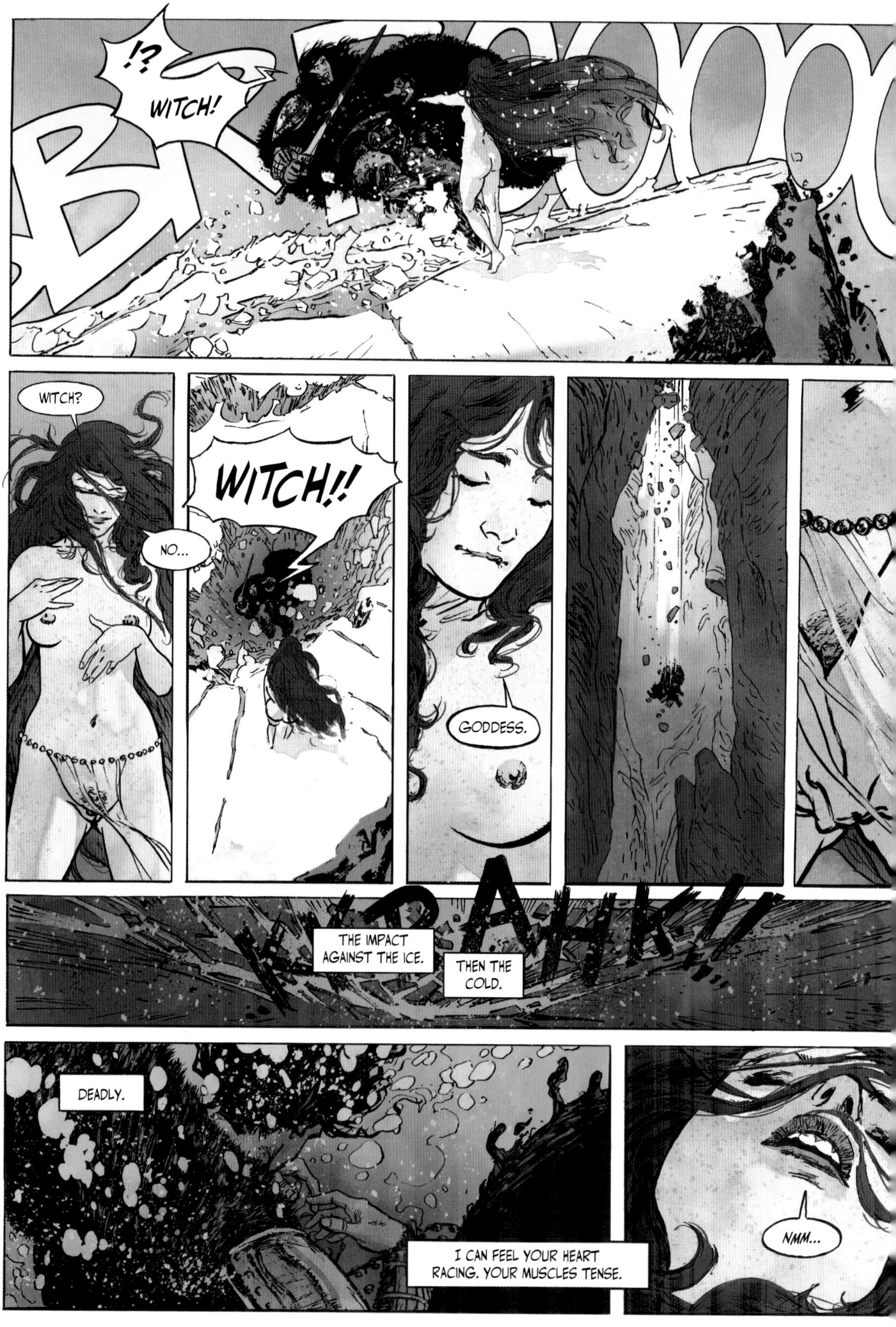
!?
WITCH!
WITCH?
NO...
WITCH!!
GODDESS.
THE IMPACT AGAINST THE ICE.
THEN THE COLD.
DEADLY.
I CAN FEEL YOUR HEART RACING. YOUR MUSCLES TENSE.
NMM...

I CAN SEE YOUR FEAR.

INSTINCTIVE.

VISCERAL.

CONAN.

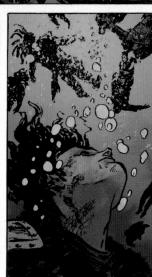

COME BACK TO ME.

QUICK.

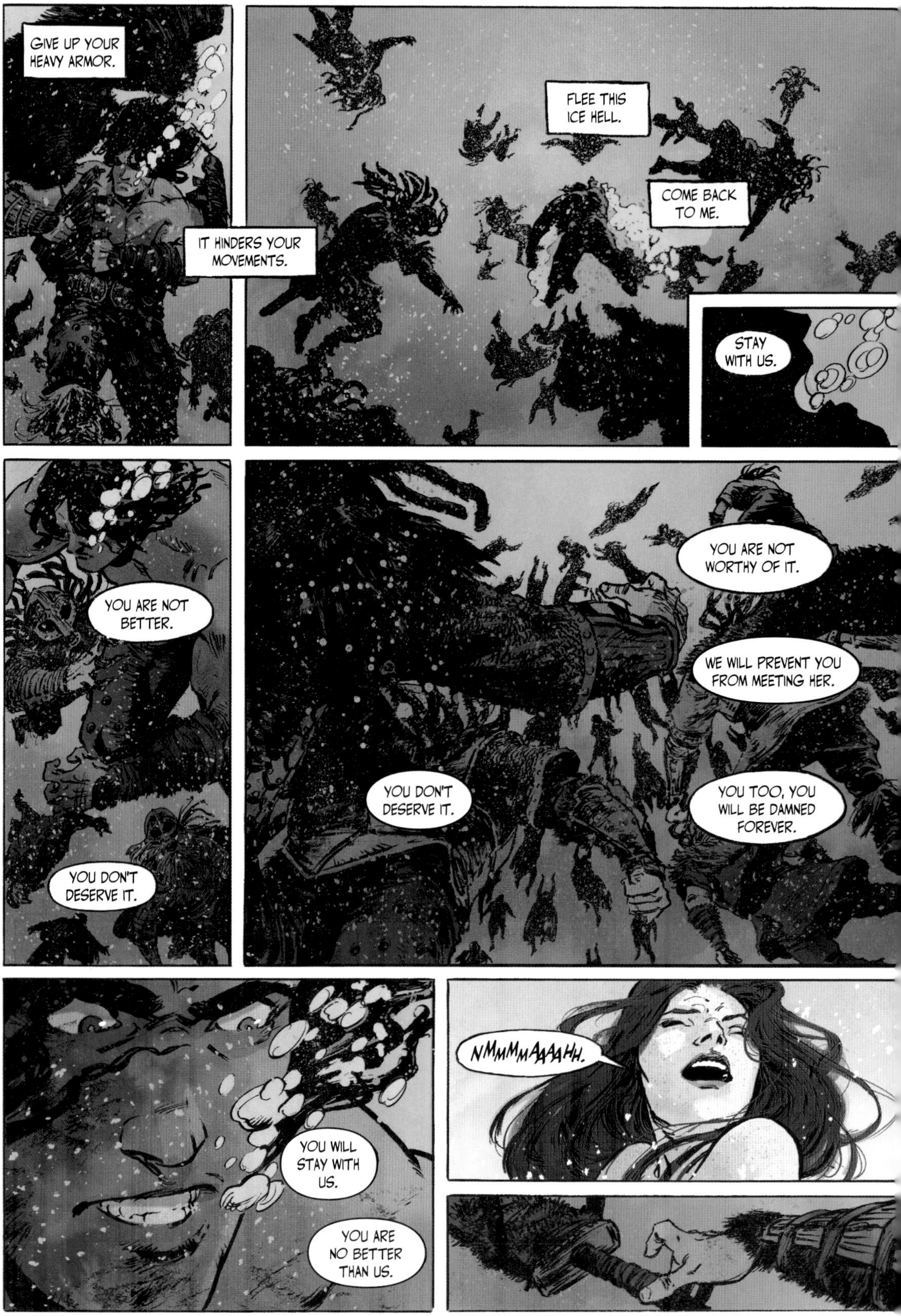
GIVE UP YOUR HEAVY ARMOR.
IT HINDERS YOUR MOVEMENTS.
FLEE THIS ICE HELL.
COME BACK TO ME.
STAY WITH US.
YOU ARE NOT BETTER.
YOU DON'T DESERVE IT.
YOU ARE NOT WORTHY OF IT.
WE WILL PREVENT YOU FROM MEETING HER.
YOU DON'T DESERVE IT.
YOU TOO, YOU WILL BE DAMNED FOREVER.
YOU WILL STAY WITH US.
YOU ARE NO BETTER THAN US.
NMMMMAAAAHH.

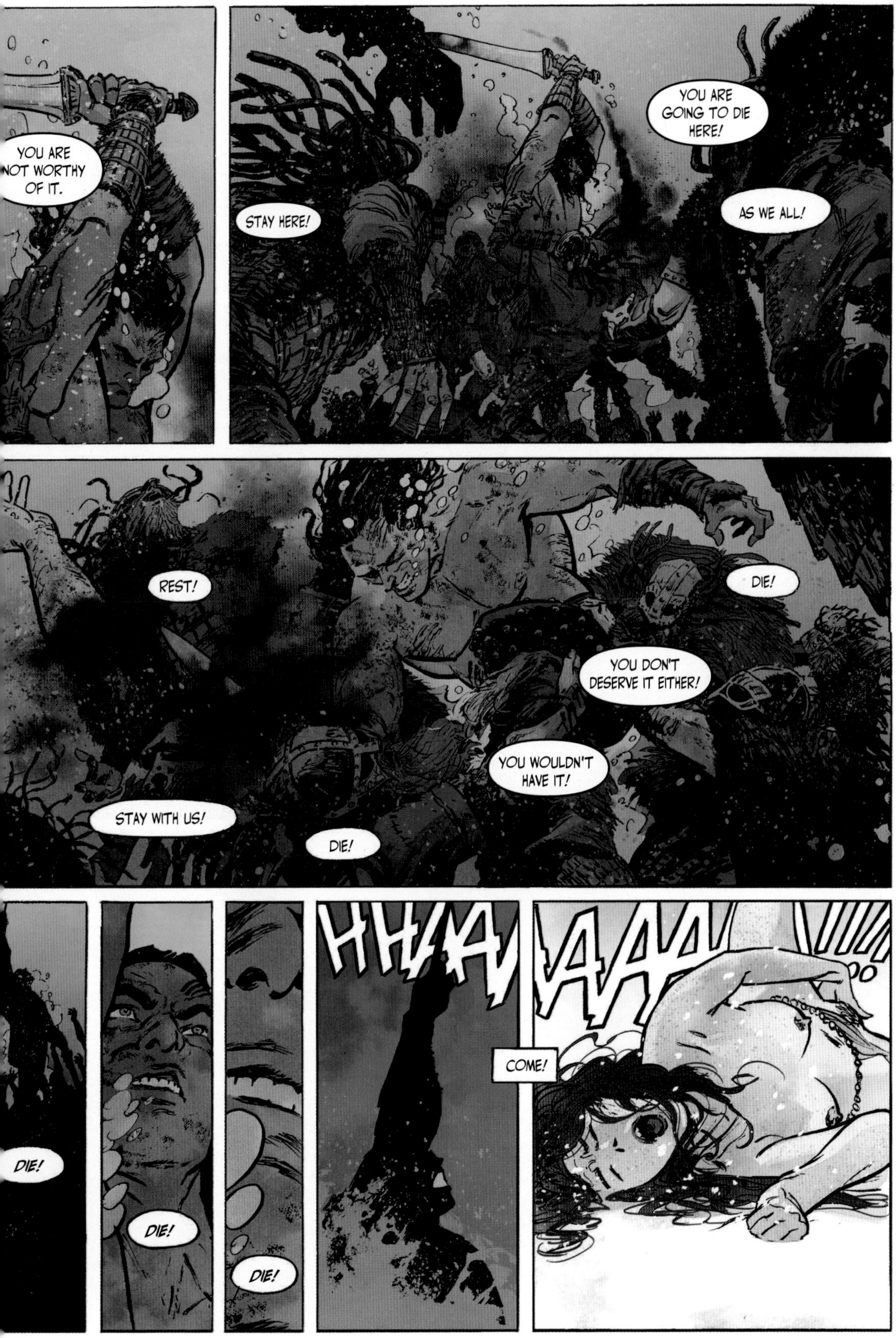
YOU ARE NOT WORTHY OF IT.
STAY HERE!
YOU ARE GOING TO DIE HERE!
AS WE ALL!
REST!
DIE!
YOU DON'T DESERVE IT EITHER!
YOU WOULDN'T HAVE IT!
STAY WITH US!
DIE!
DIE!
DIE!
DIE!
HHAAAAAAA
COME!

COME!

HNNG...

WITCH...

...WITCH!!!

YOU WILL PAY, YOU HEAR ME!!!

MMMM, COME ON!

YOU'RE MINE!!

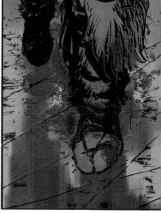

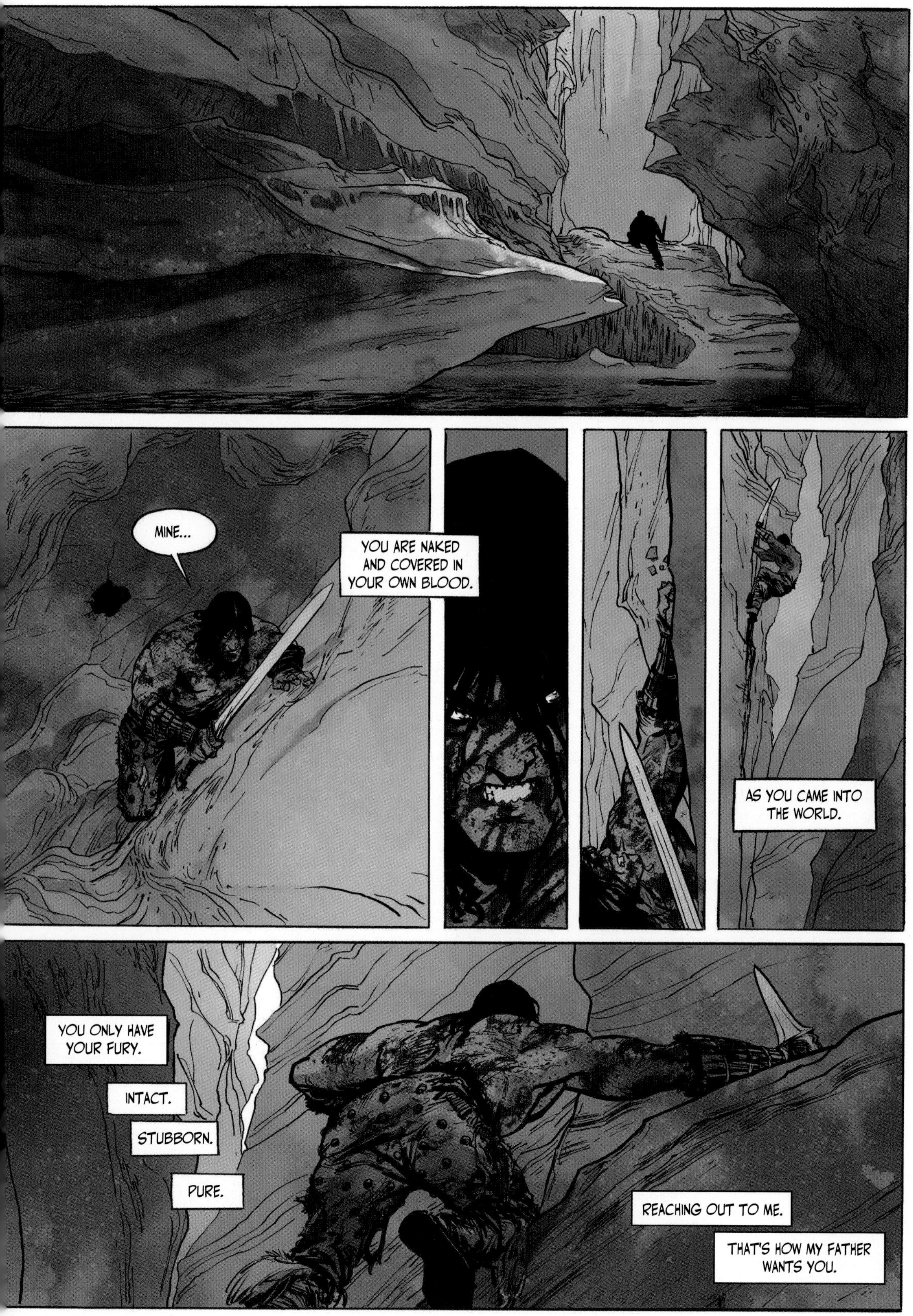
MINE...
YOU ARE NAKED AND COVERED IN YOUR OWN BLOOD.
AS YOU CAME INTO THE WORLD.
YOU ONLY HAVE YOUR FURY.
INTACT.
STUBBORN.
PURE.
REACHING OUT TO ME.
THAT'S HOW MY FATHER WANTS YOU.

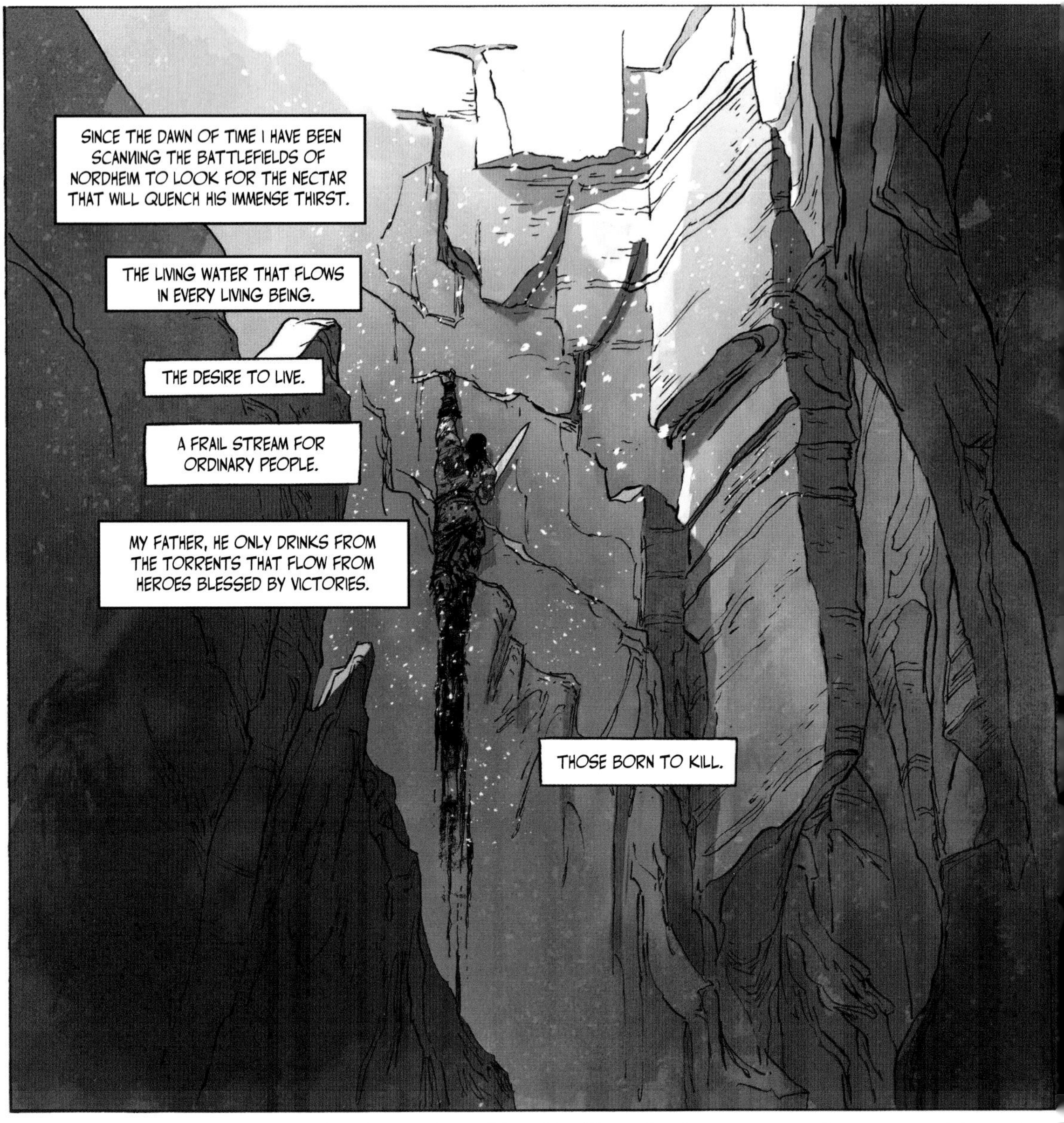
SINCE THE DAWN OF TIME I HAVE BEEN SCANNING THE BATTLEFIELDS OF NORDHEIM TO LOOK FOR THE NECTAR THAT WILL QUENCH HIS IMMENSE THIRST.
THE LIVING WATER THAT FLOWS IN EVERY LIVING BEING.
THE DESIRE TO LIVE.
A FRAIL STREAM FOR ORDINARY PEOPLE.
MY FATHER, HE ONLY DRINKS FROM THE TORRENTS THAT FLOW FROM HEROES BLESSED BY VICTORIES.
THOSE BORN TO KILL.

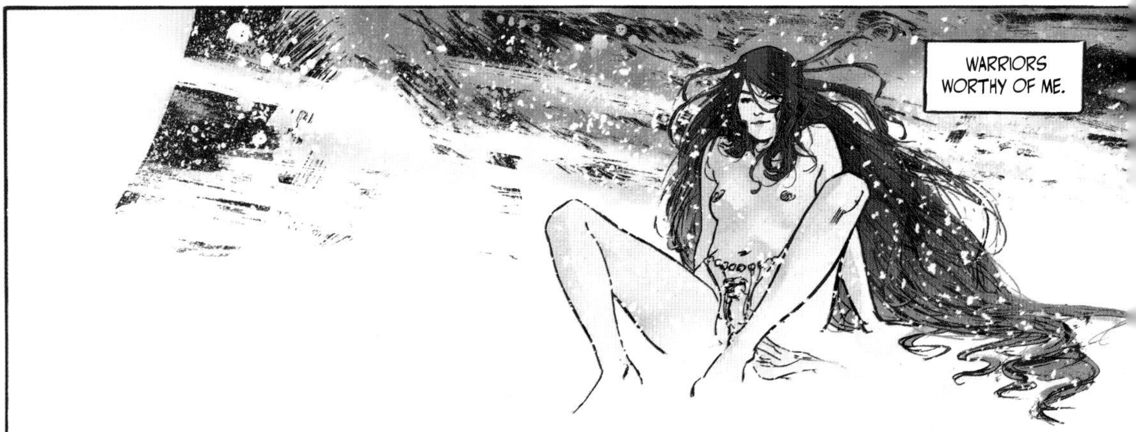
WARRIORS WORTHY OF ME.

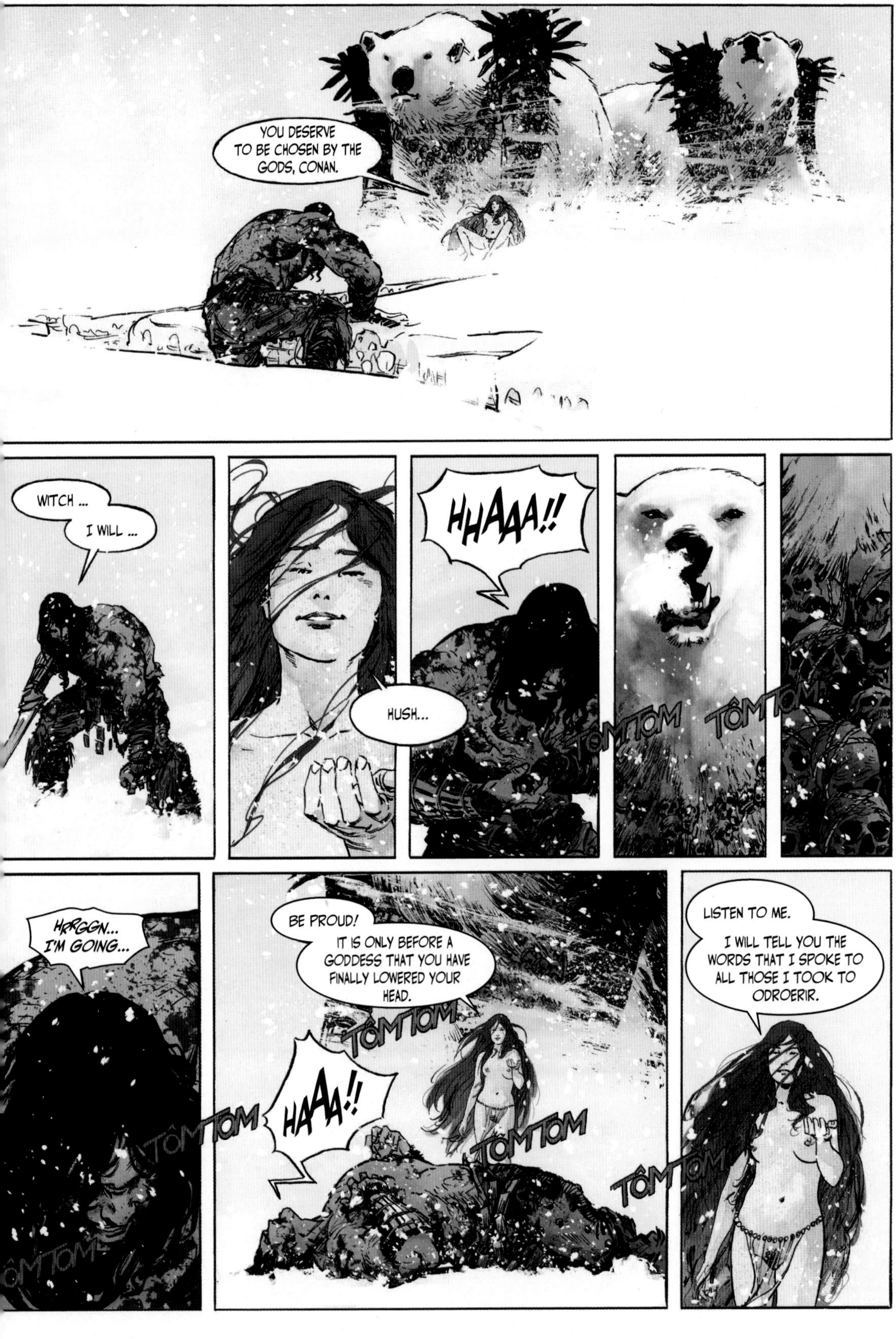

YOU DESERVE TO BE CHOSEN BY THE GODS, CONAN.
WITCH ...
I WILL ...
HUSH...
HHAAA!!
TÔMTOM
TÔMTOM
HRRGGN... I'M GOING...
TÔMTOM
TÔMTOM
BE PROUD!
IT IS ONLY BEFORE A GODDESS THAT YOU HAVE FINALLY LOWERED YOUR HEAD.
TÔMTOM
HAAA!!
TÔMTOM
TÔMTOM
LISTEN TO ME.
I WILL TELL YOU THE WORDS THAT I SPOKE TO ALL THOSE I TOOK TO ODROERIR.

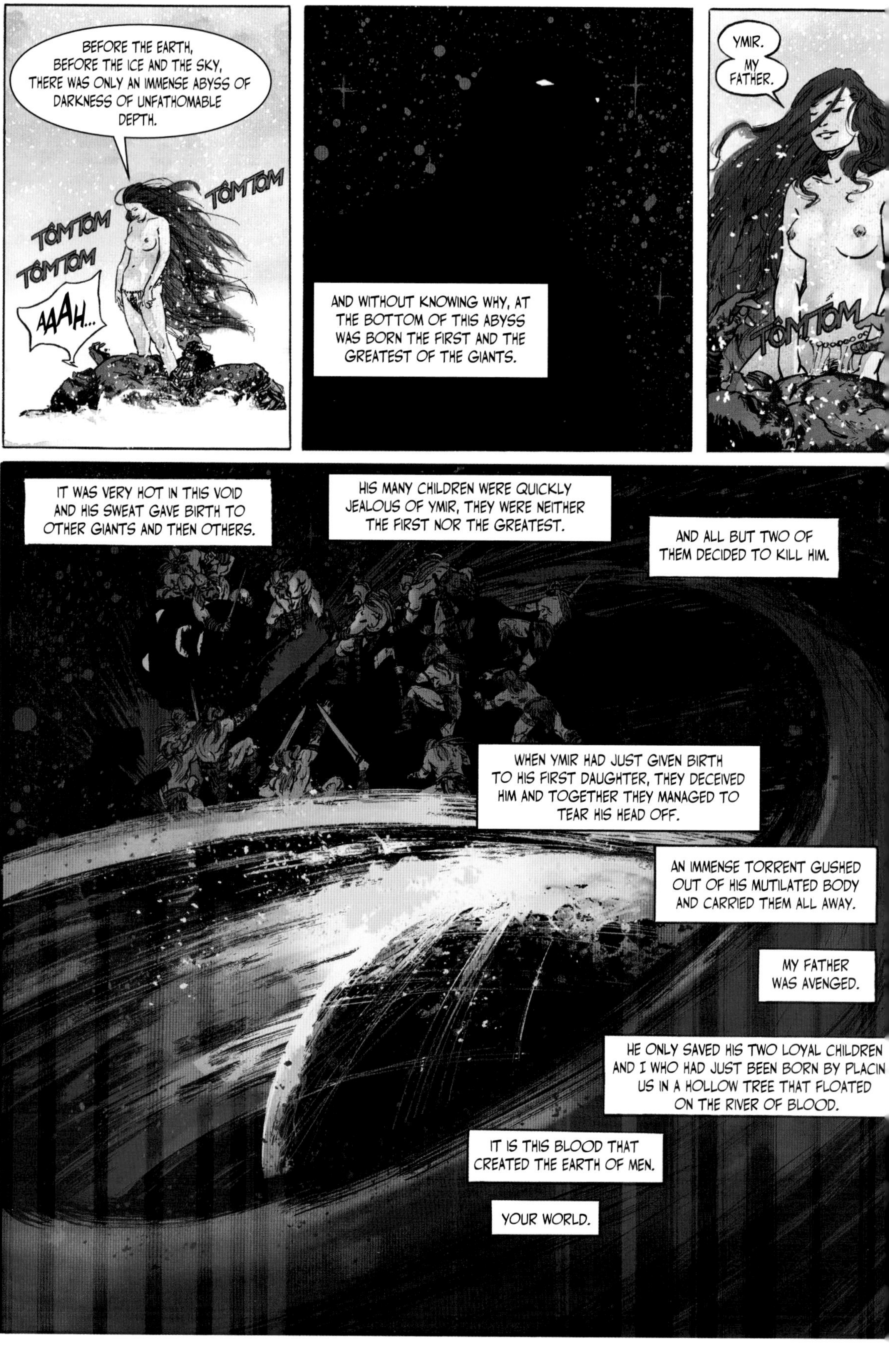
BEFORE THE EARTH, BEFORE THE ICE AND THE SKY, THERE WAS ONLY AN IMMENSE ABYSS OF DARKNESS OF UNFATHOMABLE DEPTH.
TÔMTOM
TÔMTOM
TÔMTOM
AAAH...
AND WITHOUT KNOWING WHY, AT THE BOTTOM OF THIS ABYSS WAS BORN THE FIRST AND THE GREATEST OF THE GIANTS.
YMIR. MY FATHER.
TÔMTOM
IT WAS VERY HOT IN THIS VOID AND HIS SWEAT GAVE BIRTH TO OTHER GIANTS AND THEN OTHERS.
HIS MANY CHILDREN WERE QUICKLY JEALOUS OF YMIR, THEY WERE NEITHER THE FIRST NOR THE GREATEST.
AND ALL BUT TWO OF THEM DECIDED TO KILL HIM.
WHEN YMIR HAD JUST GIVEN BIRTH TO HIS FIRST DAUGHTER, THEY DECEIVED HIM AND TOGETHER THEY MANAGED TO TEAR HIS HEAD OFF.
AN IMMENSE TORRENT GUSHED OUT OF HIS MUTILATED BODY AND CARRIED THEM ALL AWAY.
MY FATHER WAS AVENGED.
HE ONLY SAVED HIS TWO LOYAL CHILDREN AND I WHO HAD JUST BEEN BORN BY PLACIN US IN A HOLLOW TREE THAT FLOATED ON THE RIVER OF BLOOD.
IT IS THIS BLOOD THAT CREATED THE EARTH OF MEN.
YOUR WORLD.

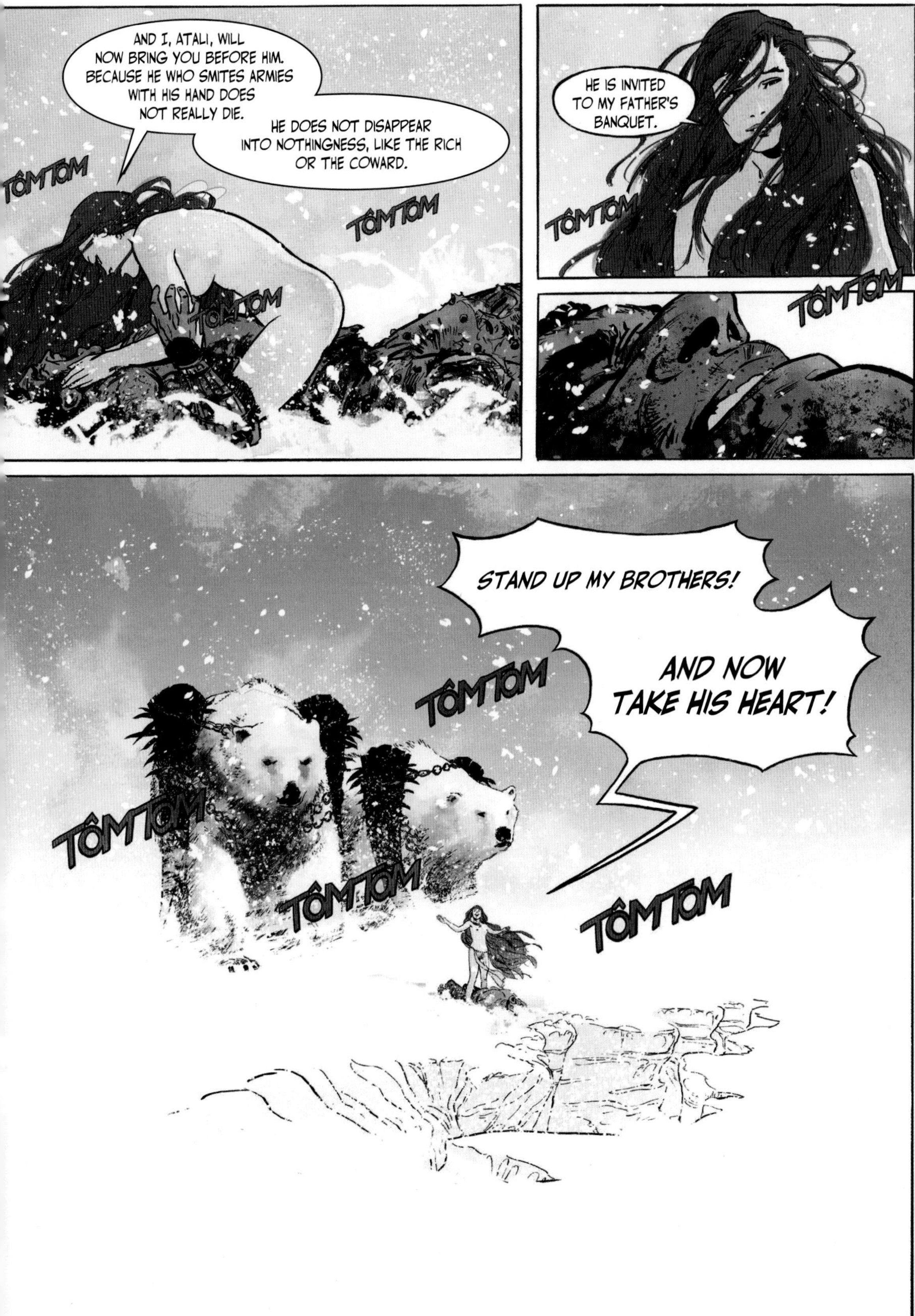
AND I, ATALI, WILL NOW BRING YOU BEFORE HIM. BECAUSE HE WHO SMITES ARMIES WITH HIS HAND DOES NOT REALLY DIE.
HE DOES NOT DISAPPEAR INTO NOTHINGNESS, LIKE THE RICH OR THE COWARD.
TÔMTOM
TÔMTOM
TÔMTOM
HE IS INVITED TO MY FATHER'S BANQUET.
TÔMTOM
TÔMTOM
STAND UP MY BROTHERS!
AND NOW TAKE HIS HEART!
TÔMTOM
TÔMTOM
TÔMTOM
TÔMTOM

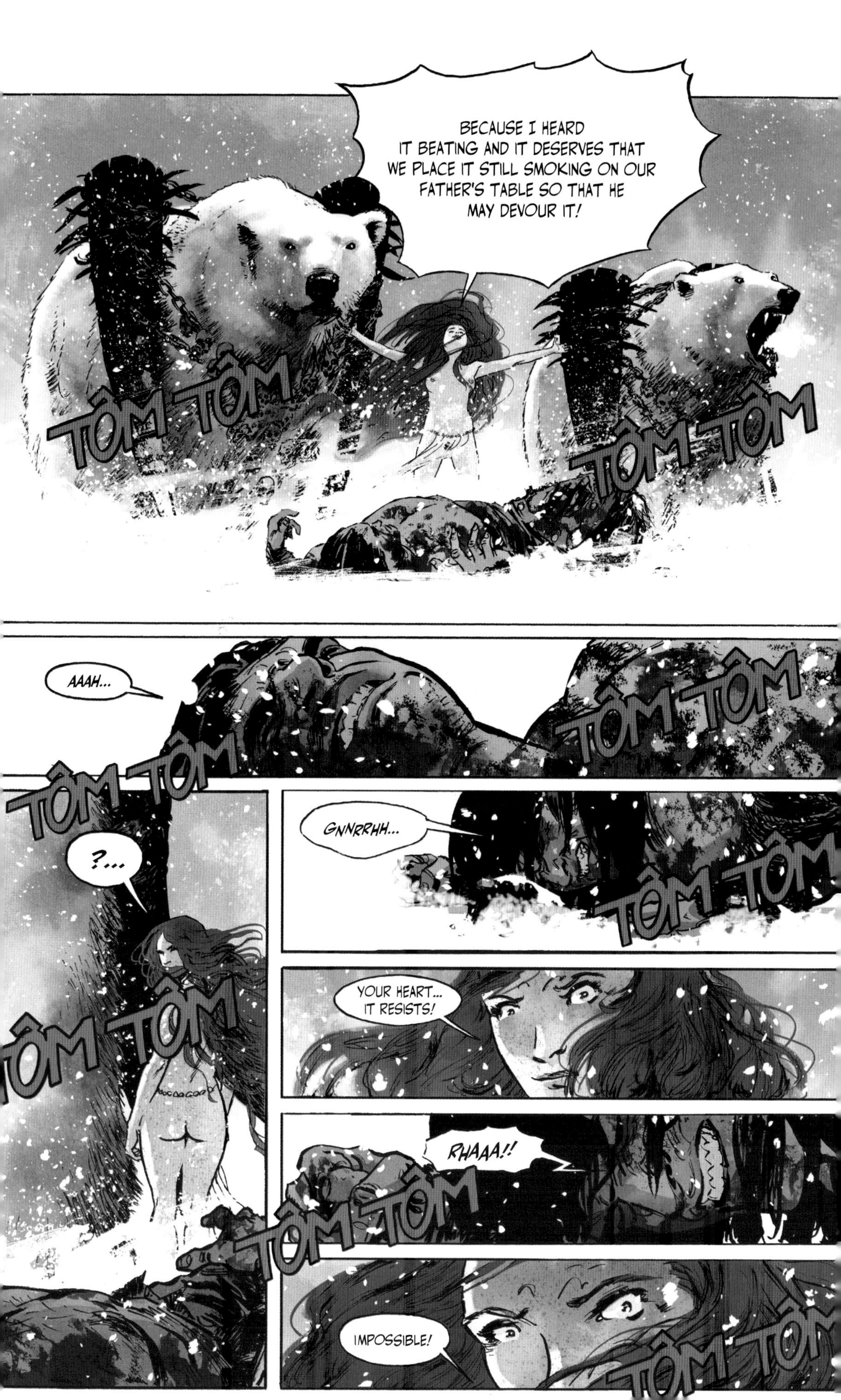
BECAUSE I HEARD IT BEATING AND IT DESERVES THAT WE PLACE IT STILL SMOKING ON OUR FATHER'S TABLE SO THAT HE MAY DEVOUR IT!
TÔM TÔM
TÔM TÔM
AAAH...
TÔM TÔM
TÔM TÔM
?...
TÔM TÔM
GNNRRHH...
TÔM TÔM
YOUR HEART... IT RESISTS!
RHAAA!!
TÔM TÔM
IMPOSSIBLE!
TÔM TÔM

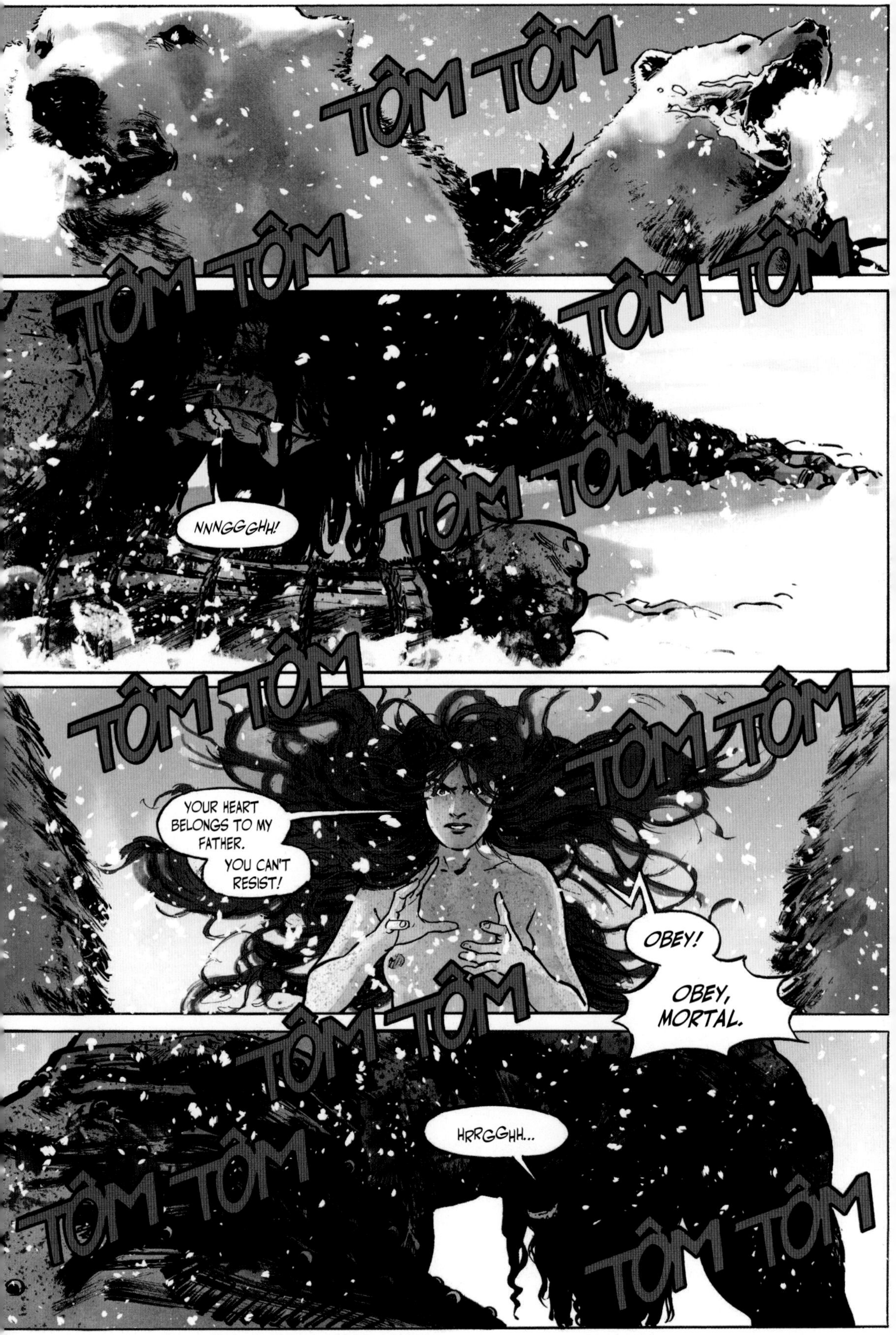

TÔM TÔM
TÔM TÔM
TÔM TÔM
TÔM TÔM
NNNGGGHH!
TÔM TÔM
TÔM TÔM
YOUR HEART BELONGS TO MY FATHER.
YOU CAN'T RESIST!
OBEY!
OBEY, MORTAL.
TÔM TÔM
HRRGGHH...
TÔM TÔM
TÔM TÔM

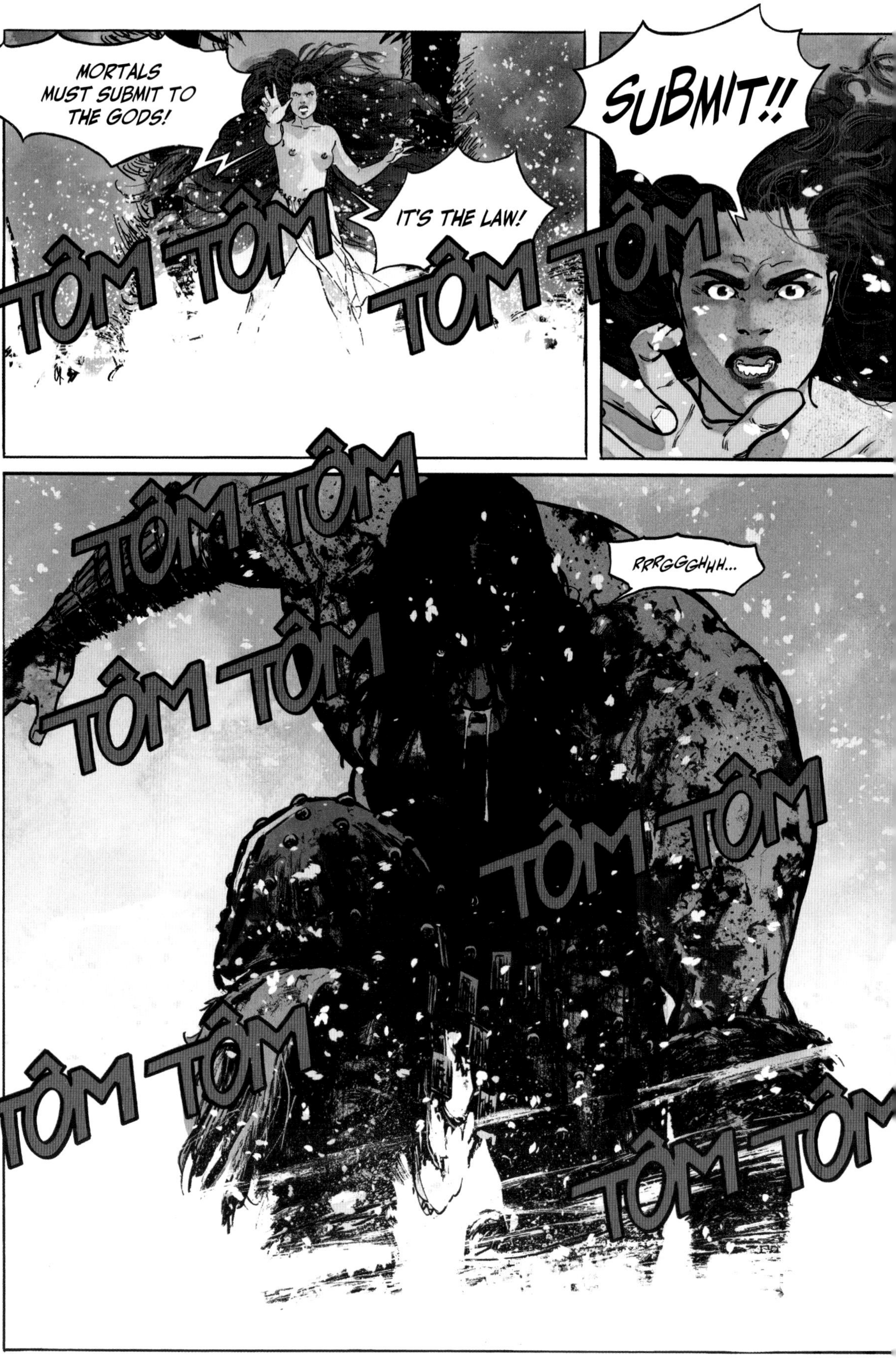
MORTALS MUST SUBMIT TO THE GODS!
IT'S THE LAW!
TÔM TÔM
TÔM TÔM
SUBMIT!!
TÔM TÔM
RRRGGGHHH...
TÔM TÔM
TÔM TÔM
TÔM TÔM
TÔM TÔM

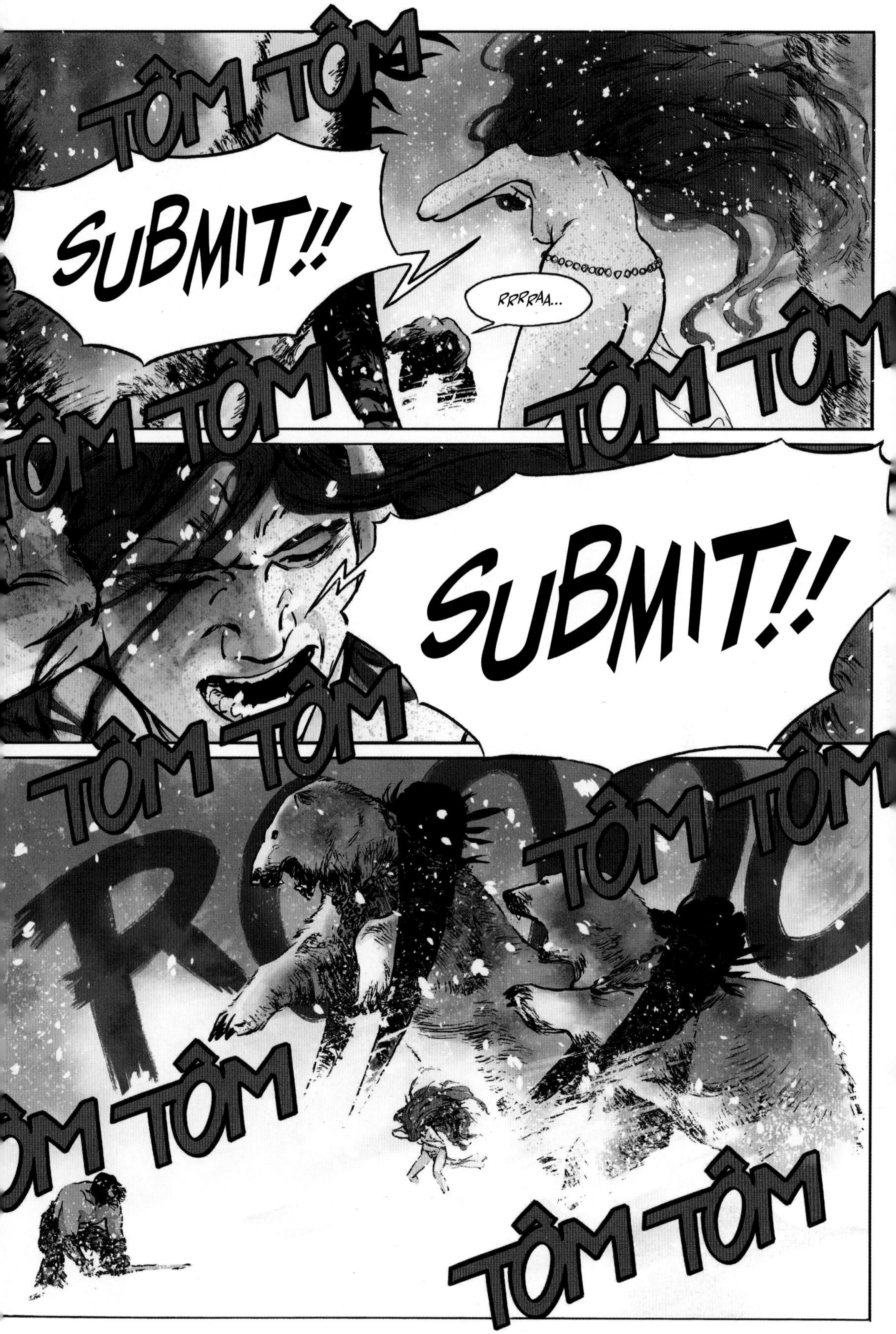
TÔM TÔM
SUBMIT!!
RRRRAA...
ÔM TÔM
TÔM TÔM
SUBMIT!!
TÔM TÔM
TÔM TÔM
ÔM TÔM
TÔM TÔM

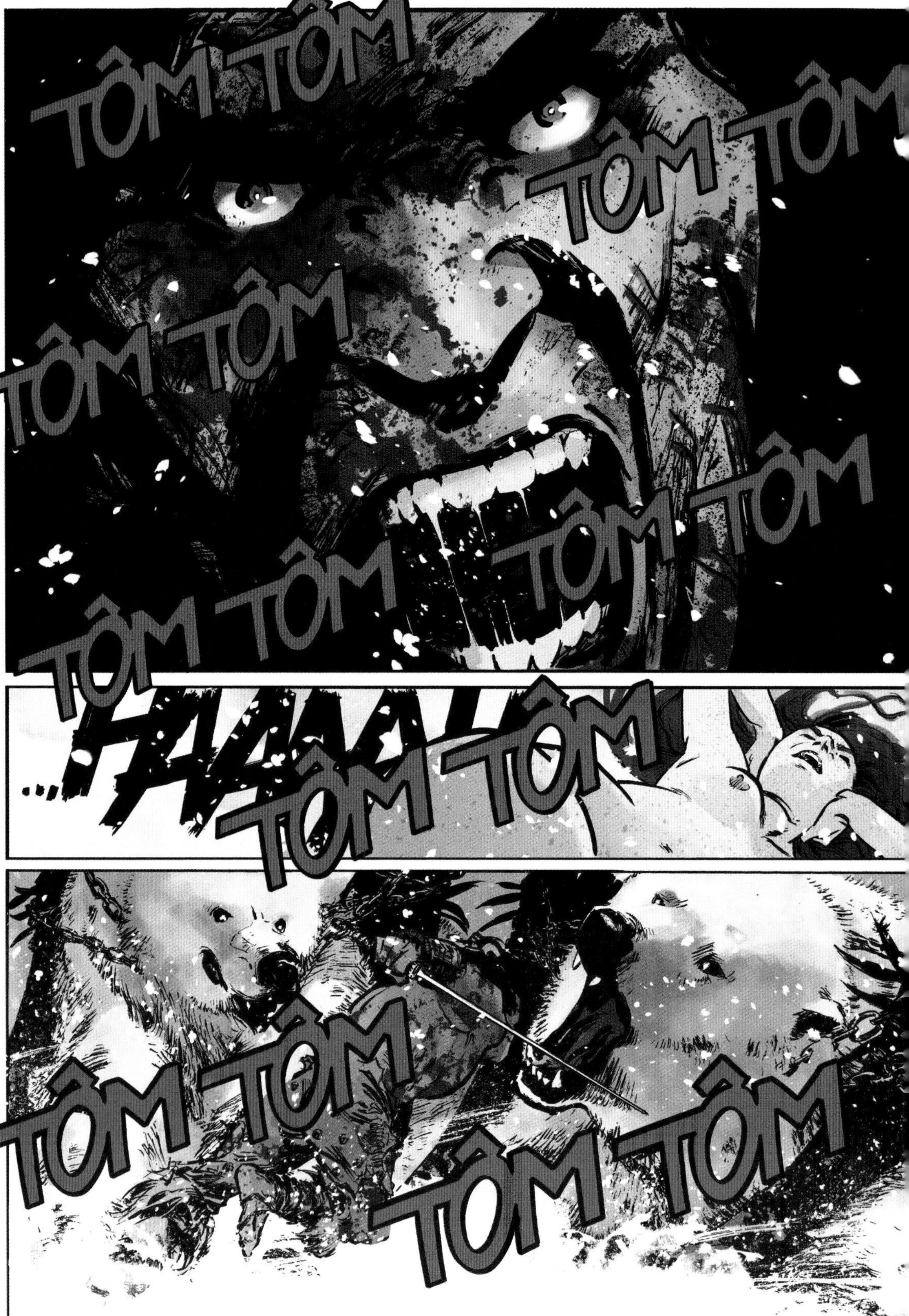
TÔM TÔM
TÔM TÔM
TÔM TÔM
TÔM TÔM
TÔM TÔM
TÔM TÔM
TÔM TÔM
TÔM TÔM

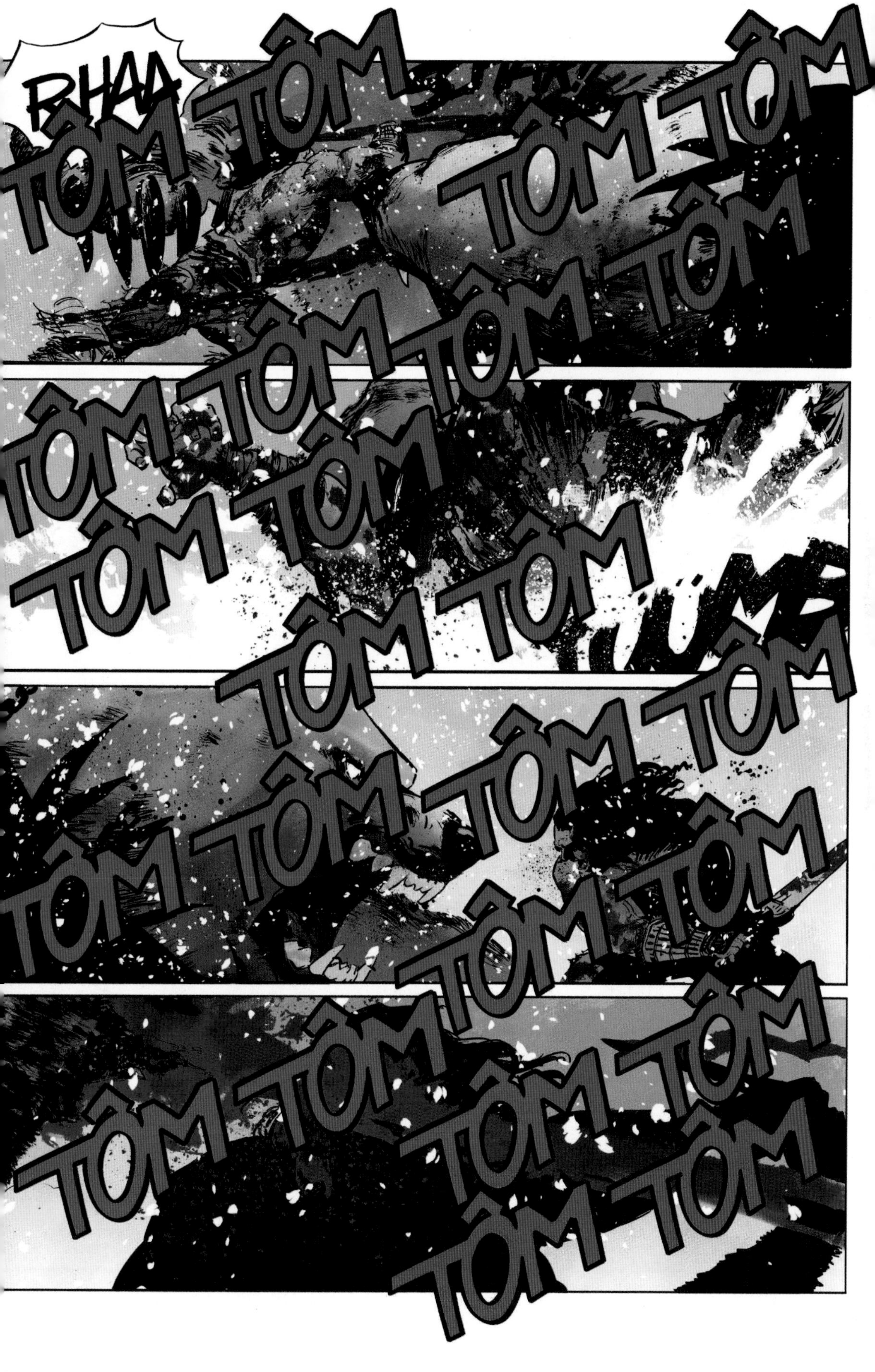
RHAA
TÔM TÔM
TÔM TÔM TÔM
TÔM TÔM TÔM TÔM
TÔM TÔM TÔM
TÔM TÔM
TÔM TÔM TÔM
TÔM TÔM TÔM TÔM
TÔM TÔM TÔM TÔM
TÔM TÔM TÔM
TÔM TÔM

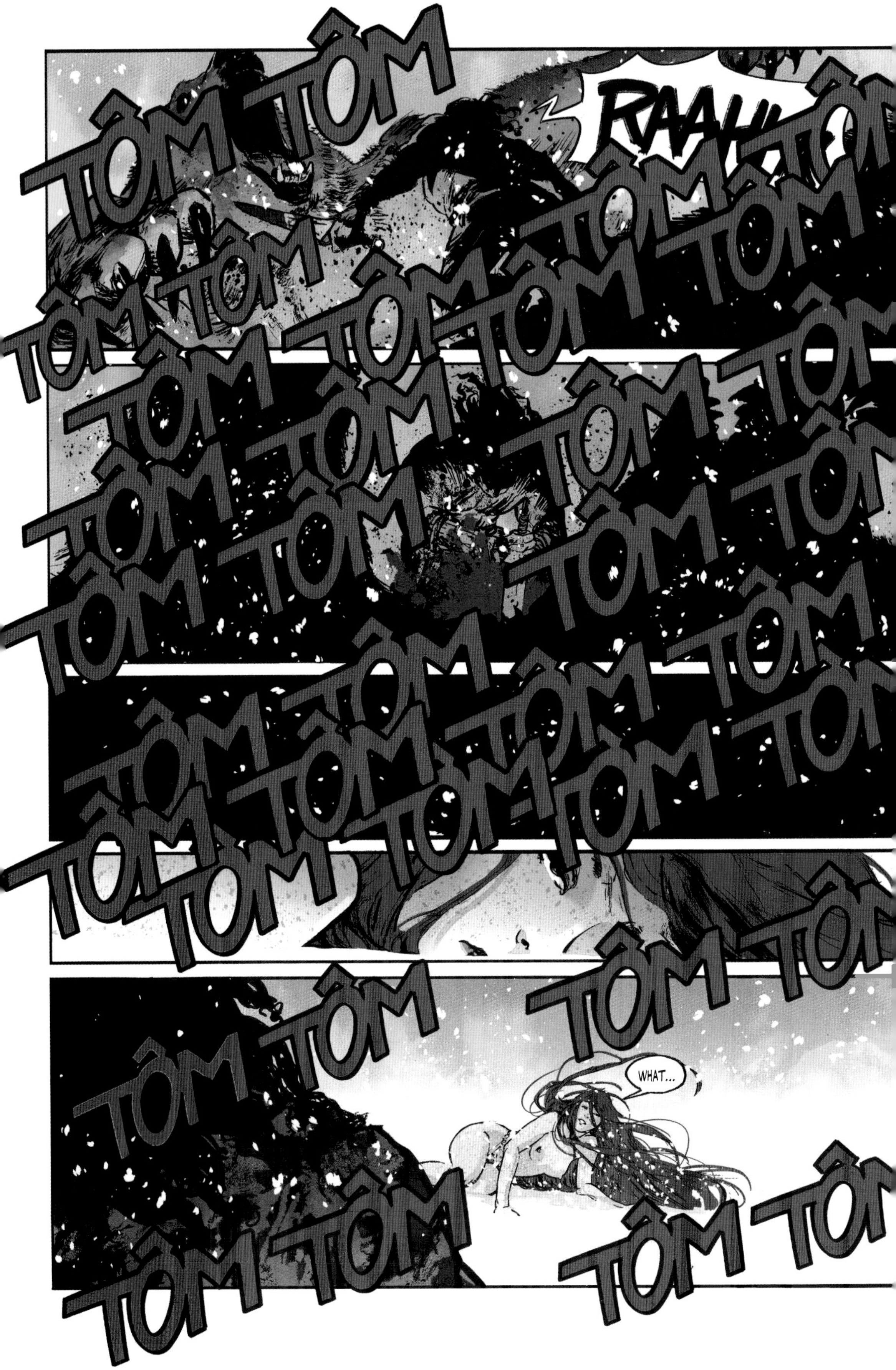
TÔM TÔM
RAAAH!
TÔM TÔM TÔM TÔM TÔM TÔM TÔM TÔM
TÔM TÔM TÔM TÔM TÔM TÔM TÔM TÔM
TÔM TÔM TÔM TÔM TÔM TÔM TÔM TÔM
TÔM TÔM TÔM TÔM
WHAT...
TÔM TÔM TÔM TÔM

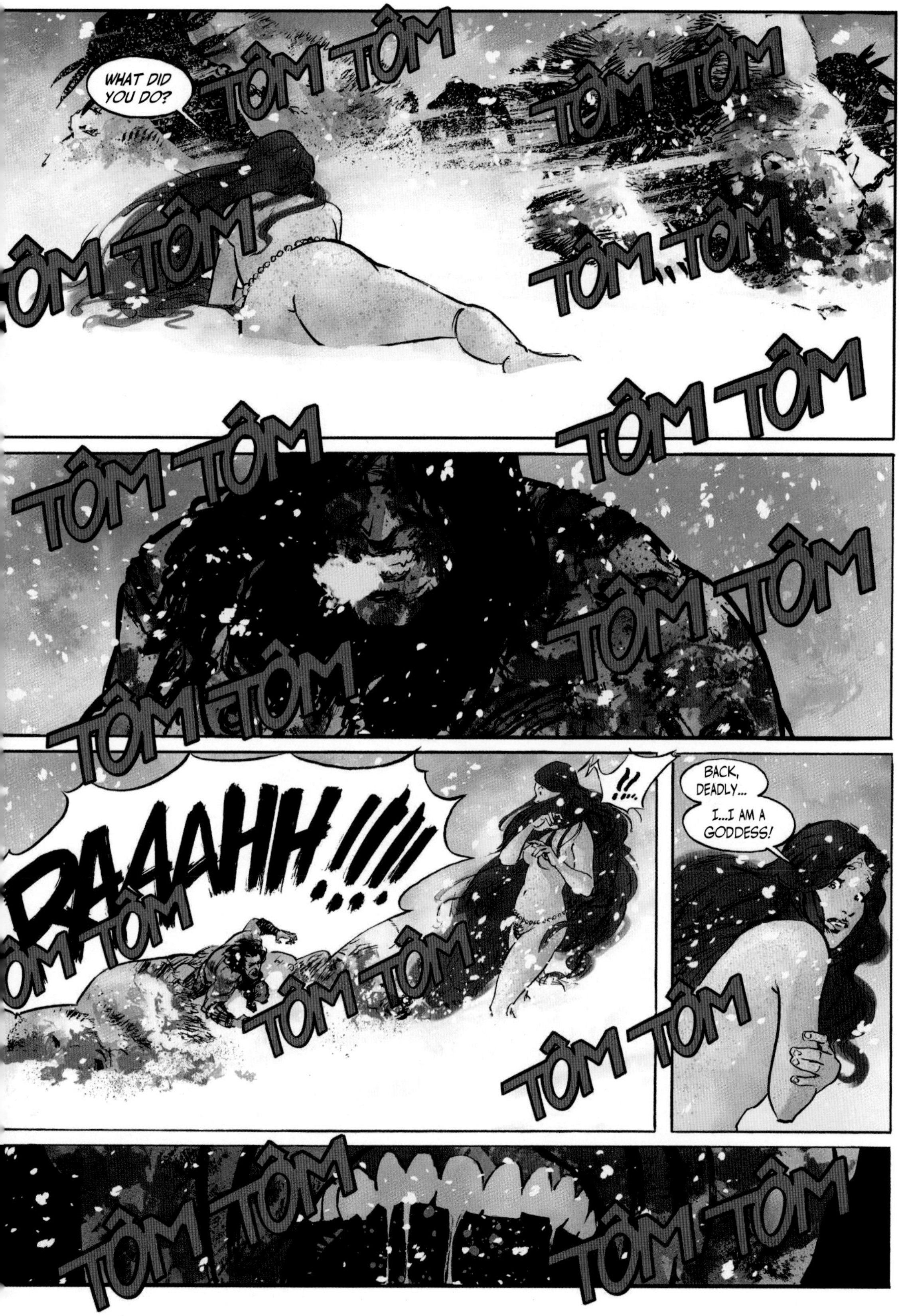
WHAT DID YOU DO?
TÔM TÔM
TÔM TÔM
TÔM TÔM
TÔM TÔM
TÔM TÔM
TÔM TÔM
TÔM TÔM
TÔM TÔM
DAAAHH!!!!
TÔM TÔM
TÔM TÔM
!!!
BACK, DEADLY...
I...I AM A GODDESS!
TÔM TÔM
TÔM TÔM
TÔM TÔM

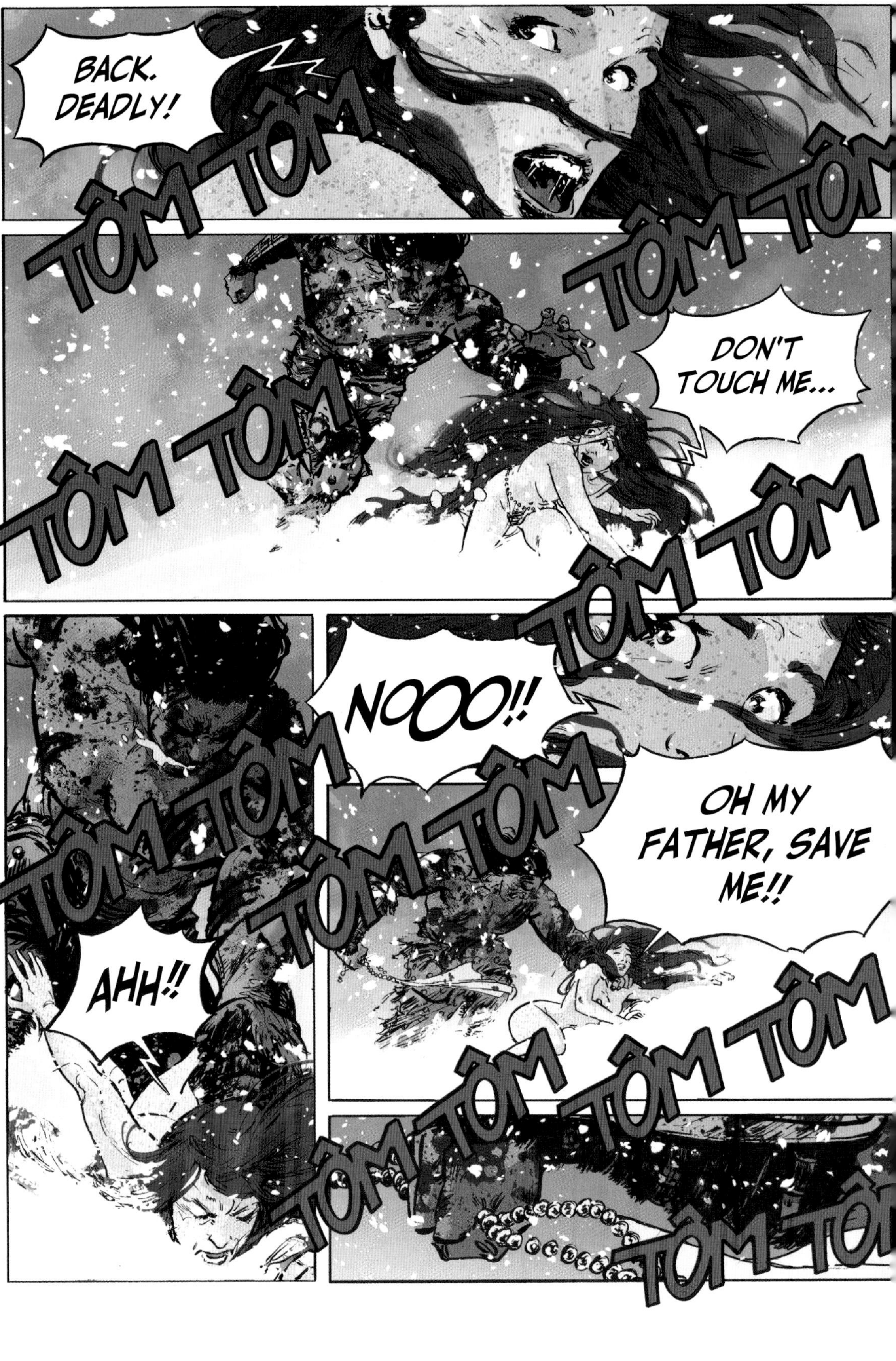
BACK. DEADLY!
TÔM TÔM
TÔM TÔM
DON'T TOUCH ME...
TÔM TÔM
TÔM TÔM
TÔM TÔM
NOOO!!
TÔM TÔM
TÔM TÔM
OH MY FATHER, SAVE ME!!
AHH!!
TÔM TÔM
TÔM TÔM
TÔM TÔM

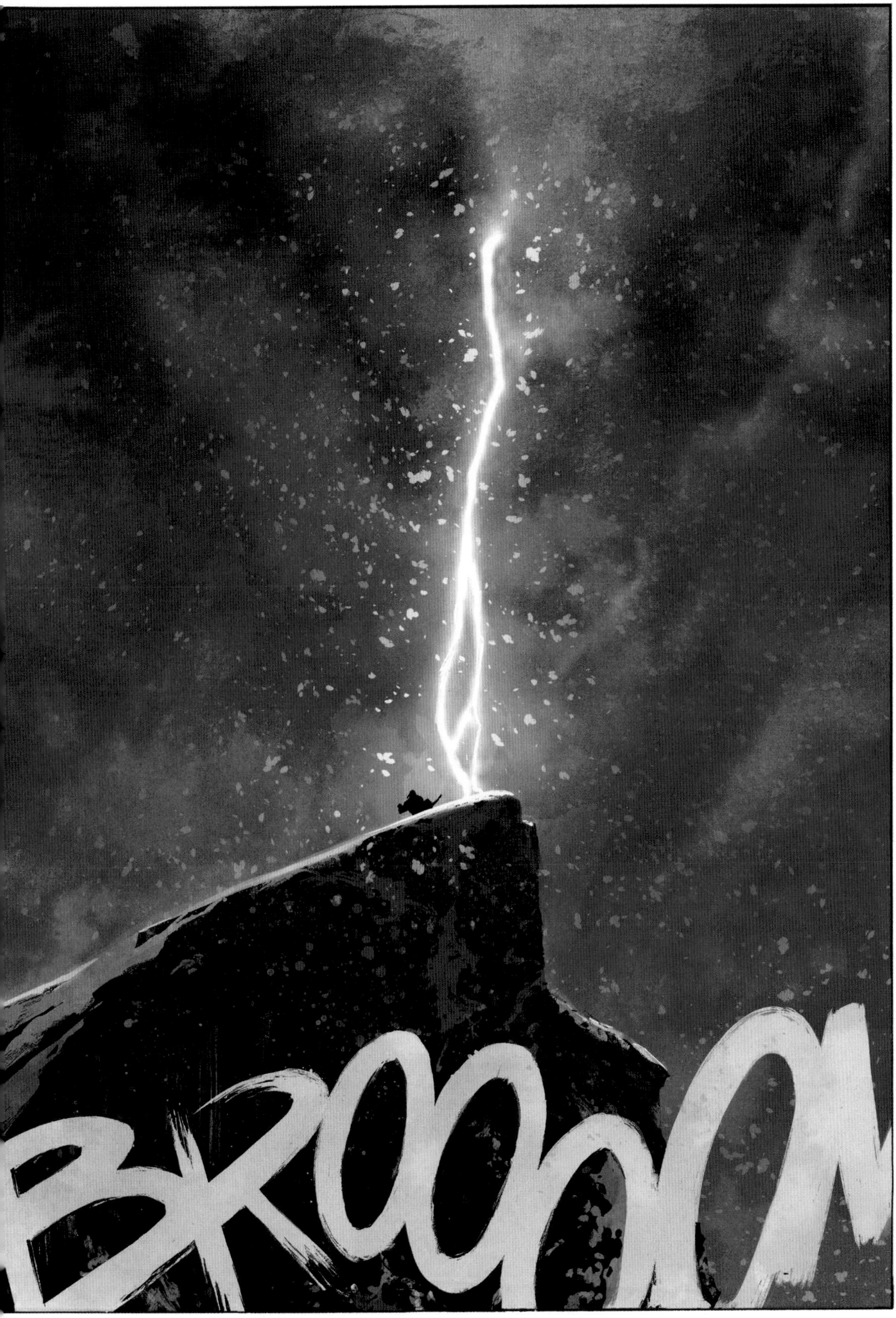
BROOOOM

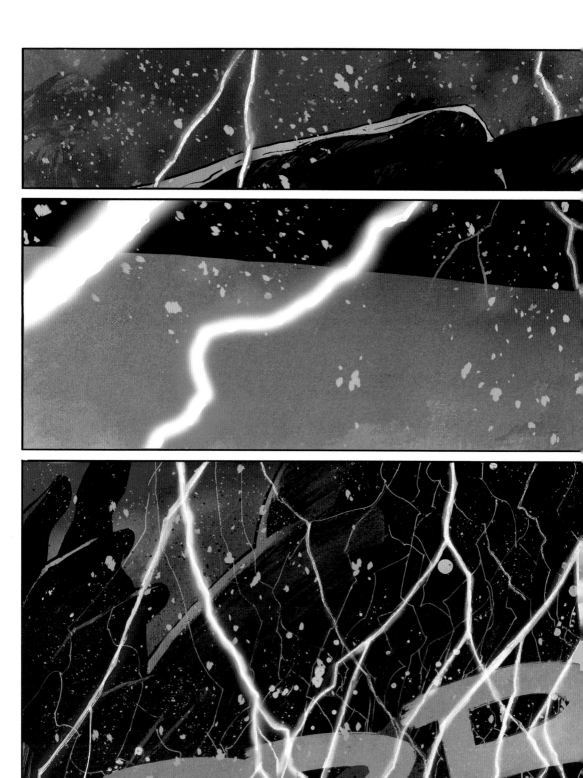

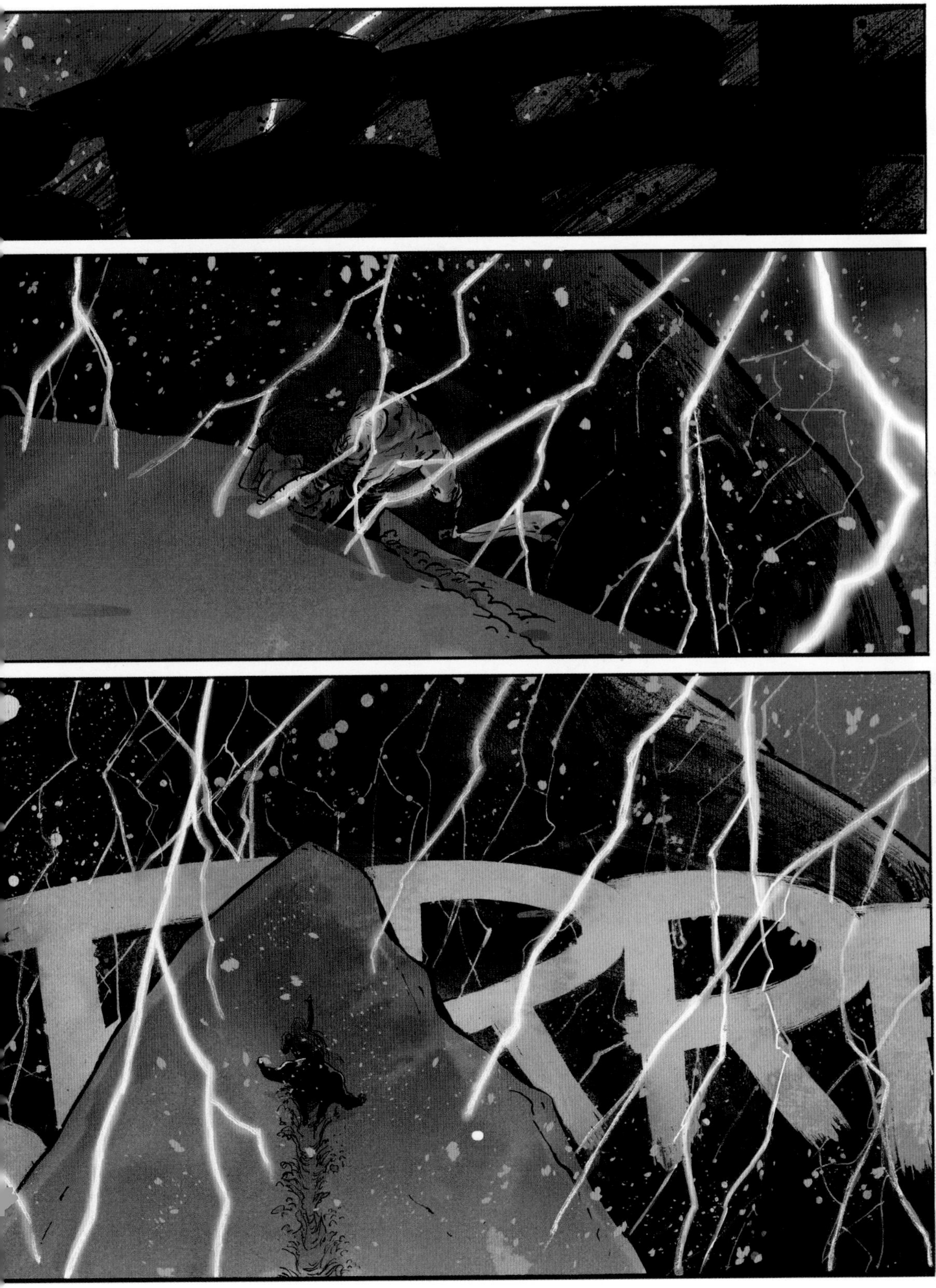
RR

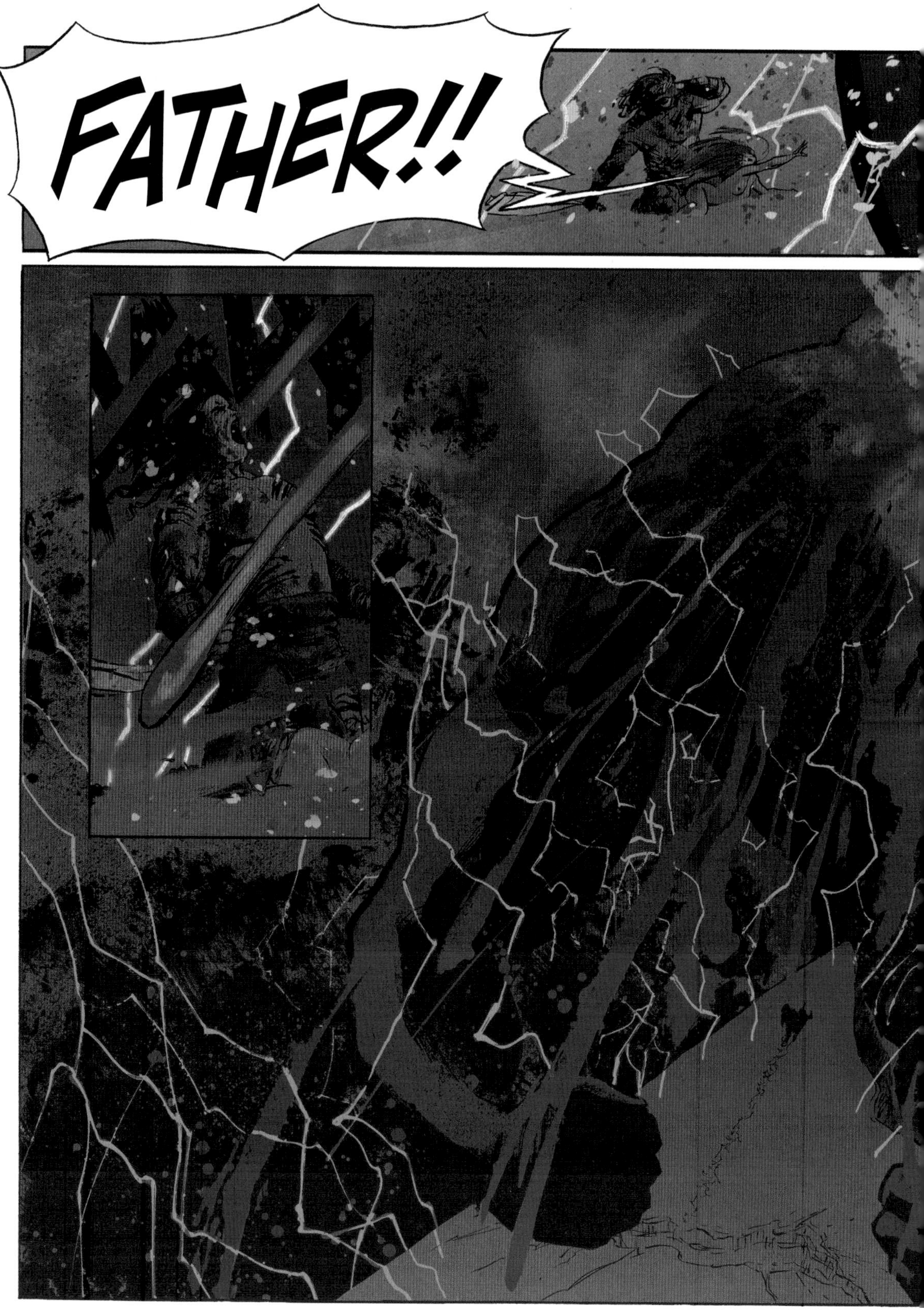
FATHER!!

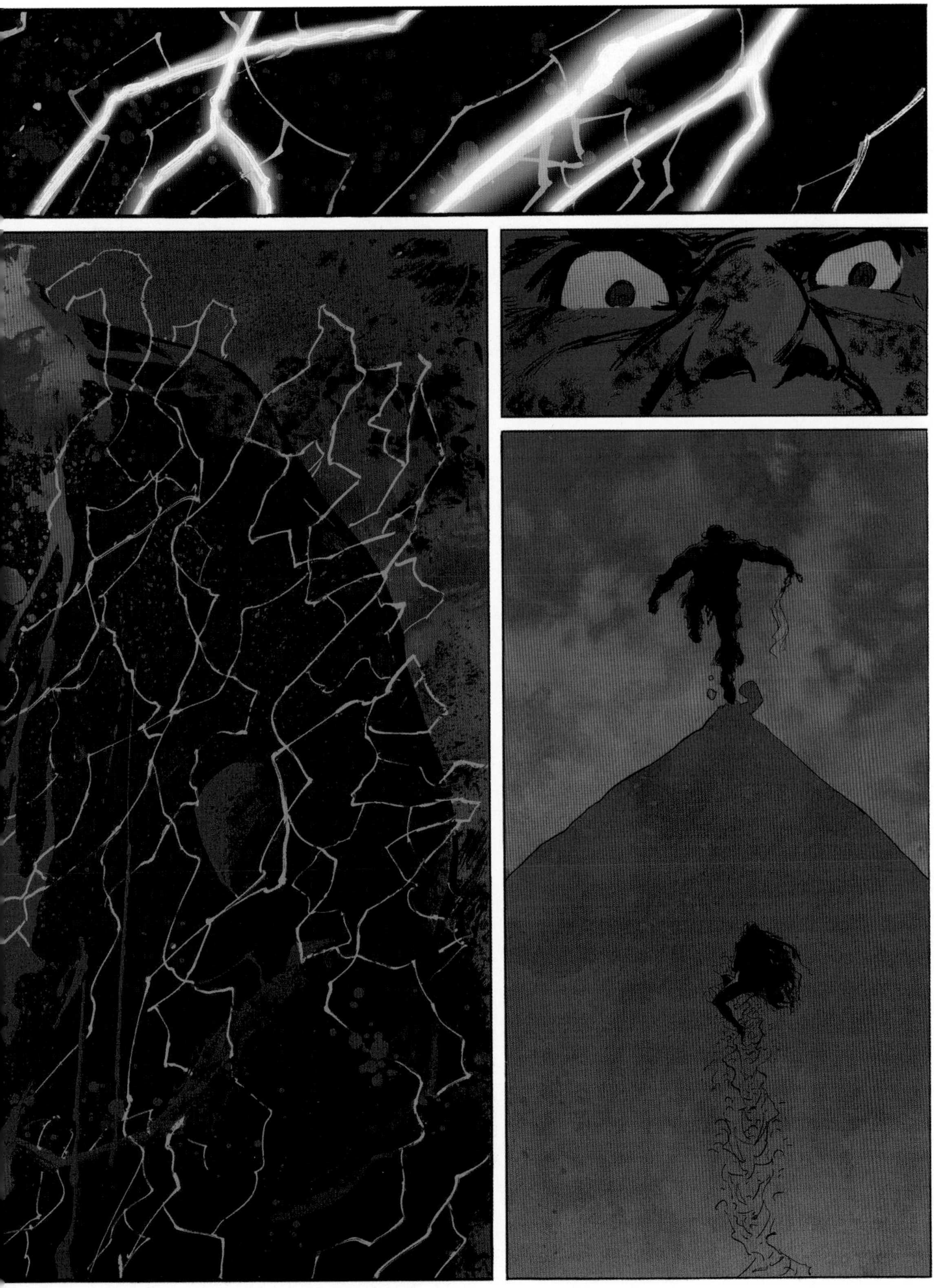

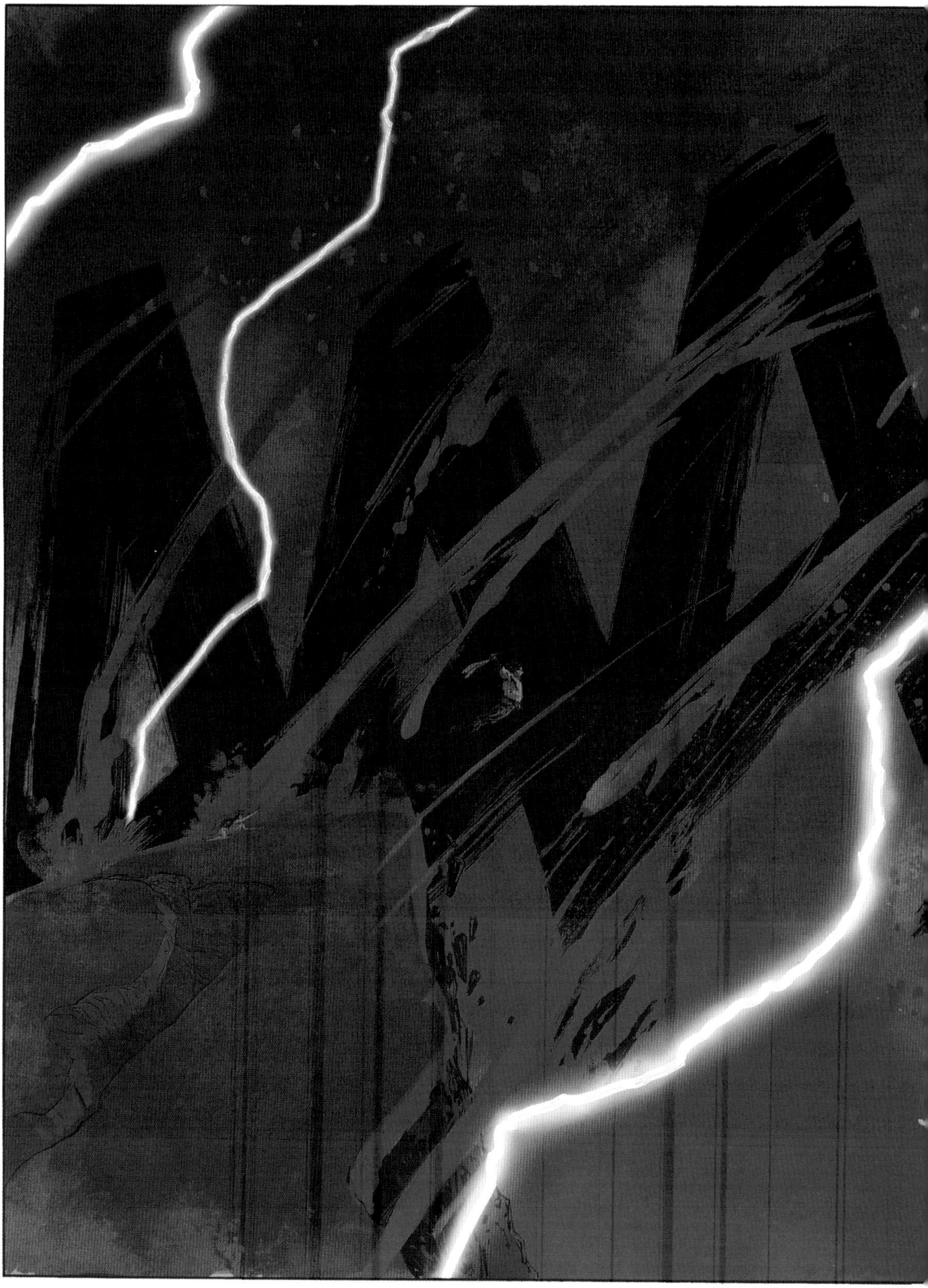

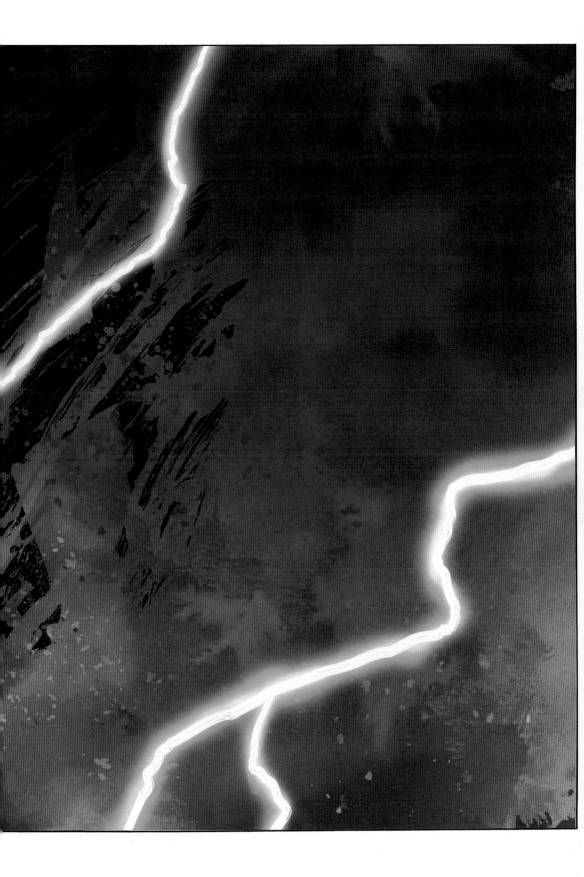

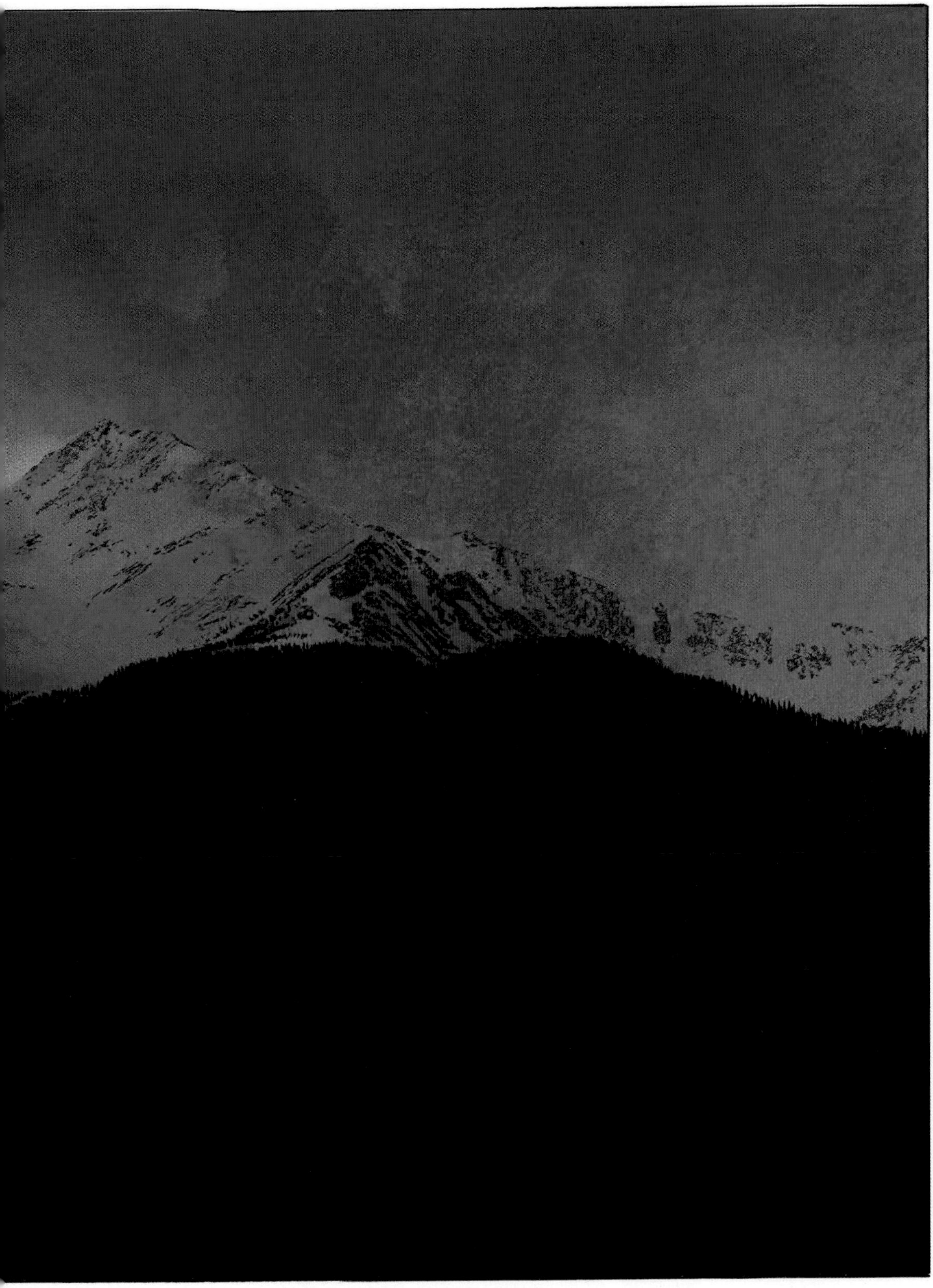

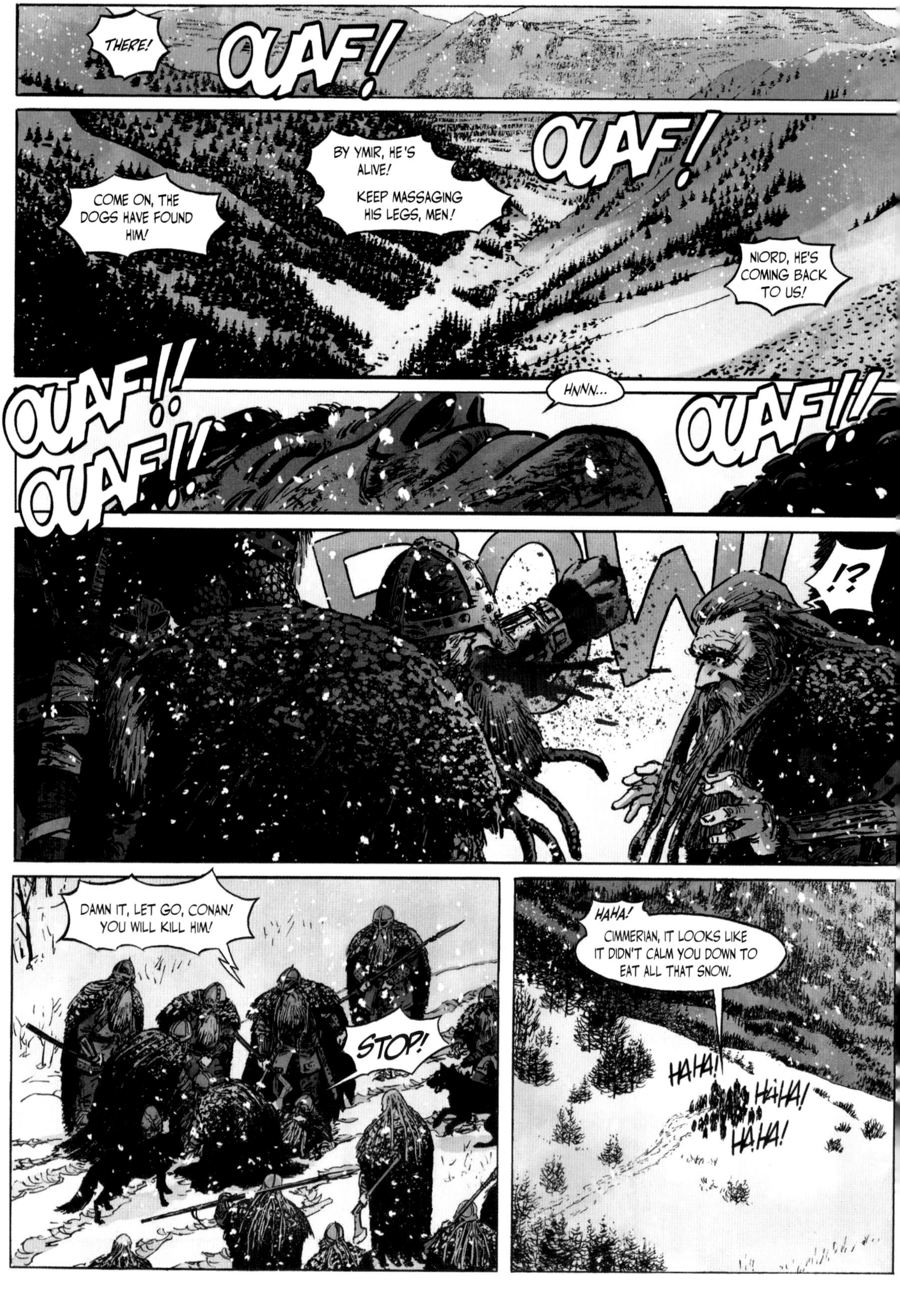

THERE!
OUAF!
COME ON, THE DOGS HAVE FOUND HIM!
BY YMIR, HE'S ALIVE!
KEEP MASSAGING HIS LEGS, MEN!
OUAF!
NIORD, HE'S COMING BACK TO US!
OUAF!! OUAF!!
HNNN...
OUAF!!
!?
DAMN IT, LET GO, CONAN! YOU WILL KILL HIM!
STOP!
HAHA!
CIMMERIAN, IT LOOKS LIKE IT DIDN'T CALM YOU DOWN TO EAT ALL THAT SNOW.
HAHA! HAHA! HAHA!

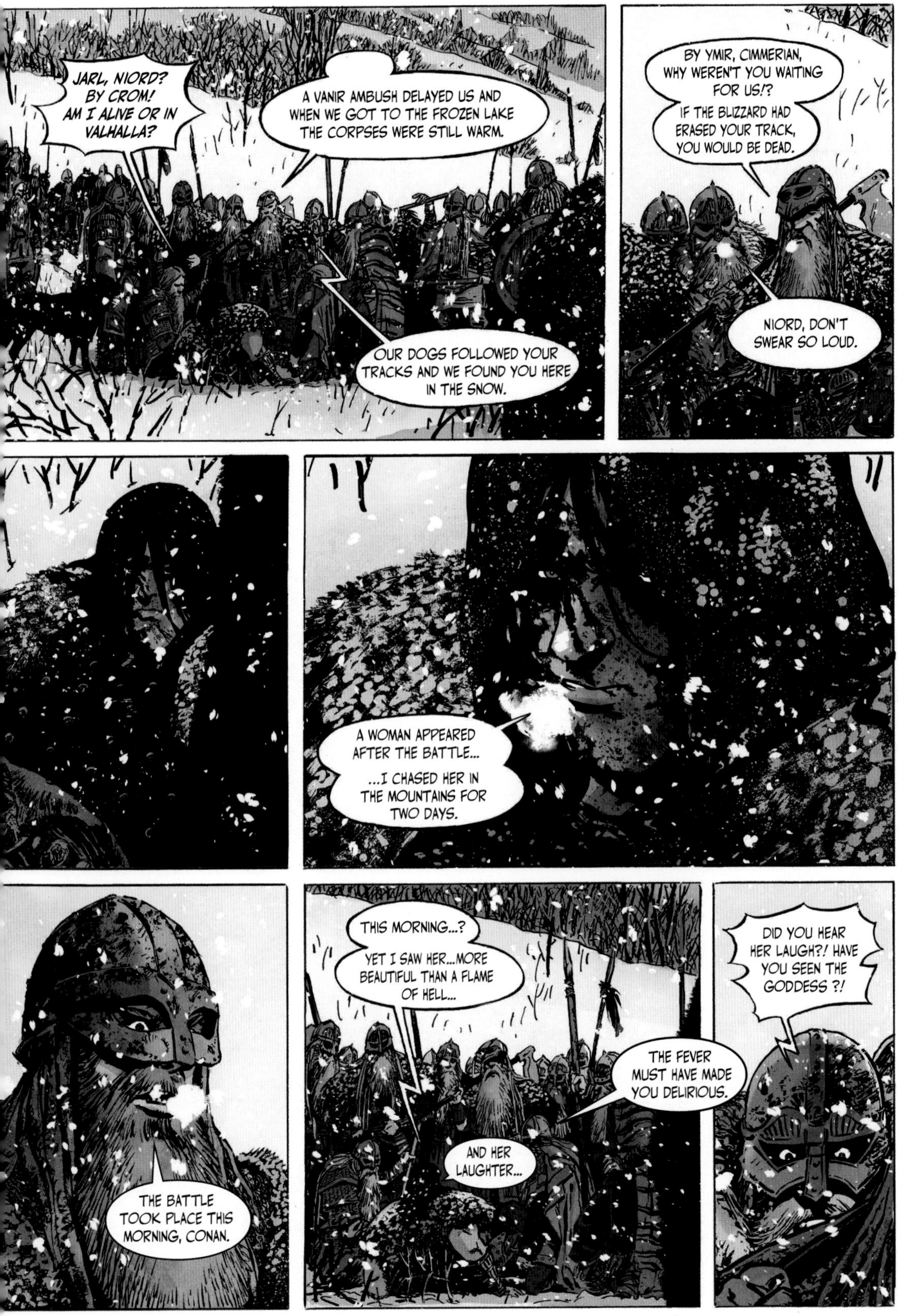

JARL, NIORD? BY CROM! AM I ALIVE OR IN VALHALLA?
A VANIR AMBUSH DELAYED US AND WHEN WE GOT TO THE FROZEN LAKE THE CORPSES WERE STILL WARM.
OUR DOGS FOLLOWED YOUR TRACKS AND WE FOUND YOU HERE IN THE SNOW.
BY YMIR, CIMMERIAN, WHY WEREN'T YOU WAITING FOR US!?
IF THE BLIZZARD HAD ERASED YOUR TRACK, YOU WOULD BE DEAD.
NIORD, DON'T SWEAR SO LOUD.
A WOMAN APPEARED AFTER THE BATTLE...
...I CHASED HER IN THE MOUNTAINS FOR TWO DAYS.
THE BATTLE TOOK PLACE THIS MORNING, CONAN.
THIS MORNING...?
YET I SAW HER...MORE BEAUTIFUL THAN A FLAME OF HELL...
AND HER LAUGHTER...
THE FEVER MUST HAVE MADE YOU DELIRIOUS.
DID YOU HEAR HER LAUGH?! HAVE YOU SEEN THE GODDESS ?!

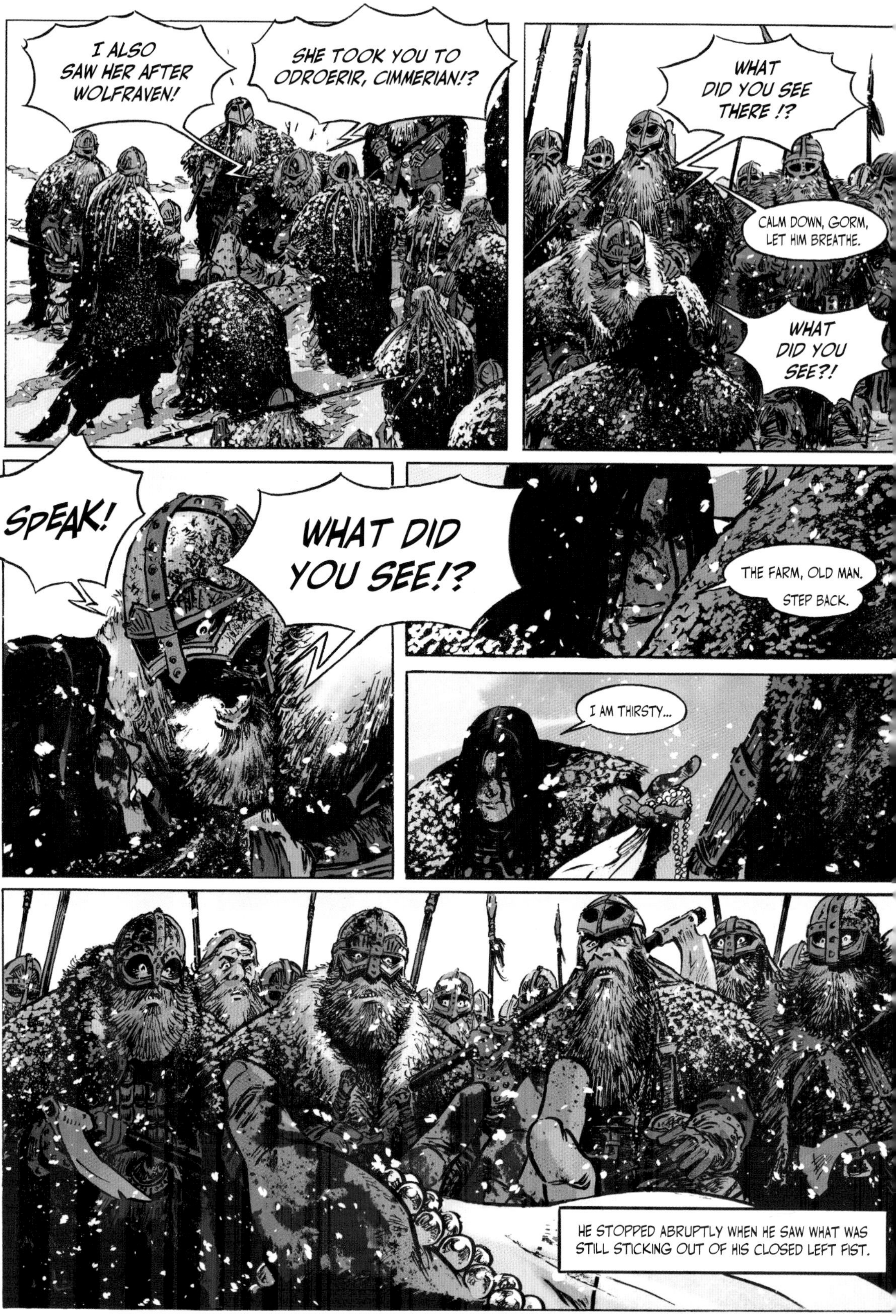
I ALSO SAW HER AFTER WOLFRAVEN!
SHE TOOK YOU TO ODROERIR, CIMMERIAN!?
WHAT DID YOU SEE THERE !?
CALM DOWN, GORM, LET HIM BREATHE.
WHAT DID YOU SEE?!
SPEAK!
WHAT DID YOU SEE!?
THE FARM, OLD MAN.
STEP BACK.
I AM THIRSTY...
HE STOPPED ABRUPTLY WHEN HE SAW WHAT WAS STILL STICKING OUT OF HIS CLOSED LEFT FIST.

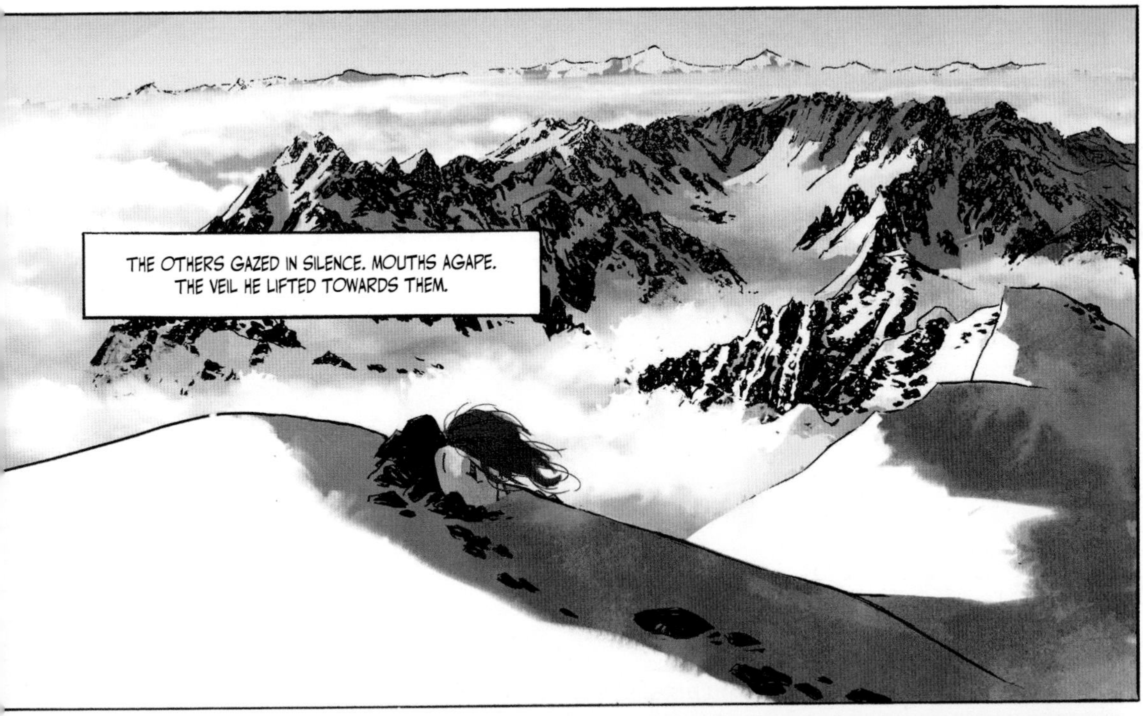
THE OTHERS GAZED IN SILENCE. MOUTHS AGAPE.
THE VEIL HE LIFTED TOWARDS THEM.

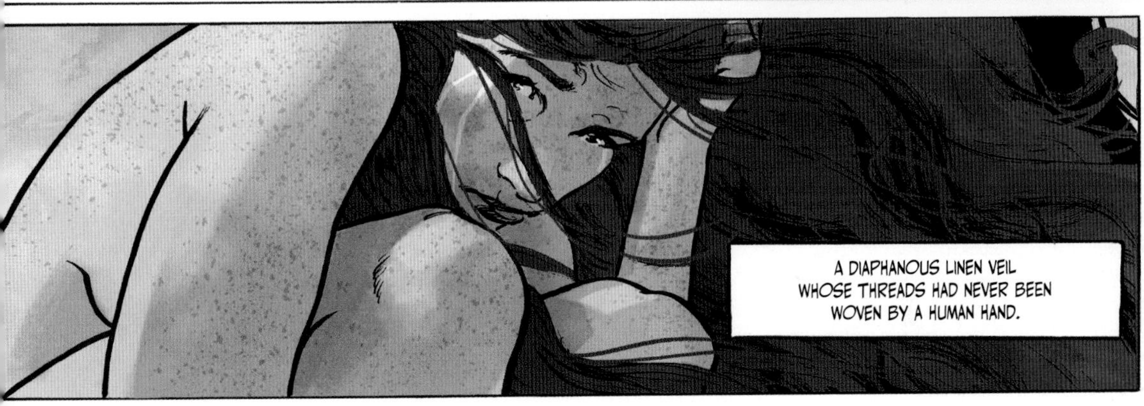
A DIAPHANOUS LINEN VEIL
WHOSE THREADS HAD NEVER BEEN
WOVEN BY A HUMAN HAND.

THE END.

THE FROST-GIANT'S DAUGHTER

By Robert E. Howard
The Fantasy Fan, March 1934

The clangor of the swords had died away, the shouting of the slaughter was hushed; silence lay on the red-stained snow. The bleak pale sun that glittered so blindingly from the ice-fields and the snow-covered plains struck sheens of silver from rent corselet and broken blade, where the dead lay as they had fallen. The nerveless hand yet gripped the broken hilt; helmeted heads back-drawn in the death-throes, tilted red beards and golden beards grimly upward, as if in last invocation to Ymir the frost-giant, god of a warrior-race.

Across the red drifts and mail-clad forms, two figures glared at each other. In that utter desolation only they moved. The frosty sky was over them, the white illimitable plain around them, the dead men at their feet. Slowly through the corpses they came, as ghosts might come to a tryst through the shambles of a dead world. In the brooding silence they stood face to face.

Both were tall men, built like tigers. Their shields were gone, their corselets battered and dinted. Blood dried on their mail; their swords were stained red. Their horned helmets showed the marks of fierce strokes. One was beardless and black-maned. The locks and beard of the other were red as the blood on the sunlit snow.

"Man," said he, "tell me your name, so that my brothers in Vanaheim may know who was the last of Wulfhere's band to fall before the sword of Heimdul."

"Not in Vanaheim," growled the black-haired warrior, "but in Valhalla will you tell your brothers that you met Conan of Cimmeria."

Heimdul roared and leaped, and his sword flashed in deathly arc. Conan staggered and his vision was filled with red sparks as the singing blade crashed on his helmet, shivering into bits of blue fire. But as he reeled he thrust with all the power of his broad shoulders behind the humming blade. The sharp point tore through brass scales and bones and heart, and the red-haired warrior died at Conan's feet.

The Cimmerian stood upright, trailing his sword, a sudden sick weariness assailing him. The glare of the sun on the snow cut his eyes like a knife and the sky seemed shrunken and strangely apart. He turned away from the trampled expanse where yellow-bearded warriors lay locked with red-haired slayers in the embrace of death. A few steps he took, and the glare of the snow fields was suddenly dimmed. A rushing wave of blindness engulfed him and he sank down into the snow, supporting himself on one mailed arm, seeking to shake the blindness out of his eyes as a lion might shake his mane.

A silvery laugh cut through his dizziness, and his sight cleared slowly. He looked up; there was a strangeness about all the landscape that he could not place or define — an unfamiliar tinge to earth and sky. But he did not think long of this. Before him, swaying like a sapling in the wind, stood a woman. Her body was like ivory to his dazed gaze, and save for a light veil of gossamer, she was naked as the day. Her slender bare feet were whiter than the snow they spurned. She laughed down at the bewildered warrior. Her laughter was sweeter than the rippling of silvery fountains, ar poisonous with cruel mockery.

"Who are you?" asked the Cimmerian. "Whence com you?"

"What matter?" Her voice was more musical than silver-stringed harp, but it was edged with cruelty.

"Call up your men," said he, grasping his sword. "Y though my strength fail me, they shall not take me aliv I see that you are of the Vanir."

"Have I said so?"

His gaze went again to her unruly locks, which at fir glance he had thought to be red. Now he saw that the were neither red nor yellow but a glorious compoun of both colors. He gazed spell-bound. Her hair was lik elfin-gold; the sun struck it so dazzlingly that he coul scarcely bear to look upon it. Her eyes were likewis neither wholly blue nor wholly grey, but of shiftin colors and dancing lights and clouds of colors he coul not define. Her full red lips smiled, and from her slend feet to the blinding crown of her billowy hair, her ivor body was as perfect as the dream of a god. Conan pulse hammered in his temples.

"I can not tell," said he, "whether you are of Vanaheir and mine enemy, or of Asgard and my friend. Far have wandered, but a woman like you I have never seen. You locks blind me with their brightness. Never have I see such hair, not even among the fairest daughters of th Æsir. By Ymir — "

"Who are you to swear by Ymir?" she mocked. "Wha know you of the gods of ice and snow, you who hav come up from the south to adventure among an alie people?"

"By the dark gods of my own race!" he cried in ange "Though I am not of the golden haired Æsir, non has been more forward in sword-play! This day I hav seen four score men fall, and I alone have survived th field where Wulfhere's reavers met the wolves of Brag Tell me, woman, have you seen the flash of mail ou across the snow-plains, or seen armed men movin upon the ice?"

"I have seen the hoar-frost glittering in the sun," sh answered. "I have heard the wind whispering across th everlasting snows."

He shook his head with a sigh.

"Niord should have come up with us before th battle joined. I fear he and his fighting-men have bee ambushed. Wulfhere and his warriors lie dead.

"I had thought there was no village within man leagues of this spot, for the war carried us far, but yo can not have come a great distance over these snow naked as you are.

Lead me to your tribe, if you are of Asgard, for I ar faint with blows and the weariness of strife."

"My village is further than you can walk, Conan c Cimmeria," she laughed. Spreading her arms wide, sh swayed before him, her golden head lolling sensuously her scintillant eyes half shadowed beneath their lon silken lashes. "Am I not beautiful, oh man?"

"Like Dawn running naked on the snows," he mutterec his eyes burning like those of a wolf.

"Then why do you not rise and follow me? Who is th strong warrior who falls down before me?" she chante in maddening mockery. "Lie down and die in the snov with the other fools, Conan of the black hair. You can not follow where I would lead."

With an oath the Cimmerian heaved himself up on his feet, his blue eyes blazing, his dark scarred face contorted. Rage shook his soul, but desire for the taunting figure before him hammered at his temples and drove his wild blood fiercely through his veins. Passion fierce as physical agony flooded his whole being, so that earth and sky swam red to his dizzy gaze. In the madness that swept upon him, weariness and faintness were swept away.

He spoke no word as he drove at her, fingers spread to rip her soft flesh. With a shriek of laughter she leaped back and ran, laughing at him over her white shoulder. With a low growl Conan followed. He had forgotten the fight, forgotten the mailed warriors who lay in their blood, forgotten Niord and the reavers who had failed to reach the fight. He had thought only for the slender white shape which seemed to float rather than run before him.

Out across the white blinding plain the chase led. The trampled red field fell out of sight behind him, but still Conan kept on with the silent tenacity of his race. His mailed feet broke through the frozen crust; he sank deep in the drifts and forged through them by sheer strength. But the girl danced across the snow light as a feather floating across a pool; her naked feet barely left their imprint on the hoar-frost that overlaid the crust. In spite of the fire in his veins, the cold bit through warrior's mail and fur-lined tunic; but the girl in her gossamer veil ran as lightly: as gaily as if she danced through the palm and rose gardens of Poitain.

On and on she led, and Conan followed. Black curses drooled through the Cimmerian's parched lips. The great veins in his temples swelled and throbbed and his teeth gnashed.

"You can not escape me!" he roared. "Lead me into a trap and I'll pile the heads of your kinsmen at your feet! Hide from me and I'll tear apart the mountains to find you! I'll follow you to hell!"

Her maddening laughter floated back to him, and foam flew from the barbarian's lips. Further and further into the wastes she led him. The land changed; the wide plains gave way to low hills, marching upward in broken ranges. Far to the north he caught a glimpse of towering mountains, blue with the distance, or white with the eternal snows. Above these mountains shone the flaring rays of the borealis. They spread fan-wise into the sky, frosty blades of cold flaming light, changing in color, growing and brightening.

Above him the skies glowed and crackled with strange lights and gleams. The snow shone weirdly, now frosty blue, now icy crimson, now cold silver. Through a shimmering icy realm of enchantment Conan plunged doggedly onward, in a crystalline maze where the only reality was the white body dancing across the glittering snow beyond his reach — ever beyond his reach.

He did not wonder at the strangeness of it all, not even when two gigantic figures rose up to bar his way. The scales of their mail were white with hoar-frost; their helmets and their axes were covered with ice. Snow sprinkled their locks; in their beards were spikes of icicles; their eyes were cold as the lights that streamed above them.

"Brothers!" cried the girl, dancing between them. "Look who follows! I have brought you a man to slay! Take his heart that we may lay it smoking on our father' board!"

The giants answered with roars like the grinding of ice-bergs on a frozen shore and heaved up their shining axes as the maddened Cimmerian hurled himself upon them. A frosty blade flashed before his eyes, blinding him with its brightness, and he gave back a terrible stroke that sheared through his foe's thigh. With a groan the victim fell, and at the instant Conan was dashed into the snow, his left shoulder numb from the blow of the survivor, from which the Cimmerian's mail had barely saved his life. Conan saw the remaining giant looming high above him like a colossus carved of ice, etched against the cold glowing sky. The axe fell, to sink through the snow and deep into the frozen earth as Conan hurled himself aside and leaped to his feet. The giant roared and wrenched his axe free, but even as he did, Conan's sword sang down. The giant's knees bent and he sank slowly into the snow, which turned crimson with the blood that gushed from his half- severed neck.

Conan wheeled, to see the girl standing a short distance away, staring at him in wide-eyed horror, all the mockery gone from her face. He cried out fiercely and the blood-drops flew from his sword as his hand shook in the intensity of his passion.

"Call the rest of your brothers!" he cried. "I'll give their hearts to the wolves! You can not escape me — "

With a cry of fright she turned and ran fleetly. She did not laugh now, nor mock him over her white shoulder. She ran as for her life, and though he strained every nerve and thew, until his temples were like to burst and the snow swam red to his gaze, she drew away from him, dwindling in the witch-fire of the skies, until she was a figure no bigger than a child, then a dancing white flame on the snow, then a dim blur in the distance. But grinding his teeth until the blood started from his gums, he reeled on, and he saw the blur grow to a dancing white flame, and the flame to a figure big as a child; and then she was running less than a hundred paces ahead of him, and slowly the space narrowed, foot by foot.

She was running with effort now, her golden locks blowing free; he heard the quick panting of her breath, and saw a flash of fear in the look she cast over her white shoulder. The grim endurance of the barbarian had served him well. The speed ebbed from her flashing white legs; she reeled in her gait. In his untamed soul leaped up the fires of hell she had fanned so well. With an inhuman roar he closed in on her, just as she wheeled with a haunting cry and flung out her arms to fend him off.

His sword fell into the snow as he crushed her to him. Her lithe body bent backward as she fought with desperate frenzy in his iron arms. Her golden hair blew about his face, blinding him with its sheen; the feel of her slender body twisting in his mailed arms drove him to blinder madness. His strong fingers sank deep into her smooth flesh; and that flesh was cold as ice. It was as if he embraced not a woman of human flesh and blood, but a woman of flaming ice. She writhed her golden head aside, striving to avoid the fierce kisses that bruised her red lips.

"You are cold as the snows," he mumbled dazedly. "I will warm you with the fire in my own blood — "

With a scream and a desperate wrench she slipped from his arms, leaving her single gossamer garment in his grasp. She sprang back and faced him, her golden locks in wild disarray, her white bosom heaving, her beautiful eyes blazing with terror. For an instant he stood frozen, awed by her terrible beauty as she posed naked against the snows.

And in that instant she flung her arms toward the lights that glowed in the skies above her and cried out in a voice that rang in Conan's ears for ever after: "Ymir! Oh, my father, save me!"

Conan was leaping forward, arms spread to seize her, when with a crack like the breaking of an ice mountain, the whole skies leaped into icy fire. The girl's ivory body was suddenly enveloped in a cold blue flame so blinding that the Cimmerian threw up his hands to shield his eyes from the intolerable blaze. A fleeting instant, skies and snowy hills were bathed in crackling white flames, blue darts of icy light, and frozen crimson fires. Then Conan staggered and cried out. The girl was gone. The glowing snow lay empty and bare; high above his head the witch-lights flashed and played in a frosty sky gone mad, and among the distant blue mountains there sounded a rolling thunder as of a gigantic war-chariot rushing behind steeds whose frantic hoofs struck lightning from the snows and echoes from the skies.

Then suddenly the borealis, the snow-clad hills and the blazing heavens reeled drunkenly to Conan's sight; thousands of fire-balls burst with showers of sparks, and the sky itself became a titanic wheel which rained stars as it spun. Under his feet the snowy hills heaved up like a wave, and the Cimmerian crumpled into the snows to lie motionless.

In a cold dark universe, whose sun was extinguished eons ago, Conan felt the movement of life, alien and unguessed. An earthquake had him in its grip and was shaking him to and fro, at the same time chafing his hands and feet until he yelled in pain and fury and groped for his sword.

"He's coming to, Horsa," said a voice. "Haste — we must rub the frost out of his limbs, if he's ever to wield sword again."

"He won't open his left hand," growled another. "He's clutching something —"

Conan opened his eyes and stared intto the bearded faces that bent over him. He was surrounded by tall golden-haired warriors in mail and furs.

"Conan! You live!"

"By Crom, Niord," gasped the Cimmerian. 'Am I alive, or are we all dead and in Valhalla?"

"We live," grunted the Æsir, busy over Conan's half-frozen feet. "We had to fight our way through an ambush, or we had come up with you before the battle was joined. The corpses were scarce cold when we came upon the field. We did not find you among the dead, so we followed your spoor. In Ymir's name, Conan, why did you wander off into the wastes of the north? We have followed your tracks in the snow for hours. Had a blizzard come up and hidden them, we had never found you, by Ymir!"

"Swear not so often by Ymir," uneasily muttered a warrior, glancing at the distant mountains. "This is h[is] land and the god bides among yonder mountains, th[e] legends say."

"I saw a woman," Conan answered hazily. "We me[t] Bragi's men in the plains. I know not how long w[e] fought. I alone lived. I was dizzy and faint. The land la[y] like a dream before me. Only now do all things seer[n] natural and familiar. The woman came and taunted m[e]. She was beautiful as a frozen flame from hell. A strang[e] madness fell upon me when I looked at her, so I forg[ot] all else in the world. I followed her. Did you not find he[r] tracks? Or the giants in icy mail I slew?"

Niord shook his head.

"We found only your tracks in the snow, Conan."

"Then it may be I am mad," said Conan dazedly. "Ye[t] you yourself are no more real to me than was th[e] golden-locked witch who fled naked across the snow[s] before me. Yet from under my very hands she vanishe[d] in icy flame."

"He is delirious," whispered a warrior.

"Not so!" cried an older man, whose eyes were wil[d] and weird. "It was Atali, the daughter of Ymir, the frost[-] giant! To fields of the dead she comes, and shows herse[lf] to the dying! Myself when a boy I saw her, when I la[y] half-slain on the bloody field of Wolraven. I saw her wal[k] among the dead in the snows, her naked body gleamin[g] like ivory and her golden hair unbearably bright in th[e] moonlight. I lay and howled like a dying dog because [I] could not crawl after her. She lures men from stricke[n] fields into the wastelands to be slain by her brothers, th[e] ice-giants, who lay men's red hearts smoking on Ymir['s] board. The Cimmerian has seen Atali, the frost-giant['s] daughter!"

"Bah!" grunted Horsa. "Old Gorm's mind was touche[d] in his youth by a sword cut on the head. Conan wa[s] delirious from the fury of battle — look how his helme[t] is dinted. Any of those blows might have addled h[is] brain. It was an hallucination he followed into th[e] wastes. He is from the south; what does he know o[f] Atali?"

"You speak truth, perhaps," muttered Conan. "It wa[s] all strange and weird — by Crom!"

He broke off, glaring at the object that still dangle[d] from his clenched left fist; the others gaped silently a[t] the veil he held up — a wisp of gossamer that was neve[r] spun by human distaff.

THE END

THE CIMMERIAN

COVER GALLERY

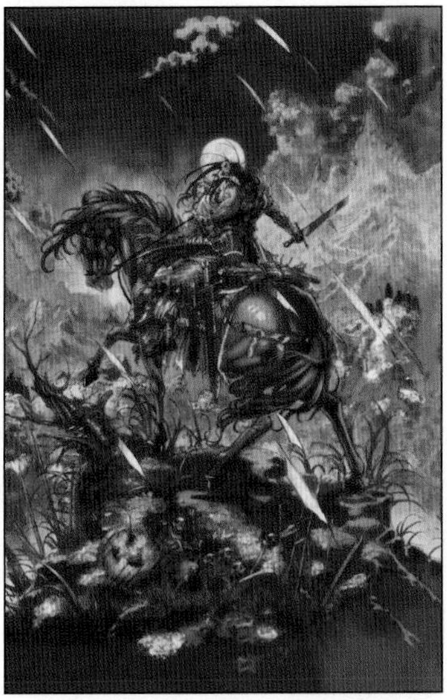

PEOPLE OF THE BLACK CIRCLE #1
COVER A BY JAE KWANG PARK

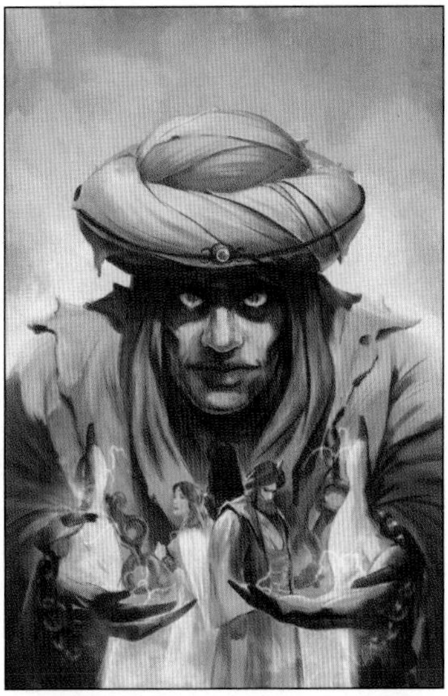

PEOPLE OF THE BLACK CIRCLE #1
COVER B BY FRED RAMBAUD

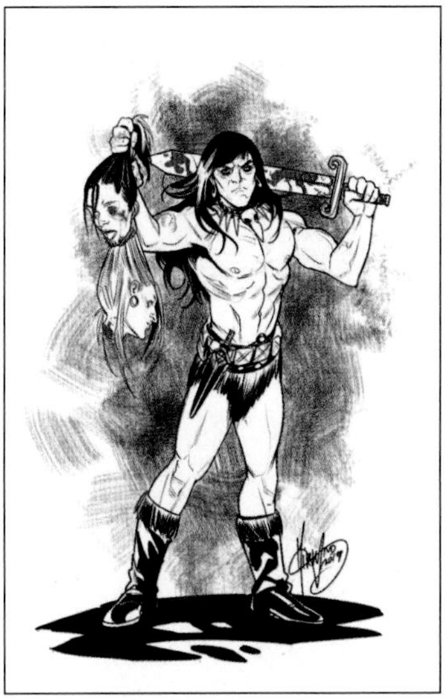

PEOPLE OF THE BLACK CIRCLE #1
COVER C BY MIRKA ANDOLFO

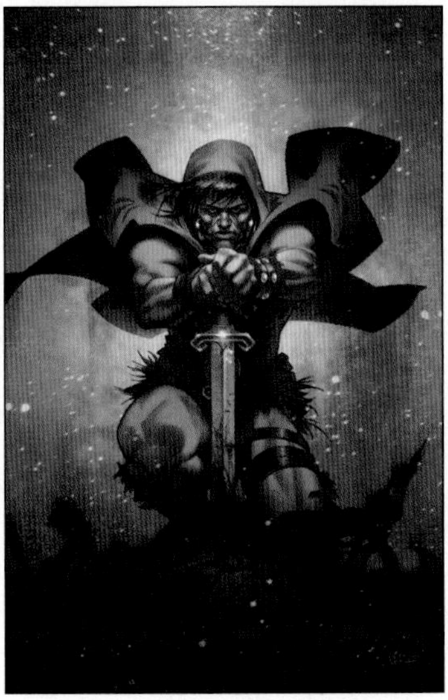

PEOPLE OF THE BLACK CIRCLE #1
COVER D BY BELEN ORTEGA

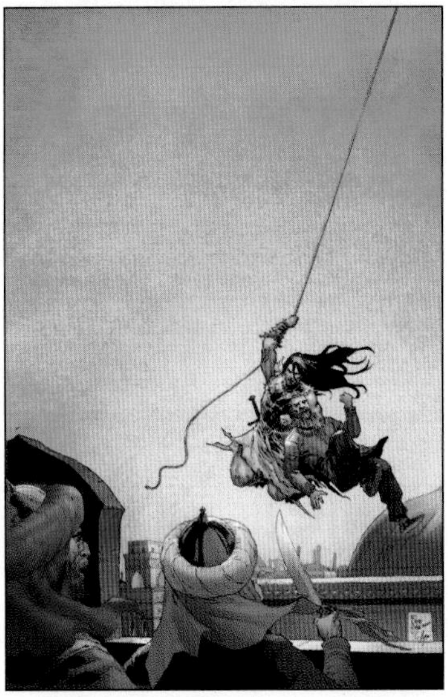

PEOPLE OF THE BLACK CIRCLE #1
COVER E (DETECTIVE COMICS #27 PARODY) BY FRITZ CASAS

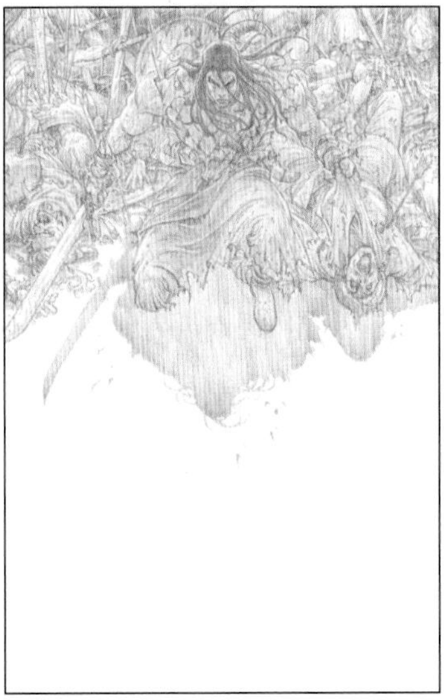

PEOPLE OF THE BLACK CIRCLE #1
ART PROOF EDITION COVER
BY JAE KWANG PARK

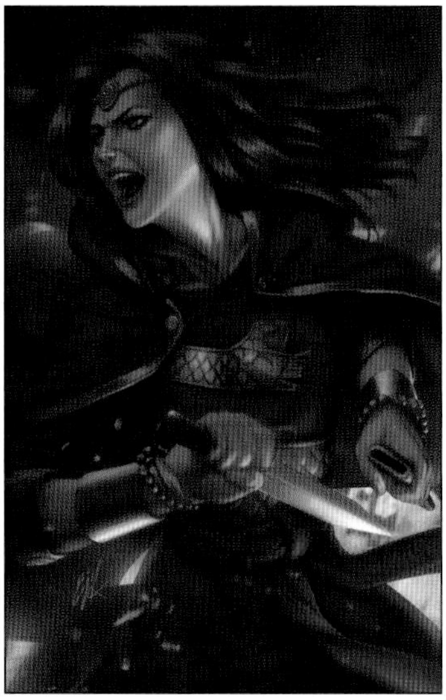

PEOPLE OF THE BLACK CIRCLE #2
COVER A BY EJIKURE

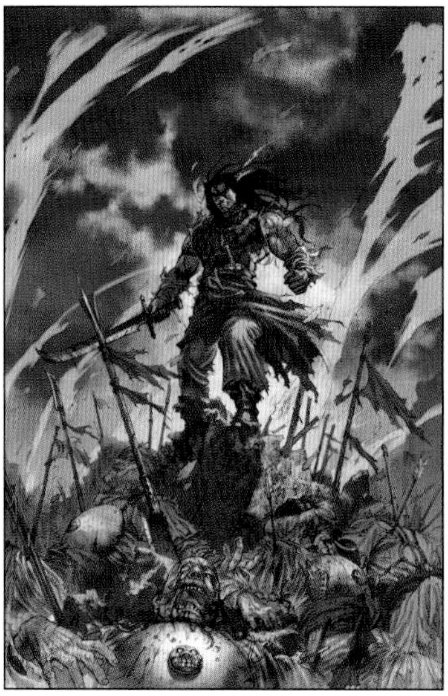

PEOPLE OF THE BLACK CIRCLE #2
COVER B BY JAE KWANG PARK

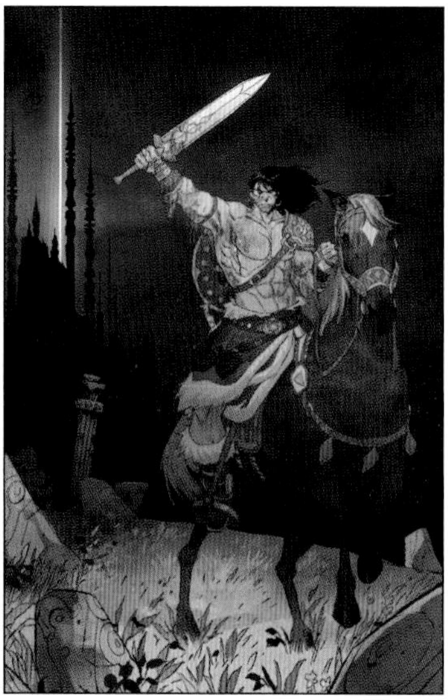

PEOPLE OF THE BLACK CIRCLE #2
COVER C BY MIKI MONTLLO

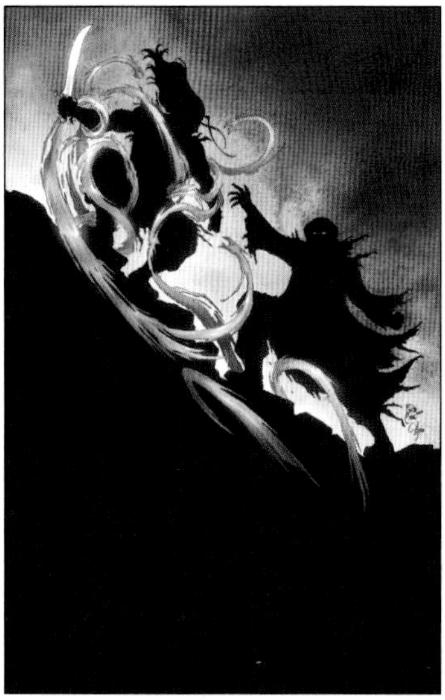

PEOPLE OF THE BLACK CIRCLE #2
COVER D (BATMAN: THE DARK KNIGHT RETURNS #4 PARODY) BY FRITZ CASAS

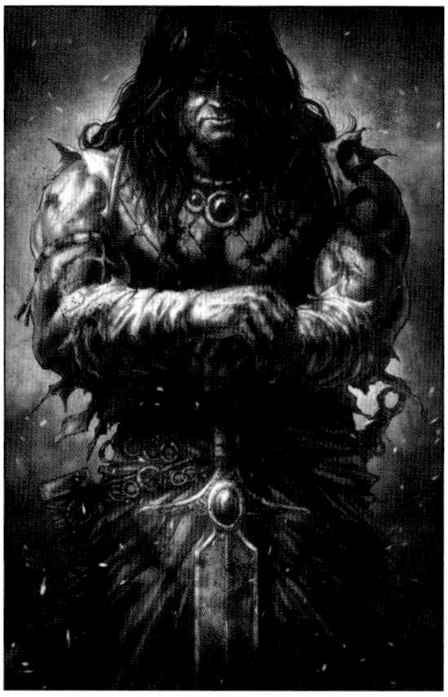

PEOPLE OF THE BLACK CIRCLE #3
COVER A BY ALAN QUAH

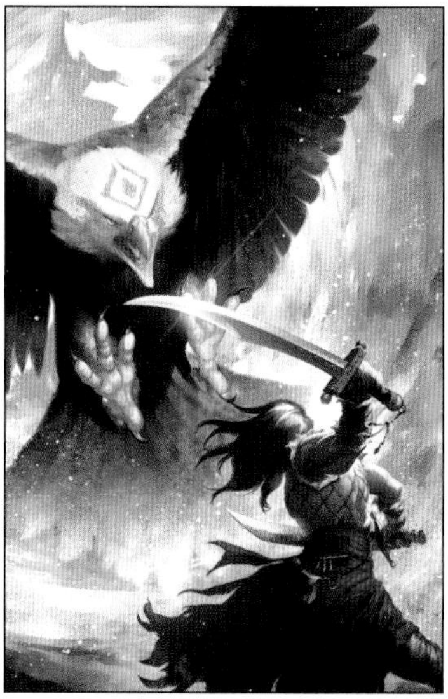

PEOPLE OF THE BLACK CIRCLE #3
COVER B BY MEGHAN HETRICK

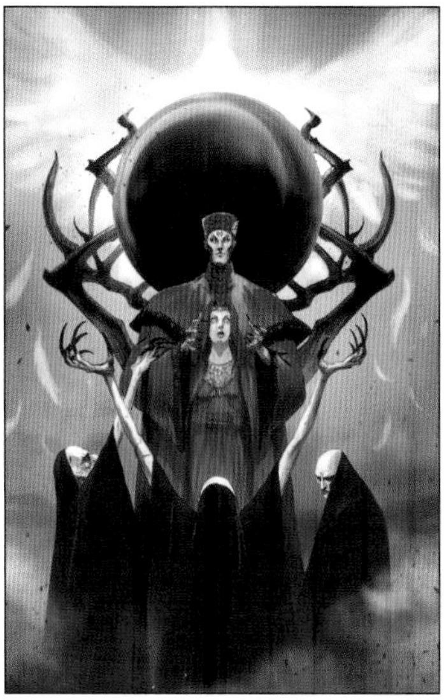

PEOPLE OF THE BLACK CIRCLE #3
COVER C BY FRED RAMBAUD

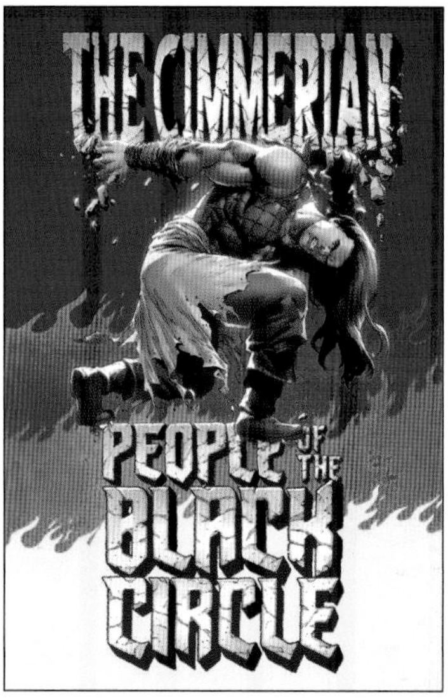
THE CIMMERIAN
PEOPLE OF THE BLACK CIRCLE

PEOPLE OF THE BLACK CIRCLE #3
COVER D (KING SIZE HULK SPECIAL #1 PARODY) BY FRITZ CASAS

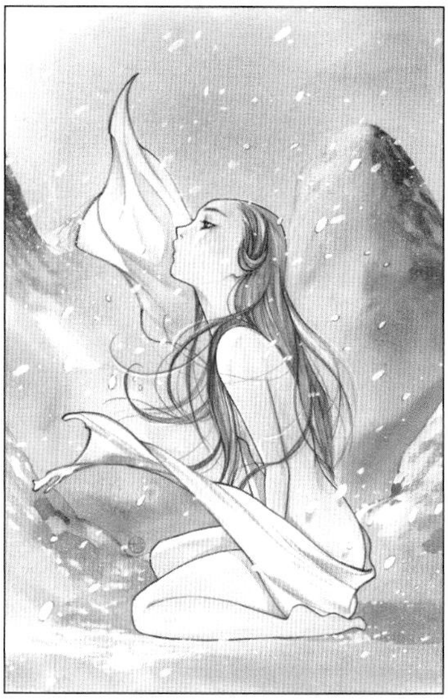

THE FROST GIANT'S DAUGHTER #1
COVER A BY PEACH MOMOKO

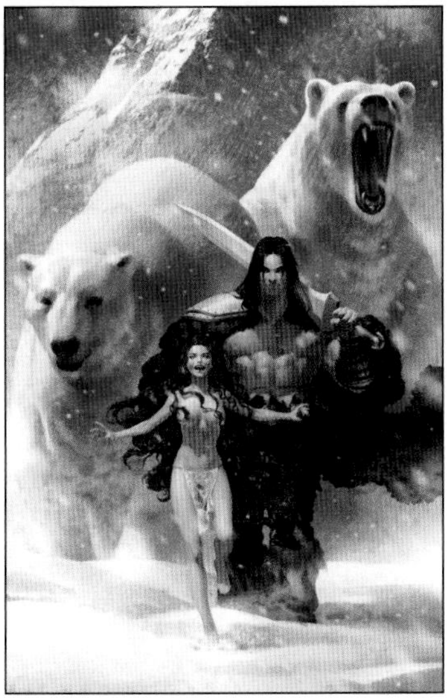

THE FROST GIANT'S DAUGHTER #1
COVER B BY JUNGGEUN YOON

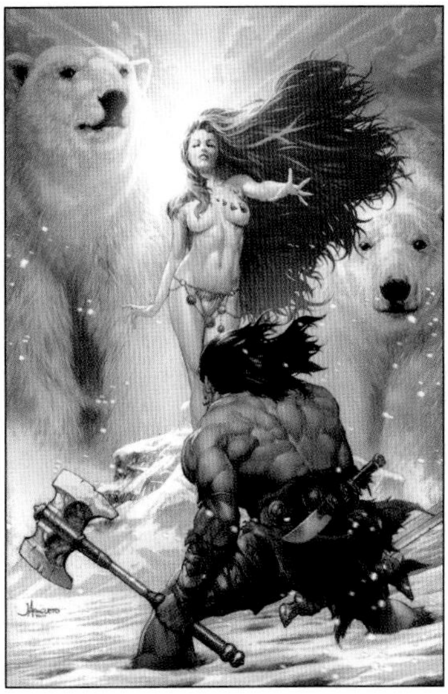

THE FROST GIANT'S DAUGHTER #1
COVER C BY JAY ANACLETO

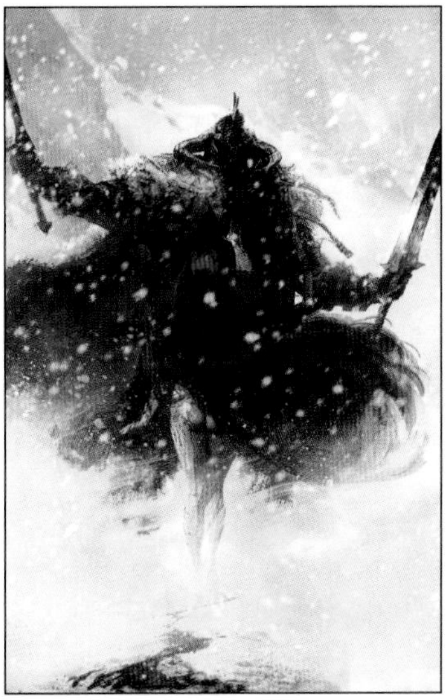

THE FROST GIANT'S DAUGHTER #1
COVER D BY ROBIN RECHT

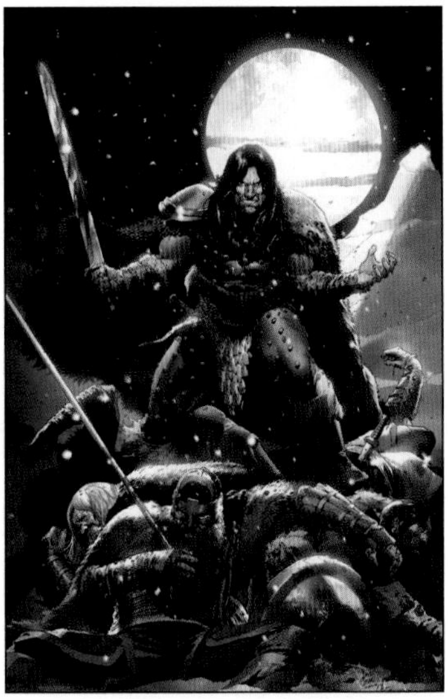

THE FROST GIANT'S DAUGHTER #1
COVER E (WOLVERINE #1 PARODY
COVER BY FRITZ CASAS

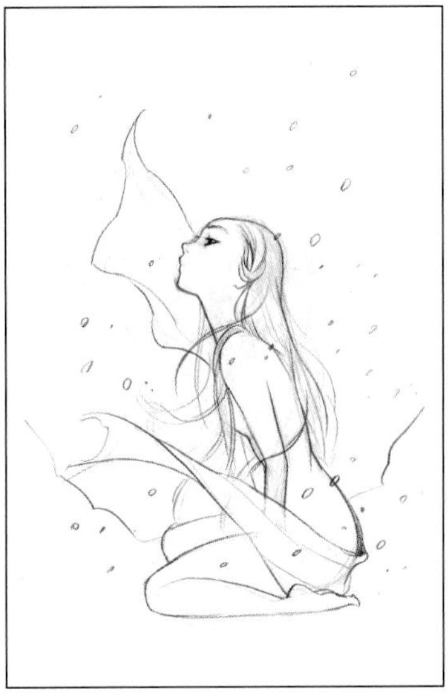

THE FROST GIANT'S DAUGHTER #1
B&W INCV VARIANT BY PEACH MOMOKO

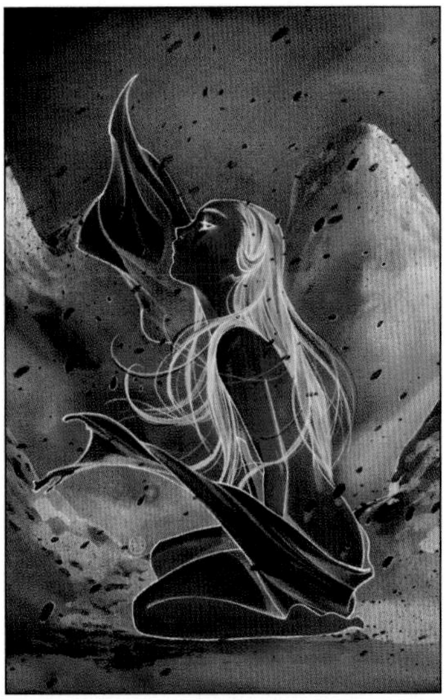

THE FROST GIANT'S DAUGHTER #1
NEGATIVE INCV VARIANT
BY PEACH MOMOKO

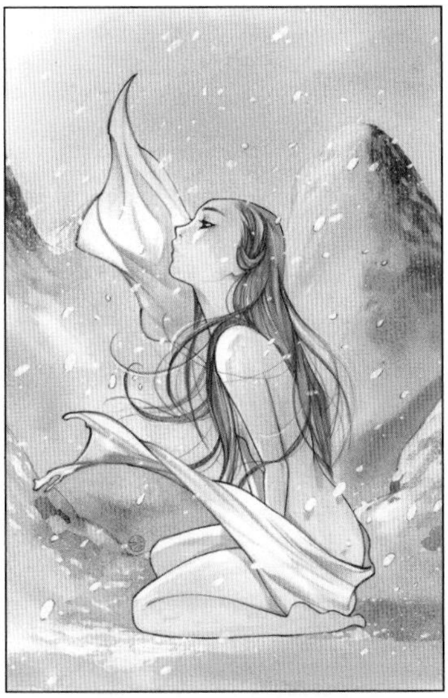

THE FROST GIANT'S DAUGHTER #1
RUBBER CHICKEN COMICS EXCLUSIVE
VARIANT BY PEACH MOMOKO

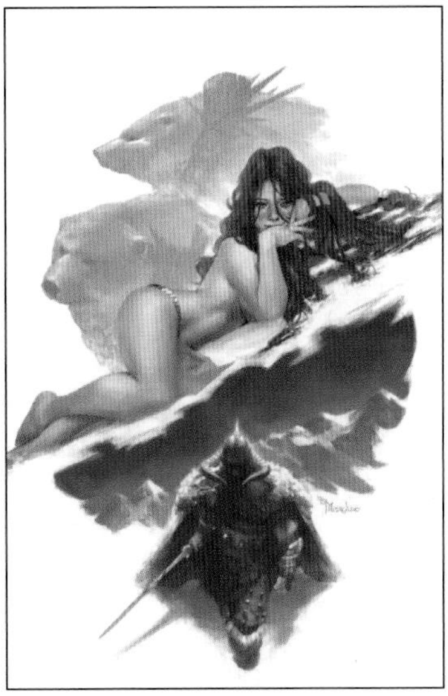

THE FROST GIANT'S DAUGHTER #2
COVER A BY MIGUEL MERCADO

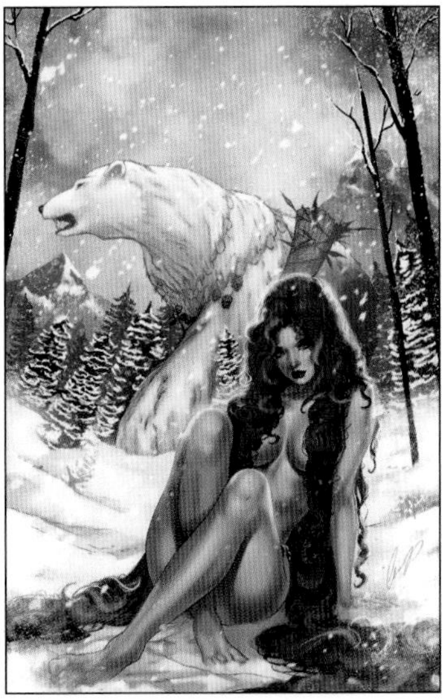

THE FROST GIANT'S DAUGHTER #2
COVER B BY ELIAS CHATZOUDIS

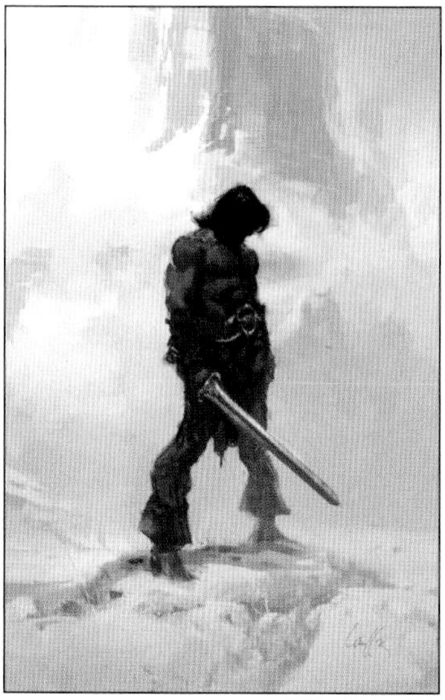

THE FROST GIANT'S DAUGHTER #2 COVER C BY MATHIEU LAUFFRAY

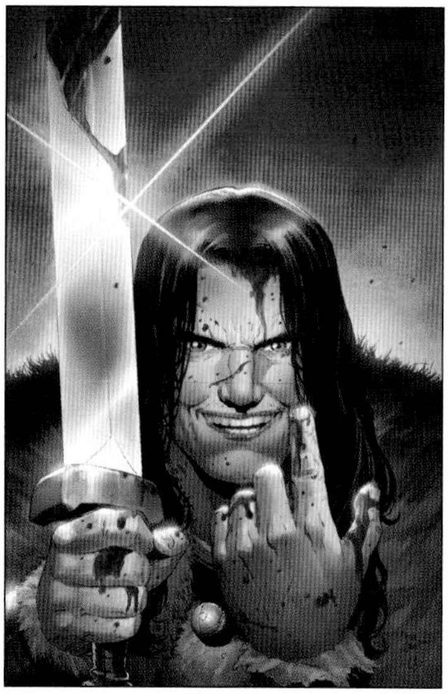

THE FROST GIANT'S DAUGHTER #2 COVER D (WOLVERINE #1 LIMITED SERIES PARODY COVER) BY FRITZ CASAS

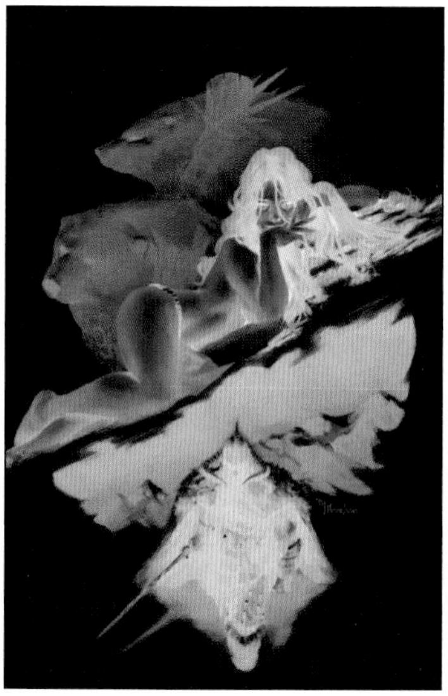

THE FROST GIANT'S DAUGHTER #2 NEGATIVE INCV VARIANT BY MIGUEL MERCADO

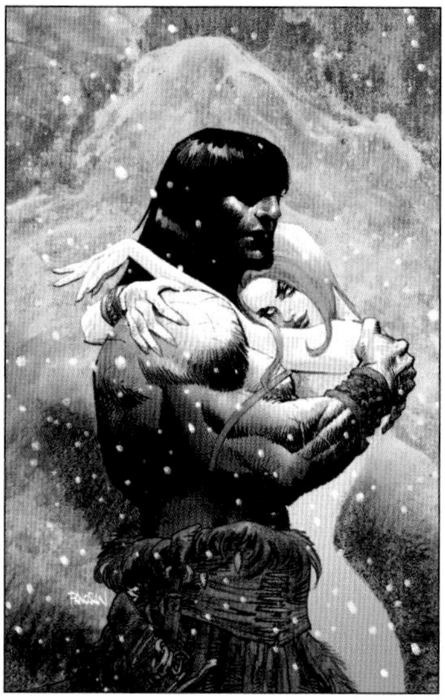

THE FROST GIANT'S DAUGHTER #3 COVER A BY DAN PANOSIAN

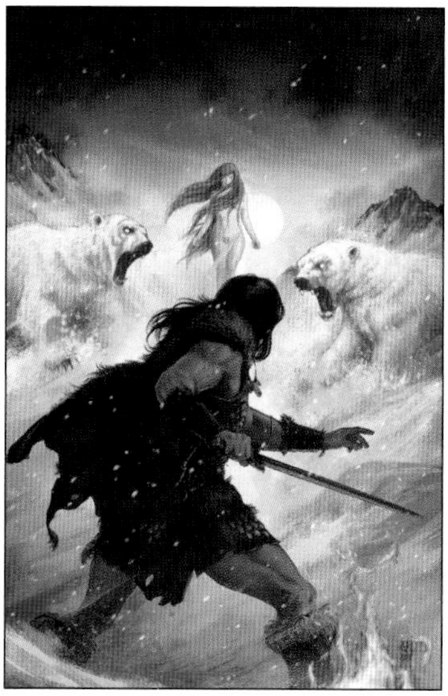

THE FROST GIANT'S DAUGHTER #3 COVER B BY VANCE KELLY

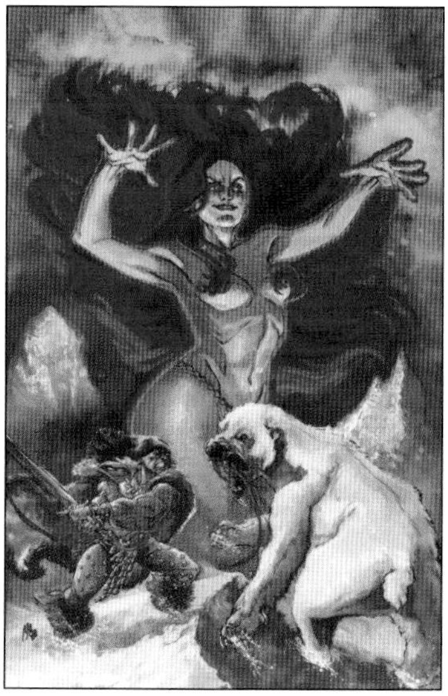

THE FROST GIANT'S DAUGHTER #3 COVER C BY ALBERTO JIMENEZ ALBUQUERQUE

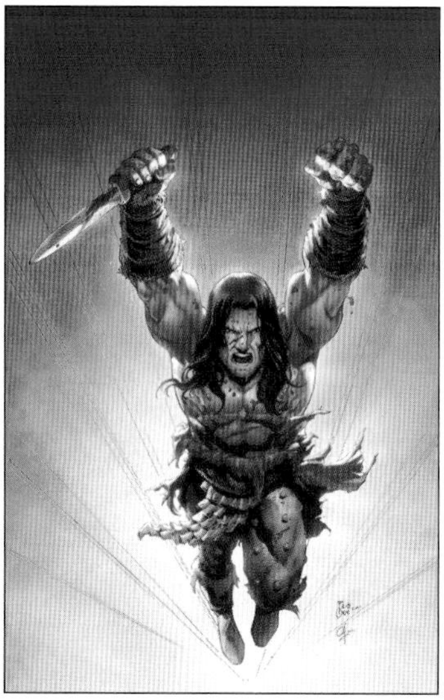

THE FROST GIANT'S DAUGHTER #3 COVER D (WOLVERINE #27 PARODY COVER) BY FRITZ CASAS

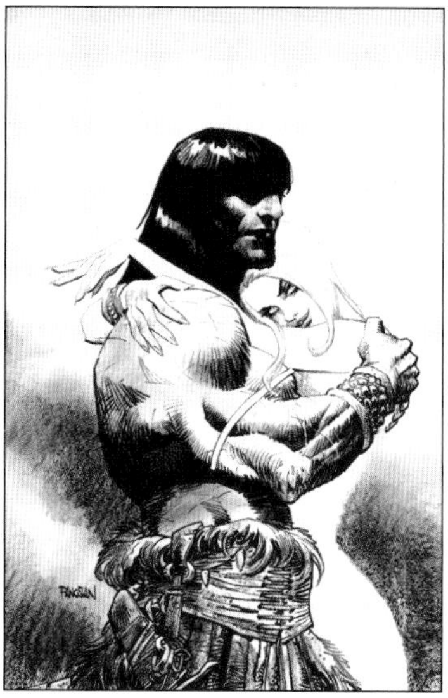

THE FROST GIANT'S DAUGHTER #3 SKETCH INCV VARIANT BY DAN PANOSIAN

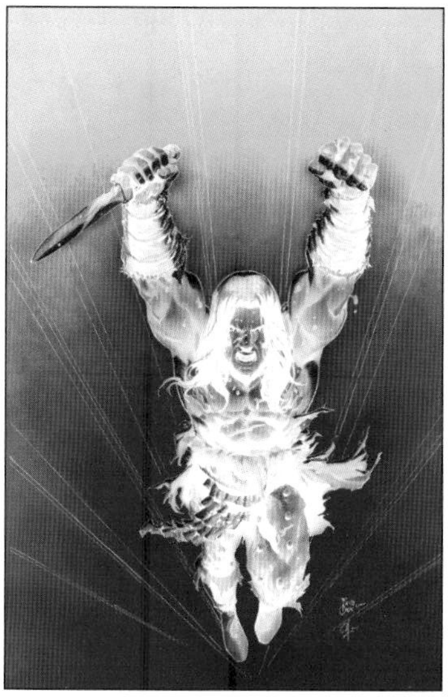

THE FROST GIANT'S DAUGHTER #3 NEGATIVE INCV VARIANT BY FRITZ CASAS

THE CIMMERIAN

EXTRAS

PEOPLE OF THE BLACK CIRCLE SKETCHES/ART ON PAGES 165–170 BY JAE KWANG PARK.

THE FROST-GIANT'S DAUGHTER SKETCHES/ART ON PAGES 171–176 BY ROBIN RECHT.

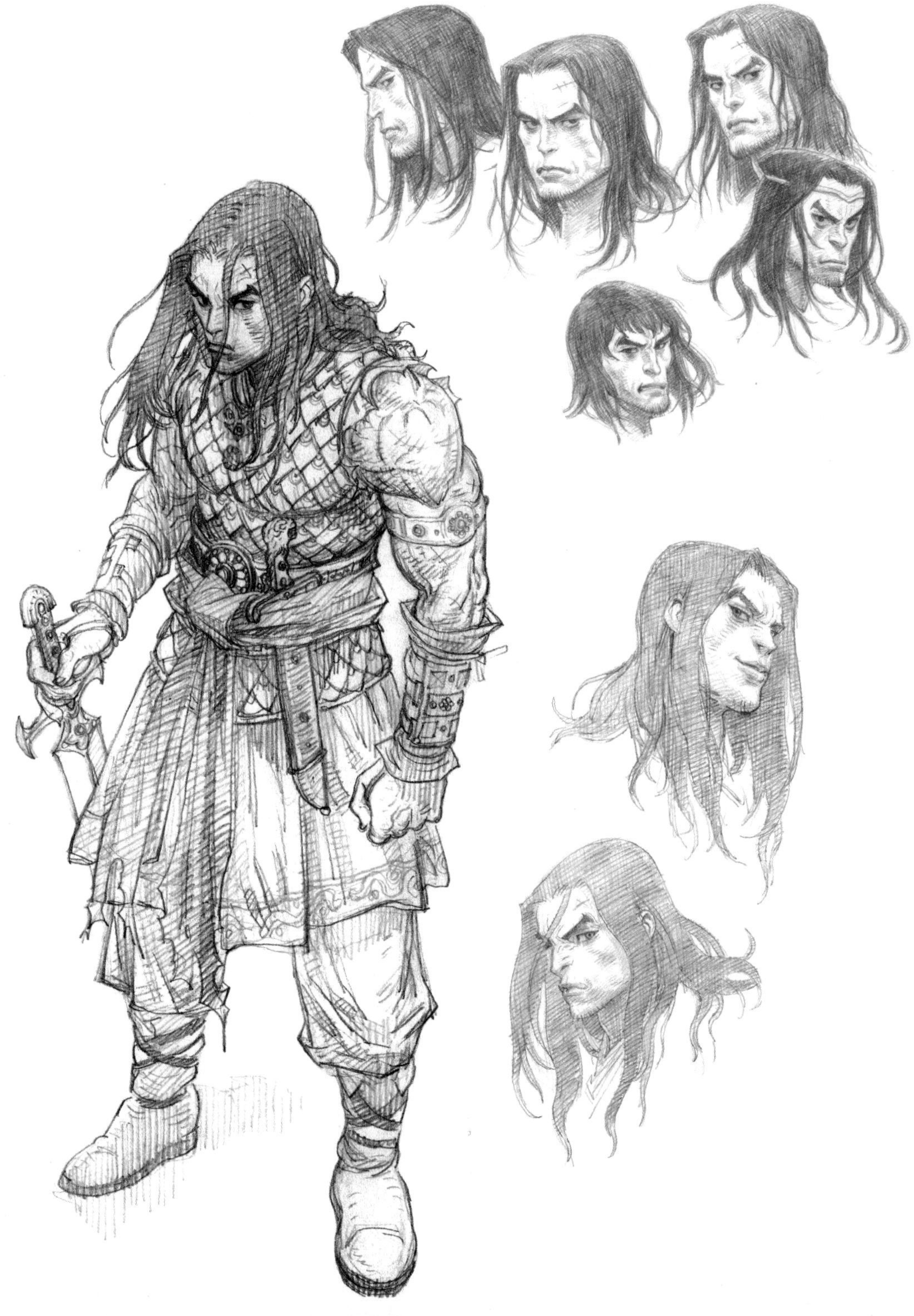

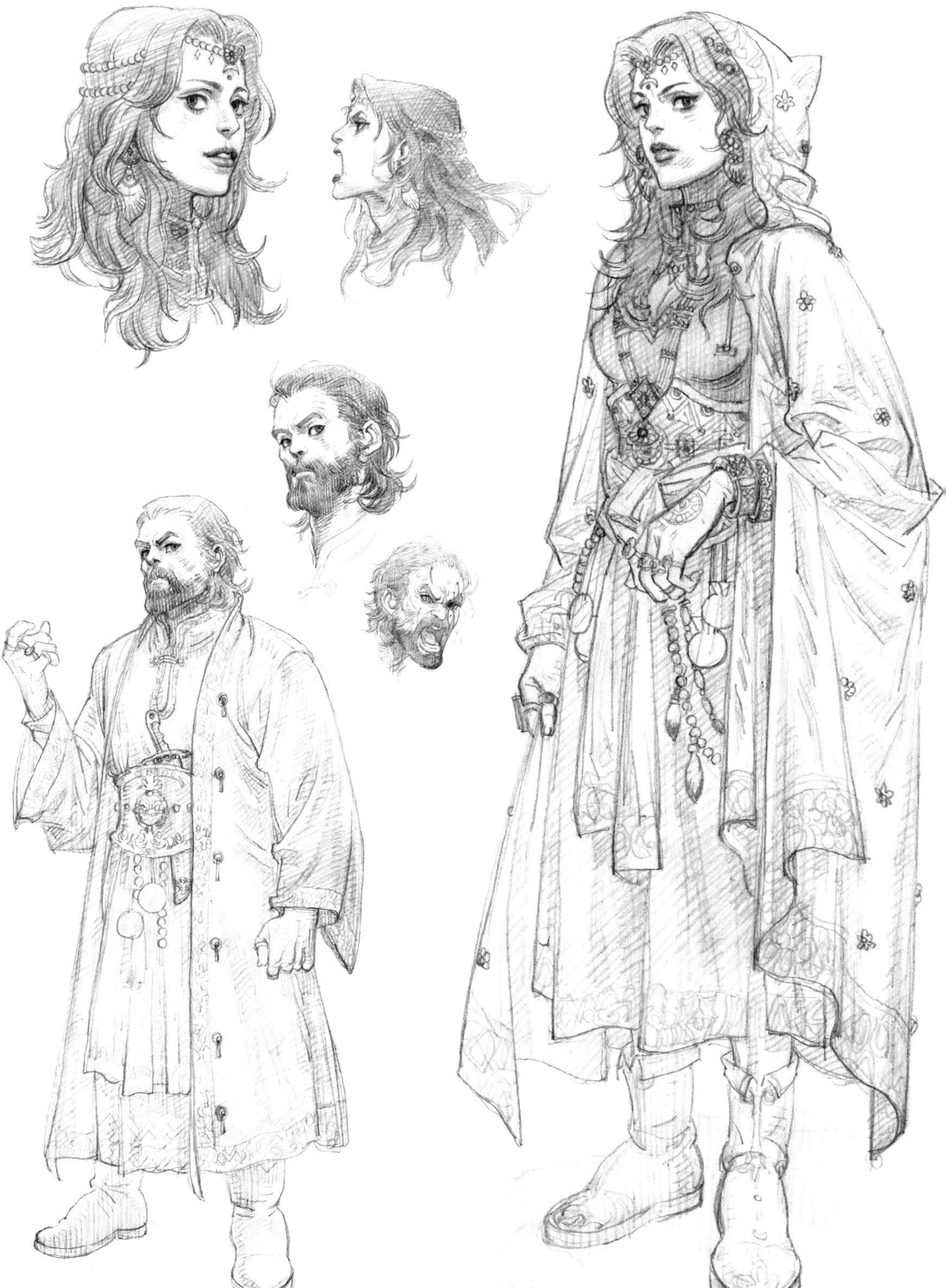

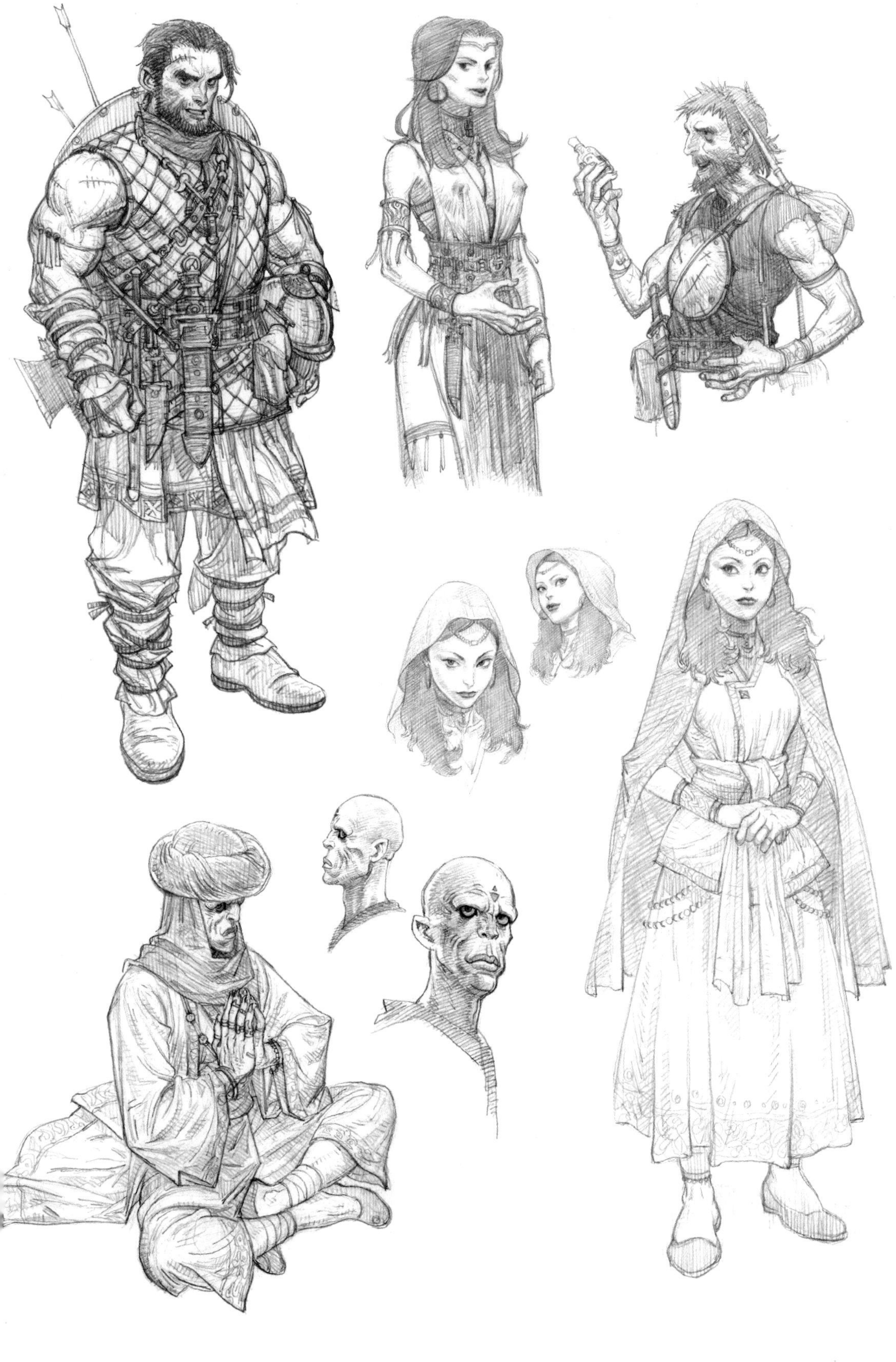

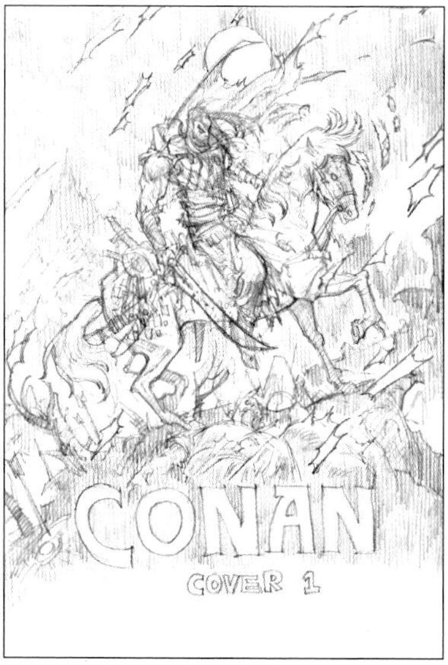
CONAN
COVER 1

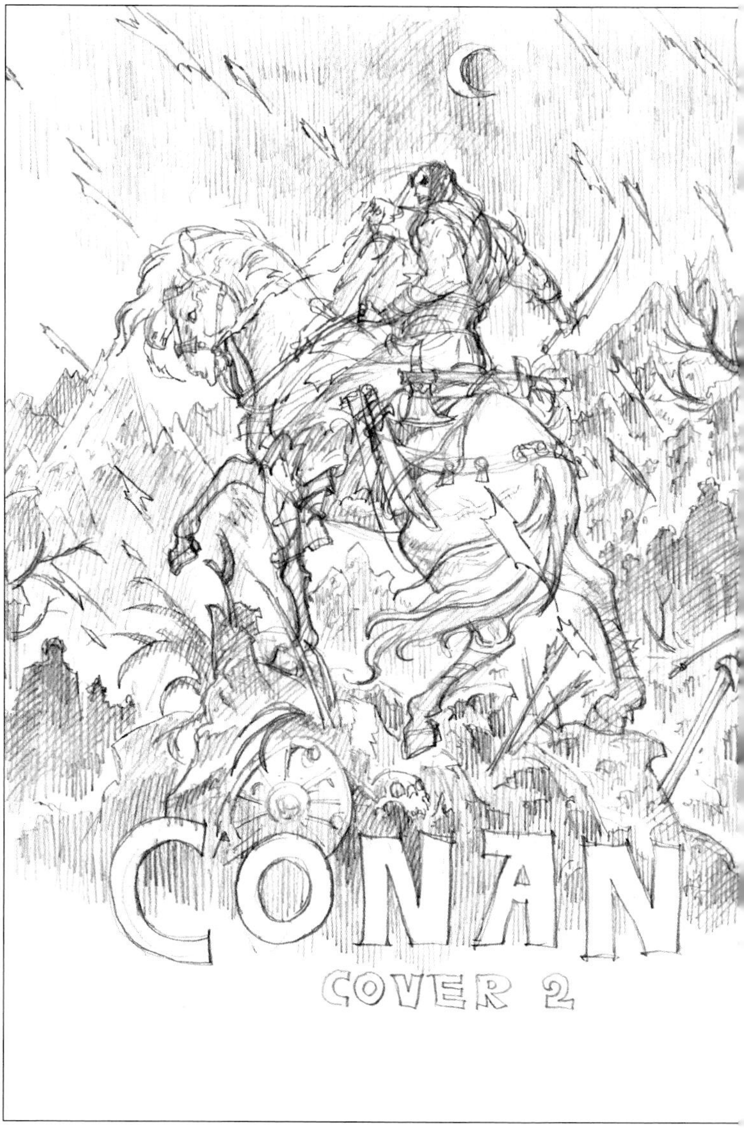
CONAN
COVER 2

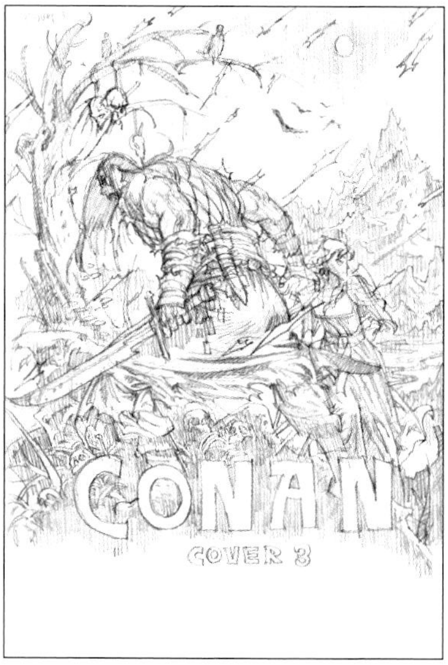
CONAN
COVER 3

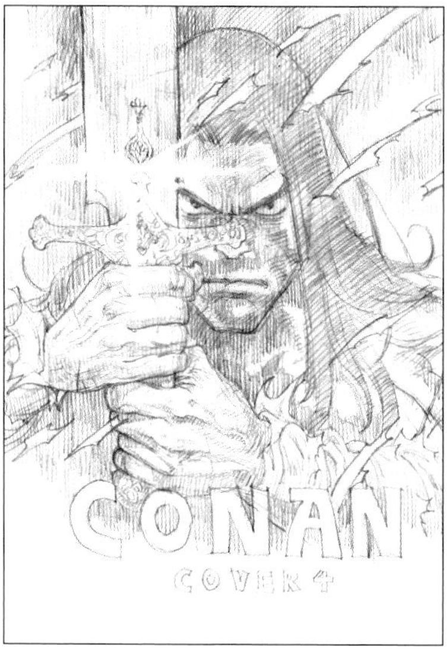
CONAN
COVER 4

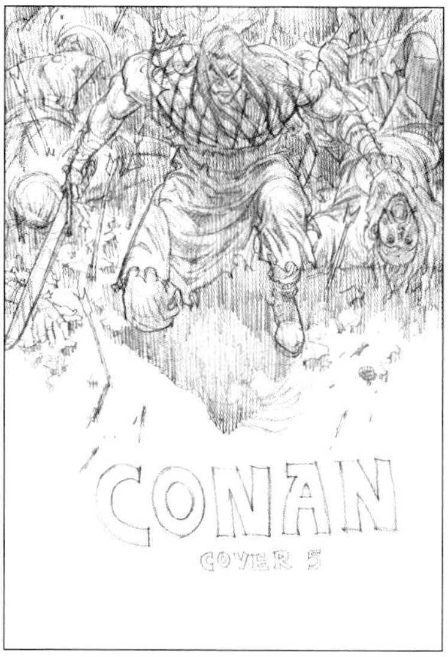
CONAN
COVER 5

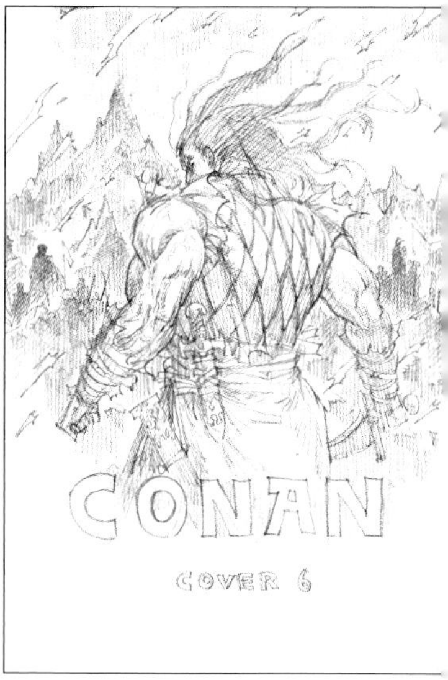
CONAN
COVER 6

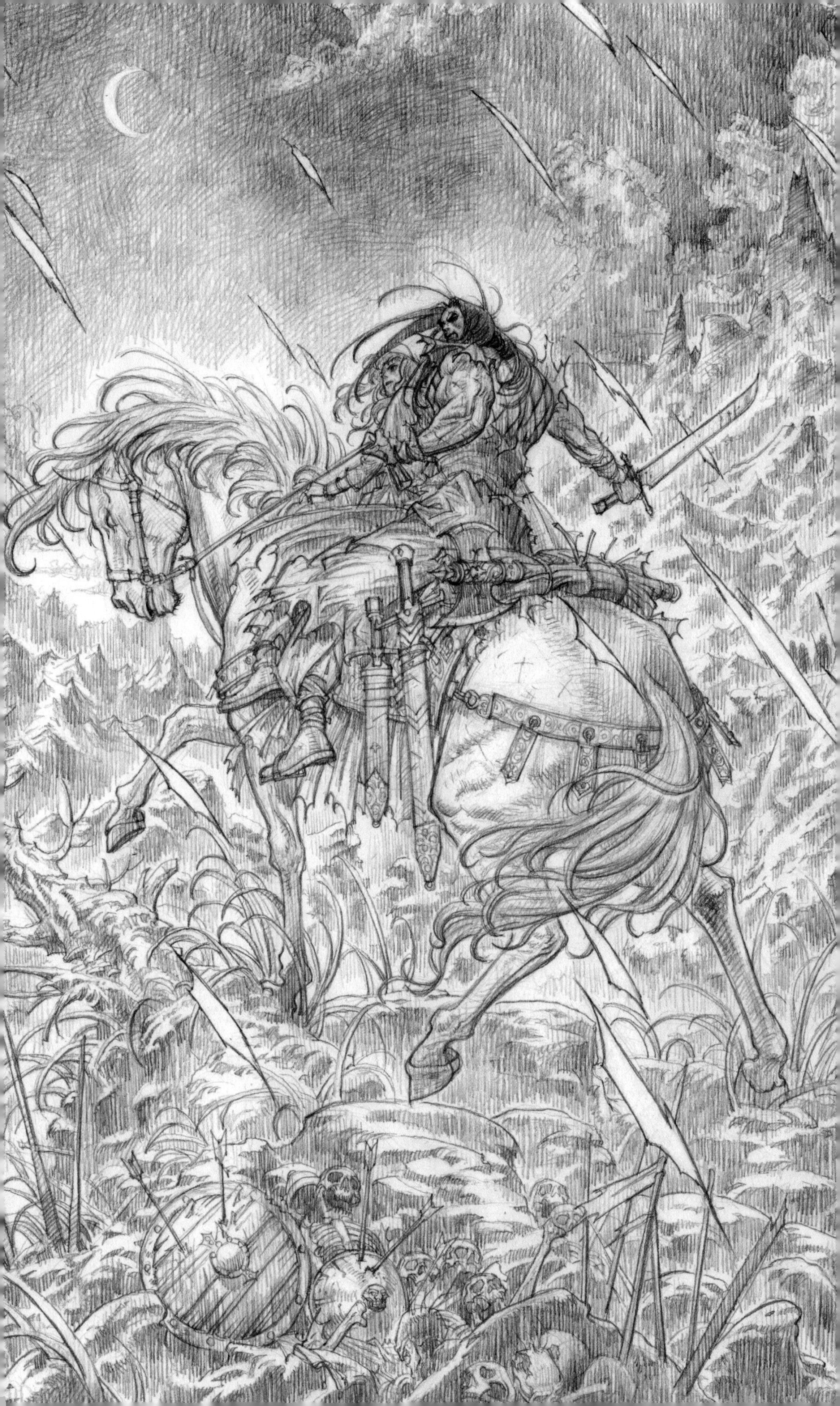

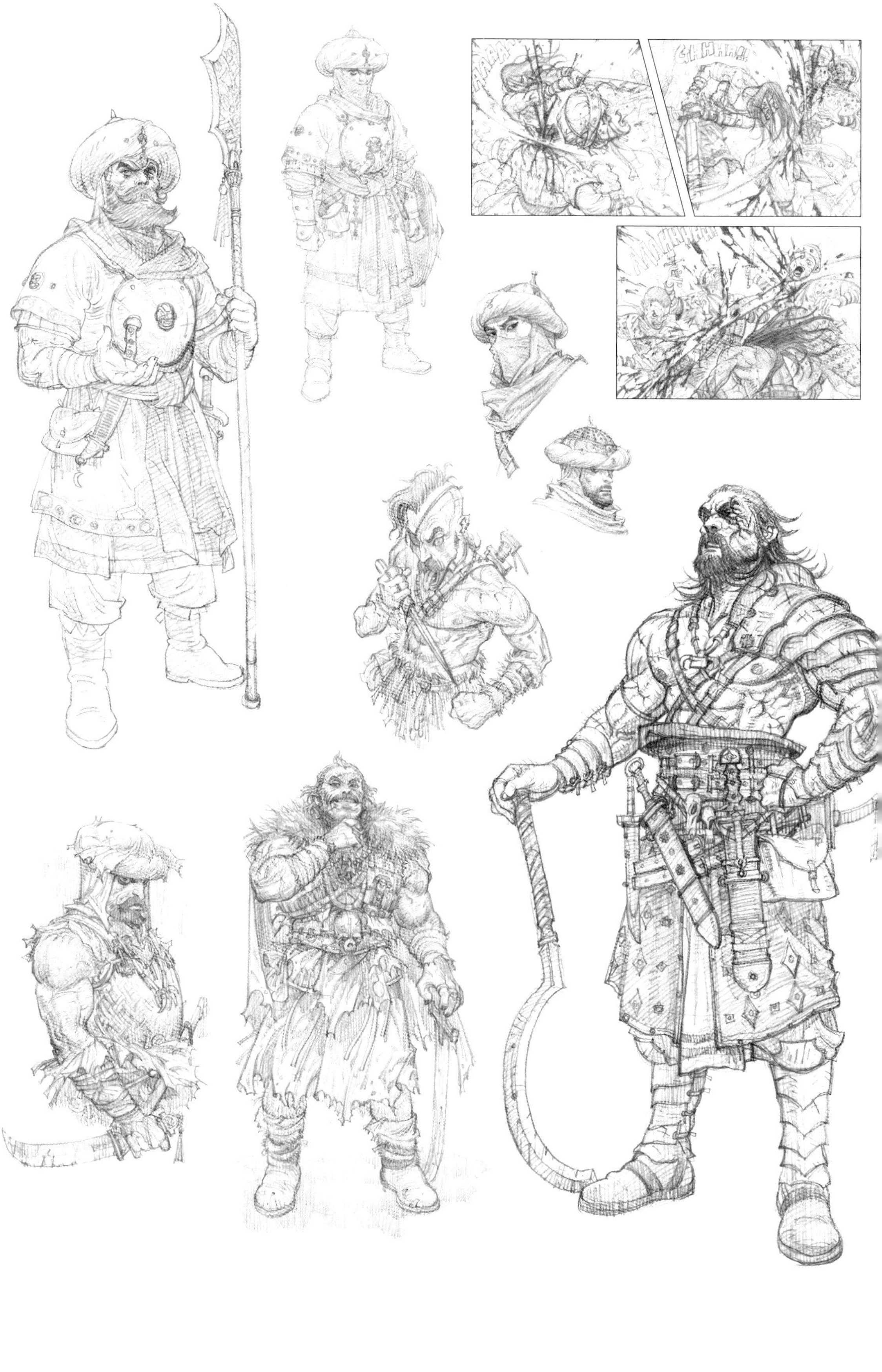
GHHHAA!!

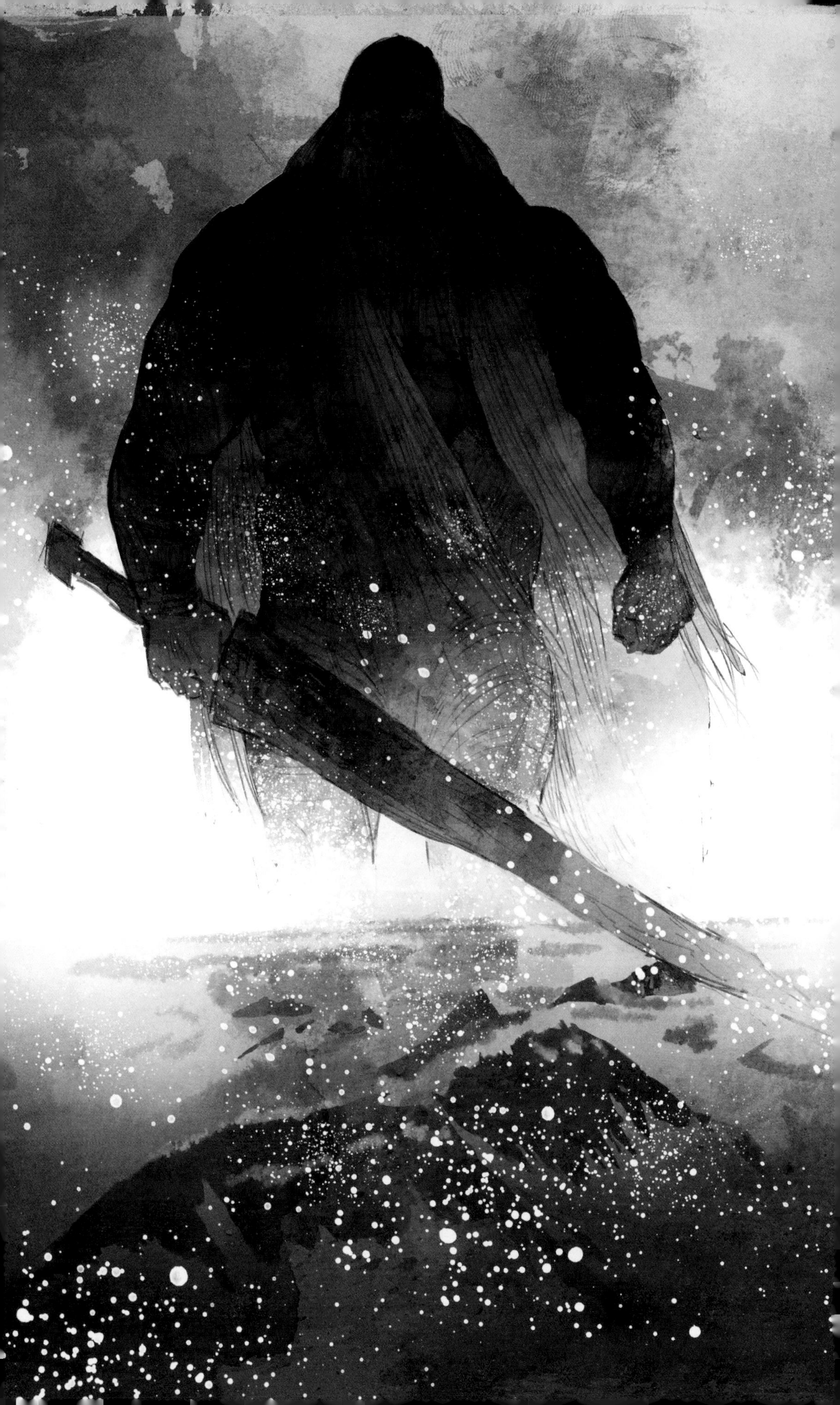

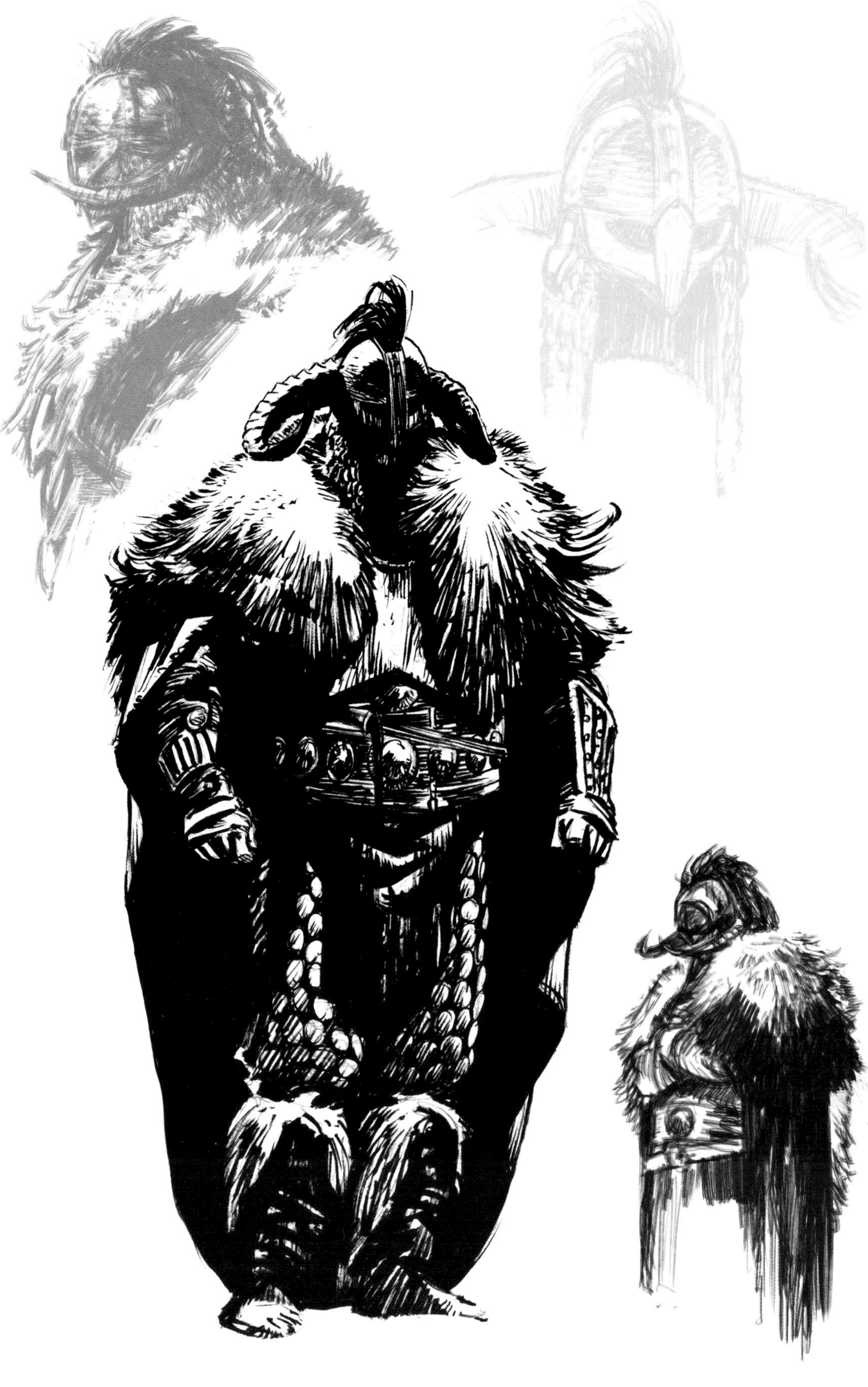

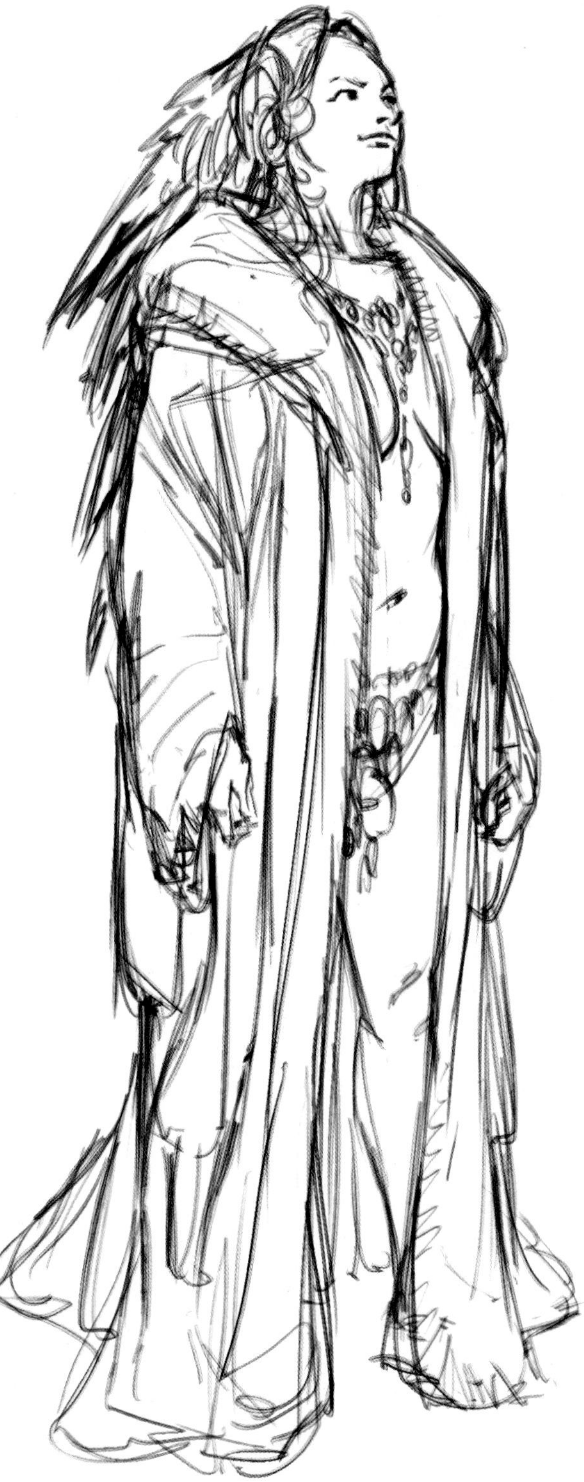

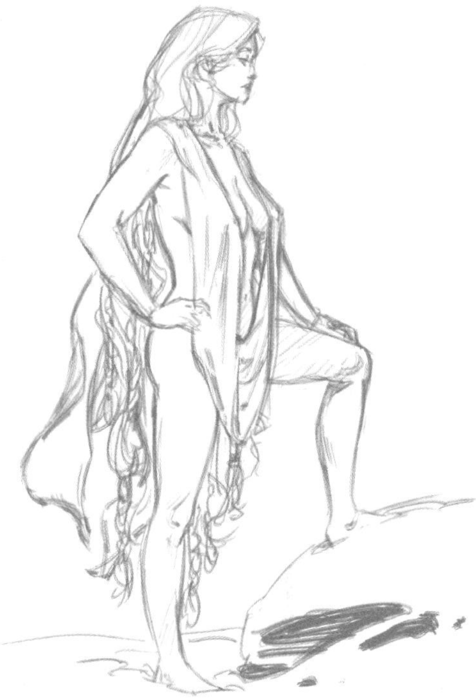

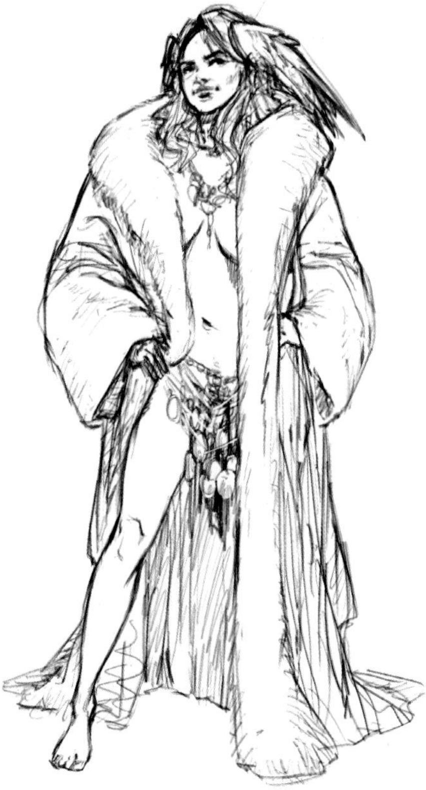

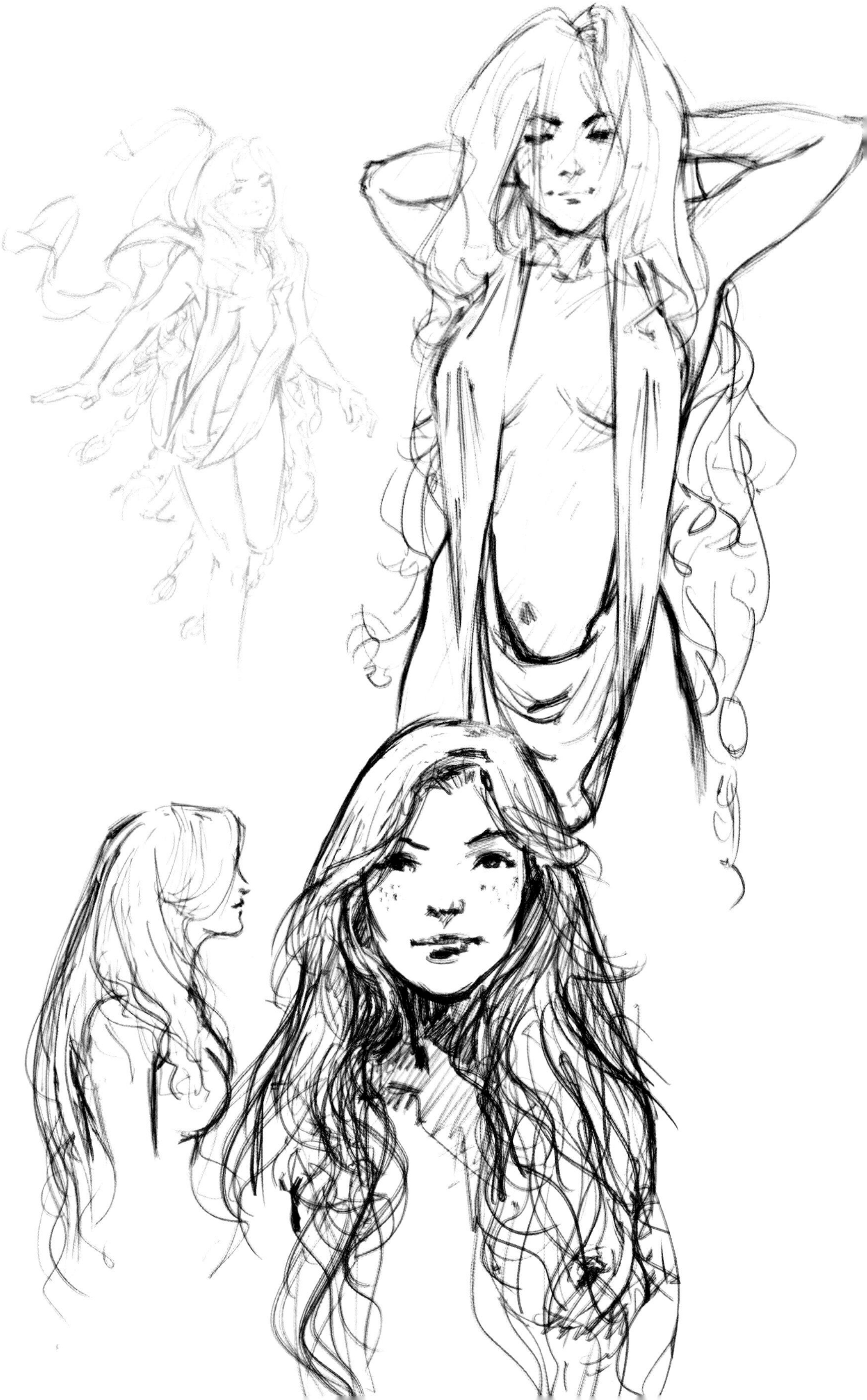

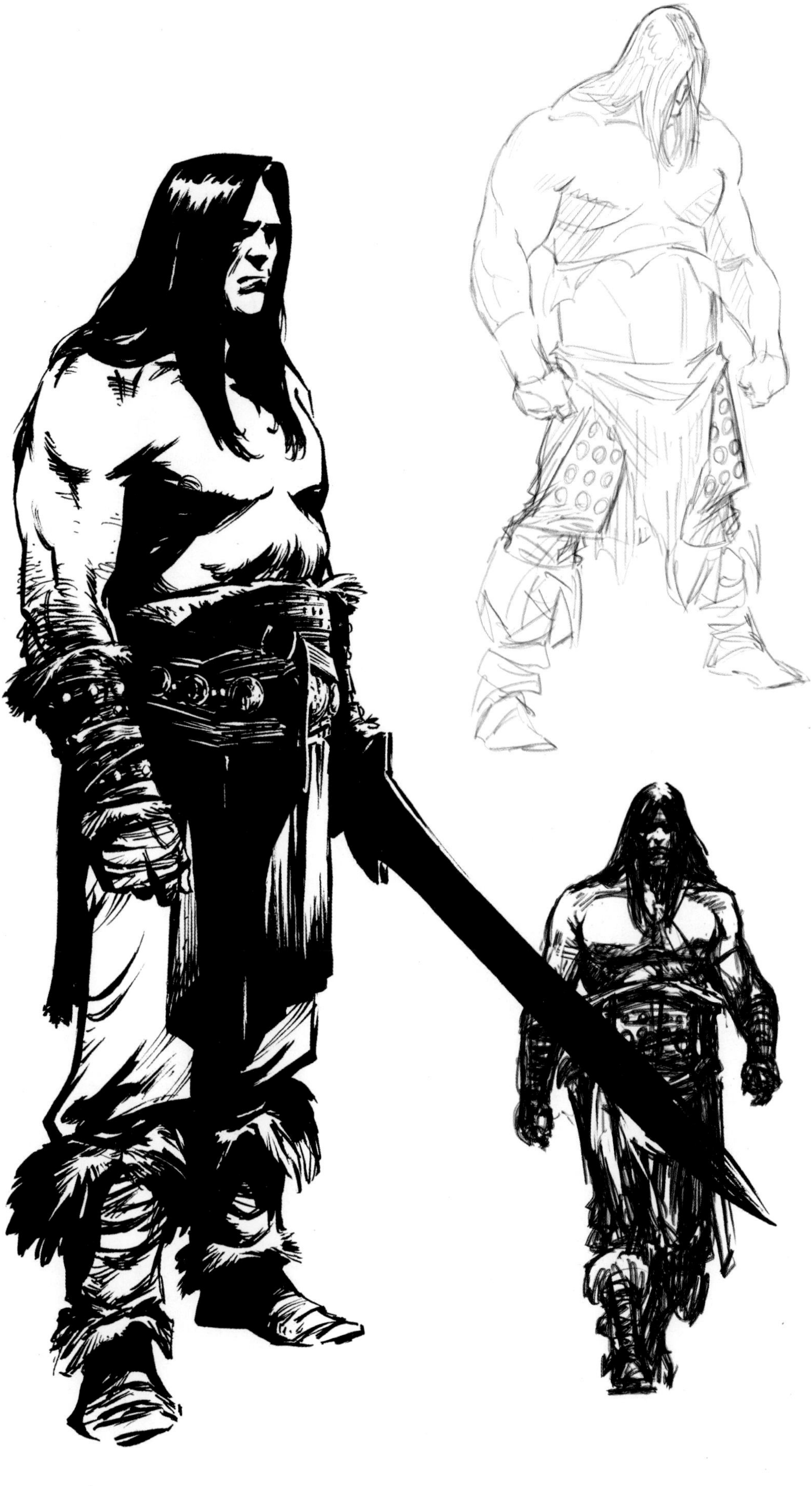

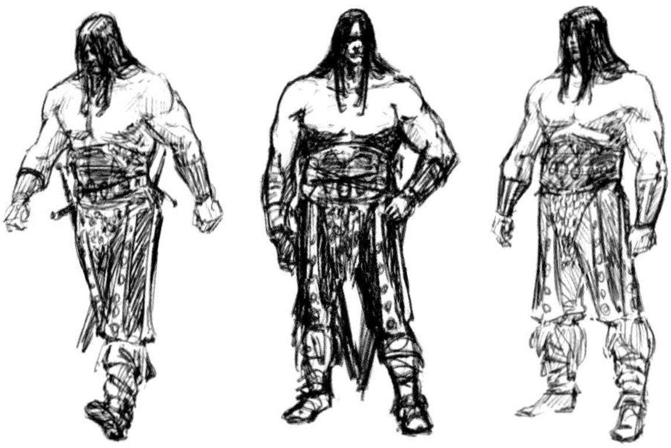

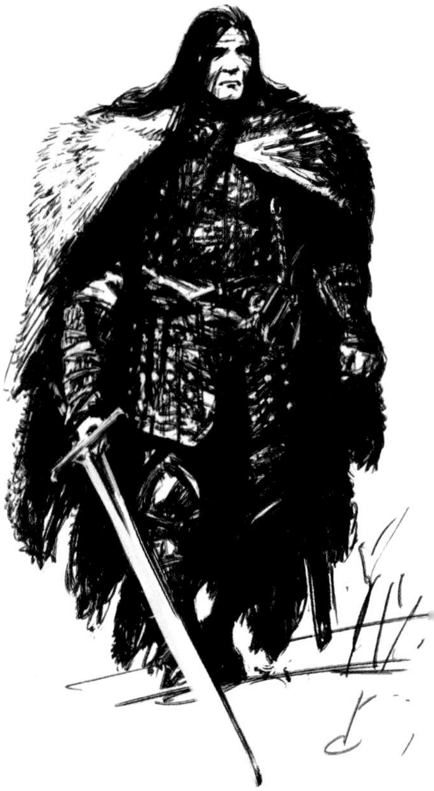

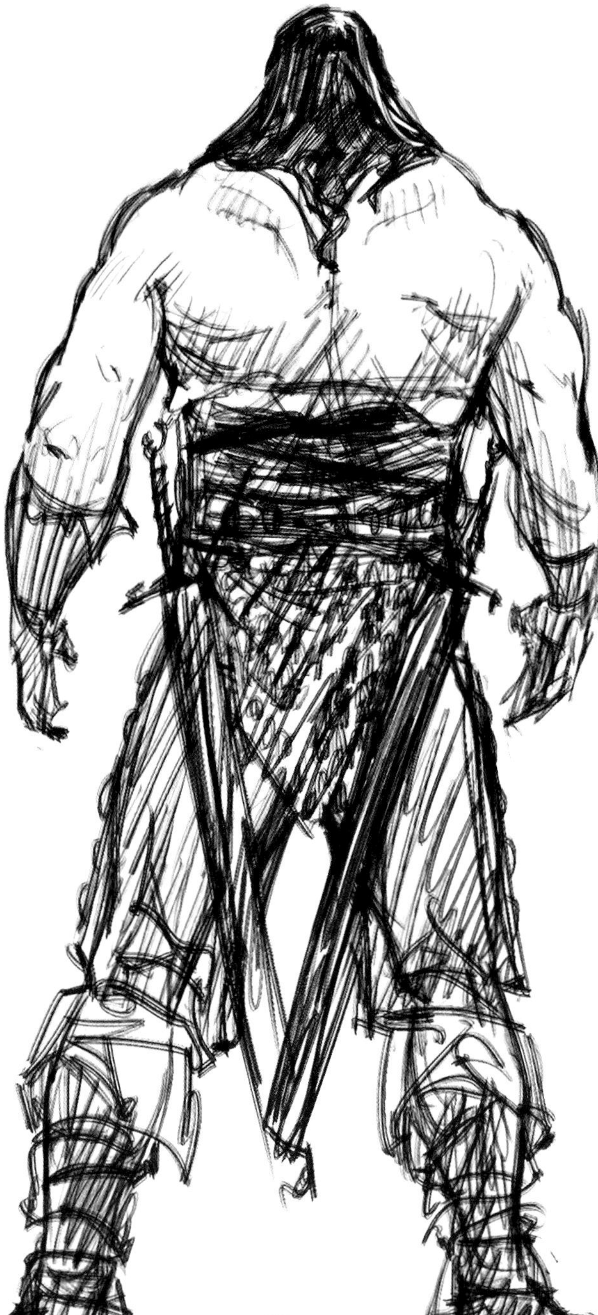

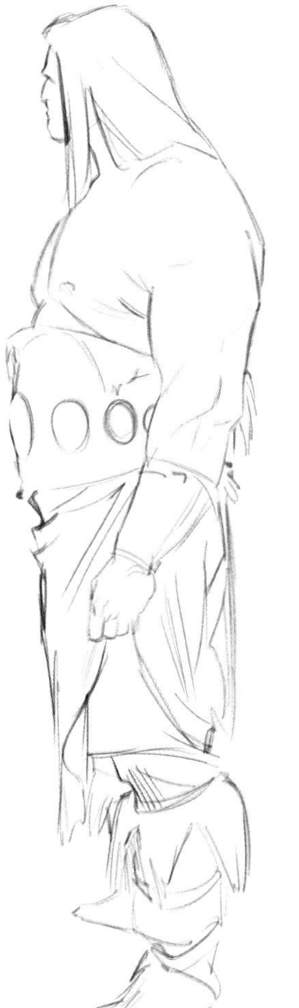

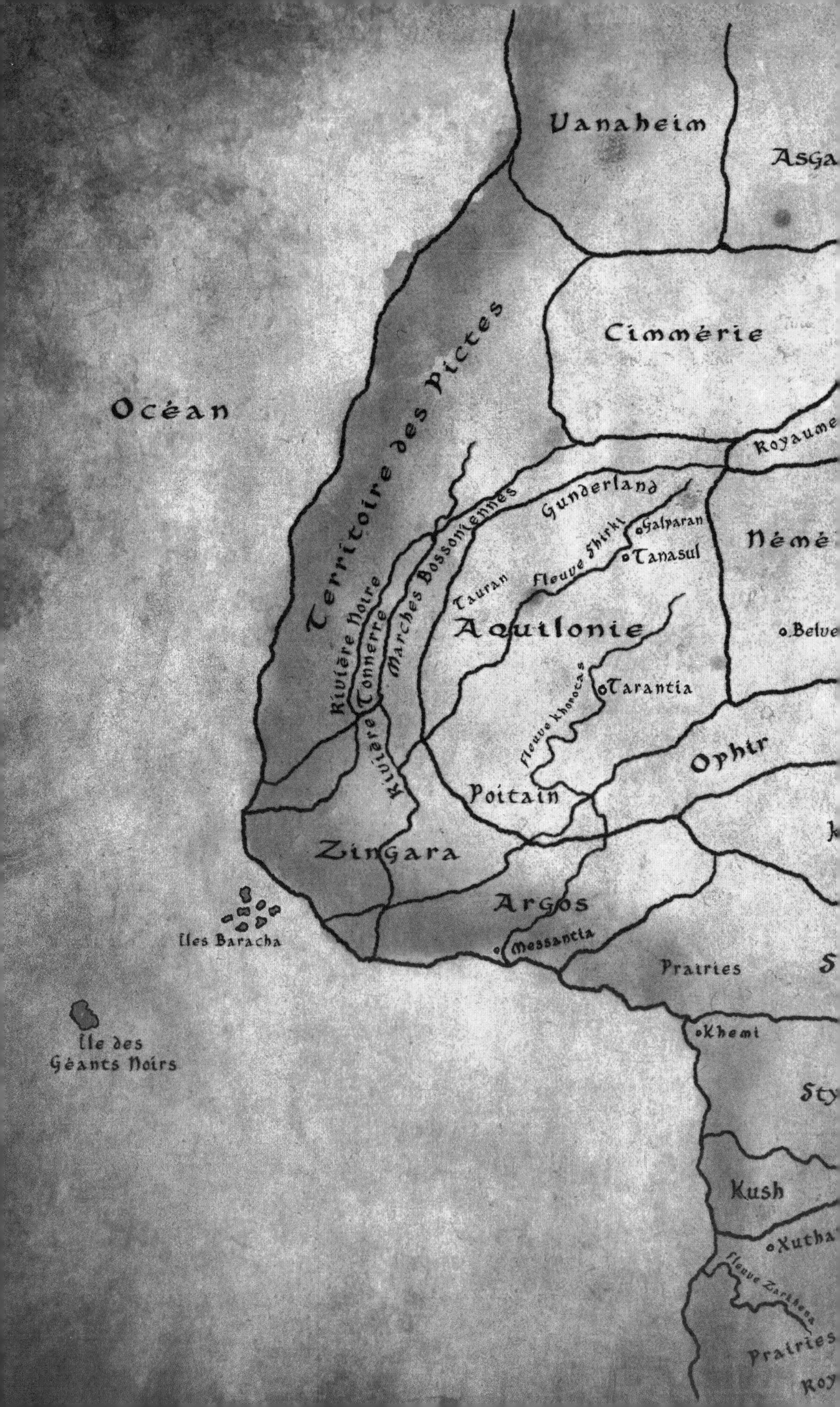

Vanaheim
Asga
Cimmérie
Océan
Territoire des Pictes
Royaume
Gunderland
Marches Bossoniennes
Rivière Noire
Tonnerre
Rivière
Galparan
Tanasul
Fleuve Shirki
Tauran
Aquilonie
Némé
Belve
Tarantia
Fleuve Khoratas
Ophir
Poitain
Zingara
Argos
Messantia
Îles Baracha
Prairies
Khemi
Île des
Géants Noirs
Sty
Kush
Xutha
Fleuve Zarkheba
Prairies
Roy